Dear Reader,

The editors at Harlequin and Silhouette are thrilled to be able to bring you a brand-new featured author program for 2005! Signature Select aims to single out outstanding stories, contemporary themes and oft-requested classics by some of your favorite series authors and present them to you in a variety of formats bound by truly striking covers.

We want to provide several different types of reading experiences in the new Signature Select program. The Spotlight books offer a single "big read" by a talented series author, the Collections present three novellas on a selected theme in one volume, the Sagas contain sprawling, sometimes multi-generational family tales (often related to a favorite family first introduced in series), and the Miniseries feature requested previously published books, with two or, occasionally, three complete stories in one volume. The Signature Select program offers one book in each of these categories per month, and fans of limited continuity series will also find these continuing stories under the Signature Select umbrella.

In addition, these volumes bring you bonus features...different in every single book! You may learn more about the author in an extended interview, more about the setting or inspiration for the book, more about subjects related to the theme and, often, a bonus short read will be included. Authors and editors have been outdoing themselves in originating creative material for our bonus features— we're sure you'll be surprised and pleased with the results!

The Signature Select program strives to bring you a variety of reading experiences by authors you've come to love, as well as by rising stars you'll be glad you've discovered. Watch for new stories from Janelle Denison, Donna Kauffman, Leslie Kelly, Marie Ferrarella, Suzanne Forster, Stephanie Bond, Christine Rimmer and scores more of the brightest talents in romance fiction!

The excitement continues!

Warm wishes for happy reading,

Marsha Zinberg

Marsha Zinberg
Executive Editor
The Signature Select Program

COLLECTION

Linda Winstead Jones
Evelyn Vaughn
Karen Whiddon

Beyond
the Dark

Published by Silhouette Books

America's Publisher of Contemporary Romance

SILHOUETTE BOOKS

ISBN 0-373-28531-0

BEYOND THE DARK

Copyright © 2005 by Harlequin Books S.A.

The publisher acknowledges the copyright holders
of the individual works as follows:

FOREVER MINE
Copyright © 2005 by Linda Winstead Jones

HAUNT ME
Copyright © 2005 by Yvonne Jocks

SOUL OF THE WOLF
Copyright © 2005 by Karen Whiddon

Visit Silhouette Books at www.eHarlequin.com

Printed in U.S.A.

CONTENTS

FOREVER MINE   9
Linda Winstead Jones

HAUNT ME   101
Evelyn Vaughn

SOUL OF THE WOLF   241
Karen Whiddon

Dear Reader,

Reincarnation is a popular theme in paranormal romance, and rightfully so. The concept of coming into each life destined to find the right person again and again, moving through the ages with that destined love guiding us, is definitely romantic.

But what happens if the *wrong* person comes back for us again and again? What if it's possible to stalk someone through one life after another? Even death wouldn't bring an end to the obsession. This is the idea that led me to "Forever Mine," which gives a different twist to those romantic words. Forever can be a very long time.

I hope you enjoy reading about Miranda Garner and John Stark, and their struggle with Miranda's otherworldly stalker.

Linda Winstead Jones

FOREVER MINE
Linda Winstead Jones

CHAPTER ONE

EVERYTHING ABOUT this lovely old house was familiar. The odors that had seeped into the walls and the furnishings over the years, the way the steps creaked when she climbed them, the angle of the sunlight that streamed through the second-story window on this brilliant and beautiful autumn day. It was good to be home.

Too bad Tony had come home with her.

Miranda Garner stood at her bedroom window and looked down on the driveway below, where she'd parked her car earlier that day. There were still a few boxes in the trunk, things she could do without for a day or two. She was so tired, she just couldn't face unloading everything this afternoon.

There had been a time when she'd had boundless energy. She'd worked at the library, volunteered afternoons at the retirement home and painted mediocre but relaxing landscapes on the weekends. There had been dinners with friends, here and at their homes, and she'd taken a few computer classes at the community college. Even after the trouble had begun, she'd managed to keep herself busy.

But lately, Tony hadn't been letting her sleep. He woke her in the middle of the night, time and again, and when she did manage to sleep he disturbed her dreams. That was the worst, when he seemed so real and solid and alive. After one of those dreams she always woke in a sweat, her heart pounding and her mouth tasting of copper, and there was no more sleep after that.

Through the open doorway she heard a step creak, much as it had when she'd climbed the stairs to bring her luggage to this bedroom, after being gone from Cedar Springs for six months. She didn't bother to turn or call out. She knew who was climbing those stairs.

"Go away," she whispered without turning to the open doorway.

Another stair squealed.

"Go away!" Miranda shouted, her voice angrier and more desperate than it had been the first time.

A few more steps creaked, and then she heard the shuffle of a shoe on the hallway floor at the top of the steps. A half second later there was another softly rasping step, just outside her door.

And then he was behind her. She felt his sigh on the back of her neck, even though he had no breath. She felt his gentle touch on the small of her back, even though he had no fingers. She began to shake, from the bones outward. "Go away, go away, go away!" She spun to face Tony, but of course he disappeared. But not before she'd glimpsed the curve of his cheek and the corners of his mouth turned up in a smile.

These days Tony was with her wherever she went. Miranda had left her family home in Cedar Springs, hoping that he wouldn't be able to follow. He had, of course. She'd moved several times in the past six months, hoping to escape him, but wherever she went he was there.

Tony claimed to love her, but if he truly loved her, wouldn't he listen to her and do as she asked? Wouldn't he leave her in peace if he had ever cared for her?

The police were no help at all, not anymore. In fact, their sympathy had long ago turned to suspicion and then contempt. They thought she was a nutcase, and heaven help her, maybe she was.

Tony was a ghost. Just over a year ago, she'd killed him.

JOHN STARK stepped into the outer office and did a quick double take. "What the hell is that?"

His secretary Claudia—invaluable personal assistant, as she insisted on being called on her bad days—grinned at him.

"Some psychic you are. Those are *flowers*. Maybe if you got out more often you'd recognize them."

John glared.

"They're from Mr. and Mrs. Thornton. Aren't they lovely?"

The bouquet was gaudy, and the blooms stunk of, well, flowers. He looked at the blooms, the scent assaulting him, and he automatically thought of death. "Get rid of them."

Claudia's cheerful smile disappeared, and she narrowed her eyes in that disapproving way she had. "We don't see a lot of happy endings here, Stark. The least you can do is enjoy this one. You told the cops where to find the kid, they actually listened to you for a change, and the boy is fine."

"It was just another job." He refused to celebrate happy endings because that meant he'd have to give equal weight to the not-so-happy cases. They far outweighed the happy, and giving them too much power would kill him, if he allowed it. "Toss the flowers out or take them home with you. If they're here in the morning I'll throw them out the window myself." That was probably a crime of some sort in Atlanta, but he didn't care. He would not have his office looking and smelling like a funeral parlor.

Claudia produced an almost comically sour face. "I guess I can take them home with me." She decided she liked that idea, and her expression changed subtly. "Jeffrey will think I have a secret admirer." She waggled her eyebrows at the mention of her new husband.

"You want to make him jealous?"

"It won't hurt to keep him on his toes, so to speak," she said. "Don't worry. I won't make him suffer for very long."

Women. John propped himself on the edge of Claudia's desk. "What have we got?"

She lifted a short stack of pink sheets and began to shuffle through them. "Yesterday was a slow day and there hasn't been much this morning. Another phone call from that girl at the television station—"

"No TV," he interrupted. His caseload was heavy enough, almost strictly through word of mouth. The last thing he needed or wanted was more exposure.

"Don't shoot the messenger," Claudia said. "I said I'd pass on the request and I did. There were also calls from a relatively desperate homicide detective in Tampa with a possible serial killer, a man in Nashville who thinks his wife is cheating on him, a woman in Charlotte who thinks her husband is gay, a lady from Cleveland who saw your picture on the Internet and thinks she's your soul mate—"

"The Internet?" John snapped. That was potentially worse than a locally aired television interview.

Claudia nodded. "Yep. There was one other call, from a woman who lives in Cedar Springs, Mississippi."

"Never heard of it."

"She also mentioned finding an article about you on the Internet, but she didn't seem at all interested in romance. She's apparently being stalked by a ghost."

John offered his hand, and Claudia placed the small stack of papers on his palm. Touch almost always triggered some sort of response, though he never knew exactly what he would see. "I hope you told the man in Nashville and the woman in Charlotte to hire a conventional private investigator. I don't take cases pertaining to personal relationships, ever. You know that."

"Yeah, but face it, it's what everyone wants. You could make a fortune just pairing people up. Steering them in the right direction. Telling them where to find Mr. or Mrs. Right." She waggled her eyebrows. "John Stark, The Love Prophet."

"Do you like your job?" he asked with a straight face.

Claudia leaned back in her chair. "Some days you are no fun at all."

He leafed through the phone messages Claudia had taken in the past two days. Some days the phone rang off the hook, and he was bombarded with requests for help. Other days were blessedly slow.

The detective in Tampa didn't need John's help; he'd have the murderer in custody by the end of the day. The poor guy in Nashville was right; his wife was having an affair. Her third. The woman in Charlotte was right, too, and he sure as hell didn't want to be the one to tell her. The *soul mate* in Cleveland was quickly approaching seventy, and John shared the honor of her obsession with Sean Connery, Johnny Depp and the Secretary of State. She wasn't dangerous, and her obsessions changed with amazing regularity.

The entire "soul mate" thing really grated on John's nerves. It was what everyone wanted. The perfect mate; a love connection on the grandest order; a destined romance that would never know pain or betrayal or heartbreak.

Hogwash.

When he touched the note with the name and address of the woman in Mississippi, it grew warm beneath his fingers. Ghosts weren't dangerous. They rattled around, they occasionally moved objects, they made startling appearances that were frightening but not deadly. They certainly did not stalk the living. Sometimes simply telling them to move on was quite enough.

But something was very wrong here. Miranda Garner was in danger; her ghost wanted her dead.

"This one," he said, tossing the discarded potential clients' names and numbers onto Claudia's desk and rubbing his fingers over the name and address his secretary had jotted down in her horrid excuse for handwriting.

"I'll call Ms. Garner—"

"No," John said sharply. "It's best that she doesn't know I'm coming." He didn't understand why, but he knew his arrival should not be announced.

Interested, Claudia leaned forward. "I'll book your flight and reserve a car."

John shook his head. While he gripped the paper, images he couldn't decipher flitted through his mind, moving so quickly and sharply he didn't have time to understand them. Most vivid was the image of a woman with long, dark hair that fell soft and intimate across his chest and his cheek, but there was also a throaty whisper; a glint of silver; the stench of cut flowers…. He lost the images quickly and completely. "No," he said as he pushed away from the desk. "I'll drive." He could get from Atlanta to anywhere in Mississippi in less time than it would take to book a flight, deal with the airport hassle, get to his destination and rent a car. "Just get me a map."

"When are you leaving?" Claudia asked.

John headed for his inner office, where he always kept a suitcase packed and ready to go. "Now."

"I'M SO HAPPY to have you back."

Miranda and her friend Elyse sat in the front parlor, drinking coffee and munching on the cookies Elyse had baked to celebrate Miranda's return.

"Are you coming back to the library?"

"Not right away." There had never been a financial need for Miranda to work. The Garner family had always had money…at least, in the past hundred years or so. Financially, the family had done well. Personally, their lives left something to be desired. In the ninety years this fine house had been standing, there had been one murder, two suicides and more divorces than Miranda cared to count. Her parents had broken the mold by daring to be happy, for a while, but their happiness hadn't lasted. Miranda's mother had died twenty-six years ago, leaving her two-year-old daughter and her beloved husband distraught and more than a little lost. Michael Garner had devoted himself to his financial concerns and his little girl, and there hadn't been a second wife or any more children.

He'd died a little more than two years ago, in a one-car accident on the winding road that led from the Garner house to Cedar Springs.

Years ago, Miranda had taken a job as librarian at the Cedar Springs Public Library, where Elyse was in charge of the children's section. She worked not because she needed the money but because she'd needed to be with people. And besides, she loved books with a passion she had never felt for anything or anyone else.

Miranda was glad to visit with her friend, but she was tired. She hadn't gotten much sleep last night. "There's so much to be done around here. While I was away something happened to the plumbing. I can barely get a trickle of water in the upstairs bathroom, and none of it is hot."

"Did you call a plumber?"

Miranda nodded. "I called Ralph's. A repairman is supposed to come by this afternoon to have a look at things."

"That's good." Elyse smiled, but the smile was forced and it didn't last. "Dammit, Miranda, you look terrible."

"Gee, thanks." She tried for a lighthearted tone of voice and a smile of her own.

"Seriously, you must've lost twenty pounds, and there are dark circles under your eyes."

"I've lost seventeen pounds, and I only have circles under my eyes because I didn't sleep well last night."

"Tony?" Elyse asked softly—gently, as if to say the name too loud might cause her friend to break in two.

In the beginning, Miranda had told Elyse about the

haunting. In those early days Tony's presence had been subtle. She'd catch a quick glimpse of him in the mirror or hear a familiar voice whisper from an empty room. Over the weeks and months since then his presence had grown stronger. Bolder. And one night, she'd felt his fingers on her throat….

Tony never showed himself or made so much as a sound while anyone else was around. Friends had dismissed her early visions of the ghost to the high emotion of the situation.

No one would believe her now if she told them that Tony was still with her, especially not down-to-earth Elyse, so she answered, "Of course not."

Elyse moved to the sofa to sit beside her friend, and she wrapped a comforting arm across Miranda's trembling shoulders. "It wasn't your fault."

"I know that." She'd been driving along the narrow road just beyond the house when Tony had appeared before her, trying to stop her from escaping by throwing his body in front of her car. She hadn't seen him in time. She'd hit the brakes, and then she'd hit Tony. He'd died moments later, but not before clutching her blouse with a bloody hand and whispering his last words.

Per sempre miniera.

Several days had passed before she'd been able to decipher what those words meant. She'd looked through foreign language dictionaries, and had finally gone to the Internet and tried different spellings at a translation site before she'd stumbled across the answer.

Forever mine. She hadn't even known that Tony spoke Italian, but it was the only thing she could find that made any sense at all.

"Get a nap," Elyse said, then she gave Miranda a quick kiss on the cheek and shot to her feet. "I have to get home and start dinner. I promised Gordon fried chicken for supper."

"Lucky Gordon," Miranda said as she rose to escort her friend to the door.

"Come join us!" Elyse offered sincerely. "Gordon is anxious to see you again."

"Maybe next week. I'm still very tired from the trip." It was more than the drive from Dallas that had exhausted her, but she didn't dare share everything. Not even with Elyse.

Elyse rubbed Miranda's arm in a gesture of friendship and comfort. "You can stay with us if you'd like, for as long as you'd like. I spruced up the guest room while you were gone. You'd love it, it's very bright and cheery. And I have plenty of hot water, I promise. This is an awfully big house for one person to be knocking around in all alone."

"Thanks, but this is home." And she wasn't exactly alone.

Since Tony didn't show himself when others were around, she had tried to keep him away by having roommates, by surrounding herself with people for as many hours of the day as possible. When that happened, he came to her dreams each and every night, and she quickly reached the point where she could not function.

If she acknowledged him during her waking hours, he sometimes allowed her to sleep.

After Elyse left, Miranda unpacked a box of books and put them on the shelf in the parlor. She dusted the desk and the collection of figurines in the entryway. A cleaning service had come once a month while she'd been gone, but once a month wasn't enough to keep this big house clean and besides…no one loved the place like she did. No one would care for it as she did.

She'd almost given up on the plumber when the doorbell rang. Duster in hand, she opened the door after peeking through the peephole and seeing a strange man standing there. He looked more bored than dangerous, and she had to admit—he was awfully good-looking for a plumber. The last repairman Ralph had sent out, before Miranda had made the mistake of trying to run from Tony, had been fiftyish and overweight, and wore the prerequisite baggy pants that came complete with almost two inches of exposed butt crack.

She threw the door open. "I thought you would never get here."

The man on her doorstep lifted finely arched eyebrows. Man, those eyes were blue, the bluest she had ever seen. "You're blond," he responded oddly, sounding surprised.

He was dressed suitably enough, she supposed, in well-worn blue jeans and a dark gray T-shirt and work boots. His hair was short and dark. Not a warm brown dark, but black as night. His looks were very much Black Irish, and the coloring suited his features. She didn't care what he looked like, as long as he got her hot water working. The cold shower she'd taken this morning had shocked her into awareness, but the misery had been more intense than she'd imagined it could be.

She stepped back so he could enter the house, and he did. He'd parked his black pickup truck in the driveway, behind her sedan, but had come to her door empty-handed. "Where are your tools?"

He cocked his head and tapped one finger to his temple.

"Great," Miranda muttered. "A comedian." She turned to look at him as she backed toward the stairway.

"The problem is upstairs," she said, pointing with the feather duster. "The bathroom is the third door to the right, and the hot water heater is in the basement. I don't know where you want to start, but…"

He just stared at her, his gaze locked on her face in a way that was absolutely mesmerizing. An odd shiver worked up her spine. She felt almost as if she knew him, but of course she didn't. He did not have a forgettable face. If any man had ever looked at her with eyes like that before, she would've remembered.

Her stomach sank. "You're not the plumber, are you?"

As soon as she said the words, books she'd just placed on the bookcase in the parlor flew off the shelves and into the entryway, where they banged into the wall. The walls of the old house rumbled and the ceiling shook, and a figurine she had just dusted spun off its table and then slammed to the floor, shattering into a thousand pieces. An unearthly wail filled the house and her head. A cold wind whipped through the entryway, ruffling her hair and the duster and chilling her to the bone—very much like the cold shower had done.

The man who was most definitely *not* a plumber leaned in so she could hear him above the noise. He gripped her wrist and shouted, "I don't think your ghost likes me."

CHAPTER TWO

JOHN WAS LESS CONFUSED by the ghost's antics than he was by the fact that Miranda Garner's hair was blond and short. She had one of those trendy hairstyles, where the pale strands looked mussed all the time. It was unexpectedly sexy, but his newest client should have long dark brown hair, silky and slightly wavy.

He was more disturbed by the fact that he'd been wrong than he was intrigued by a passably pretty woman who looked as if she hadn't slept in a week. When he'd touched the paper with her name and phone number written on it, he'd been so certain she was the dark-haired woman.

Her soft hair had fallen across him, and she'd laughed….

A thick book hurtled through the air, tumbling end over end, headed directly for the blonde's head. John already had a good grip on her wrist, so he yanked her out of the way. Startled by the sudden motion, she squealed and dropped to her knees. She wrenched her wrist from his grasp as she fell, and the duster she'd been holding went skittering across the hardwood floor.

As suddenly as the disturbance had begun, it ended. The house went quiet. The cold wind died as the ghost retreated.

John offered his hand to assist Miranda Garner to her feet. "I believe he's done, for a while."

She looked up at him, her green eyes accusing, her cheeks flushed pink. She did not take his hand, but struggled to her feet without assistance. "Who the hell are you?"

"John Stark," he said, retrieving his offered hand. "Sorry if I startled you, but you were the one who called me."

Her eyes widened, and she brushed back a wisp of fair hair that had fallen across her cheek. "I thought maybe you'd call or send a letter, not…stop by."

"Slow day," he explained.

Miranda Garner looked at him the way women often did, as if he were an oddity, a freak and a danger. She wondered if he would see into her soul when he touched her, if he would uncover all her secrets or whisper some dreadful prophesy into her pretty ear.

"Let's get a few things straight," he said, his voice and his demeanor completely businesslike. "I don't do séances, Ouija boards or tarot cards. I don't talk to dead people or read auras. I can't guarantee you that I can help with your problem, or that I will see whatever it is you need me to see. I don't control my gift, it controls me."

"I have a ghost," she said softly.

"Yes, I already know that," he said too gruffly.

"Can you send him away?"

Miranda Garner sounded so desperate and looked so fragile, she touched something deep inside him, and that was a very bad sign. He never, ever allowed himself to become emotionally involved with a client.

He had known from the moment he'd touched that

piece of paper with her name, phone number and address scribbled on it that she would be trouble. If she thought he was going to come in here and be her knight in shining armor, she had some seriously mistaken ideas.

"Can you?" she asked again, before he had a chance to contemplate an answer.

"I don't know." How was he supposed to concentrate on the spirit who was haunting her when he could not get past the fact that he'd been wrong about something so simple as her hair color? "Did you recently dye your hair?" he asked. "And perhaps cut it?"

"I don't see what that has to do with—"

"I'm curious. Humor me."

She cocked her head and looked at him, hard. Yep, she thought he was looney. "This is my natural hair color, and I've worn it short for years."

"Oh." He dismissed the vision of her as a brunette, with long hair that swept across his body. Everyone was allowed a malfunction, now and then. Even him. "Tell me about your ghost."

THE MAN UNNERVED HER. When she'd called John Stark's office, she certainly hadn't expected that he'd jump in his truck and drive from Georgia to Mississippi. If she had, and if she'd known how intensely he would look at her, she never would've made that call.

But if he could get rid of Tony...

What choice did she have but to trust John Stark, this odd man who called himself a psychic? Since she didn't know him and would never see him again once this job was over, she had nothing to lose if he thought she'd lost her mind. "A year and a half ago, Tony Cochran walked into the Cedar Springs Public Library looking for books on the history of the area. That's my specialty, area history."

"You're a librarian?"

"Yes." What kind of a psychic was he that he didn't already know that? "Anyway, I escorted Tony to the local history section, we talked for a while, and then he invited me out for coffee. Tony was cute and smart, and he…he had a really nice smile." Her heart hitched. That smile had fooled her. "We talked about history and local architecture and the Civil War, and of course we talked about Vera Lavender."

"Who?" he asked.

She should not be annoyed. Very few people who weren't from the area remembered the once well-known actress who had been born in Cedar Springs and had died here. And yet she *was* annoyed. "Are you sure you're psychic?"

A muscle in his jaw twitched. His lips hardened slightly. "Positive."

Miranda sighed and waved off Stark's lack of knowledge. "Tony and I had a lot in common, I'll put it that way. A couple of days after we had coffee we went out to dinner. The next week we went to a movie." It had all progressed so normally, for a while. "Before much time had passed, we were seeing one another regularly."

The change in the relationship had been gradual, but looking back she could see the problems had been there from the start. "After a few weeks of friendly dinners and lunches and movies, Tony turned possessive. He started showing up here in the middle of the night, checking to make sure I was where I should be and that I was alone. One day at work he publicly accused me of having an affair with some poor guy who was simply asking about the library's true crime section."

"Were you?" Stark asked.

"Was I *what?*"

"Did you make a habit of picking up men in the library?"

"No," she answered curtly, insulted that he would assume such a thing.

"No reason to glare at me, Ms. Garner." The psychic had made himself comfortable in a chair by the window, leaning back with his long legs thrust out and his fingers steepled. "It's part of my job to absorb as many details as you can possibly give me before I begin."

Miranda sighed deeply, reaching for control. She'd had so little control, in the past year. "Tony and I dated for a few weeks, and then I told him I couldn't see him anymore. He didn't take it well."

"I assumed as much," Stark responded.

"After I ended the relationship, it seemed Tony was around more than ever. I'd be shelving books in the library, and I'd turn around and find him right there, just a few feet away. He called at all hours of the day and night, and—"

"Please tell me you called the police."

"Of course! But Tony hadn't actually done anything illegal. The cops talked to him a couple of times and told him to back off, but…"

"He didn't," Stark finished when she stumbled over her words.

Miranda shook off the past, as best she could. Those unnerving days had been just the beginning of her troubles.

"He came here one night. It was raining, and he kept banging on the door begging me to let him in." Her breath came too hard. "I tried to call the police, but he'd cut the phone lines."

"No cell phone?"

Miranda shook her head. "No signal out here. You have to get beyond the curve in the road before you can get a halfway decent reception."

Stark snagged his cell phone from his belt and checked for a signal. He cursed mildly before turning it off. "You're right."

"Of course I'm right."

He looked directly at her, those blue eyes doing their best to see right through her. "It was raining, you didn't have a phone," he prompted.

The doorbell rang, and Miranda almost jumped out of her skin. She rushed to the door to answer; the plumber had finally arrived. Stark had risen from his chair and followed her, and now stood propped casually in the parlor entrance, watching.

The plumber, the same overweight older man who'd come to her aid last year, looked pointedly at Stark, and at the books Tony had tossed about, and at the broken figurine. The disapproval in his eyes was easy to read. Miranda didn't care to try to explain. She told him what her plumbing problems were and sent the repairman to the basement.

Hot water first, trickle upstairs later.

When she heard the cellar door off the kitchen close, she turned to John Stark. He smiled, for the first time since he'd come to her door. "He thinks you and I had a violent lovers' spat."

Miranda shuddered. "I don't care what he thinks." She tried for a prim voice, but there was a bit of a tremble in her statement. "Can you help me?"

"I don't know. You haven't finished telling me what happened."

"I thought you were a psychic," she snapped. "Don't you know everything?"

"Hardly."

She wasn't sure why she'd even bothered to call John Stark's office. There had been a small article on the Internet about him, at some off-the-wall Web site she'd found herself reading primarily by mistake. A typo in her web browser had taken her there, and she'd ended up intrigued by a byline. *Psychic solves crimes and answers questions of the heart.*

A year ago she hadn't believed in psychics, and she still wasn't sure that she did. But a year ago she hadn't believed in ghosts, either, and look what Tony had done to her. Calling John Stark's office was proof of just how desperate she had become.

"A year ago," he prompted with a wave of his hand. "It was raining. Tony was here."

"I heard him around back, rattling at the kitchen door, so I left by the front door." Her heart began to beat too fast, just as it had that night. "I dropped the keys in the driveway as I was running for the car, and when I bent down to pick them up I was so afraid that he was going to get to me before I reached the car. I think he would have killed me."

Stark nodded once, in agreement with her assessment of what might've happened that night.

"He didn't, though. I made it to the car, started the

engine, pulled out of the driveway. I had left the driveway and was on the road, when he jumped in front of
my car. I would've stopped if I'd seen him in time," she
said quickly, as she had many times on that night and
in the days to follow. "But I didn't see him until it was
too late."

"How did he get ahead of you?" Stark asked, skeptical as all the others had been at first.

"As you can see the driveway is quite long, and the
road twists and turns. Tony must've heard me leaving
and run through the woods, taking a shortcut in order
to reach that curve in the road before me. He did, just
barely. And he's been with me ever since."

"Getting rid of a ghost is usually simple work," Stark
said unemotionally. "Tell them they're dead and no
longer belong on this earth, tell them to go away—"

"I have told Tony to go away a thousand times!" she
interrupted hotly. "I don't need a professional to tell me
how to order a man to leave me the hell alone!"

He gave her a small, reluctant smile. "I'm not imply-
ing that you do, Ms. Garner."

"I'm surprised he caused a ruckus while you were
here," she said, trying to calm her voice and force her
facial expression to blandness. "He's usually quiet when
others are present." It was for that reason that everyone
dismissed her visions as posttraumatic stress, guilt or
plain old hysteria.

"Your ghost revealed himself to me because he
knows I'm not leaving until he's gone," Stark said in a
matter-of-fact voice.

"How can you say that? We haven't come to any sort
of agreement."

Stark smiled at her, and she was immediately disarmed. He didn't look at all weird, as she'd expected he might when she'd read that Internet article, but was a fairly normal above-average good-looking guy with a nice smile. He even drove a pickup truck, for goodness sake, and wore jeans and work boots. The only truly unusual feature was his eyes, and they were extraordinary. They seemed to look right through her, and were such a vibrant shade of blue she could hardly tear her gaze away.

"We will come to an agreement," he said with confidence.

"How can you be so sure?"

He lifted his eyebrows slightly. "I said I don't know *everything,* not that I don't know *anything.*"

He'd said he wasn't leaving until Tony was gone, which was a relief. "So, you can send him away today? Now?"

"Not likely," he said absently. "It will take some time."

Her heart hitched, a little. "You expect to…to stay here?"

He nodded. "It's the only way to get the job done, Ms. Garner. I need to discover what's holding your ghost here. When that's done, perhaps he will move on, as he should've a year ago."

She found herself wringing her hands, and she couldn't stop. "He says he loves me," she admitted in a lowered voice.

Stark's jaw went hard. "I'm not a romantic, Ms. Garner, but I do know that love and terror do not go hand in hand. This ghost has terrorized you for a year. There is no love in that."

IT WASN'T A GOOD HOUSE. John feathered his fingertips against the wallpaper in the upstairs hallway, as he carried his bag to the spare bedroom where Miranda Garner had grudgingly told him he could sleep.

People had a hard time coming to grips with the fact that things were good and bad, just like people. This house had absorbed a lot of bad energy over the years. John could hear the screams that had echoed in this house, he could feel the death. There had been some happiness to cut the chill of the horror, but the misery remained more steadfast than the joy.

He stopped when he came to an antique side table and his fingers brushed against the polished wood. The dark-haired woman flashed into his mind again, only this time she wasn't laughing. She screamed, she begged him to stop…and then blood bloomed on the front of her white nightgown, and the screaming abruptly stopped.

The table had been new then, and the woman's prim nightdress and dated hairstyle told him that whatever had happened to her had happened long ago.

John yanked his hand away from the table. He wasn't here to solve an old crime. He was here simply to send Miranda Garner's ghost away so she could live in peace. Nothing more.

But he found he couldn't make himself move away from the table. He laid a trembling hand there again, and this time the images that assaulted him were very different.

She was smiling this time, and her dark hair was unbound and hanging over her shoulders and down her back. A thick lock of dark hair fell across her face, almost hiding one brown eye.

She perched on the edge of this very table, her arms draped loosely around his neck, her narrow skirt pushed up so she could wrap her legs around his hips. He unbuttoned a few of the pearl buttons down the front of her silk blouse. The column of her throat was pale and tempting, her lips were parted as she moaned softly.

"YOU HAVE TO LEAVE HIM," he said as he opened her blouse. Afternoon light shone into the hallway, from the small window that overlooked the back lawn and from the windows of the bedrooms that opened onto the hall, so he could see her well. The sheen of her perfect skin, the swell of her breasts, they mesmerized him, as usual.

"I will," she said breathlessly as he lowered his head to lay his lips on her shoulder. "I can't stay with him another minute. I love you. I love you with all my heart."

He had waited so long to hear her say those words, and he wanted to believe her. But she had lied to him before.

"When are you going to tell him?"

"When he gets home," she whispered. "I promise."

She had promised before to leave her husband for him, he remembered that as he reached beneath her skirt to stroke the soft skin of her inner thigh, to slip his fingertips into the top of her stocking. She had broken that promise many times. He hated her for that, but he loved her, too. He had not known it was possible to love a woman and hate her at the same time, but this woman was maddening. He wanted her; he needed her. But at times like this he wished he didn't love her quite so much.

*She closed her eyes and smiled and reached out to
stroke the erection that strained his trousers, and he forgot how infuriating this woman could be.*

"YOUR ROOM'S ON THE LEFT," Miranda Garner said.

John yanked his hand away from the table. His mouth
was dry, and he could still feel the vision of the woman
on this table. He didn't normally *feel* anything. He saw,
he listened, he even smelled…but he was always distant
from whatever happened. No matter how disturbing the
vision might be, he watched from a distance. He did not
participate.

Ms. Garner's footsteps on the stairs were loud
enough; he should've heard her long before now.

John didn't turn to face the woman who had hired
him. It wouldn't do for her to see the erection that now
strained his jeans. He continued on down the hallway.

"Interesting house, Ms. Garner," he said indifferently.

"You might as well call me Miranda," she said reluctantly. "It seems we're going to be living together for a
short while."

Her words did nothing to ease his discomfort.

CHAPTER THREE

MIRANDA WASN'T yet convinced that John Stark could help her. He'd spent most of the evening muttering to himself and handling all sorts of objects that caught his attention. Books, furniture, pictures that had hung on these walls for many years. His hands were never still… his fingers traced and touched and prodded almost everything. He had stayed downstairs for most of the evening. They'd shared a simple meal, sandwiches and soup in the kitchen, and since then he'd barely said two words to her. Unless some of that muttering was meant to be a communication of some kind.

It was long past dark, and she was tired. Heavens, she was so sick of being tired all the time! If John Stark could send Tony away, she'd be able to sleep again.

Since she'd agreed to pay this man for his time, she apparently wasn't thinking well, either. Tomorrow morning she would pay him for the day and send him back to Atlanta. Damned if he wasn't as disturbing as Tony, in his own way.

He had been standing behind the parlor sofa for a good fifteen minutes, eyes closed and mouth occasionally working gently as if he were talking to himself, when his eyes flew open and he looked at her.

"There was a woman who lived in this house back in the forties," he said sharply. "She's interfering, somehow. She's blocking me from seeing what I need to see. She's getting in the way."

"Are you telling me I have another ghost?" Miranda asked, alarmed.

"No, she's not a ghost," he explained. "But I keep seeing her." He didn't seem at all pleased by that fact.

"If it's the forties you're seeing, then the woman is probably my great-aunt Vera."

"Vera," he repeated. "Yes, that's it. She was an unusual woman."

Miranda smiled gently. Unusual didn't even begin to describe her great-aunt. "Vera Lavender. I believe I mentioned her earlier. She was an actress. She acted and danced in a number of moderately successful motion pictures. Her husband was her partner, at least for a while."

"Fred and Ginger," Stark said lowly.

"Not quite so well known, but that's the general idea."

Stark glanced around the room. "We're a long way from Hollywood."

Miranda's smile faded. The success of that handful of musicals was the fun part of the tale. What came after was not so much fun.

"They were famous, for a while, but when their fame began to wane Vera and her husband moved here. This was her home, after all, and here in Cedar Springs she would always be a star, no matter what Hollywood thought of her."

"She preferred to be a star in Mississippi rather than a has-been in Hollywood," Stark muttered.

"Yes. I can't say that I blame her."

He looked at her, his blue eyes accusing. "You're not telling me the most interesting details of this story."

"Don't you already know?" she snapped.

"I know some. Not all. I'd like to hear you tell it."

"Vera and her husband, Phillip, moved here after her parents died. They passed within six months of one another, and her little brother—my grandfather—went to Virginia to live with relatives. The house was empty, and I suppose to Vera it was also home. Phillip didn't like it here, by all accounts. He would've preferred to be a washed-out actor in Hollywood. As a matter of fact, he traveled there often."

"Vera did not go with him."

It was a statement, not a question, and still Miranda answered, "No, she didn't."

"She took a lover."

Miranda felt her face turn warm, and likely red as well. In the beginning there had been those who'd believed BJ Oliver had broken in here that night, uninvited. But too many people had seen them together…too many people had known the truth. Her aunt had died long before her own birth, and still Miranda felt shame for the woman. They shared blood, after all. "She was lonely here, and yes…she took up with a local man. BJ Oliver was an artist. Not a successful one, I'm afraid. He painted pretty but unexciting pictures, and worked as a handyman on the side to make ends meet. He killed Vera in a jealous rage."

John glanced away from her. "Are you sure it was Oliver who killed her? Why not the husband? If she was having an affair…"

"Vera's husband was on his way home from Hollywood when she died. He didn't get here until days later. Besides, after Oliver murdered Vera he took his own life. Their bodies were found in the upstairs hallway. She'd been stabbed in the chest numerous times. He was lying on top of her with a bullet in his brain. The gun was still in his hand."

"Someone might've reconstructed the crime scene to look like…"

Miranda clenched her fists. "This is a fascinating conversation, Mr. Stark, but it has nothing to do with getting rid of my ghost."

"I'm afraid it does," he answered halfheartedly. "Why are there no pictures of your aunt Vera? She was famous, you'd think there would be a number of photographs and memorabilia on display."

"My father moved everything to a room upstairs," Miranda explained. "He got tired of having this conversation every time someone stopped by and saw the photos."

"May I see them?"

Miranda still didn't see how this could have anything to do with Tony, but she led John up the stairs and down the hallway to a rarely used spare bedroom. "Everything's in here." She opened the door and John walked in slowly, almost as if he were afraid.

He walked to a collection of photos that was arranged on the dresser, and laid the tip of one finger on one of the most flattering photos of the decidedly beautiful woman.

Miranda stood in the doorway, watching.

As a child, she had been fascinated with Vera Lavender. Miranda Garner had been pale and plain and gawky, and the woman in the photographs was so beautiful and elegant. There had been more than one night when she'd sneaked into this room to delve into the trunk where some of Vera's old clothes had been stored. She'd played dress-up, and pranced around the room pretending to be someone she was not…and never would be.

She felt Tony touch her throat, and the whisper in her ear was so close she caught her breath and held it.

"John Stark is not who he pretends to be," Tony whispered. "He's dangerous. He wants to hurt you. He killed you once, Miranda, and if you let him, he'll kill you again. Be careful, love. Be careful."

A frightened noise escaped from her throat, and Stark turned to look at her. "What's wrong?" he asked, one small framed photo still caught in his hand.

Dangerous… It could be true. She didn't know John Stark nearly well enough to trust him. At this point, she was afraid to trust anyone! "Nothing," she said as Tony backed away. "Nothing at all."

It DIDN'T MAKE SENSE, not yet, so John said good-night and went to bed without telling Miranda Garner what he had discovered tonight. Until he knew more, there wasn't much to tell. Not much she'd care to hear, anyway.

Miranda was a skittish woman, easily startled and shy and standoffish. Her body language very clearly told him to keep his distance; no man would need to be psychic to decipher the crossed arms and clenched hands. Hard to believe that in her most recent past life she'd been the outrageous actress Vera Lavender.

Vera had been a passionate woman, and she'd loved to laugh. When she loved, she did so deeply. When she laughed, she didn't hold anything back. She'd embraced life with her own sort of abandon, making her mark in her short lifetime. Vera had danced like an angel unfettered by the bounds of gravity, she'd sung with passion, and she'd died a horrible death, here in this house.

She was the dark-haired woman of his vision.

John unpacked, making use of the empty drawers in the antique dresser against the far wall. His bed was a tall four-poster, which was squeaky but surprisingly comfortable. Good thing, since he was likely to be here for a few days.

Somehow the present-day haunting was tied to Vera Lavender and the horrible way she'd died. But the situation was complicated, and some unexpected interference was getting in the way of his visions. He wasn't seeing everything he should, and half of what he did see wasn't making sense.

He closed his eyes, hoping for sleep to come easily. If he had no luck putting things together tomorrow, he'd call Lara Hilliard. Ghosts were Lara's specialty, and she could talk to them in a way he could not. She and her team could come in here and make sense of what was going on in a matter of hours.

He should have thought of Lara earlier. That's who Miranda Garner needed to hire. Not him. He couldn't help her.

He had never been able to help her.

SUNLIGHT CAME THROUGH the opened bedroom window at an angle that told him it was afternoon. A cool breeze wafted through the window. The sun would soon set, and it would be night again.

He was on his back in the four-poster bed where they

made love on many an afternoon, and Vera sat beside him. Gentle hands caressed his bare chest, and her hair fell in a thick wave across her face. She was trying her best to look happy…but she wasn't happy. She was never entirely happy.

She was a fabulous dancer, but in truth she could not act at all. At least, she couldn't fool him with that false smile.

"Can I trust you, Johnny?" she asked softly.

"What do you mean? Of course you can trust me."

"This thing with us has happened so fast. I haven't known you very long at all. Why is it that I sometimes feel I can't live without you?"

"Because you love me?" he asked, half-teasing.

"I can't love you, you know that. But I do want you."

Vera tried to hide her unhappiness as she always did, in passion, touching, kissing, in caressing and then undressing herself quickly when he reached for her. Sunlight on her bare body was fascinating. The swell of her breasts, the curve of her waist and her hip, the perfection of her face. He had never known a woman as beautiful as this one could exist, much less that such a creature could desire him.

"Come away with me," he whispered as she pressed her bare body to his.

"And where will we go?"

"I don't care."

"How will we live?"

"We'll find a way." He didn't care what kind of house they lived in. He didn't care if their clothes were rags or the finest fashions, whether they had money or not.

But she did. He was good enough for Vera in bed, but not anywhere else.

He pushed her onto her back and spread her thighs with his knee. When he was inside her, she loved him, whether she would admit it or not. When the realities of life intruded, she was not so sure.

"Make love to me, Johnny," she whispered. "Everything else can wait."

He pushed inside her, and she wrapped her legs around his hips. Vera made love with abandon, the same way she danced and sang and laughed, and whether they were in his bed or down by the pond, he could almost forgive her for offering him her body but not her heart.

JOHN WOKE with a start. The room was dark and quiet, and there was no afternoon sun, no open window...no Vera.

He'd been so sound asleep, he couldn't imagine why he'd awakened from the dream. It was just as well that he had. The dream had seemed too real, too tactile.

The house creaked, as the wind outside picked up. Perhaps a storm was coming in, and that's what had disturbed his sleep. And then he heard the sound that had, no doubt, awakened him.

Miranda Garner was talking, her voice growing louder and more insistent and more afraid with each passing second. John leaped from the bed and reached for his jeans as he finally made out the words.

"Go away!"

And then she screamed.

IN THE SEMIDARKNESS of her room, Tony's ghost took on an eerie glow. His face, in particular, shone malevolently as he descended upon her. He had appeared to her before, many times; he had shaken her bed and entered her dreams; he had wrapped his hands around her throat.

But he had never before looked so angry.

"Go away!" she said again, as she backed away from the bed.

"He's going to kill you," Tony said, "just like before." A long knife appeared in his ghostly hand. "He stabbed you again and again, until the last of your breath left you and there was nothing left to kill, and still he thrust the knife into you."

Tony tried to demonstrate, swinging the ghostly knife at her breasts. Miranda screamed as the image of the knife passed through her. She felt no stab, but there was a decided chill around her heart. Tony continued to advance on her, and she stepped back and away from him.

She glanced behind her when a chill touched her back. The window had been closed when she'd gone to bed, she was sure of it. But it was open now, to allow a cool autumn wind to rush into her room. With every step she took, she was closer to that opening.

The doorknob jiggled loudly. Tony turned and looked toward the locked door, and he smiled. "You were smart to lock him out. You can't trust him, Miranda. I love you. No one will ever love you the way I do. Don't let him come between us."

John Stark called her name frantically, and a moment later the door buckled and creaked as he threw his weight against it. "Miranda?" he yelled again. "Unlock the door!"

Tony stood between her and the door, menacing and misty and glowing. When she tried to inch around him, he moved with her, always between her and escape. The door creaked again. It was solid oak, and would not be easy to break down, but John was trying to do just that.

"Don't let him in," Tony commanded. "He'll kill you if you give him the chance."

"Miranda!" John shouted again. "Open the door."

Who could she trust? The ghost who had been haunting her for a year, who had stalked her before his death, who had all but robbed her of her sanity? Or the flesh-and-blood man she barely knew who had come here to help her?

Miranda closed her eyes and rushed through and past Tony. The space he occupied was cold, so cold it touched her very bones, but she pushed through it. She ran to the door on bare feet, and her fingers fumbled with the lock before she managed to work it. When the door was unlocked, she threw it open and flung her arms around John Stark's neck.

She didn't know why she felt such a strong need to hold this man she barely knew, but once she had her arms around him she didn't let go. She held onto John Stark, and after a moment he wrapped one strong arm around her.

"It's okay," he whispered. "You're all right, Miranda."

Relief rushed through her, warm and tangible. Holding on to John, hearing him whisper those reassuring words…she liked it. His arms around her not only made her feel stronger, saner and less alone, they also warmed her to the pit of her soul.

Tony was gone, at least for now. He always preferred to torment her when she was alone.

She did not know John Stark as well as she should,

but at the moment he was all she had. He was the only person, the only thing standing between her and Tony.

A psychic, a stranger, a man. Her last chance.

"Can I trust you, Johnny?" she whispered. "Can I trust you?"

CHAPTER FOUR

Miranda Garner's father had worked out of this study when he'd been living. It was an impressive office, in an Old South kind of way. The desk was massive and fashioned of gleaming dark wood that had been well-loved over the years. The chairs were made of burgundy leather, slightly worn but not shabby. Bookshelves crammed with books—old and new—climbed to the ceiling.

John knew without being told that Miranda did not spend much time in this room. It had been her father's domain and still was...and always would be.

On the desk sat a photo of a gap-toothed little girl with blond pigtails and green eyes. It was hard to believe that the little Miranda in the photo and the frightened woman seated beside him were one and the same.

Someone had actually written a book about Vera Lavender—her life and her murder. The book had been self-published and bound cheaply, but the story was there in its entirety. What was known of the story, at least.

A subdued Miranda sat beside him; each of them had claimed one of the red leather chairs. He was pretty subdued himself; he hadn't actually looked her squarely in the eye since she'd thrown her arms around him and repeated that question from his dream.

Can I trust you, Johnny?

No one had called him Johnny since the age of twelve.

"That's him." Miranda reached past him to place a fingertip on a grainy black-and-white photo of the man who'd murdered her great-aunt. BJ Oliver. Nowhere did it say that the *J* in BJ stood for John, but he knew that to be true. Why else would the Vera in his dreams have called him *Johnny?*

BJ Oliver was an ordinary-looking fellow, brown-haired and square-jawed, not pretty but certainly not ugly, either. There was a sadness about him, even in this photo that had been taken long before his entanglement with Vera Lavender.

John touched his own finger to the photo, and Miranda jerked her hand away, as if it would be unwise for their hands to come too close. He delved deep into his mind to try to learn for himself if this man truly had murdered his lover and then killed himself…but got no answers to his questions. He was psychic, not omniscient. There would always be questions to which he had no answers. Why did he so desperately want BJ Oliver to be innocent of the crime of murder?

He nodded and flipped through the pages. Another man's photo caught his attention. The smile that had been flashed for the photographer was wide and bright and false. Thick blond hair was perfectly styled, to suit the era in which the man had been a minor and short-lived star.

"Phillip Lavender," Miranda said. "He was much better looking than that BJ Oliver fellow," she mused. "I don't know why Vera would turn her back on a man like this one for a…a poor artist who couldn't hold a candle to her husband in any way that I can see. Phillip adored his wife and was extremely distraught after her murder."

John felt a moment of indignation for the poor artist as he touched one finger to the photo. "You don't know how Vera's husband treated her when no one was watching." He knew, though. He knew too well. "Phillip saw his wife as a possession, not a partner. A thing he owned, no different than a car or a suit. He said he loved her, and he did in his own way. Phillip loved Vera the same way he loved his gold watch and his favorite tie. As long as she did as she was told and brought him pleasure, he loved her. When she didn't…when she didn't please him, he no longer loved her."

"This is fascinating," Miranda said dryly, "but what does it have to do with Tony?"

"I'm not sure," he muttered.

"I don't care about something that happened almost sixty years ago. I want my ghost gone—nothing else matters." She squirmed. "It's becoming apparent that you're not going to be able to help me," Miranda said primly. "It was a mistake for me to call you, and it was certainly a mistake for you to come here so impulsively. I'll write you a check for the services you've rendered thus far, and you can leave this afternoon."

"No," John said halfheartedly as he leafed through the book.

"I hired you. I can fire you," Miranda snapped.

"I'll leave after you've retained the services of some-one else," he said. "I won't leave you alone in this house."

"I've done fine alone for the past year."

John lifted his head and looked Miranda in the eye. She was pretty, and she was stronger than she gave herself credit for. But she was *not* fine. "I don't want to scare you, but…"

"But what?" she prompted when he faltered. "Go ahead. Scare me."

"Tony wants you dead," he said as gently as possible.

MIRANDA MADE A FRESH PITCHER of iced tea while John made some calls from the parlor phone. She tried not to allow her hands to shake, while she went about the simple chore, but the shaking started and would not stop. More than her hands shook—she shivered to her bones.

She wasn't at all surprised to hear that Tony wanted her dead. He was always whispering in her ear about the two of them being together forever. Forever mine, he'd said as he lay dying, in a rasping voice that still reminded her of some macabre Valentine's Day greeting even though at the time she'd had no idea what his words had meant.

Miranda did her best to ignore the soft voice that whispered to her now. At least she didn't see Tony this afternoon. Instead there was just a whisper, and a breeze that might or might not be the touch of his hand, a chill against her ear that was nothing more than his ghostly breath.

"I'm not the one who wants to hurt you," her ghost whispered. "It's Johnny. Don't trust him…don't let him touch you…I'm the one you can trust. The only one. Don't you remember? You gave me your heart…"

"I did not," she muttered as she mindlessly stirred the tea. "I never gave you my heart."

"Think back, love. Remember. You're mine, now and forever. You swore it to be true and I won't let you go now."

What could she have said to Tony to make him think she was literally offering him her *heart*. They had never even come close to a romantic relationship of that type. Miranda swore to herself that if she got out of this alive and ghostless, she would never so much as look at another man. It would be best that way, since she obviously had the worst of luck where the opposite sex was concerned. How could she have been so wrong about Tony? For a while she'd been so certain he was a nice, normal, gentle man. It hadn't taken long for her to discover the truth about him.

He had been obsessive and cruel, in life and in death.

"Bad news," John said as he walked into the room.

Startled by the sound of his voice, Miranda twitched and sent the spoon with which she'd been stirring the tea spinning to the floor. She twirled around to see John standing in the doorway, leaning against the doorjamb as if he didn't have a care in the world. How was it that the appearance of a flesh-and-blood man made her jump more than the whisper of a ghost?

"What?" she snapped. Just what she needed, more bad news.

"Lara is on a job, and she won't be able to get away for a week. Possibly two. She's involved in some sort of research project and can't leave. Think you can stand me for that long?" A hint of teasing crept into his voice.

Miranda turned back to her tea that did not need any further stirring. Since the spoon she'd been using was on the floor, she grabbed another one from the drawer and began to stir anyway. John said Tony wanted to kill her. Tony said the same thing about John. Like it or not, she knew Tony a lot better than John Stark, and while he had scared her witless and she wanted him gone…he had not physically harmed her.

"I appreciate your offer to stay, but it's not necessary," she said calmly. "You obviously can't help me with my problem, so you might as well go home. I don't mind staying here alone for a few more days." So why did her heart lurch at the very idea?

"I'm not going anywhere until Lara and her team arrive," John insisted. "I suppose you could kick me out of the house, but I'd just camp in the front yard anyway."

She felt John coming up behind her, the same way she always felt Tony. This sensation was different, though. It was warm and reassuring. Comforting and calming. If he whispered in her ear she wouldn't feel a chill. Instead she'd feel the warmth of his breath, the heat of his lips…

"I need to be here, and I knew that without doubt the moment I touched the message with your name written on it. Should I have called and made arrangements? Of course. But I didn't call because I knew that it would be dangerous for you to be forewarned." John's voice was deep and warm and real. "I know now that Tony would've been a more serious threat if he'd known I was coming. For some reason he didn't want us to meet. I believe he would have tried to find a way to kill you before I arrived, if he could've managed it. He isn't that strong yet, but he grows stronger every day. Every day, Miranda. You know that as well as I do."

Tony was growing stronger, and at least John didn't think she was crazy because she saw a ghost. She

couldn't forget that John had saved her last night, that
he had not only frightened Tony away…he'd made her
feel safe for the first time in a year.

"All right," she said. "You can stay until your friend
arrives. Who knows? Maybe you'll discover something
new before she gets here."

John laid a hand on her shoulder, and even though
she'd known he was close she jumped when he touched
her. Yes, he was warm, and like the voice—the touch
was real.

He let his hand fall, perhaps because he knew that his
touch disturbed her. "You need to get out of this house
for a while," he said softly.

"It doesn't matter where I go," Miranda said. "Tony's
always there, taunting me. Whispering into my ear.
Touching me." She shuddered.

John's hand skimmed down her arm, and she didn't
jump or step aside, not even when he took her hand in
his. "Ignore him. We're going for a walk."

THE LAND SURROUNDING the Garner house was wooded
and lush. It was good to get away from the city, even
though he loved Atlanta and always had. There was
something soothing about this copse of trees, and
when they turned the path and saw the pond sparkling
as the sun set and cast its rays onto the water, he felt
an odd sense of familiarity, as if he had known that
pond would be there long before they'd taken the turn
in the path.

From the dream, he remembered that Vera and
Johnny had come here, sometimes just to sit and talk,
other times to make love.

John felt as if he had been here before, too, or else he'd been in a place very much like it.

Miranda was pale and shaken, as she had been since he'd met her. What had she been like before Tony had come into her life? Before torment had shaken her? What had the little girl whose photo still sat on her father's desk been like? He wanted to know. She was pretty and smart and he could very easily imagine that she had a wonderful laugh.

The sun only emphasized Miranda's paleness and the circles under her eyes. She needed a good night's sleep more than any woman he'd ever known. Simply surviving the past year had been a feat, and yet she did not realize that fact. She was stronger than she knew... stronger than anyone could ever know....

"You seem familiar to me," she said as she looked out over the water.

"Do I?" She seemed vaguely familiar to him, as well, though he did not tell her so.

"Yes, in an odd way you do."

Déjà vu, past life memories, a simple and vague similarity to someone she had known in the past...there were many different explanations for that feeling of familiarity.

He couldn't dismiss the sensations that were growing inside him, and he couldn't ignore that they grew stronger every day. There was something about Miranda Garner that made him want to wrap his arms around her and hold her close. He wanted to protect her, from Tony and from everything else. Perhaps he felt protective because he had connected in a very deep way with the man who had been her lover in another life...the man who had loved her and hated her and killed her.

Miranda turned away from the pond and pointed into a thick copse of trees. "I was exploring one day, and I found a heart and some initials carved into a tree just beyond the edge of the growth. VL and JO."

"Vera Lavender and Johnny Oliver."

"I suppose. Do you think the *J* in BJ stands for John?"

"I do," he said, without telling her how he knew, without telling her that they had likely carved that heart just after making love…or just before. There was great passion here, lingering in the air. Passion, not love.

"I never showed anyone else that carving. There's still lots of interest in Vera in these parts and I know there are some who would like to know it's there, but the heart seems so personal I just didn't want to share it. BJ Oliver murdered her, but…I think she loved him, very much. I think she had to, in order to deceive her husband the way she did. That doesn't make what she did okay but… It just doesn't seem right for curious people to take a moment that was probably pure and romantic, and sully it by taking photos and scraping off bark as souvenirs."

"I understand."

She looked him in the eye. "Do you?"

He nodded. Somehow, it was true. Not everything was meant to be shared.

"Vera was lonely," he said. "When Phillip was gone, even when he was here, she felt lost and apart from those around her. She put on a happy face for everyone, she hid her loneliness in grand gestures and great exuberance, but she was a very lonely woman, until she met BJ Oliver."

Miranda looked up at him, and at least for this moment she did not question what he could do. "I wouldn't mind showing it to you," she said almost reluctantly. "If you're interested."

"I am."

They walked away from the pond, taking a narrower, overgrown path and then leaving the path and making their own way through tall weeds. Miranda led the way, and long before they reached the edge of the growth a wind kicked up and the tall weeds began to dance. Miranda's hair was caught in the wind, and short curling strands whipped around her delicate face.

She stepped into the shadow of the tall trees and very easily found the faded and worn carving on the trunk of an ancient tree. "Here." She traced the heart outline with her finger, her movements slow and gentle, almost reverent. "Why would a man who loves a woman do such a thing? How could a man who claims to want only the best do such violence?"

"May I?" John asked, standing close to Miranda and laying one finger on the carving, as she did.

With a jolt of knowledge that came to him with a physically painful sharpness, John knew that the man who had carved this heart had adored Vera Lavender to the depths of his soul. He'd loved her, he'd wanted only to get her away from this place before it was too late....

But she always denied him. If someone dropped by and her lover was here, she treated him as if he had come to paint a fence or trim tree limbs or cut the lawn. More than once she had greeted visitors with Johnny's sweat mingled with hers, with the flush of lovemaking on her cheeks, with his scent still in her nose and her body trembling from his touch. And she didn't even look directly at him. When others watched, she denied Johnny with a completeness that cut him to the bone.

No wonder he hated her.

The cracking sound above their heads was all the warning they had, before a limb came crashing down. John grabbed Miranda's arm and pulled her sharply away from the tree, a split second before the thick branch crashed into the ground. It landed with a thud and a crack, directly onto the spot where they'd been standing moments earlier.

Momentum took them both to the ground, and Miranda squealed as she fell. John covered her body as best he could, looking up to see what might've caused the limb to fall. There wasn't enough wind to bring it down, and the tree was healthy…the limb that had fallen was not dried or diseased.

Overhead he heard a soft trill of laughter, and Miranda heard it, too. She shuddered beneath him and whispered, "Tony."

CHAPTER FIVE

*J*OHNNY LIFTED HER easily and perched her on the table in the upstairs hallway, and she laughed. Not because he'd said or done something funny, but because she was so happy. She could not remember ever being so happy, not in her entire life.

She quit laughing when her lover began to unbutton her blouse. "You have to leave him," he said.

"I will," she said as Johnny pushed her blouse aside and kissed her shoulder. A trill of pure sexual sensation fluttered through her body. "I can't stay with him another minute. I love you. I love you with all my heart."

"When are you going to tell him?"

"When he comes home," she whispered. "I promise."

She had planned to leave Phillip so many times, but she always chickened out when the time came. She loved Johnny, he made her happy, he made her laugh, in bed he made her scream in pleasure. But he had nothing to give her but love. That should be enough, and at times like this when he was minutes, maybe seconds, from being inside her, she believed it was enough. But when she was faced with the reality of walking away with nothing…she wasn't sure she could. Ever.

The house belonged to her, but Phillip controlled the

money. Every penny she'd made as a dancer, as an actress, was in Phillip's hands. She didn't want to be poor.
She hadn't loved her husband for a very long time, but
she still felt bound to him in a way she could not explain.

But that didn't mean she didn't love this man. It was
extraordinary; she had never known it was possible to
love anyone as much as she loved her Johnny.

Johnny reached beneath her skirt, and his fingers
teased the top of her stockings, flickering over bare
flesh. She was perched precariously on the table. If he
did not hold her she'd surely fall, but she knew Johnny
would never let her fall. She spread her thighs as he
lifted her skirt, and reached out to stroke his erection.

"You're never going to leave him." Johnny caressed
her intimately as he shared this awful truth. At times like
this it was nice to pretend that they had a future, but she
was afraid of the unknown, and he knew it.

"I don't want to talk about this now," she whispered.
She wanted him so badly, she ached. Her body, her
heart…he made her ache in ways she had not known
possible.

"You never want to talk about this," Johnny said.

"Make love to me," she said as she began to unfas-
ten Johnny's belt. She knew how to end this discussion
that would never have a satisfactory ending. Sexual
heat had brought them together and it would keep them
together. Some days it seemed that they had more, but
if this was all they had was it enough? Could she make
it be enough?

He growled at her and unfastened his trousers, and
with anxious hands he pushed her skirt out of the way
and pulled her underwear down and off. She couldn't

wait to have him inside her. Her body trembled, and she grew damp.

He pushed into her, and as they became one she knew everything was going to be all right, somehow. She did love him. Maybe he didn't believe that she knew how to love, but she did.

She was so scared. Like it or not, she had to tell Phillip. She had to leave everything she knew behind for this man.

"I do love you," she said as he pushed deep and completion teased her with a pulsing and a tingle and a shudder. "Oh, Johnny." She threw her head back, opened her eyes, and looked up into his face.

It was John Stark's face.

MIRANDA CAME AWAKE with a start, sitting up and gasping for air. It only took a moment for her breath to come more easily and her heartbeat to begin to slow. A dream. Just an ordinary dream. She'd slept deeply, and Tony had not been there, plaguing her dreams as he so often did. Johnny…John Stark had been there. But it hadn't really been him, and she hadn't been herself….

She combed her hair with trembling fingers and slipped from the bed, trying to leave the dream and the memory of the vivid images behind. In its own way, this dream was as disturbing as any of the nightmares Tony had invaded. At least in those nightmares she knew who she was.

She didn't have erotic dreams about men she'd just met.

Three-thirty. Too early to rise…too late to plant herself in front of the television with a cup of decaf to watch an old movie. Maybe if the dream faded and she could shake it off, she could go back to sleep.

She never slept in the dark, anymore. Tony appeared too solidly and too frequently when she slept in the dark. Two night-lights and a dim bedside lamp burned in her bedroom, as if the faint illumination could chase away the demons of the night. Miranda sat in front of the mirror and brushed her hair, studying her face in a critical way. She hadn't bothered to look at herself this closely in almost a year, because she had not cared.

There was new color in her cheeks, an aftereffect of the dream, she supposed. She could not remember ever being so sexually aroused, not in real life or in fantasy. She'd felt John's fingers on her skin, the rough fabric of his trousers against the palm of her hand, and she had experienced a response that seemed real…not at all a fantasy.

Tony appeared behind her, as a ball of light first, then taking form. This had happened so many times, she was no longer surprised.

"Go away," she whispered without passion.

Tony ignored her, as always, and wrapped his hands around her neck. He did not squeeze, but the grip was threatening. She could feel his fingers there, cold and menacing. It was not the first time he'd touched her this way.

"No man but I will ever touch you, love."

"You're not a man," she answered softly.

"Of course I am. I'm just caught in another place. I'm terribly lost without you."

"You're dead."

"Yes, I am. And all I want is to touch you."

"You will never touch me," she said, her voice trembling.

She felt the hands tighten around her throat, as if the

fingers were real. Never before had he felt so solid. "You want *him,* is that it?" Tony no longer smiled. This was the face he had shown her when she'd tried to send him away, so many times. The face was petulant, and angry and not quite sane. "It's always *him.* You know that it was wrong to let him touch you as if you belonged to him. So wrong. I tried to forgive you."

Had Tony somehow invaded her dreams? Even though the encounter with John wasn't real, had Tony been there, watching? It was another invasion of her life, one of so many. "I didn't let—"

Tony continued as if he couldn't hear her. "So many times, over and over again. No matter what I do to keep you contented, you always turn to *him.*"

"You're not making sense, Tony."

"I won't allow it to happen again."

His hands tightened until Miranda could no longer breathe. Tony had touched her before, in his ghostly state, but never like this. Never with such force that he took her breath away.

"I'm getting stronger, you see," he said in a whisper. "Every day that you hold me here, you make me more powerful. I won't live again, but I have come back for you, love. You won't need anyone else when I'm here. Just you and me, that's how it should be."

Tony could choke the life out of her, here and now. How do you fight a ghost? How do you rid yourself of someone who's already dead?

She couldn't do it. John Stark could.

Tony's hands were wrapped so tightly around her throat she couldn't call out, so Miranda reached out and grabbed for a bottle of perfume. At first she missed, and her fingers flailed against the dresser, but finally she was able to grasp the small bottle in her hand. She threw it against the door where it broke without making anywhere near enough noise to wake the man down the hall.

Tony didn't like her attempts at rousing the only other person in the house, and he pulled her away from the dresser and cursed in a soft, misty voice. But he could not restrain her entirely and keep both hands around her neck. A burst of energy carried her forward again, and she grabbed for her brush as Tony once again pulled her away from the dresser. She threw the hairbrush and it banged against the door much more loudly than the bottle of perfume. Tony yanked her back sharply and she fell to the floor. The chair in which she'd been sitting was knocked onto its side, and Miranda landed on her knees. Hard. Tony did not let go. He stood over and above her, squeezing the last breath out of her.

The room spun and began to go gray, and while she tried to grasp at Tony's hands she could find no grip. He could affect her, but she could not affect him. She didn't have the strength left to throw anything else, and even if she did…nothing was within reach. Miranda began to slump onto the floor. She was going to die, right here, and Tony was going to harass her into the next life. She would never be rid of him. Never…

"Miranda!"

A sharp knock sounded on the door. Miranda tried to answer, but she couldn't. John continued to knock on the solid oak door.

Maybe she didn't know John Stark, maybe he was a stranger to her. But tonight when she'd gone to bed she'd realized without doubt that she could trust him more than she had ever trusted Tony. That's why she hadn't locked the door.

Her head spun dangerously. *Johnny.*

HE HAD HEARD NOISE from this room…and the stink of a flowery perfume drifted through from the bedroom.

Miranda did not answer, but that only made John more uneasy. If he ran into her room and she was simply asleep, having a nightmare and talking in her sleep, she'd toss him out of the house long before Lara arrived.

But what choice did he have? Something was wrong—and he knew it. Dream, ghost, or reality, something was *wrong.*

Last night the door had been locked, but tonight it opened easily when he twisted the doorknob. Miranda slumped on the floor, a misty shape hovering over and all around her. The mist was wrapped around her body, and it was choking the life out of her.

"No. I won't allow it." John bent down and scooped Miranda off the floor and up…away from the ghost. The angry spirit could touch her, but not him. He didn't know why. He didn't care why. He only cared that Miranda gasped and took a breath as he carried her toward the open door.

The spirit stayed behind as John carried Miranda down the dark hallway, or else it became quiet and still again.

It wasn't supposed to be this way. Ghosts, restless spirits, the dead who refused to move on…they were everywhere. At worst, they made a little noise and rattled about in the night. In most cases, the living were not even aware that spirits were around them. What allowed Tony to physically touch Miranda? What held him here?

Not love, John knew that much. He didn't pretend to understand romance and the incomprehensible complexities of love, but he did know that murder and terror were not among the requirements.

He carried Miranda to his room. There were other bedrooms in the big house, but they'd been empty for months and were stale and musty. Besides, he didn't think he could leave Miranda alone. Not until Tony was gone for good.

Would he ever be?

He laid Miranda on the bed, and her thin nightgown draped around her body. "Talk to me," he said gently as he patted her cheek. "Come on, Miranda, look me in the eye and say something so I'll know you're okay."

If she didn't wake up he'd have no choice but to drive her to the nearest hospital. And how would he explain this? *No, those are not my handprints around her throat. A ghost choked her. Not me. Never me.*

Sounded like a good way to land in jail.

Miranda's eyes opened slowly and she looked at him. She was rational and clear-eyed, which was good. She was also scared, which was only natural.

"I dreamed about you," she said, her voice slightly raspy.

Remembering his own odd dreams and visions since he'd come to this house, he started slightly. "Oh," he responded ineffectually.

"The man in the dream was you but...not exactly you." She closed her eyes again.

"It was just a dream," John said, trying to sound cool and unaffected even though he was neither.

"But it seemed so real," she whispered. "I could almost…" she wisely hesitated. Perhaps she had been affected by tonight's ghostly threat, but she had not lost her mind completely.

"Go to sleep, Miranda," he said. "He's gone." *For now.*

"Stay with me," she responded. "I don't think Tony can hurt me when you're here. I don't know why, but…"

"I'll stay."

She reached out as if to grasp the front of his shirt. The problem was, he wasn't wearing one. Her hand fisted at his chest, just above his heart.

"How do you kill a dead man?" she whispered.

MIRANDA SLEPT DEEPLY for the first time in months. It had been a year since she'd slept so well. More than a year. Since Tony had come into her life, she hadn't come anywhere near to feeling this relaxed and rested.

Morning sun slanted across the bed. Not her bed, Miranda realized as she came awake. John Stark's bed. The room was silent, but for the gentle rasp of his even breathing. No ghostly chill cut the warmth of the sunshine, no cold unliving fingers touched her. Tony was not here.

Instead of slipping from the bed as she knew she should, Miranda stayed beneath the covers with a sleeping John Stark lying beside her. Did Tony have some kind of fear of John that kept him away? Had last night's visit sapped his energy?

Was he gone at last?

She couldn't make herself believe that Tony was

gone for good, but she could enjoy this moment of peace. Peace, serenity, sanity…simple things that were not appreciated until you didn't have them anymore.

John made a noise in his sleep and rolled over to face her. He snorted, and sighed, and opened his eyes.

And sat up quickly, obviously surprised to find her in his bed.

"Sorry," he said as he swung his legs over the edge of the bed and presented his bare back to her.

A very fine back, Miranda had to admit. John wore flannel pants which covered his legs, and she found herself wondering if his legs were as well sculpted as his back. She had not enjoyed such natural, warm thoughts in a very long time, and they felt good.

"I didn't intend to fall asleep," he said. "I just didn't want to leave you alone."

"Thank you for staying with me." Miranda drew the sheet up to cover her breasts. Her nightgown was modest enough, but in the morning light it seemed much too thin for modesty.

John glanced back, and there were a thousand questions in his eyes. He only asked one. "Did you sleep?"

"Very well, thank you."

He nodded and glanced away, obviously embarrassed by the too-intimate setting. She should be terribly embarrassed herself, but instead she felt relief and ease and an unexpected familiarity.

"Your ghost tried to kill you last night," John said gently. "Do you remember what happened?"

"I'm afraid so." She remembered too well what those hands at her throat had felt like.

Just as clearly, she remembered the dream she'd been

having before Tony had awakened her. It was silly to hang on to a fantasy when her world was falling apart, but what she remembered was oddly comforting. She felt closer to John than she'd imagined was possible, and if a dream caused the aberration…maybe she should just enjoy the feeling while it lasted.

He turned his head to look at her again, and she was reminded sharply that John Stark was a very fine-looking man, one who was willing to help a woman everyone else had branded as crazy. "I won't leave you alone until Lara Hilliard and her people get here and she sends Tony away," he said.

"Can she do that?"

John nodded. "Yes. You really should have called her in the first place. This sort of thing is definitely up her alley."

"But I didn't call Lara Hilliard. I called you."

He turned his gaze to the uncovered window, to study the fine, autumn morning beyond the panes of glass.

Miranda added, "I'm not sorry I called you, John."

He didn't look at her as he answered. "Neither am I."

CHAPTER SIX

J OHN WATCHED Miranda sip coffee. She looked better this morning. A little brighter, a little more well rested. A touch of color rose in her cheeks, and an emerald sparkle danced in her green eyes. Should he tell Miranda that she was Vera Lavender reincarnated? Should he inform her that he'd been channeling her lover—the murdering, suicidal artist/handyman—and that the accompanying visions and dreams had been extraordinary?

He wasn't sure how much she could take at this point, and until he knew more it didn't make much sense to upset her, especially when she was so obviously having a good day.

"He isn't here," Miranda said softly, her gaze raking over the kitchen from corner to corner. "Some days it seems like he's always right behind me, or just around the corner, or hovering on top of me. But this morning…" Her eyes met his. "Do you think he's gone?"

John wanted to be able to tell her *yes,* he wanted to make her smile. But he had to tell her the truth, above all else. "No. Tony was weakened by last night's appearance, but he's not gone." He suspected using the words "murder attempt" instead of "appearance" would upset her, though she was dealing with the reality well enough.

"I thought you didn't talk to ghosts," she teased.

"I don't. I'm not talking to Tony, but I can feel him in the house. He hasn't gone, Miranda."

Her easy smile faded some but did not disappear. "I didn't really think so, but still, this is nice." She closed her eyes. "I had forgotten what it's like not to be haunted. To sip coffee without shaking and take deep, even breaths and think of anything other than what my ghost might say or do next."

Miranda was beautiful this way, eyes closed, heart at ease, lips turning up just slightly into a half smile. If he had met her in any other way, in another place and another time…

The truth washed over him in a shock wave that made him dizzy. He *had* known Miranda in another place and another time. Not just one, either, but more than he could comprehend at the moment. He had loved her, he had made her laugh and scream and cry.

And he had killed her.

John jumped up from his seat at the table and headed for the coffeepot and a refill, primarily so he wouldn't have to look into Miranda Garner's eyes while he regained his composure.

She'd looked at him with those eyes before as she'd taken her last breath, blood covering her nightgown… her apron…her silk gown…her bare body…her corset….

The doorbell rang and Miranda left the kitchen with a quick, easy step. John was tempted to follow her, but it wasn't as if Tony was going to ring the doorbell before his next attack. The ghost had been seriously weakened; though to be honest John had no idea how long it would take Tony to rebuild the strength that had been sapped last night.

Another female voice drifted to the kitchen, and quickly moved nearer. "I smell the coffee. I swear, Miranda, you make the *best* coffee."

Miranda tried to convince the woman that she'd be happy to serve coffee in the parlor, but the visitor would not relent and was soon stepping into the brightly lit kitchen. Her curious eyes immediately lit on John, and her smile brightened.

"So this is the man who belongs to the truck out front? How rude of you not to arrange a proper gathering to welcome your visitor to Cedar Springs." The woman's smile stayed in place throughout the light-hearted chastisement.

John stepped forward to introduce himself, but Miranda intercepted. She circled around the nosy woman.

"This is my good friend Elyse. We used to work together at the library."

"And will again one day, I hope," Elyse said as she offered her hand for a shake.

"John Stark," John said as the woman shook his hand for a moment too long. "I'm…"

"A friend from Dallas," Miranda said before he could say too much. "I wasn't expecting him to stop by. It was quite a surprise."

"And here I was feeling sorry for you because you were out here all alone," Elyse said, her Southern accent pronounced. "My goodness. No wonder you didn't want to move in with me and Gordon."

Miranda looked at John with pleading in her eyes. She silently begged him not to tell her friend who he was and why he was here. The pain he felt was much too deep for something so trivial as her obvious embarrassment. Lots of people denied who and what he was. To be a psychic in a world that valued only that which could be touched and weighed and explained in a logical manner was not always an easy thing. He understood that.

And still it hurt. The more he thought about it, the more the contempt she showed him hurt. It hurt in a way that only an oft-repeated slight can, like salt being poured into an open wound, like he was being pounded in the same sore spot, again and again. She was ashamed of him, she was embarrassed by who he was. So she lied, to her friends and to herself.

When Miranda had denied him in the past—and she had, many times—he always killed her for her disloyalty.

JOHN PACED and muttered and gave her the oddest glances. He had been this way since Elyse had departed, hours ago. No, he had been this way since just before Elyse had arrived. Something was wrong, and he refused to tell her what.

For a moment she had suspected that perhaps he was hurt by her little fib about why he was here, but that didn't make any sense at all. Like her life made so much sense, these days.

Maybe he hadn't slept as well as she, or he was picking up something odd from Tony's ghost. Every time she asked him what was wrong, he waved her off without even looking her way.

"Would you please sit," she said in desperation. "Just watching you is making me dizzy."

"Then don't watch me," he said absently.

"Fine." She stood slowly. "I'll poke around the fridge and see what we have for supper."

Miranda left the room; John followed her. She stopped in the long hallway and spun to face him. "I can't watch you, but you're following me to the kitchen?"

"I'm not leaving you alone. We don't know when Tony will show up again."

"This is ridiculous. Why are you so annoyed at me?"

"No reason. Why would I be annoyed? I should be very happy, in fact. After all, I'm just a *friend* from Dallas stopping by for, what, a little recreational sex? At least, I assume that's the cover story. Men don't drive from Dallas to Cedar Springs just to say hello."

So, that *was* it. Surely he understood why she'd been forced to lie. "What did you expect me to tell Elyse?" Miranda snapped. "That you're the psychic I hired to take care of my ghost problem?"

"It's called the truth," he said sharply.

She supposed it might look pretty bad, when examined under a certain light. "I can't let word get out that I hired a psychic. Everyone in town already thinks I'm half-nuts, and if they know you're here…"

"As soon as Lara gets here, I'll be gone," he said. "I certainly wouldn't want you to be further embarrassed by my presence."

"I didn't say—"

"You didn't have to, and I should be used to it by now."

She had the oddest urge to kiss John. To touch his face and lay her mouth over his and rest her body against his, to tell him that it didn't matter who he was. The kiss would take away the pain of rejection, at least for a while. She stood very still and held her breath, waiting for the urge to pass.

It didn't.

"I'm sorry," he said, the heat of his argument gone in a flash. "I'm just…there's something going on here I can't explain."

"Can't or won't?" she asked. She didn't know John Stark well enough to discern such a subtle distinction for herself, and yet she was quite sure that he was hiding something from her.

"Does it matter?"

A slight, brief chill caressed her neck. Tony. Her response was to take a step closer to John. Her sharp intake of breath told him what was wrong.

"He's back," John whispered.

Miranda nodded and moved closer to John. He was warm and alive and real, and he was here to protect her from Tony. As if he knew what she needed, he wrapped his arms around her.

"I am sorry that I reacted the way I did. It's not important," he said.

Somehow she thought that maybe it was, in a way she had not expected and John would not admit.

"I won't let him hurt you," John promised.

"Thank you." She hid her face against his chest, and the chill at the back of her neck disappeared.

"He's not as strong as we are," John reminded her. "We are alive and he is not. This is our realm, our world, our reality. Tony doesn't belong in it."

It was a simple affirmation, and also a true one. Miranda realized that as she held onto John, soaking up his warmth and finding comfort in the strength of the arms that encircled her.

She should feel awkward, to rest in the arms of a man she hardly knew. Then again, they had shared a bed last night, and they'd battled Tony together.

Maybe together they were strong enough to keep Tony away.

Miranda lifted her head, rose up on her toes and pressed her mouth to John's. He was surprised by the move. In a way, so was she. And yet it felt so right, to kiss him. To press her soft lips to his, to hold on a little bit tighter. She responded to the simple kiss in a way she hadn't even dreamed of in a long while.

Well, she had dreamed....

After the surprise passed, John kissed her well and deeply. Her body responded, and she pressed herself closer to him. She wanted more. She wanted John to take her to the bed they'd shared last night and make love to her, as he had in that dream.

Of course, she couldn't tell him that. She couldn't ask him to make love to her and make her forget....

He pulled his mouth from hers and raked his fingers through her hair. "You're scared," he said gently. "You don't know what you want. I won't take advantage of you."

Miranda sighed. She had forgotten that she didn't have to ask John anything out loud. He knew. He always *knew.* "I feel good here," she whispered, grasping onto his shirt with one tight fist. "Whole and safe and..." *Loved.* She couldn't say that. It was too soon for such a word to be spoken between them. "I don't want the feeling to go away just yet."

She didn't have to be psychic herself to know he was tempted, to know that he wanted her. He wrestled with the decision for a moment. "When Tony is gone for good, if you still want me I'm yours."

LATE IN THE EVENING, Lara called to check on the situation. She was intrigued by the strength of the ghost... but not enough to leave her current situation. Tony had begun acting up again, in a nonthreatening way. A breeze wafted through the parlor where John and Miranda sat, even though no window was opened. The wind outside was brisk; thunderstorms had been predicted, and it looked as if the weather forecast had been correct. The old house was solid, but it shook under the force of the wind. In the distance thunder rumbled.

Every now and then Miranda swatted at an invisible pest, trying to shoo her pesky ghost away. Still, it was nothing compared to the thick mist that had tried to choke the life out of her.

When Tony regained his strength, what would he try to do? If only Lara and her team could send the ghost on before it got to that point.

John glanced at Miranda, and then quickly lowered his eyes to the book in his lap—the Vera Lavender biography. To say that things were strained between him and Miranda was an understatement. The dreams, the kiss...the past lives of which she was blessedly unaware....

All along John had believed that he was channeling BJ Oliver in his dreams and visions, but apparently it was more than that. He had *been* BJ Oliver, Vera's Johnny, the lover who had killed her and then himself when she'd refused to leave her husband for an uncertain life with him.

It was more than that, he knew that now. They had been re-creating this same scenario, in one form or another, for hundreds of years. Every time he and Miranda came close to happiness, every time they reached for what they wanted and deserved…their lives ended violently.

In Venice, that had been the first life to go horribly wrong. Scotland; Russia; the wilds of a new and uncertain country; on a cold mountainside; in a fine drawing room.

He always died with her blood on his hands.

Miranda had lit several candles earlier, afraid to be caught in the dark if the power failed. Apparently Tony was more solid, at least visually, in the darkness.

Sure enough, a clap of thunder sounded, and the lights flickered and went out. In the soft candlelight, he saw Miranda jump.

"It's all right," he said, remaining calm.

"The electricity is usually out for no more than fifteen minutes when these storms move through," Miranda responded, sounding not quite as confident as she'd intended. "It'll come back on shortly."

"I'm sure you're right." John set his book aside and watched Miranda in the candlelight. She jumped slightly, as if she'd been touched, and clasped her hands tightly in her lap. Head down, she muttered something he could not quite understand. Go away, perhaps. He had heard her say that before.

Fifteen minutes came and went, and the electricity did not come on. The room remained dark, but for the flickering light of the candles. Half an hour, forty-five minutes. The storm arrived at full force, rocking the house and shaking the windows.

And Miranda became more and more scared, as the minutes passed.

"Perhaps we should go to your friend's house," John suggested.

"You want to drive in this weather?"

"It might be preferable to sticking around here," he said calmly. "I'm feeling uneasy about staying here tonight."

"What difference does it make? Tony follows me everywhere. I tried to run, it didn't work."

"Yes, but tonight he wants you here, in this house," John said. A chill walked up his spine. Tony wanted him here, too. But why?

Miranda nodded her head and rose almost jerkily. "I'll get my purse. We can take my car. It's closer to the door." She took a flashlight from a desk drawer and turned it on before dousing the candles.

John followed her as she walked into the kitchen, where she grabbed her purse from the counter and delved inside for the keys. They didn't run for the front door, but they walked briskly, anxious to escape. As they reached the entrance to the old house, John took Miranda's elbow to guide her. She was scared, more scared than she'd ever been, and Tony was all around her.

She threw open the front door as a bolt of lightning split the sky. The thunder cracked, and at the end of the long drive a tall pine fell with a crackle as resounding and loud as the thunder. They watched as the pine fell, landing across the driveway.

Miranda stood in the open doorway, stunned and more afraid than before as the wind and rain blew against her. "We're trapped," she said. "It's too far to walk in this storm." Another bolt of brilliant lightning proved that point.

She turned into him and John dutifully wrapped his arms around her. "It will be all right," he said as he pulled her inside and closed the door. As he held her, he had a vision of the night to come. There wasn't much in this world that made him shudder, but this vision chilled him to the bone.

Unless they found a way to send Tony away tonight, neither of them would live until morning.

John felt an odd shifting inside him, as he held Miranda. The shifting wasn't painful, but it was curious. His head swam and his knees tried to buckle. He faded, he was displaced...he changed.

He looked down at the woman in his arms, and he smiled—as he often did when he held her.

"Vera, darling, what have you done to your hair?" He lowered his lips to her throat and kissed her. Her skin was so soft, and it tasted so good. Until he'd found her, he hadn't known anything so fine existed. Not for him. She shuddered beneath him, she shivered and held on tight. "I like it," he whispered.

CHAPTER SEVEN

"John," Miranda said softly. Her heart thudded. He had looked at her so strangely right before he'd kissed her throat. "What's wrong?"

He continued to kiss her throat, scattering gentle kisses here and there. "What's wrong?" he asked darkly. "You know very well what's wrong. There was a time when you said you couldn't love me, but that's changed. Now you tell me again and again that you love me, but you still won't leave Phillip. I think you only love me when I'm inside you." One hand skimmed down past her stomach to rest between her legs. "Is that love?" he whispered as he stroked her through the thickness of her jeans. "You've ruined me. Half the time I can't think straight. I lose my temper, I daydream when I should be working…I haven't painted a decent picture in months because I can't *concentrate*. I wasn't like this before I met you, Vera."

Vera? Again, Miranda's heart thudded hard. "John, listen to me. I'm not Vera. I'm Miranda. Remember? Vera's dead."

His body jerked like he'd been shot, and he pulled his hand away from her. Slowly, his head pulled away, too. "Dead," he whispered. "What have I done?" He took two steps back and looked down at his hands. "This is your blood…her blood, on my hands. Always on my hands. It's my fault. I never should've touched her. I never should've…"

Miranda didn't know what to do, so she relied on old movies for inspiration. She drew back her hand and slapped John across the face, hoping to bring him to his senses. The sound of her hand smacking against his cheek was loud in the foyer. His head snapped around, and then immediately he turned on her. His hand reared back, he took a step forward and she prepared herself for the blow that was to come.

But the blow never came. He stopped, almost as if he were frozen, and then the hand fell. "Miranda?" he whispered. "What happened?"

"I was just about to ask you the same question."

For a long moment, several silent seconds where it seemed the wind tried to blow the sturdy house away, John stared at his hands. "Time is bending," he said in a low, gruff voice. "Shifting and bending and merging."

Since he'd called her Vera, that possibility was as frightening as Tony choking the life out of her. Miranda was just about to decide that running to town through a raging storm was preferable to staying here.

John lifted his head and stared at her, hard and flinty. "There's something you're not telling me," he said, accusation in his voice. "Something to do with Phillip. Tony," he said quickly, correcting himself. "Tony. You bound yourself to him in some way, and it keeps us coming back again and again, caught in this cycle where nothing is ever as it should be."

Outside the walls of the dark house, a very close clap

of thunder made her put aside her urge to run. "You're not making any sense," she said when the boom had faded.

"No, for the first time in days I am making sense. This isn't the first lifetime in which Tony has stalked you. It isn't the first time he's made us miserable. He considers you his, because you gave him permission to own you, heart and soul."

Her heart skipped a beat. Reincarnation had once been as unreal to her as ghosts, woo-woo for flakes and those who dealt in fiction. But at this point she wasn't going to dismiss anything as impossible. In a way, what John was saying rang true. "Tony said, once, that I had given him my heart."

"That would do it," John said. "Words are powerful. Spoken in the right circumstances, that might very well—"

"I never said anything even remotely resembling the presentation of my heart," she interrupted.

"Not in this lifetime," John said calmly. He turned and walked into the parlor, where he relit the candles. They gave off a better glow than the flashlight he carried, though it was not a particularly steady light.

It struck her like a thunderbolt that she had seen him this way before, in candlelight, afraid for his life…and for hers.

"We're caught in a triangle," John said as he walked slowly toward her. "I don't know how old it is. Hundreds of years, surely, maybe a thousand or more. We repeat this triangle again and again, we make the same mistakes over and over, and in the end we always lose. Tony always wins because you allow him to win. You gave away that which you should have guarded more closely. Your heart. Your very soul. Long, long ago, you allowed him to convince you that it was right that you give these precious possessions into his keeping, but he was not a worthy keeper of such treasures."

"You're scaring me," she whispered.

"Good," John rasped. "You should be scared. You should be absolutely terrified. I am. In every life, Tony, Phillip, Adair, Carlo…the same soul with a different name, he comes back to claim what you gave him, and you and I end up dead."

She wanted to deny that such a thing was possible, but deep down she quivered and knew that John spoke the truth. "How do we make him stop?"

"Take it back." He tipped her head back so she was looking him in the eye. "In every life you give me your body, but you can give nothing more because he has it. He hoards what is yours to share. Take it back."

"I don't know how."

The house began to shake, a cold wind circled around her, and then Tony was behind her, whispering in her ear. "He killed you before, love, and he'll kill you again. Ask him if he's ever had your blood on his hands. Ask him how many times he's taken your life because you refused to give him what he wanted."

John had looked at his hands in the foyer and mentioned blood. Her blood. If he had been BJ Oliver in his last life, then he'd murdered her before.

She drew away from John, and he did not try to pull her back. "I don't know who to trust."

"Trust me," he said.

"Trust him and he will kill you," Tony said. "I

would never hurt you. I've loved you forever, Miranda, and I will love you until the end of time. *Per sempre miniera.*"

Forever mine.

Miranda turned to face Tony, a misty light that fought to maintain his presence here. "Show yourself to me," she said. "You've done it before. I know you can do it again."

"Miranda, don't," John said. "Invite him into your life and he'll never go. You'll never have a moment's peace."

She lifted her hand to silence John, as Tony did as she asked. The ghost who had stalked and terrorized her for a year took form close to her. He shimmered. Miranda lifted her hand and gently touched his cheek. "Let everything that happened in past lives go," she said. "I never meant to bind you to me. I never meant to ruin your life and mine. I'm sorry that I burdened you with such a hardship. I'm so sorry."

"It was never a hardship to keep your heart and soul," Tony said. "The keeping of them made you mine."

"I want them back," she said gently. "I want my heart and my soul returned to me, now. I release you from whatever bonds I created between us by making such a gift."

She dropped her hand, "I don't love you," she said softly. "I don't think I ever did."

He disappeared, slowly and completely.

The storm was moving away, but the electricity had not yet come back on. Miranda turned to John. "Tony's gone."

John nodded. "Yes, he is."

She stepped into the arms of this man she was meant to share at least one lifetime with, and he embraced her.

VERA PRIMPED before the mirror, making sure her hair and her makeup and her nightgown were just right. Johnny would be here soon, and even though he had been here just this afternoon she was already anxious to see him.

It was scary, but she'd made her decision. When Phillip returned from Hollywood, she'd tell him that she wanted a divorce. She loved Johnny, at least she thought she did. He kept telling her that somehow they would make it work. Maybe he was right.

The front door opened and closed, and she ran to the stairs. Since she'd left a light burning in the hallway for Johnny's return, she could see her husband climbing the stairs.

"Phillip," she said, her heart pounding unnaturally. "I didn't expect you back for several days."

"Obviously," he answered, lifting his head so she could see his eyes. They were red and swollen and so angry.

Somehow, he knew.

Vera backed away a few steps. Someone had seen Johnny here and started a rumor, or maybe some nosy body had seen the way she'd looked at her lover, when she thought no one was watching. All she had to do was convince Phillip that what he suspected was wrong... even though what he suspected was very, very right. "I don't know what you heard..."

"I didn't hear anything," he said as he reached the upstairs hallway. "Well, grunting and moaning and whispers of love, as I arrived home early in order to surprise my lovely wife. Other than those disgusting noises I didn't hear anything at all. What I saw as I crept up the stairs, on the other hand, was quite startling."

This afternoon, when Johnny had made love to her

in the hallway and she'd decided that she had no choice but to leave what she knew behind to be with him…Phillip had been watching. She could talk sense into her husband, she'd always been able to reason with him. He didn't look at all reasonable, at the moment.

"It was nothing, Phillip," she said as he approached her. "I was lonely, and you're away so often. I faltered, that's all." Now was the time to tell him that she was leaving, but she couldn't make herself do it. Not now when he looked so sad and angry and betrayed.

Phillip grabbed her and set her on the table in the hallway, where just this afternoon Johnny had made love to her. The arrangement of fresh flowers fell, water splashing over the table, fresh blooms spilling across the table and onto the floor. "Do you think I will ever let anyone else have you?" he asked as he grabbed her nightgown and shook her. "You are mine, Vera. Forever. Don't you understand what forever means?" With that he reached into his jacket and pulled out a knife.

Vera screamed, but she soon stopped. Her husband was going to threaten her, to frighten her, but he'd never hurt her. Not Phillip. He loved her.

She believed that his love for her would save her, even as Phillip stabbed her again and again. She screamed, until she couldn't scream anymore. He pulled her from the table and threw her to the floor, so that she stared up at the ceiling while her husband cried and cursed and killed her. Eventually he stopped stabbing her and he went away, crying still.

She should've died quickly, but something kept her hanging on and she was still alive when Johnny arrived. He ran up the stairs expecting to find her in bed,

*and instead he discovered her lying on the hallway floor,
crushed flowers all around her and blood staining her
gown and her body. She tried to call out to him, but she
couldn't speak.*

*"Vera?" he asked in an odd voice. He dropped to his
knees and touched her bloody gown as if he could not
believe what he was seeing. "I'm sorry. I'm so sorry. I
never should've left you here alone. Who did this to
you?" He lifted her gently and held her in his warm embrace. For a moment, just a moment, she thought everything was going to be all right, now that she and Johnny
were together.*

*"It was your husband, wasn't it?" Johnny asked.
"He found out about us. Oh, Vera, I'm so sorry...."*

*She saw Phillip coming up behind Johnny, and she
opened her mouth to warn the man she loved. But no
words came out, not even when Phillip lifted the gun to
Johnny's temple. Johnny was holding her in his arms
and telling her how sorry he was when Phillip pulled
the trigger....*

JOHN WOKE UP with a start, the dream/vision so star-
tlingly real he could still smell Vera's blood and the
fresh flowers that had been spilled all around her. No
wonder the stench of fresh blooms always made him
gag.

Until now, he'd seen what had happened only
through Oliver's eyes. He'd felt the anger and frustration, and that made it easy to believe that Vera's lover
had killed her. It was a relief to know that he had not.

The lights had come on again. He and Miranda were
both sleeping in the parlor; he in the not-so-easy chair,

she stretched out on the sofa. Just as well. He wasn't ready to be alone, not yet. Neither was Miranda, apparently, though she seemed to be sleeping peacefully enough, at the moment. He watched her, and oddly enough that pastime comforted him, deep down. She was so beautiful, and even though she had hidden her laughter and passion…they remained. They were waiting for the right man to let them loose.

He was that man. He knew it in a way he had never known anything about his own life.

The house seemed quiet enough, but he wasn't entirely convinced that Tony was gone. It was true that words had power, and that to give away one's heart and soul were foolish and not so easy to undo. Such precious things were meant to be shared, not presented on a silver platter for safekeeping.

He left the chair, stretched and walked toward a sleeping Miranda. She woke before he reached her, and she smiled up at him.

"I didn't kill you," he said without preamble.

Her eyebrows arched slightly.

"Well, BJ Oliver didn't kill Vera. He found her, dying. Phillip killed them both."

She sat up slowly. "He was in Hollywood."

John shook his head. "He came home early and found out about Vera and BJ, and he couldn't bear the idea of letting her go." He sat on the couch beside Miranda, as she stretched and came awake. "She was going to leave her husband, uncertainties and all. She did…love Johnny."

"Vera must've loved him very much."

Miranda leaned in and kissed him, much as she had

that afternoon. It was an easy kiss, arousing and natural. Without Tony's ghost between them, without the fear that John himself might somehow do her harm, it was easy to let all his fears go and just enjoy the kiss. He had to admit…he liked it. Very much. The kiss went on and on, growing deeper and more intimate, and he fell into it so easily, as if he'd kissed Miranda just this way a thousand times.

Rain pattered on the windows, and the old house creaked on occasion, as old houses often do. Other than that, there was no sound beyond their breathing and the rasp of annoying clothing.

The kiss changed. Miranda's lips parted, her tongue teased his, and she reclined on the couch, drawing him down to lie atop her. She wrapped her legs around his hips, and only the soft rasp of denim—his and hers— kept him from making love to her here and now. Her arms draped around his neck and she held onto him as they kissed. He was hard; she was ready; this was right. She rocked against him, in a subtle, almost unconscious way, inviting more, asking for everything.

Just as subtle was the way she pushed him away. Of course she pushed him away. He barely knew her…he knew her to his soul. He had just met her…he'd known her forever.

John reached for a touch of control. The woman was trying to drive him crazy. Another part of his brain went elsewhere. Did he have a condom in his bag upstairs? Maybe. Surely.

Crap, Miranda was messing with his head the same way Vera had messed with BJ Oliver. One surprise after another…never knowing what might come next….

"This couch is not suitable for proper lovemaking," she said as they reached a sitting position. She kissed him again, whipped her shirt over her head, and leaped from the sofa to run from the room. John followed, and from the foyer she laughed. He had always wanted to hear her laugh this way.

In the entryway he saw that her bra was draped over the banister. Her shoes were discarded on the stairs, one and then another.

And Miranda Garner was perched on the hallway table, smiling and wearing nothing but a pair of unbuttoned and unzipped blue jeans.

CHAPTER EIGHT

OUTSIDE, A CRACK of thunder split the sky, the brilliant flash of lightning filled the house, and then the electricity went out again.

There were no candles lit here on the second floor. After his eyes adjusted to the darkness, he could see Miranda sitting on the table. Still smiling, still waiting.

Of course, she was not Miranda. Not entirely.

And Tony wasn't entirely gone.

She had dealt the ghost a mighty blow, asking for the return of the heart and soul he had hoarded for so long. They were rightfully hers, after all. But Tony had possessed them for so long he continued to crave them. Miranda alone could not fight off the man who had haunted her for centuries.

But together, they could send him away.

John walked to Miranda and wrapped his arms around her nearly naked body. She was so smooth, so warm and inviting. He was tired of dreams and visions; he wanted the reality of Miranda beneath and around him.

Tony shimmered behind her, and the annoying ghost whispered something in her ear.

"Go away, Phillip," Miranda whispered, her eyes on John's face.

"Yes, Phillip," John said. "Go away."

Miranda wrapped her legs around him and placed her mouth against his neck, where she suckled gently. Her breasts pressed against his chest, and the way she moved against him told him very clearly what she wanted. Everything. Now.

He was so tempted by her, more tempted than he had ever been. But Miranda would never forgive him if he made love to Vera before he ever made love to her.

John ran his fingers through the short strands of her hair. "Miranda, do you know where you are?" he asked.

Calling her name triggered something. She blinked and her body stiffened slightly. "Johnny?"

"John," he said, stroking her bare back. "Come on, Miranda, come back to me. You know who you are, and you know who I am. Vera's dead, remember?"

Miranda squirmed, but she did not let him go.

"Of course she is," she responded in a sensible voice. "Vera's been dead…" Miranda drew back sharply, and her arms shot up to cover her exposed breasts. "I'm naked!"

"For the most part, yes," John said, calling upon amazing restraint.

Miranda backed slightly away, but she didn't jump down from the table. "Did you…"

"No, you did it yourself."

She glanced around the hallway as if she couldn't remember getting here. And she probably couldn't. "This has never happened before. A lot of very strange things have happened to me in the past year, but nothing like this. Why now?"

John was beginning to understand what was going on

here, and it went beyond a simple haunting. Nothing like this had ever happened to him. He hadn't even known it was possible. "Tony's haunting has made the walls between this life and the last one too thin. Time is bending, circling around. The most recent past life is slipping in on us, trying to repeat, to live again. Apparently you can tempt history into repeating itself, if you're not careful, and that's what's happening here."

Miranda dropped her arms and slowly fell into him to wrap those arms around him. "I don't want to die," she whispered, her heart thudding against his.

"I won't let that happen."

She lifted her head and glanced around sharply, but she did not let him go. "Tony's back."

"Just barely, but yes. He's here, and you and I are going to send him away once and for all."

"How?"

"We're going to rewrite history."

THE IDEA of tempting history into repeating itself was farfetched, and a year ago she would have dismissed it as absurd. But Miranda couldn't let herself dismiss anything, these days. She had to ask herself the same question she'd been struggling with for days. Who did she trust?

This life and the last one were blurring, she knew that, and still Miranda hung onto who and what she was. She had been a librarian with a dull and safe and ordinary life, until Tony had shown up to ruin it all. She had hidden here, in this family home, afraid to take too much of what life had to offer. Afraid to take a chance on love and passion, maybe remembering on a soul-deep level that in the past it had always been love that led to the end.

Was John worth the risk? Love, passion, life. The way he held her, the way they faced this moment together, made her think—*yes*.

She thought that John would tell her what to do next, in order to send Tony away once and for all, but instead he kissed her, and she couldn't help but kiss him back. Even now, she wanted him. She'd wanted him from the first moment she'd laid eyes on him. She'd thought he was a plumber, then, come to fix her water heater.

They had been here before, just like this, and the memory that was not entirely her memory made her body react almost violently to the kiss. It was a dream, a deeply sleeping memory, a past life come to life that made her react this way. She leaned into John, her body clenched and unclenched as she threaded her fingers through his hair and hung on. If she…or Vera, whatever the case might be…had removed the jeans as well as everything else as she'd run upstairs, she'd be unzipping John's jeans and begging him to come inside her.

He touched her breast, gently at first, harder when she reacted almost violently to the caress. Heaven above, she wanted him more than she'd ever wanted anything else, in this life or any other.

"I know what you want," she whispered against John's throat, her lips barely kissing his as she spoke. "If I give my heart and soul to you, then Tony will go away."

"No," John said, his voice low and rasping. "I don't want you to give me anything."

A surge of disappointment washed through her. John did want her, she knew that without doubt. Physically, at least. Perhaps he wanted her body but not her heart and soul. Perhaps all they had ever shared was physical love.

"Your heart and soul are yours to keep, Miranda," he said as he pulled her close. "They are meant to be shared, not given away. Share yours with me, the way you share your body. Combine them with mine so we blend the souls and hearts together."

A squeak on the stairs told her Tony was here.... No, Phillip was here, solid and dangerous and intent on murder. And yet she didn't look that way. Her eyes remained on John's face. He was right; together they were stronger than they would ever be apart. Arms and legs entangled they did merge, not physically—not yet—but in every other sense they were one. Heaven above, she felt him inside her in a way she had not imagined possible, and she laughed with pure joy.

"How could you do this to me?" Tony whispered in her ear. "You're *mine.*" The glint of a silver knife caught her eye as he lifted it high. Her ghost remained misty, but the knife looked very real.

"I'm not yours," she whispered, unafraid. "I belong to no man." She held onto John and buried her face against his shoulder, turning her back on the ghost with the knife. "Go away, Tony." Her voice was no more than a breath, and yet as soon as she spoke the words he did as she asked. He vanished.

In the dark, with the rain pounding against the roof and the windows, John lifted her from the table and carried her to his room. There was no one in the world but the two of them, no thought on her mind but holding him until dawn, and beyond.

It was too soon, but past lives were indeed melding into this one, and she knew her feelings without doubt. "I love you," she said, draping her arms around his neck and holding him close as he carried her down the hallway. A flash of lightning lit the way for them.

"I have always loved you," he said as he carried her into his room and gently placed her on the four-poster bed.

When she thought of how close she had come to sending John away, she was as afraid as she had ever been. She grabbed his shirt and dragged his face down to hers. "Think we'll make it work this time around?"

"As strongly and surely as I've ever known anything…" He drifted down to join her on the bed. "Yes."

"YOU CAN'T BE SERIOUS," Elyse said in a hoarse whisper. "You've known the man less than two weeks! You can't just up and move to Atlanta on a whim! You can't even *think* of marrying the man, and you certainly can't expect me to sit back and let you run off to some courthouse somewhere and legally bind yourself to this…this strange man."

Miranda smiled. When she'd told Elyse that John was not an old acquaintance from Dallas but a new one, her oldest friend had been shocked. Elyse had always known Miranda to be cautious where men were concerned, especially in the past year. "It's not a whim. I haven't been happy here for a very long time. John makes me happy."

Elyse gestured wildly with her hands. "There are lots of men in Cedar Springs who would love to make you *happy* if you'd give them the time of day. Sex is no reason to sell the house you've lived in all your life and get married to a man you barely know, no matter how cute he might be, and leave your friends behind and…" Elyse ended the tirade with a snort.

John walked into the parlor with Lara Hilliard trailing behind him. Miranda had been a little dismayed to find that the ghost hunter was an attractive young woman, and that she and John had known one another for years. But it hadn't taken her long to realize that John and Lara were friends, nothing more. Lara was fascinated with the house, and there were indeed ghosts here that needed to be released.

But not Tony's. Tony was well and truly gone.

Miranda smiled when she saw John. He smiled at her. Elyse grunted in open disgust. "You'll be back in six months, when the excitement of this new relationship has faded, and by then the house will be sold and what will you do?" Elyse muttered, but she did so loudly enough for everyone to hear. "Oh, all right," she finished. She looked at John, and her eyes flashed. "So, Mr. Stark, what are your intentions? How are you going to take care of my friend? If you're a gigolo planning to live off of her money, I swear…"

"I have a job," John said. "I don't want Miranda's money."

"A job," Elyse snorted. "What *kind* of a job?"

John didn't answer, but instead looked at her and waited. Miranda smiled. "John is a psychic," she said. "An extraordinarily talented psychic who makes a very good living helping people. I feel quite confident that he cares nothing about the Garner family money."

Elyse was silent for a moment. "A psychic," she repeated softly.

"Yes," Miranda answered. "A psychic." She would never deny him again. Not in this life, not in any life to come. They were past that challenge, at last.

"And what are *you* going to do in Atlanta while he's…psychicing?" Elyse asked.

"I'll help out around John's office and travel with him on occasion." And have babies. Not right away, but within the next few years…babies. They had never gotten that far before, and she wanted babies more than she'd imagined possible. She hadn't discussed that with John yet, so she didn't want to bring it up now.

Of course, it was always possible that he already knew exactly what she wanted from their life together. It was difficult to hide things from a psychic lover, not that she'd ever tried to hide things from John—or ever would.

Sometimes she knew what he was thinking, just as he knew her mind. An aftereffect of the joining that night they'd sent Tony away, she imagined.

"I also have the urge to get back into painting," she added.

"But…" Elyse began.

"I love John," Miranda said before her friend could come up with another argument. "I love him, and I'm going to marry him, and eventually the two of you will be the best of friends."

Elyse was not so sure about that, and neither was John.

But Miranda knew that one day her husband and Elyse would be friends. She wasn't sure how she knew with such certainty that this would come to pass…but she did.

After Elyse and Lara had gone, John wrapped his arms around Miranda and smiled—that bright smile she had learned so quickly to love. "Teach me to paint?" he asked.

"I didn't know you were interested in art."

"Neither did I," he muttered.

He placed one large, warm hand over her stomach. "Babies, huh?"

"Yeah. I want three."

"Well, you're going to get…"

She silenced him with a kiss, a long, deep kiss that distracted them both, and within a matter of minutes they were on the couch, fumbling with buttons and zippers.

And then she remembered why she'd kissed him. "Some things are supposed to be a surprise," she said as John pulled her blouse over her head. "Just because you *can* see everything, that doesn't mean you're supposed to…"

He shimmied her trousers down, freed himself and then he was inside her.

Miranda threw her head back and shifted her hips up to meet his thrust, and a startling vision filled her head. While John held himself deep inside her body, and she responded with ribbons of intense pleasure that never ceased to surprise her, she smiled. "Oh, John," she whispered, her heart swelling with love. "Twins…."

Dear Reader,

I'm so pleased to write the story "Haunt Me" that...well...it's scary! My first published books, for the Silhouette Shadows line, were dark romances, so Halloween anthologies are a kind of homecoming for me. And this particular story allowed me to explore several topics that have fascinated me for a long time: romance between a married couple, near-death experiences and the idea of astral projection. *Especially* astral projection. I mean...imagine it! The astral world has far fewer limitations than the plane on which we usually exist. Could adventures on the astral plane allow us to mingle with loved ones who have passed? With people from history or from the future? With other kinds of beings we can't even define? With characters from our favorite fictitious worlds, even? The possibilities are exciting and endless.

And exploring them in story form has all the fun and none of the scary part. Well...not unless you count the Monster! Definitely be careful of what kind of emotions you feed the Monster.

I hope you enjoy reading David and Charis's story as much as I enjoyed writing it.

Sincerely,

Evelyn Vaughn

HAUNT ME
Evelyn Vaughn

Much thanks to the writing community—
the friends—whose caring helped me through my own abyss:
the Wyrd Sisters; the Writers of the Storm;
the Witches in Print; Denise Little; my agent, Paige Wheeler;
my kind editors at Silhouette; and the ladies of NTRWA
and DARA. Who would have guessed cards and flowers
can communicate so much love?
Special thanks, too, to Juliet and Toni and Deb for reading
and critiquing, despite my truly twisted writing schedule.

In memory of my dad,
John Bruce Jocks
The Nomadic Rhymer
1923–2004

You said I killed you—haunt me, then! The murdered do haunt their murderers. I believe—I know that ghosts have wandered on earth. Be with me always—take any form—drive me mad! only do not leave me in this abyss, where I cannot find you! Oh God! it is unutterable! I cannot live without my life! I cannot live without my soul!
—Heathcliff
Wuthering Heights

CHAPTER ONE

HEATHCLIFF WAS A JERK.

The quiet beeping of a monitor. The rhythmic hush of the respirator. White walls, white sheets, white floors...and occasionally a nurse's flowered scrubs, more blasphemous than cheerful amidst the sterility.

Charis had made up her mind about Heathcliff when she'd been forced to read *Wuthering Heights* for high school, then again for college. She hadn't veered from that opinion when her artsy friend Diana insisted on renting the movie. By the time Charis was pushing thirty and had joined a reading group at her local bookstore, she had the guts to argue it out loud. Mr. Famous Romantic Hero was a bully and a selfish jerk.

Tubes. Wires. Numbers and displays. Technology seemed such a cold way to keep a human being alive. Especially this human. Especially when he shouldn't be.

Alive.

Some idiot named David Fields had been crazy enough to argue back. "Don't you believe in passion?" he'd asked. "Emotions that push a person beyond reason? A love so powerful that you don't care whether or not you're selfish, so necessary that you'd sell your soul—hell, you'd sell your best friend's soul—to keep from losing it?"

Paper-wrapped footsteps beyond the doorway—her face lifted in bleary hope for a doctor. Had something changed? Was there even a chance? But it was someone else, an old man crumpled with despair, being led toward another of the ICU rooms.

Charis had been a never-married and glad of it, back then. From what she saw of friends who'd wed too young and were having trouble with rebellious children or broken marriages, she felt increasingly smart for having resisted that complication. She'd told David-the-idiot exactly that. But as with her opinion on the novel, he took her argument as a challenge.

Two years later, they'd married. Soon, they'd celebrate their four-year anniversary. Charis hadn't known such happiness existed. True, they had their little problems. Happily ever afters weren't immune to minor conflict. But David was great, really. Even if she wasn't as enthusiastic as him. Even if maybe she disappointed him, now and then. Every day, David told her he loved her.

And *Wuthering Heights* remained their favorite book.

"'Because misery, and degradation, and death, and nothing that God or satan could inflict would have parted us,'" Charis read. Her voice rasped, hoarse, but she didn't dare stop. The familiar scene, in which selfish Heathcliff berated his dying Cathy, felt like a magic charm. If she just kept reading, David might still open his eyes. David might sit up. David might argue with her, once again, like he always had, about ridiculous passions and limitless love. "'*You*, of your own will, did it. I have not broken your heart—*you* have broken it….'"

Her throat felt like sandpaper. Trying to swallow, she made the mistake of looking up. Her world swooped at the shocking sight of David's swollen, bandage-wrapped face, the tube down his throat—the brace—halo, they called it. It was too much metal and plastic, too much whiteness, too little *David*. She squeezed his limp hand around the hard clamp of a pulse-ox monitor. It didn't feel like his hand. It felt lifeless.

She made herself look back down to their book.

The book was safer than the horrible place that reality had become since the phone call…yesterday? Maybe the day before that. She didn't know or care what time it was, anymore. Her ability to care was dying, on the bed beside her.

…Accident…

…Teenager ran a red light…

…Children in the crosswalk…

…We think your husband pulled into the intersection to protect…

She forced the words in order to keep from weeping, desperate now for the familiarity of Heathcliff's selfish pleas. "'So much the worse for me, that I am strong. Do I want to live? What kind of living will it be when you…?'"

But the lines had taken on a horrible new familiarity. Always before, Charis could distance herself from the book's desperation. Heathcliff was, after all, a jerk—and so unlike David. David was selfless. Heroic, even. In this day and age, who would guess that there were still heroes?

…Head trauma…CT scans aren't good…agonally breathing…won't be long now….

Stupid damned hero. He could have stayed safe, but his selflessness had killed him. The doctors had said as much. All that was left was the wait. Loss had become too real now, a force that didn't discern between the worthy and the unworthy. Between people who'd chosen wisely, and those who'd chosen poorly. Between people who were kind, and those who were selfish.

None of it mattered in this cold, horrible place. Here, loss was loss. Lives could be fragmented no matter their worth.

God, she was tired. Normally the ICU had strict visiting hours, but the nurses and doctors had made an exception for Charis, for her deathwatch. They'd brought water and snacks and begged her to rest and let her friends or family take over, but Charis refused to give up a minute, a second, a breath with David.

Not if these were the last she'd get.

It had been hours. Or days. Her eyes could hardly focus on the familiar words in the book. Her dry lips moved, but she got no more help from her throat. Desperate, she bowed her head onto her arm across the bed rail, just for a minute. She wished David smelled more like David and less like antiseptic, less like blood. She desperately wished she'd been more of what he'd wanted in life….

But no, she couldn't go there.

She thought of *Wuthering Heights.*

"What kind of living will it be when you—oh God! would you like to live with your soul in the grave?"

She startled awake to alarms from the monitors that crowded the tiny, sterile room. Even as she blinked into comprehension, nurses were drawing her away from the bed, making space. The book wasn't in her hand anymore; she must have dropped it. Doctors bent over David, talking about BP and ICP and dilation like it was algebra homework and not her husband's life—*her* life—withering away in front of her.

"No," rasped Charis, recognizing the truth even as she protested it. She'd been staring at those monitors long enough over the last day or two to recognize what the falling numbers and flattening lines and buzzing alarms meant. *No.*

"Run the tape," ordered the older doctor, while a younger doctor squeezed on the IV bag and pinched open David's eye and shook his head. Machines continued to wail impersonal protests.

No.

A nurse rubbed Charis's back in mute sympathy. Was that part of her job, too? Charis strained away from her. "David—"

Don't leave me! Even now, she couldn't force such dramatic words from her throat. Charis wasn't the kind of woman who wailed protests in hospital rooms. Charis was discreet. Pragmatic.

At this moment, she hated her pragmatism almost as much as David always had.

"Paddles," said the younger doctor.

"No," insisted the older one. "Call it."

"Is there a DNR?"

Horrified, Charis forced her gaze from David long enough to turn, long enough to recognize the Do Not Resuscitate order that lay, unsigned and forgotten, on her purse in the corner. So much for being the efficient one. She should have handled that; it was the right thing to do. She and David had talked about this, back when it was comfortably abstract. He wanted to donate his organs, the damned hero. He didn't want to be a vegetable….

She could do it now. Snatch it up. Scribble her signature as her final, brave tribute to the man she'd loved.

But she couldn't move. She couldn't sign it. Not yet. He might force her to say goodbye, but she wasn't about to volunteer it.

Maybe she was as selfish as Heathcliff, after all.

Turning back to the bed, Charis saw that the paperback novel had been kicked underneath.

"Paddles," repeated the younger doctor, but the older one said, "Don't be a sadist. I'm calling it. Eleven o'three."

So that she could always know, to the minute, when her world had ended.

"You can go to him," whispered the nurse, and Charis numbly did as she was told. The nurse snapped off the alarms, the sudden silence drowning. Echoing. Awful.

Charis took David's hand, still warm, no more limp than it had been a few minutes ago. She stared into his swollen, battered face, searching for any sign of life, willing him to open his laughing dark eyes, silently pleading, praying....

It didn't make sense. How could she still be here in this cold, sterile world of machines and strangers, if he wasn't?

"Don't leave me," she whispered at last. He'd wanted emotion? Her words were suddenly thick with tears and desperation, and she couldn't stop them. "You can't be that selfish. Don't leave me, David. Don't do it. I can't let you go."

"It's better this way," said the older doctor from the doorway, even as the younger one hovered. "Perhaps Dr. Bennett wasn't as clear as he should have been about one's chances after severe head trauma. If your husband had survived...."

But Charis ignored him, bent across the rail, pressed her face into David's gown-covered shoulder. "I'm not letting you go," she slurred. Some part of her was aware how ugly this was—her wet words, her cruel insistence. How *indiscreet*. But her need won out. "I don't care, I don't care, I don't care. You can't come into my life and change everything and then leave. Please. *Please*. Don't make me stay here alone…."

Which is when the monitor quietly beeped.

Everything in Charis went still. David was alive?

"Yes," breathed the younger doctor in triumph.

"Oh, God," muttered the older one. "God forbid."

"He's alive?" Charis whispered, gulping back her misery, afraid to hope.

"For all the damned good it will do him," snarled the older doctor—and left.

Charis stared into the swollen wreckage that had been David's face…and horror slowly settled across her, turned in her empty stomach, tightened into her throat.

He was still gone.

"Dr. Smit is old school," murmured the younger man—Bennett? "Not all surgeons are on track with the new guidelines…."

His noises meant less than nothing against a truth that her eyes, her heart could see. David was still breathing, thanks to the tubes. His heart was still pumping, thanks to the fluids the younger doctor had been pushing since the accident. But damn it….

He wasn't there anymore!

She'd lost him anyway. And worse, she hadn't let his body go with him. The guilt of it welled up inside her like vomit—she staggered back, stumbled out of the tiny ICU room, slumped against the white wall across the hallway. What had she done?

He was a hero. He always had been. But she was a coward.

She was supposed to have loved him, no matter how rarely she'd been able to say it.

What had she done to him?

Vaguely, she became aware of the open doorway into the next room, of the old man she'd seen before, now pressing his lips to his wife's blue-veined hand. As if in a dream, she became aware of his weeping. "Kathy," he said, through desolate tears. "Kathy…."

Like from the book. Charis whispered, "'How can I live without my heart? How can I live without my soul?'"

But better that kind of fate than what she'd done. She shrank away from the stranger's pain, from her own cowardice—

And something cold washed past her.

It felt real, as real as a current of invisible water. Cold, and ugly, and pitiless. She recoiled from it, bumped back against the wall, stared at—

At nothingness.

At linoleum, and glass, and glaring white.

She stretched out her shaking hand—and again, she felt it, like thick, diseased liquid sliding icily past her fingers. It was *real*…and then it was gone. Rather, it was past. She shuddered, afraid whatever it was might linger for a lot longer than it should.

If that had been David's ghost, it had been the exact opposite of what she would have expected from him….

But exactly what she deserved.

CHAPTER TWO

He didn't hurt.

That was the first thing Dave noticed. Or maybe it was just the first thing that struck him as *worth* noticing. He usually tried to show a macho, tough-guy face…but secretly, he didn't much like pain.

Luckily, when he'd seen the Corvette speeding toward the red light, and the kids crossing the street beyond him, he hadn't had time to worry about pain or anything else. He'd barely had time to recognize the danger, to punch the gas….

A gunning engine. A rush of motion. A crash, a lurch, a blur, screaming metal, screaming bystanders, spraying nuggets of glass.

Oh, crap. He'd been in an accident, hadn't he?

He glanced over at himself, where he lay in the hospital bed beyond several rushing, strangely lit doctors. Wires. Tubes. Screws? He looked bad. *Really* bad.

Then it occurred to Dave that he shouldn't be able to do that. To see himself, swollen and bandaged and unconscious, his wife Charis weeping beside him in thick, mustard-colored shadow.

Uh-oh, he thought. *This can't be good.* In the six years he'd known her, Dave had never seen Charis cry. Not at sad movies. Not when the cat died. Never.

It had kind of bothered him, never being sure what she felt. In fact, they'd fought about it this morning....

"Show me something," he'd challenged, trying to keep it light, like a joke, but failing. It wasn't a joke. "Show me anything."

She'd set her jaw with that cool control that so grated on him. "Maybe you aren't looking closely enough."

Dave blinked away the abrupt, disconcerting memory and the bare wisp of emotion it brought. Strangely, he couldn't work up much upset over that, now. Rather, he *could*—he still felt things—but it felt safer than it should. One step removed. Like watching something really dramatic on television.

That's when Dave realized he might be dying. His first instinct was to fight this death. He had too much to live for. What about Charis? But even as he moved toward his body, toward where she wept uncharacteristically over him, real pain struck.

His arm, bent ways arms didn't bend. His legs, trapped and bleeding in the wreckage of metal, waiting for a rescue crew with a blow torch. And his head—he remembered glimpsing a bloody smear against a spider-webbing of broken glass on the car's windshield, like stained glass in the sunshine, before unconsciousness had eased him from the encroaching agony.

That agony surged back when he even thought of returning to his body, and he stumbled farther away. Nope. Wherever he was now was much better. In fact, he felt great! And...

He looked down at himself—the himself standing there, not the one in bed. And he looked great, too, especially contrasted with the other version. He glowed with a bright, turquoise light that shimmered like the Northern Lights, and that looked healthy, too.

Like a step-by-step instruction manual, the cliché began to unfold. Aware of a brilliant light to his side, Dave pivoted toward it. Illumination and comfort poured from a beautiful tunnel, beckoning him, drawing him. Figures emerged from it and he knew them all with the certainty of his heart, even the grandparents who had died before he was born. His parents were there, parents he'd lost as a teenager. After only a moment's stunned surprise, he stumbled into their waiting arms. Others surrounded him with silent, tangible welcome, and he was home. Right here in the hospital.

All the love, the acceptance that he'd missed for so long was his. Damn! This whole dying business was definitely underrated.

Except…

Even through this rush of well-being, something niggled at him. As his mother drew him toward the tunnel, toward the light and contentment and pure peace, Dave looked over his shoulder.

Charis….

"Don't leave me, David," she sobbed, from where she lay across the body that, weirdly, had to have been his. Her words sounded faint and warped, as if he were hearing them from under water, but he definitely heard them. He'd needed words like that from her for so long, he wasn't about to turn away now. "Don't do it. I can't let you go…."

She *did* love him. Really.

"I'm okay," he told her, and he knew it was the truth, but she didn't seem to hear him. "Char, it's okay. Really."

"David," said his mother softly. "We have to go now."

His mother had always called him David, too.

"She'll be fine, son," said his father.

Dave knew they were right. Somehow he understood beyond doubt that the pain Charis felt was natural but temporary, that their separation was an illusion. The very real presence of his parents proved that, as surely as the way that the doctors, the walls, even his wife were fading toward insubstantiality. Everything except his deceased loved ones and the brilliant, glittering light were dimming into illusion. Charis's words faded into wisps of sound.

But he heard her, all the same. His heart, his soul, heard them. "I'm not letting you go," she sobbed. "I don't care. I don't care."

"It's okay," he insisted to her deaf ears, even as he backed a step closer to the light.

Then he sensed a wash of something opposite of the light. Of darkness, cold…of evil. He spun to look.

"Hurry," insisted his mother, but what Dave saw wasn't okay at all.

Charis, the doctors, even the hospital walls…though real, they all had a strangeness about them, a color or shadow or distance like a faded photograph. Only his parents, still lingering just inside the brilliant tunnel's mouth, seemed fully solid and real as they reached be-seeching hands toward him.

His parents—and the Creature.

The explorers who first viewed a platypus must have felt something like Dave as he watched the Creature that snuffled across the ICU room behind Charis…well, they would if platypuses were the size of rhinos, had no obvious legs or eyes and exuded a menacing aura of pure evil. This thing, or Thing, was solid and gray-black and malformed, and it stank of wrongness and corruption. It seemed to have more than one gaping mouth, and perhaps…*were* those eyes, multiple eyes like a spider's, behind the stretched, stained membrane that seemed to coat it?

Despite its lack of feet, it was shambling toward the bed where Dave's former body lay.

It was approaching Charis.

"Hurry," insisted Dave's father, repeating his mother's words.

But Dave turned his back on his parents to step between this Thing and his wife. *"No."*

And that's when—

On his honeymoon, in Hawaii, Dave had tried surfing. Of course Charis had protested and called him reckless, but he'd loved it—or he had until a towering wave had broken right on top of him, slamming him and his board downward through water and sand, rolling him until he didn't know up from down or light from dark.

As soon as he said "No," it felt just like that.

The world exploded around him, slapped him silly, but instead of water he drowned in a rush of memories and hopes and dreams and regrets and noise and light.

On that beach on Oahu, the wave had suddenly receded, spitting his bruised body onto solid sand as the world righted itself into air, sunshine and one angry bride. This time, when he opened his eyes, Dave was on his knees on oddly lit linoleum. He saw that the Creature was retreating from him, scuttling back like a roach from light. From his own turquoise light, in fact. It moved with a grotesque slither that, like a snake's, hid uncanny speed. Was it afraid of him? Good!

"Yeah! You *should* run!" Dave called after it, pumping a fist. "Let's hear it for the dead guy!" Triumphantly, he twisted toward the tunnel, toward his parents.

But they weren't there. Somehow, when the world disintegrated around him, his mother, father and even the tunnel had vanished.

Dave turned all the way around, but apparently he'd

delayed too long. Either that, or he wasn't dead after all, and if that was the case, why wasn't he in that twisted body of his?

Not that he was in any hurry to go *there*.

"Well…damn," he muttered. "Now what?"

Adding insult to injury, Charis backed away from his bedside. Hello…what about her not letting him go? He should have known that wouldn't last; God forbid Char be impractical. Still, backing away until she bumped against the hallway wall, she bled a dirty, sulfuric color that he belatedly recognized as…pain? It hurt her to lose him, of course, just as it had hurt him to lose his parents. He hadn't realized at the time how right that pain had been, like the pain that accompanies childbirth or…or sacrificing oneself for a good cause. He hadn't realized it then, and clearly she didn't either. But somehow…

Somehow he'd figured she could handle it. Char could handle anything…even when he wished she weren't quite so competent.

Anything that she could see, anyway.

But while Dave had been distracted, the Creature circled back from a different angle. Its maws widened greedily, emitting slimy black tendrils that slithered out, tonguelike, to slurp across the dirty aura radiating from Charis. She simply bled more pain to replace it, even muddier.

The Creature shuddered with satisfaction, extending more tongues.

Was it feeding on her suffering?

"Get away from her!" Again, Dave shouldered between Charis and this…this Thing. For a moment one of its black tongues brushed past his arm, leaving a streak of pain like fire. He caught his breath—out of habit, apparently, since he doubted this ghostly version of him was really breathing. The Creature's essence dizzied him, a stench like rotting bodies, a roiling mass of fears and angers and agonies and so much more. If we were what we ate, then this Thing…

This Thing hungered for everything horrible.

"Get…" Dave struggled to stay conscious against the burn of its touch, not wanting to even imagine what kind of venom it secreted. "Get back."

Again it retreated, avoiding his aura only sullenly. Maybe it wasn't so scared of him after all. He felt half-hidden, malformed eyes on him and on Charis behind him, as if it were merely waiting for him to falter.

As if it could wait eternally.

Then, to Dave's momentary relief, it abruptly turned away from him and Charis—and toward another target entirely. Dave saw just how solid the old lady in the next room seemed as she hugged the old man who wept over…her. Rather, over her corpse. The version he'd noticed—still moving—was one of the few things free of the strange lighting that cast across Charis, the doctors, everything else. The old woman seemed as real as his parents had, as real as he did. But she seemed exhausted. The light she projected was nearly invisible.

Her husband's aura was a blurry mixture of sulfur and gray…which seemed to draw the Creature like blood would draw a shark.

And the Creature, Dave finally noticed, had no aura at all. It put out no light, reflected no light. If anything, it absorbed light. Its presence was a hulking absence outside their door.

"It's all right, my love," the old woman insisted, holding and kissing an earthly husband who couldn't hear or feel her. She wore a sweat suit and a chenille robe instead of a hospital gown, as if she'd been there long enough to have her own clothes. "A few years barely make a difference, really. I'll be with you always, I promise, and when you come I'll be waiting for you."

Making a motion as if sniffing the air—as if this monstrosity had a nose—the Creature charged at the pair of them. Dave took off after it, despite the burn that still throbbed on his arm from its touch. It was either that, or watch this Thing….

Well, whatever it meant to do, he couldn't watch it without acting, no more than he'd been able to simply watch that drunken teenager mow down those school-children. No matter what.

Just because Charis annoyed him when she said he was reckless didn't mean she was wrong.

The Creature slithered nearer the grieving couple but kept a wary gaze on Dave, sizing him up with countless eyes hidden behind lumps in its mottled, black-gray membrane and tasting the air with its tendril-like tongues.

"Lady, get back," called Dave, slowing his step to circle the Thing.

She looked up, saw the Creature and gasped. But she didn't move. "I can't leave him yet."

The Creature vibrated with apparent ecstasy at this old couple's suffering and uncertainty. It seemed to salivate at her exhaustion. Dave moved even closer, eying it, a contest of wills. "No offense, ma'am, but I think you already have."

"Yes…." With a final, defeated kiss, she stepped back. The Creature continued to watch her, but Dave kept himself between them. "Oh my! I can finally breathe again. I'm tired, but I can stand. You don't know what a joy it is to stand! And the pain is gone. It would be such a relief, if only…"

Feeling the Creature's focus move from her to her living, grieving husband, Dave understood exactly what she meant. The only thing that really sucked about dying, once you got there, was your loved ones' pain.

As the woman came to terms with her death, she seemed less appetizing to the Creature. But her husband, bleeding his despair…

Dave made a decision and stomped at the Creature, like he might stomp at a wild animal he had to somehow, against all odds, chase away. When it didn't move closer, Dave tried the other foot, dangerously close now. He waved his arms. He'd heard that with some bears, it didn't hurt to look as big as you could, so it seemed worth a try. "Get! Go on!"

Instead, it snarled. The snarl hit him like a blast of sleet and icy numbness, and he shuddered with the uncertainty of just how dangerous this Thing might be.

Then, as if it heard something he didn't, it seemed to look elsewhere. With a sudden burst of speed, it hugged the wall and skittered disjointedly away, down the hall and off to other areas of the hospital.

"Holy—" But Dave didn't finish the exclamation. It seemed rude around this nice old lady. Instead, he turned back to her—and was surprised to see the bright tunnel opening for her. People emerged from it with short, excited steps, watching her like long-lost relatives at an airline terminal.

So that's what had scared it?

"My darling," she sighed to her husband, kissing his bent head as he wept over the shell she once had been. "Take care of yourself. Enjoy the life you have left, the children. Remember your medications…."

"Mama," said one of the ghostly figures from the tunnel—and finally the woman turned away from the man.

Dave had never thought of an old woman as radiant, until he saw the joy that lit her face at the sight of her dead son. With a wordless exclamation, she threw her arms around the boy, sobbing her joy as throngs of other loving figures surrounded her. "My baby," she wept, laughing at the same time. "Oh, my baby…."

Together, the crowd of them filtered back into the tunnel.

Dave looked back for Charis—and felt disappointment slump his shoulders as he saw what she was doing. She seemed to be talking to one of the doctors, a pen and paper in her hand. There he lay, freshly dead, and she was taking care of the paperwork?

That's what he got for falling in love with someone he wanted to save from herself. Sometimes, you failed.

At least he'd tried. "I'll miss you, anyway," he whispered, and the pain no longer felt distant. It was hard in his throat. "I hope you find joy with someone, Char. Really. I'm sorry… I'm sorry it wasn't with me."

Damn it. If he continued this way, he was going to cry. He'd already lost his Firebird today, then his life. His macho, tough-guy facade could only handle so much.

So he turned away from Charis—from life itself— and he followed the old woman into the tunnel.

Or he started to. But he walked into what felt like a wall.

"I don't think it's your time," said one of the old lady's relatives, patting him on the shoulder as she passed him, entering something he could not. "Not quite yet."

Then the light was gone and Dave, stunned, stood alone. There was Charis, still dotting *i*'s and crossing *t*'s with the doctor. Other doctors and nurses and random health workers moved about as well—Dave could see them through the glass ICU windows and oddly, even when the blinds were pulled, he could see shadows or auras that hinted at the people beyond. But they only saw the corpse that was his body.

Or was it a corpse? He moved closer, for a better look.

The pain forced him to back up.

Macho facade or not, he was starting to panic. "Charis?" he shouted, and put everything into it—his whole soul. *"Charis!"*

If this had been a movie, she would have at least sensed him, wouldn't she?

She did not.

He guessed they hadn't had that kind of bond after all.

That hurt almost as much as the accident had.

"Kiss me again, but don't let me see your eyes! I forgive what you have done to me. I love my murderer—but yours! How can I?"

—Heathcliff
Wuthering Heights

CHAPTER THREE

CHARIS WAS STANDING at the window of David's ICU room, looking out across a gray parking lot, when the ghostly reflection of a man's face from behind her appeared in the glass. For a moment her heart leaped with foolish anticipation. She spun.

But of course it wasn't David. The exhaustion had to be getting to her. In fact, the person who hesitated in the doorway of the ICU room wasn't even a man. He was a teenager.

A teenager bruised brown and yellow and purple, his pale face mottled with healing abrasions, confined to a wheelchair. He glanced nervously from her to the bed where David lay, deathlike, then back.

Charis had never seen the kid before.

"I'm sorry," she said, and her voice rasped in her throat from disuse. She'd spent the last four days with David, sleeping in the reclining chair near his bed, holding his still hand, alternately sitting and standing. The only times she'd eaten had been when the nurses brought her someone's untouched tray, or when her best friend, Diana, had shown up in the waiting room with a care package for her. And Charis had barely spent any time with Diana, since David wasn't supposed to have more than one visitor at a time. "You must have the wrong—"

"Mrs. Fields?" The boy's voice cracked.

Okay, so maybe he had the right room after all. "Do I know you?"

"I'm Todd Vernon." The name sounded uncomfortably familiar, but Charis still didn't place it until he added, "I'm the one who…who ran into your husband."

A wounded sound escaped from Charis's throat, startling her as much as it seemed to startle Todd Vernon. *This* was the monster who'd gotten drunk, run a red light, nearly mowed down a cluster of schoolchildren? This was the person who'd stolen her husband from her?

He looked so…young. Scrawny. Vulnerable.

She felt herself start to shake, a twitch in her wrists, her fingers. She doubted that was from exhaustion.

"I'm being transferred to the rehabilitation hospital," Todd continued quickly, his gaze finding and then veering from the bed. "I didn't want to leave without…without apologizing. To you and your husband, I mean. My parents' lawyer said not to, but I—"

His increasingly panicked eyes glistened suspiciously.

Forgive him. The voice was in her head—it had to be—but it sounded so remarkably like David's that she looked more closely at him, laid out in the bed, his rising and falling chest the only sign of life.

David was being transferred today, too.

He was being transferred to the long-term care wing. Dr. Bennett, the younger of the two physicians who'd worked on him, would have her believe this was a good sign. David's blood pressure was back to normal. The swelling in his brain had gone down. When he came out of the coma, Dr. Bennett insisted, they'd have a better grasp of what could be done toward his recovery.

But the older Dr. Smit, who'd visited only twice, gave her the respect of a more honest assessment. David might never come out of the coma, and if he did, the brain damage threatened to be so severe as to rob him of speech, of muscle coordination, of organized thought. She might never, never have the man she loved back. Dr. Smit had even used the "n" word—nursing home.

After he'd left, Charis had thrown up.

Todd Vernon continued to babble about how stupid he'd been, how he had no excuse, how if it hadn't been for David he would have hit those kids, and he had a younger brother almost the same age. He spoke of how sorry he was, how sorry, how sorry. But he, the one who'd had a choice in this, was awake, talking, facing a full recovery and probably some community service. Her David…

Char, damn it, forgive him.

No, she thought firmly, in response to what had to be an imagined plea. She would have spoken the word, but her stiff silence was all that was keeping her from throwing herself at that stupid, murderous teenager and beating the crap out of him, trying but never succeeding at showing him exactly what kind of pain he'd caused.

Todd swallowed, hard, and looked down. "Anyway. I wanted to say that."

Then he wheeled himself backward out of the room, turned the chair with the ease of a kid already adjusting to his temporary inconveniences, and rolled away past the large glass wall.

Ice princess. It's what David had called her during that last, awful fight, the morning of his accident, and suddenly Charis was back in their kitchen, wishing now that she could have stopped him from leaving.

"*Because I'm the one who always plans our anniversary,*" *David complains, stalking to the front hall for his jacket, his briefcase. "Maybe I'd like just a little indication that it's important to you, too."*

"Of course it's important!"

"Then you *plan it for once. Surprise me."*

Charis feels herself tense at the very idea. David always goes all-out for their anniversary getaways, finding incredible hotels, reserving cozy restaurants, arranging treats like string quartets or carriage rides that are so over-the-top romantic that they almost embarrass her, except for how much she enjoys watching his enjoyment. She can never come close to the sort of weekend he would plan. She will get it wrong, and he'll be disappointed, and she really, really doesn't want him disappointed on their anniversary. "I wouldn't know where to start."

"Figure something out." He hesitates in the doorway, his clear gaze especially cutting. "Unless you don't want to."

What a relief. He's so much better at this kind of thing. "I don't *want to."*

She's surprised by how his eyes flare in annoyance, by the bitter edge to his voice. "Nice job softening that one, Char."

"Softening…?"

"It takes two to make a relationship work."

But—their relationship does *work, except for moments like this. She's never been happier in her life than when she's with him. Why does he require restaurant or bed-and-breakfast reservations to prove it? "We* are *two people."*

"Sorry, Ice Princess. I meant two people who care."

"I do care!"

"Then show it. Show me something." He laughs, but not convincingly. "Show me anything."

Beyond marrying him, he means? Beyond the love-making, the living together, the quiet times? He knew she wasn't one for big gestures when he met her.

She clenches her jaw. "Maybe you aren't looking close enough."

"Maybe I shouldn't have to."

Unsure what else to say, but hurting like hell, she says, "Screw you."

That's the last thing she says to him. Screw you. *But of course, standing there in the doorway to their house, she doesn't know….*

"Nice spontaneity," says David, "but I'm late for work."

She watches him go out to his car, his shoulders stiff, his step tight. She finds herself holding her breath when he stops without unlocking the door. He's about to turn around, to apologize, to promise her the best anniversary weekend ever.

Instead he says, "I'll call you later."

And with a beep of the remote key, he unlocks the door, gets in and drives away.

That's the last thing he *says to* her. *But of course he doesn't call. He never makes it to work.*

IT WOULD BE just like David to take the high road and forgive Todd Vernon. Maybe Charis could have, too, if it had been her he'd hit. But forgive the boy for David?

David lay there, nothing moving but the rise and fall of his chest. His eyes were taped shut. He was being fed through a tube. Though scans showed he had brain functions, he might never walk, talk, reason again. Never touch her face. Never draw her into laughter or arguments or passion of any kind again.

"Rot in hell, Todd Vernon," Charis whispered.

"Mrs. Fields?" She jumped before she recognized Jed, the evening nurse. "Are you all right, Mrs. Fields?"

That was a stupid question to ask in ICU, wasn't it? Even more stupidly, she muttered, "I'm fine."

Fine and dandy. No use showing otherwise, right?

"I need to bathe him," explained Jed, carrying in a basin full of supplies. "Why don't you go stretch your legs, get something to eat? It's a beautiful afternoon."

Charis blinked. "Leave?"

The nurse smiled. "It will only take half an hour."

Her sense of responsibility stiffened her. "Shouldn't I...help?" Charis had no nursing experience. She didn't really want to stare at the open wounds and broken bones of David's tortured body—every time she even glimpsed them felt like a cattle prod to her gut. But...

For better or worse. She'd bathed him more than once during the better times. Bathed *with* him anyway....

A SPLASHING of water echoes off the bathroom's tile walls. The air thick and hot with more than just steam. David thick and hot behind her, his wet arms circling her, the hair on them dampened to dark, straight brush strokes. She leans her head weakly back into the solidity of his chest, trying to let go. That's what he calls it, anyway.

"Let go, Char," he murmurs against her wet, exposed neck. "Just trust me and let go."

Instead, her hand tightens into a fist, sending a gush of suds from the sponge she's been drawing indiscriminately across them both. Doesn't he understand that the more he asks, the worse it is?

She does want him, him and everything he brings her. She's never been happier than since she met him, loved him, married him. It's just that she can't simply—

More splashes. She begins to drift away in the sensation of his hands on her, his lips on her. Then he whispers again, "Let go."

Damn it.

"Make me," she challenges, not wholly teasing. And oh, he accepts the challenge. He succeeds, too. Finally.

But she can't help but worry that she's somehow disappointed him. Again. He thinks everything should happen so easily, like in a sweeping, romantic novel....

"ONCE THE WOUNDS have better healed," Jed suggested. "For now, though, there's not much you can do to help with this. Go on." His eyes were gentle but firm. "I promise, he'll still be here when you get back."

So he understood. The two times she'd had to rush home over the last few days, for a quick shower and change of clothes, she'd gone over the speed limit. Her heart felt compressed with dread. *What if David died while she was gone?*

Because she was gone?

Maybe everyone visiting the ICU thought that.

So after a few more owl-like blinks, Charis forced herself to stand and leave David's room. She scanned the nurses' station and the walls of glass-fronted rooms, most with their blinds down, some open to show patients alone or with vigilant friends and family. It felt odd to realize that she and David were just one couple of many, their suffering downgraded from life-shaking tragedy to another mere misfortune. It almost felt...comforting? But that wasn't right or fair to anyone.

A stooped old man stood at the nurses' desk with a

huge spray of flowers. Yellow gladiolas and white lilies and pink roses mixed with narcissus and carnations in a burst of natural beauty. They'd been beautifully arranged, with a big pink bow and a little cheerful birdhouse and two fake birds mixed in with the blooms.

The old man looked familiar, but his familiarity didn't nauseate her like Todd Vernon's name had.

"…people loved her so," the old man was telling the nurse. "I've got more danged flowers than I know what to do with."

"We all miss Kathy," agreed the nurse sadly, accepting his flowers. Now Charis recognized the man. He'd lost his wife in ICU, the same day that David had died and then revived into…into whatever purgatory David's existence had become. "You're kind to think of us, Mr. Wells. Your wife was so—" But a ringing phone interrupted her.

The old man lingered, as if unwilling to leave before he knew what she'd meant to say about his wife. Perhaps he was clinging even to mentions of her. He looked frail and white-haired and easily as alone as Charis had felt this week.

Unsure what she meant to do, but unwilling to leave him standing there while the nurses conferred about an incoming patient, Charis went to Mr. Wells's side.

"They're beautiful flowers," she said, and the polite words felt fake in her mouth, despite that she meant them. "I'm sorry for your loss."

Wells turned haunted eyes on her for a long, solemn moment. It was a moment of recognition that went deeper than mere names, the look that people in hospital waiting rooms or the fringes of the ICU often shared. Desperation, hope, fear, resignation. A recognition of shared humanity.

"I remember you," he said. "You're the one whose husband saved all those children, aren't you? It was on the news. My sons were talking about it."

Charis nodded, only vaguely surprised to hear that. Messages from reporters had filled her answering machine. She'd erased them. "That's David for you," she said.

The bitterness in her own voice surprised her. But Mr. Wells suddenly smiled for her, the expression weary on him, as if he hadn't had much cause for smiling lately. "Would you do me the favor of joining me for a cup of coffee, Mrs. Fields?"

"I don't know…they might need me…." Charis glanced toward David's room, with its pulled blinds. She could see her reflection across the horizontal lines, hollow-eyed and pale with wrinkled clothing and uncombed hair. She looked even worse than poor, frail Mr. Wells. And standing off to one side, his arms folded and his shoulders wonderfully broad and his mouth set with disapproval as he eyed them both, stood—

David!

Charis spun with a sob of relief to where the reflection showed him standing—but of course nobody was there. When she glanced back at the window, both confused and embarrassed, his reflection had vanished as well. She'd imagined it.

David lay, all but lifeless, behind those blinds, having his bandages changed and his body cleaned.

The real sounds of phones ringing and machines beeping and low conversations and nurses prepping for an incoming patient—"bicycle…no helmet…another head injury…"—taunted her.

Charis shuddered—and not, this time, from the Cold. That's how she'd come to think of the awful wash of ugly, icy dread that she'd sometimes encountered here, over the last few days. She couldn't explain the Cold as blowing vents, because it never seemed to be in the same place. She couldn't explain the Cold as the result of, say, spilled rubbing alcohol or sprayed disinfectant, because its presence gagged her like nothing clean or good. She couldn't explain it at all, unless...

Maybe her shudder was related, after all.

"Mr. Wells," she heard herself asking with a shaking voice—and she *must* be exhausted, to say something so stupid and so embarrassing to a complete stranger. "Do you believe in ghosts?"

CHAPTER FOUR

"Yes!" screamed Dave from the room's doorway. He spread his arms to embrace the triumph of this moment and wished he were embracing his wonderful, wonderful wife—but he'd already tried that once, and the whole stumbling-right-through-her thing had freaked him out. Still, way to go Char!

She, of all people, *got* it!

"*Yes!* I'm a...well, maybe not a ghost exactly. I mean, there's probably some technicality about the body dying first, right? But that's close enough, hon. God, I love you."

And he did love her, *damn* he loved her, Ice Princess or not. Hell, he'd known she was an Ice Princess from the minute he met her, and it hadn't even slowed him down.

He'd kind of liked the challenge of thawing her out.

And now she was living up to his highest hopes by grasping the seeming impossibility that—

"No," Charis said to the old man then, answering her own question...and David stopped spinning to frown. Her voice sounded no more odd than it had since he'd gone ghosty—noise from the living already seemed monophonic, like a cheap speaker—but that's not why he frowned. He just saw it coming— "No, of course you don't. Why would you? Only an idiot would believe in something like that. I'm sorry, Mr. Wells...."

David felt like he'd been gut-punched.

Only an idiot. And God forbid Charis ever, ever risk looking like an idiot.

"No, hon," he protested, crossing toward her. "You had it. You *had* it. I'm here. If you just try, maybe…"

But as ever, nobody heard him. Mr. Wells said something about coffee and some quiet, and she agreed, and they headed off together.

"Charis!" Dave called after her, following.

Or he started to follow her. As usual, he didn't even make it to the elevator before he felt a powerful lurch in his solar plexus. With a rush, he was jerked into a backward blur.

Into *pain.*

That's because he was suddenly too close to his body again.

Dave scrambled away from it, where it lay corpselike on the hospital bed, being bathed by a male nurse.

He scrambled away from the head-cracking, arm-shattering, soul-wrenching pain that struck him whenever he got too close to the damned thing. He dropped, exhausted, to the indistinct floor, with his back braced against the weirdly lit white wall. For some reason, while he could go right through people, wheelchairs, food carts and anything that didn't sit in one place too long, the walls and floors were less penetrable.

Just now, he didn't give a damn why that was.

Soon, he could breathe again without his chest imploding—or, at least, he could mimic the memory of breathing, since he wasn't sure if this new, ghostly form of his needed oxygen or not. It didn't seem likely.

He half lay, half sat there on the floor in defeat, and he glared at the physical shell to which he seemed permanently attached. He looked down at himself and his pale, fluctuating glow of turquoise, then back at the shell.

Then he slapped the floor beneath him in fury and frustration. *"Damn!"*

To him, his shout seemed to ricochet off the walls, off the ceiling, off the floor in otherworldly reverberations. But in front of him, the nurse continued to matter-of-factly sponge off his clinically naked body with nary a recognition that the thing on the bed wasn't Dave at all. Dave had already tried everything—pushing people, which led to diving through them; trying to throw things, which he couldn't even pick up; screaming in their faces. But he was invisible to them. Invisible and silent and all but dead.

Even to Charis.

He'd hoped that if anybody would recognize the real him, the him that wandered this ward of the hospital trapped somewhere between life and death, it would be his wife of four years. The woman he loved. The woman he'd sometimes thought might be his soul mate. But nope.

Charis never had been that fanciful….

"Why do we all assume that it's really Cathy's ghost?" The woman at the book discussion group, the one with the solemn expression and the funny name, wears her hair up in a bun. Dave has always thought the hairstyle a cliché for unimaginative movies and TV shows where the straight-laced ice princess ends up tossing her glasses aside, kicking off her pumps, unbuttoning her high-collared blouse to show some cleavage and letting down her hair. But there the reality sits, sans spectacles.

Except that he doubts this one will be kicking off her beige sling-backs anytime soon. He says, "Of course it's Cathy's ghost."

"Of course? Isn't it more likely Mr. Lockwood is having a nightmare?"

"Oh, come on." Dave leans forward, bracing his elbows on his knees as if he can change her mind through sheer proximity. Also…she smells surprisingly good. *"Where's the fun in that?"*

The woman—Charis, right?—stares at him as if she's never heard the word "fun" before. Poor, inhibited Charis.

"Like haunted houses at Halloween?" prompts Dave. *"Horror movies? Campfire stories? Ghosts are fun."*

Just as he's really starting to feel sorry for her, she simply shrugs him off, turns to the others and says, *"Show of hands, how many of us have ever had a nightmare?"*

Of course everyone in their group of seven raises their hands. Dave can see where she's going with this, even before she pointedly asks, *"And how many of us have seen ghosts?"*

Only one person raises her hand. It's Charis's friend Diana. Unexpectedly—well, Dave didn't expect it—Charis laughs. *"Oh, Di, not your YaYa's kitchen again!"*

The two friends momentarily bicker about an incident they both, clearly, already know. Dave hardly hears them. He's still blinking, stunned by the way his insides lurch when Charis laughs.

Whoa.

Some women, especially the kind he usually dates, laugh easily. Dave also laughs easily, so he of course assumes it's a good quality in a human being. But with her…

Hearing Charis laugh is like spotting a red cardinal amongst a treeful of brown sparrows. Her laugh is a gift. It's special.

He wants to hear it again. Suddenly he notices just how pretty she is…or would be. If she'd just let her hair down.

And maybe unbutton her blouse a little.

"Was it fun?" she demands of her friend, as their de-

bate winds to an end. "*Even if it really was your grand-mother's ghost, would you call the experience fun?*"

Diana sighs in defeat. "*I wouldn't use that word, no. Maybe...poignant.*"

Charis turns back to Dave, her eyes flashing triumph, because she did hear his point and she disagrees and she's not the kind of woman who backs down. He likes that, too. "*It's more likely that Lockwood dreamed Cathy,*" she insists.

"*Except that I don't read books like* Wuthering Heights *for reality,*" Dave argues right back. "*I get plenty of reality in my day-to-day. I read books for something extra. Call it poignant, call it fun, call it drama, whatever. The point is to feel something, anything, intensely. Cathy's ghost is exciting. A nightmare? Like you say, everyone gets nightmares.*"

"*But if it's not realistic, isn't it a waste of time?*"

"*And if you don't risk wasting a little time now and then, how do you experience anything new at all?*"

"*I try new things!*" Charis protests, while the others in their group exchange arched looks or grin at the entertainment.

The words tumble out of Dave's mouth before he's even thought them through. "*Then go out with me.*"

She gapes at him. But he's determined that, before the week is over, he'll hear this woman laugh again. He'll see her smile. And it will be just for him....

"Mom?"

Dave's eyes snap open.

The voice—clear for once, instead of sounding like something underwater—would've caught Dave's attention even if it weren't a child's. But as he rolled to his feet, he clearly saw a little boy, maybe eight or maybe nine, standing just outside another of the ICU rooms. *Clearly.*

Oh, damn. Dave knew what it meant when he saw and heard a person this solid, now that he'd gone all ghostly himself. It meant that they'd died.

Even after four days, Dave had a new and more positive perspective on death—a continuation of the life process, another stage instead of an end. But still…a kid?

The boy radiated fear—which was apparently thick and dark blue—and his voice spiked upward. *"Mommy?"*

"Hey, buddy, it's okay." Dave hurried past the nurses' station, slowing before he reached the wide-eyed kid so that he wouldn't scare him further. "Look, your mommy's right there. She's fine."

Well…if you could call her hand-wringing panic over the kid's still body on its gurney *fine.*

"But she looks funny." The kid wiped an arm across his nose and straightened his shoulders, his aura lightening as he tried to buck up. "Like…like someone needs to adjust the picture."

Good description. "That's because she's, uh…" *Alive.*

Luckily, Dave didn't have to finish his attempted explanation, because as suddenly as the boy had appeared, he vanished.

The body on the gurney moved. *Thank God.*

"Good for you, buddy," Dave muttered—and tried not to feel jealous of a child. It's not like he wanted back into his own wreck of a body, was it?

The broken one being bathed like an infant. By a guy.

Another voice, from across the hall, grumbled, "What the hell is this? Damn it, I've got *meetings.*"

A bad day for the ICU, Dave guessed, turning his attention to the businessman sitting at the foot of a bed in which his body was receiving CPR. Dave had only seen four people—or spirits, whatever—pass through here, including Kathy Wells. Now he had two more showing up within a breath of each other?

Or maybe just one and a half.

"You may have to take a miss on the meetings," Dave suggested gently, crossing the hall to the open doorway.

But the fury in the businessman's eyes made him take a quick step back. What he'd noticed about this in-between place, that people put off colored auras, reflected in a twisting, bloodred corona around this man. It felt hot, tangible.

"Not these meetings," insisted his fellow ghost. "I sold my freaking soul for these meetings, and nothing, *nothing's* going to get in my way. This deal could set me up for life."

"Um…yeah. About that—"

Dave was saved from trying to explain further as the tunnel appeared—the same old tunnel, glowing with that same, glittering, blissful illumination that felt like music.

The one he could no longer enter, even when he tried.

Several figures emerged, opening their arms for the man.

"Rick," greeted an elderly man, and a sleekly slim girl said, "Daddy?"

"Who the hell are you?" asked Rick, backing away from them. "You look like my—but no, you can't be. And you! I don't have any children."

"I was never born," explained the girl simply. "But that's all right, Daddy. We can be together now."

Rick shook his head. "No."

The older man put a hand on his shoulder—all the

ghosts *could,* apparently, touch each other. "Ricky, I know it's a shock. But—"

Rick spun away from him, smacking him away. Hard. "I said *no!* Get off me, old man!"

Wow, Dave hadn't yet seen anyone this resistant to passing.

"It's all right," insisted the old man gently, taking no offense at all. "You just need some time to adapt."

But Rick was staring at his body—his worldly body—and the doctors who surrounded it. "The hell!"

More faintly, they heard the doctor say, "It's no use. Hold compressions."

"What? No! Don't hold compressions!" That, of course, would be Rick.

"Time of death…"

"You'd better goddamn start compressions again, or I'll sue! I've got meetings, damn it! I've got a reputation!"

Dave felt the chill, singeing cold across his back, just in time to whirl on the slick, lumpy, multieyed Creature.

As usual, he had to gulp back nausea at the very sight and stench of it. It was wrong. It was evil. It was an abomination. And, clearly, it was hungry as ever.

"Back!" Dave stomped at it, waving his arms as if he wasn't wholly grossed out…but damned if it wasn't slower than usual to retreat. Did it smell some particularly tasty emotions off Rick the Businessman, making it hungrier than usual?

Or, worse…was it getting accustomed to Dave?

Behind him, Rick bellowed, *"What the hell is that?"*

The Creature sludged to one side, as if to circle the obstacle Dave presented. Dave edged that way, too, staying between it and the businessman. "Rick, you'd better listen to your family and get to safety."

"Please, Daddy," pleaded the little girl who'd never been born. Miscarried? Aborted? Dave guessed it wasn't his concern.

"Hurry, sonny," pleaded Rick's grandfather.

"Like hell," snarled Rick.

The Creature slimed closer, mindlessly stubborn as a shark. This time when Dave stomped at it, increasingly afraid that he wouldn't be able to repel it this time, it didn't retreat. Instead, it extended one of its long, dark, tonguelike tendrils, slow, experimental…

And then whipped it across Dave's gut.

Cold—so cold it seared him, and sharp, like a saw-toothed blade—the tongue cut deep into him. Dave gasped back a cry as he dove to the side, away from this Thing. What the—?

It usually ran from him.

He'd thought he was immune!

"Hurry," pleaded Rick's grandfather. "If you stay, you'll just keep losing life-force like that young fella there until you just…vanish."

What? Keep losing what *until he what?*

Think about that later.

In any case, Rick wasn't having it. "Screw that!"

Dave dragged himself back to his feet, one arm pressed hard across the burning wound in his gut, his eyes fixed on the mutated, membranous Creature. It flexed its way closer to Rick, and Dave hated putting himself in danger for someone that stubborn, that stupid.

But he couldn't just stand by and watch the Creature…well, do whatever it was this Creature was intent on doing.

Not even to Rick.

"Would you just *go?*" Dave demanded, limping between the ghostly idiot and the hungry Creature yet again. The pain in his gut was fading from scream-worthy to merely whimper-worthy. *"Please?"*

Rick said, "I've. Got. Meetings!"

And then Dave heard something that sent a rush of horror through him. It was the same boy's voice he'd heard before, little, young, scared.

"Mommy!"

Worse—the Creature's veiled eyes slid toward the sound.

"In every cloud, in every tree—filling the air at night, and caught by glimpses in every object by day—I am surrounded with her image... The entire world is a dreadful collection of memoranda that she did exist, and that I have lost her!"

—Heathcliff
Wuthering Heights

CHAPTER FIVE

CHARIS FELT strangely…nervous. But maybe it was just the caffeine.

"Not surprising you'd be hearing things," soothed Hank Wells, over their cardboard cups of cafeteria coffee. "Sitting with your husband day after day, and him in that state. At least my Kathy could chat with me, when she wasn't sleeping. Until near the end, anyhow. There toward the end, she wasn't talking much. Maybe she gave up…."

Charis flushed, realizing that she'd been unburdening to this kind old man almost nonstop…on the day of his wife's funeral. God, could she be more selfish?

"How long was your wife in the hospital?" she asked, basic courtesy taking over where her stunted instincts had failed miserably.

"Three days," he said—but the sharpness in his tone contradicted him. "That's what the doc told us it would be, anyhow. 'Three days,' he said. 'Simple operation.'

But that was months ago. He said she'd be home in three days, and she went home again. Not the way we'd hoped."

"I'm…" But she didn't want to insult him by simply saying she was sorry. *Sorry?* Why not face that there were no words? She reached across the table and squeezed his old hand with its worn wedding ring.

He met her gaze and nodded his acceptance of what she couldn't say. Their shared humanity, shared mortality linked them as words couldn't. "We wouldn't have done it, if the so-called doctor hadn't assured us how simple it would go. Then the operation took too long, and then she, she just didn't heal up from it. Turns out her breathing medicine 'interfered with the healing process,' they said. Well the doc knew she was on that medicine before he ever cut into her. He prescribed it his goddamned self—"

He stopped and shook his head, closed his eyes. "Excuse my French, Mrs. Fields."

"It sounds warranted!"

"My Kathy never did like profanity, warranted or not." He took a deep, shaking breath. "But as far as I'm concerned, that doctor of ours murdered her, as surely as if he'd held a pillow over her face. He knew we trusted him, fools that we were. A week before she died, not long before she stopped talking altogether, Kathy looks at me and says, 'Three days, Hank.' Because that's what we were told, before it became months of her just getting sicker and sicker. Broke my heart."

Charis wasn't sure if his eyes were glistening with tears or not. She couldn't see clearly through her own.

Hank squeezed her hand. "Whatever happens, Mrs. Fields, you keep an eye on those doctors. Some of them are fine individuals—I wouldn't be walking without them, and they saved our firstborn's life. But some of them…"

Then he stiffened, and took his hand back.

Charis wiped at her eyes, confused, while Hank stood.

"I'd best get back to Kathy's and my guests," he said, looking past her, with a definite chill in his tone. "You take care of that husband of yours. And don't you give up hope. That was the hardest part…watching my sweet Kathy give up hope."

Charis looked over her shoulder—and recognized, among a cluster of doctors buying sandwiches, Doctors Bennett and Smit.

"Goddamned murderer," muttered Hank beneath his breath as he turned away, whether Kathy would have approved or not.

The sense of nervousness that Charis had blamed on caffeine intensified to full nausea. Was the doctor who'd so badly botched poor Kathy Wells's operation one of the men working on David?

Which one?

She wanted to ask it, "Which one?" But Hank was already several steps away. She'd have had to call the question out to him. Even if he answered, he might've just been speaking from grief. And by the time Charis realized it didn't matter how silly she looked, that she should call out to him, Hank was even farther away— and Bennett and Smit were heading toward her.

Oh, God.

If only she weren't so tired, so confused. Maybe she could find Hank's number in the phone book and call him. Maybe she could ask then, keeping in mind that his story was wholly subjective, and find out…

"Mrs. Fields," greeted Dr. Bennett. "May we join you?"

But no matter how exhausted and confused she felt, Charis knew she didn't want that. She stood. "I'm sorry, I really need to get back to David. Perhaps another time?"

Dr. Bennett nodded. He always seemed so optimistic. Was he optimistic to the point of giving bad advice, such as when he'd insisted on treating David even after Smit deemed it unnecessary, even cruel?

Of course, if Bennett hadn't continued treatment, David might not be alive now. But was that really a good thing?

Was David even alive, in any way that counted?

"We'll take that for you, Mrs. Fields," offered the older man, Dr. Smit, and politely relieved her of her tray. He eyed not just the coffee cup but the half-eaten doughnut lying on a napkin. "If I may offer a word of advice?"

I really need to get back to David. Why did she feel that so strongly? It didn't make sense.

Charis nodded, more unsettled than ever.

"Don't forget your own health, during this trying time," he advised, like a kindly grandfather. "Get more sleep, watch your diet, make sure you exercise instead of just sitting with your husband day in and day out. You won't be of any use to him if you fall ill yourself."

"Dr. Smit," explained Bennett, "is quite the advocate of active wellness."

The older doctor looked to be in his sixties. He seemed very fit. Charis guessed it worked for him. "I'll keep that in mind," she said.

Dr. Bennett said, "If you have any questions about the transfer to the long-term care wing, feel free to call me. Anytime."

Charis nodded, but she was already backing away.

Sensible or not, she really needed to get back to David. *Now.*

As soon as she reached the carpeted corridor, she broke into a run. She still wasn't sure why. She didn't believe in psychic warnings or supernatural instincts. If something had gone wrong upstairs, there was no way she would sense it from the cafeteria.

No way.

And yet when she saw that both elevators were on other floors, Charis shouldered through the metal door into the stairwell and ran up the concrete steps rather than wait. Like her pounding pulse, she couldn't deny the fear that choked her. Something was wrong. *Something was wrong.*

She rushed into David's room, half-expecting to find doctors and nurses crowded around him, to find his monitors screeching and flatlined, to find him gone forever.

And she didn't want that, *God* she didn't want that.

Or that's what she thought—until she saw Nurse Jed tucking the cotton blanket over David's now-clean body.

"See?" Jed said, with a friendly grin. "I told you he'd be fine while you were gone."

Stunned, Charis stepped dumbly to the side of the doorway, so that Jed could carry his empty basin out. She stared at David, so blank and bandaged and quiet— and now freshly dressed in a new hospital gown, like some mannequin.

Fashion for the Persistent Vegetative State.

Once Jed left, she began to shake with awful understanding.

She wasn't relieved.

Why wasn't she relieved? But she knew that already. The only real relief would be to find him improving somehow. That seemed so unlikely, no matter what Dr. Call-Me-Anytime Bennett suggested, that of the alternatives...

God.

Charis wished she could be sure it was just her knowledge of her husband that made her resist the idea of him continuing on like this for weeks, months...

years. Bathed like an infant. Fed through a tube. She wished she were sure he would prefer death to this. Because if it was just her...

Oh, God. She was definitely as selfish as Heathcliff in *Wuthering Heights.*

No. That wasn't her. She wouldn't let it be....

"No," INSISTS David Fields on their first date. "I'm the one who invited you. I'm the one who pays."

Charis shakes her head—and not just to protest the unfairness of that outmoded custom. Something about David Fields makes her vaguely dizzy, like being at a high altitude or breathing nitrous oxide. Some of it is how handsome she finds him...his thick, dark hair and brows and lashes; his stubborn jawline; his bright, lively eyes. But she's been around good-looking men before, better-looking men than him, without losing her balance this severely.

Her light-headedness stems from something less easily defined than appearance...from something far more integral to this *man.*

She clings to practicality even more desperately, in response. Practicality makes sense. "I probably earn just as much as you do, and we're both taking the equal risk that we won't enjoy each other's company—"

"Not me," he interrupts with a grin and a waggle of his eyebrows. He is sitting to her immediate right, instead of across the table from her. She can feel the warmth off him, and she likes it. "I've already enjoyed this date far more than..." Again he reaches for the check, which she has covered with her hand, but she slides it away. "Than whatever amount that says."

"I wouldn't have gotten the appetizer if I'd realized you meant to pay for everything."

"I enjoyed the appetizer," he insists.

"So did I, so I should pay for part of it."

He sizes her up, candlelight soft on his gray suit. David Fields cleans up beautifully. "Is this so that you won't feel indebted to me? Because I have no intention of taking advantage—"

"Oh, please!"

He grins, teasing her now. "What if my manly ego can't handle having a girl pay?"

She snorts.

He laughs. "Okay, so this is really about fairness to you? Women like you really exist?"

She narrows her eyes, warning him how close he has come to being annoying. That's another thing about him that has kept her off balance all evening.

He holds her gaze as he covers her hand, over the check, with his own. Gentle. Warm. "Then…how about a deal? I pay for this date, and you pay for the next one?"

The next one. Only as he says it does she realize how foolishly, how desperately she has hoped there will be a next one.

"Okay," she agrees—and his answering smile creases his face, crescents his lively eyes, makes her want to laugh. She lifts her hand and lets him have the check.

"Our next date at McDonald's," he adds then, holding the check away from her like some childish game of keep-away. Now she does laugh, right there in the restaurant….

HE'D BEEN so full of life, of passion. And now…

"I miss you," Charis confessed to the stillness of him. "I'm starting to think I see you—in windows, or mirrors, or across the parking lot. Sometimes I think I hear your voice…."

That happened especially in the deep of the hospital's never-silent nights, when illusions were easiest to believe. Worse, her heart leaped every time, as if on some deep level she hoped that was *exactly* what she was hearing and seeing.

When the inescapable truth lay right in front of her.

"Maybe I'm going crazy," she admitted, tugging uselessly on his sheet as if a little more tautness would bring him comfort. An overly bright, jingly lullaby played out then, through the hospital—marking that a baby had been born in the maternity ward, the nurses had told her. It felt jarring. "I'm going crazy, and here you are, missing it…."

But a wave of uncharacteristic despair stole her voice.

Her mouth gaped wide, wider than would have seemed possible. Despair closed her throat, pushing upward, upward, until she thought she'd never breathe again. It gagged out of her in a long, jerking sob—and then she gasped air, and she was still alive, damnably alive.

Whether she wanted to be or not.

With breath, she had the strength to truly sob, wet and sticky and convulsing and ugly. She crumpled over David's immobile body, muffled her wail in his blankets. Nothing should hurt like this. It wasn't fair. She wanted things to be how they'd been. She wanted God to give him back. She wanted the hurting to stop.

But it wouldn't, it wouldn't, it wouldn't….

At some point, she slid off of David's body onto her knees on the linoleum floor, beside the wheels of the bed, beside the receptacle of his urine. Only that last, ugly detail gave her the strength to push away, to crumple into the reclining chair instead, to curl into a ball and hide her sticky, burning face. Her nose was stuffed up. Her throat burned. She'd never felt so exhausted.

Finally, finally, she slept….

"Will you get into the damned tunnel?"

Startled, Charis turned toward the familiar voice—and there he was. *David!*

It didn't make sense. Strangely, he wore the clothes he'd worn to work the morning of his accident; khaki pants, a pressed shirt, his stupid fish tie. Even more strangely, he was scooping a little boy into his arms.

But she didn't dare question it, not any of it. "David?"

He spun—and stared in instant, unmistakable recognition.

It was him. *Him!* His hair stuck to his forehead. His eyes slightly wild. His mouth open with his panting breath. But him.

"Char," he whispered, a tremble to his raspy voice. Then his gaze moved past her shoulder and widened. Charis felt something cold behind her, and she turned....

And she screamed.

CHAPTER SIX

IT WAS—

God, how *could* it be her? Standing there, staring at him, as real and solid as if he could reach out and touch her!

"David?" she whispered, her voice exactly the way he remembered it.

Dave stopped midspin, so that the socked feet of the little boy he held swung with the force of his aborted turn. Charis! His throat tightened with recognition, with hope, with a love as powerful as the day he'd married her. "Char…"

Then he saw it, that huge Thing with which he was in a desperate game of keep-away, moving in. Damn, this was getting old! Whenever Dave got between it and Rick the Businessman, the Creature had gone after the child. When Dave moved between it and the little boy, the Creature simply moved back toward the businessman. It had an alien quality Dave thought of as mindless—but even mindless determination made it dangerous, if it could outlast him.

And now there were *three* people to protect?

With the sucking sound that usually accompanied the Thing's low, lumbering movements, it sludged into action. Charis turned, saw it and screamed.

"*Charis!*" yelled Dave.

The how, the why, the when—all of that could wait. Dave had one priority now. Her. Child still dangling from his arms, Dave lunged for his wife and her frightened, desperate, apparently tasty aura.

The Creature, with a silent kind of triumph, veered away…straight toward Rick, who never had gone into that damned tunnel of light.

"Oh my God," wheezed Rick, his horror palpable, somewhere behind Dave. "Oh. My—"

Charis tipped her face up to Dave's, only a breath away now. Her eyes were bright with confusion at this strange, sudden meeting. And it *was* a meeting; it was *her.* He could count every eyelash, could see that tiny chip in her front left tooth, and he wanted nothing more than to lose himself in her brown gaze, to drown in her nearness, to just touch her, *be* with her, until this eternity in which he'd found himself finally dissolved into nothingness. *Char—*

"No!" screamed Rick, behind him.

And Dave stuffed the little boy into Charis's arms. *"Hold this!"*

"What?"

Their hands brushed as he handed off the kid, barely a suggestion of the touch he'd been missing so badly. Then Dave spun and bolted toward where poor, stubborn, stupid Rick was backing away from the advancing…Thing.

"David!" But he couldn't let Charis distract him at the moment. He had a big…slithering…membranous…

He had a monster to stop.

Even as he got close, the sheets of cold that reeked off of the Thing knotted his stomach.

"Get back," Dave warned it, sidling around its high, lumpy girth. "I'm warning you. Rick may be a jerk—"

"Hey!" protested Rick.

"But I'm not letting you hurt anyone," Dave continued. "Rick, get into that damned tunnel or I swear…"

"Come on, sonny," pleaded Rick's grandfather.

But Rick had other plans. "No," he panted. "I need to get to my meetings."

And he took off running.

"No!" warned Dave.

"David!" screamed Charis again. "Look out!"

And yes, the Thing got damned close to Dave's feet, for a minute there. But even as he dodged it, Dave feared something else.

Rick didn't even make it as far as Dave usually did before whatever force it was that kept a spirit near its body caught him and flung him back like some otherworldly bungee. One minute, Rick was racing for the strangely lit elevators. The next, he'd been thrown bodily into the wall, beside his corpse.

And that corpse of Rick's—it was definitely finished. The doctors and nurses, blind to the drama playing out right beside them in this overlapping but distinctly different world, had already turned away. They shook their heads as they left the room.

Rick hit the wall, dropped to the floor—

And the Thing slid onto him.

Again, Charis screamed. In four years Dave had never heard her yell like this—and don't think he didn't take that as an insult—but now she was like a banshee. Still, he couldn't have turned to her if he'd tried.

The sight of Rick, whose screams outstripped even Charis's, held Dave dead still. The Creature *devoured* the man. One minute, Rick had been slumped across the shadowy hospital floor. The next, the Creature swallowed him, as inexorable as a jellyfish wrapping a fish or…or quicksand, drawing its victim deeper and deeper.

Rick's feet went first. Then his legs. Then his thrashing, twisting waist vanished beneath gelatinous appetite and gaping maws while his arms flailed helplessly….

"Help me!" shrieked Rick, his voice cracking with the pain of it. "My God, help…!"

Shaken out of his shock, Dave leaped for him, inches from the glacial stench of the Thing. It hurt just to be near it, the opposite of reaching into a hot oven. He had to try three times before he caught one of Rick's flailing hands. Grabbing it with a double-handed grip, bracing his feet too near a slimy streak the Thing had left on the floor, Dave pulled with all his strength.

He didn't need all his strength.

Only Rick's upper half—his shoulders, arms, and head—pulled free. Everything else was…melted.

Rick's screams hit a pitch that surely didn't exist in the real world.

Dave let go. Fast. He choked back vomit, twisted away, stumbled. This wasn't…this couldn't…

Like a spreading puddle of ooze, the Creature slipped across the last of the businessman. Silence washed across the ICU ward as it shrouded him completely.

The Thing shuddered with pure satisfaction.

Then the stench it put off finished the job that Rick's mutilation had started. Trying to stagger farther from the Thing, for safety, Dave doubled over and dry-heaved. After all, he hadn't eaten anything in days. Not since…

"David!"

Another scream? Half-lost in his own failure, he tipped his attention blearily up from the floor between his knees—

And Charis tackled him clumsily to the ground, rolling him away from a long, probing tentacle just as the Thing licked across Dave's leg for another burning taste.

"Damn!" yelped Dave. Between the nausea, the searing pain, the weight of Charis on top of him and the way his head walloped the linoleum—or whatever this otherworld's version of linoleum was—he hurt in more ways than he could count.

But he also had Charis.

Oh, heavens. He had his arms full of Charis. And the sensation was…

Wow. Nothing he'd ever experienced while he was alive.

He blinked blearily up at her, then said "damn" again and scrabbled backward, Charis still in his arms, in case the Thing was still coming after them. This time, it was not. Sated with the businessman it had just devoured, it slid off to its own matters, leaving a trail of putrid slime behind it.

Dave's grip on Charis tightened, guilt-ridden and grateful. Then, suddenly, he sat up. "The kid! Char, you were supposed to be watching the kid!"

"Didn't you hear me scream?"

"Which time?"

"He vanished," she explained coolly. Now that was the Charis he remembered—except that, despite her calm act, she was trembling. "David, he just disappeared! Where—?"

"Shhh." With another gulping breath of relief, Dave twisted toward the gurney where the child had been brought in. The kid—as strangely lit and indistinct as everything else from what used to be his own world—was sitting up, his parents holding him, seeming to weep from joy. Their auras were bright, clean. "Look. He disappeared because he's not dead."

At first Dave didn't notice Charis stiffen. He was busy turning toward the tunnel of light, spiraling into a smaller and smaller diameter. "I'm sorry," he said to the old man.

The little girl, the one who'd never been born, wept into the old man's side, but Rick's grandfather nodded glumly and turned back toward the vanishing tunnel.

Dave called, "What exactly happened to him?"

"You saw it," said the old man, trudging away in a trick of perspective. "It ate his soul."

His…*soul?*

Was that even possible?

"Best make up your mind, before the Critter comes after you," warned the haunting voice of Rick's grandfather. "It's built up quite an appetite, 'round here."

Then the tunnel, too, had vanished, taking the pair with it.

Dave and Charis were alone.

Her eyes, when he met her gaze—so near, so real—brimmed with tears. "'He's not dead,'" she challenged, repeating his earlier words. "*He's* not dead? What does that mean, David? Does that mean you…?"

New horror twisted, deep inside him. "What about *you*, Char?"

His voice actually cracked. He'd hated these last few days, being alone, unable to talk to her, to touch her. But the idea that her own life might have been cut short…

"No," she reassured him, framing his face with her hands. "No, David, I'm okay. I think I'm sleeping. I think…"

He followed her gaze through the semitranslucent walls to his room, where his own corpselike body lay unmoving—and where her own form curled, still and quiet, on the accompanying recliner. Even as they stared, her form shifted and again stilled.

Relief warred with disappointment in Dave's gut.

She was alive, safe, thank God. But that also meant this…this *visit*…would be temporary and he would soon go back to whatever it was *he* was. But not yet. Not yet.

With her in his arms, he missed her already.

But not yet.

"I think I'm dreaming," Charis whispered, and turned her attention back to him, held his gaze hungrily. "I know I am."

That's when he kissed her.

Across the boundaries of life and death itself, Dave Fields kissed his wife.

I have not one word of comfort. You deserve this. You have killed yourself. Yes, you may kiss me, and cry, and wring out my kisses and tears; they'll blight you—they'll damn you. You loved me—then what right had you to leave me?

—Heathcliff
Wuthering Heights

CHAPTER SEVEN

DAVID'S LIPS pressed onto hers, and Charis surged into his embrace.

Really. *Into* his embrace.

Into him, as he flowed into her.

The sensation was electric, all-encompassing, *whole*. Because somehow, in this strange place, they weren't two bodies forced to stop at clothes, at skin, at bones. Or…they weren't merely that. They were also two souls, and souls really could exist in the same place at the same time. Mingling. Bonding. Charis felt completed, full, as if she'd been unfinished for long and lonely lifetimes and now, now…

David.

She lost track of how long they kissed, soul to soul. Apparently, in dreams, one didn't have to breathe. Even when they drew back, to stare at the confirmation of one another's presence, she felt wrapped in his essence. In him.

And it was him. *David!* After days of believing that

she'd never see him again, those were his bright, intense eyes; that was his blocky jaw; those were his lips, parting as if distracted on the way to a smile. These were his arms around her. If this was a dream, then dreams were worth far, far more than she'd ever credited them.

"Wow," she heard him mutter. "Holy…wow."

That was his raspy voice, all right. That was his smile, half awe and half delight, which didn't make sense, since all those things were of the body. As warm as his embrace felt, as solid as his arms seemed around her even as their souls mingled, this *wasn't* his body, was it? David's body lay over there, oddly shadowed as if to visually emphasize its separation from wherever this was. So this David…

Oh, God. What *was* he?

Despite her need to hold him, to continue to savor the unmistakable reality of this reunion, Charis could only teeter on the edge of impossibility for so long.

So she repeated what he'd said about that other… ghost? About the little boy who had clung to her neck during the nightmare preceding this dream, only to vanish, leaving her arms feeling cold and empty. "*He's* not dead?"

David glanced toward the gurney where the strangely lit child still moved, tended by parents, by doctors, by people who'd succeeded where David's doctors seemed to have failed. "Obviously."

"And you?"

He frowned. "I don't *know,* Char. You've talked to the doctors a lot more than I have, lately."

Oh, God. Had nobody told him? "You were in a car accident," she admitted, tightening her hold on his arms as she forced the necessary explanation. "You're in a coma. You broke your arm, and some ribs, and punctured a lung, but the worst part is that you suffered head trauma. At one point your heart stopped—"

Dave's fingers, pressed gently against her lips, silenced her. "I know that part. I can hear what people say, if I listen closely. I even heard you talking about putting me…"

But he swallowed hard, scowled and looked past her shoulder at nothingness.

Real nothingness. Almost everything here seemed insubstantial—everything except him and his obvious distress.

And the other ghosts.

And the monster. *The Cold.*

"The nursing home?" she finished for him, guessing.

"Easy for you to say."

"No! It's not easy for me to say. And that was just Dr. Smit trying to keep me from getting my hopes up. Dr. Bennett says there's still hope for…for your recovery…or at least…"

The laugh that barked out of him held little humor. "You really suck at false optimism, Char."

It sounded like an accusation, which stung. She *wanted* to hope for the best, damn it. She *did.* But sitting with his inert form, day in and day out, collecting information about the dangers of muscle atrophy and bedsores and a dozen other ailments a man in his late thirties shouldn't be facing was hardly encouraging.

"At least you're not dead," she suggested, though it sounded lame even to her. And rude, as if she were flaunting the fact that she was more alive than him. "And that…that Thing…"

She knew on an instinctive level that the lumpy, shambling, membranous monstrosity which had eaten that other ghost was what she'd been sensing since her first day at the hospital, cold and wrong and curdled with death. If the idea of putting David into a nursing home could be real, then why couldn't *it* be?

"No." David's hold on her tightened, and she curled gratefully into him with something nearing desperation. She didn't want to wake up, separated from him again. She didn't want to ever wake up to that. "The Thing didn't get me, either."

"What *was* it?"

"I've got a theory," he admitted, and she closed her eyes to savor the precious sound of his voice as she listened. "Wherever this is—this dream world, this spirit world, whatever—energy seems more distinct here. Remember how your friend Diana talks about seeing auras?"

"Yes, but she talks about crystals and pyramid power, too." And astral projection. And dream interpretation.

And soul mates. Her friend often spoke of soul mates.

"I think that's part of why the living look so strange here. I'm seeing them through the haze of their auras, different colors for different emotions. Some emotions are strong, and bright, and alive. Greens, and blues, and yellows. But others look kind of, well…still. Dirty. And not—" His breath warmed her neck in a wry chuckle. "Not in a sexy way."

Charis smiled, eyes still closed, face still pressed into his shoulder. *Don't go,* she thought. *Please don't go.*

No matter how selfish or controlling that was.

"Anyway, whatever that Thing is, it seems drawn to the dirtier colors. Hatred. Anger. Fear. Like that older woman who died the day of my accident. She was already exhausted and depressed from her hospital stay, and that Thing… I think it *smelled* it."

"Kathy Wells," guessed Charis, her heart speeding as she thought of Hank. *Not his Kathy!*

"It wanted her, but something distracted it. Either that, or it's scared of the tunnel. Just not scared enough." He took a deep breath, needed or not. "Then there was this man who died of a fast-moving cancer yesterday, very religious. His family was there. And although they were sad, it was kind of a healthy sadness, you know? They knew everyone dies sooner or later, and they were all so secure in their faith. And the Creature didn't even show up! But people like Rick, the guy who got, uh…melted? He was so angry, he buzzed with it. Did you see that color he gave off? A dark brown, like drying blood. I think that attracted the Thing. And the little boy…"

The one who'd vanished from her arms? "I didn't see any colors. Not on anybody."

"Didn't you? He was really scared. His family, too. They put off a kind of muddy blue the Creature seemed to like."

"It's drawn to the living?"

David held her gaze. "It's even drawn to you, Char."

But she knew that already, didn't she? She'd felt the ugly chill of it, more than once.

David said, "I guess even you've been kind of emotional these last few days, huh?"

And after she'd fought so hard to keep herself together. "I'm sorry."

"For what? For *caring?*"

His question embarrassed and confused her, so she changed the subject. "But why is it drawn to unhappy emotions? Does it…?" But she knew that already, too. "It *feeds* on us?"

David nodded. "Whatever it is, I don't think it's natural. Those ghosts who show up to collect their loved ones when they die? They all seem surprised to see the Thing. And usually pretty scared of it, too."

"The ones in the tunnel," Charis remembered. "They were there to collect Rick's soul?"

"If he'd just gone through the tunnel, he would've been safe."

But that emphasized his own danger, didn't it? "Unlike you," she said.

"Hey, I've done just fine for myself. Sure, the Thing's gotten one or two licks in, when I got careless, but nothing I can't handle."

"For how long?"

David's jaw set at that, and his dark brows lowered. He clearly didn't want to think about that. David had often annoyed her that way, refusing to face facts.

And, as ever, she pushed it. "The old man from the tunnel. He said that the Creature would be coming after you."

"Well, I'm not dead yet."

Charis's throat tightened. "Yet?"

"What—you're in a big hurry to be widowed?"

"No! I just want to understand what's going on. Is that so terrible?"

He let go of her to scrub his hands through his thick hair. "I *don't know* what's going on, Char. It's not like I got a manual, or like gate-agents met me when I showed up here. *Obviously* I'm not dead or I'd be in a coffin instead of ICU. But clearly I'm not completely alive, either, or I'd be back in my body. What else do you want me to tell you?"

She could think of one thing, and her eyes stung to have to ask it. "Why are you angry at me?"

"Because you're talking as if this is my fault!"

"Isn't it?" Oh heavens. Had she actually *said* that? Clearly, from the way David's eyes widened in bright accusation, she had. Wherever they were, truth must ride much closer to the surface—even the uglier truths.

"And here I thought it was the fault of the guy who plowed into me. Speaking of which, I heard you with Todd Vernon. Way to go with the forgiveness, there!"

"Wait—you think I should forgive the person who did this to you?"

"He's just a kid. He's going to have to live with this his entire life."

"Good!"

"You didn't have to twist the knife."

"He didn't have to drive drunk."

David shook his head. "You can be such an Ice Princess!"

"And you never think before you act. The only reason he plowed into you is because you pulled into his—"

She clamped her teeth shut, too late. She felt seasick from all the emotion roiling between them, almost visible, and she didn't want the damned monster coming back, but something about this place seemed to tease the words right out of her.

"Yeah, I pulled into his path so he wouldn't plow into children. You think I should've let *them* get hurt instead?"

"No!" Of course she didn't! She was proud of him. So why hadn't she simply said that? "I…I don't know…."

"Look," said David.

Which is when she woke.

CHARIS SAT UP with a gasp. "David!"

Where was he?

But of course David wasn't there to answer her, or accuse her, or taunt her. Not the man she'd just been dreaming about, anyway. The only David here was the one in the hospital bed, his jaw drawn, his eyes taped shut, far too many tubes and wires running into and out of him. What had just happened? What…?

Charis rose and swayed, wrapping her arms around herself when she felt suddenly cold and alone. Had she just *dreamed* all of that? In two steps, she stood unsteadily by David's bedside. Had *none* of it been real?

She moved slowly, automatically into the routine she'd adopted over the last few days, an attempt to make him more comfortable. She dipped a sponge on a stick into his ice water, then slid it into his mouth, running it along his gums, over his tongue. To think that someone mass-produced things like this! Then she used a finger to slide petroleum jelly onto his drying lips.

Everything else, the physical therapist and the machines seemed to be doing.

Only then, out of chores, did she extend a tentative hand and brush her fingers across David's thick, dark hair. It felt strange to her. It could have been anybody's hair. His skin, suntan fading the longer he lay here, was mere epidermis. After only four days of unconsciousness, this barely seemed like David at all. And that scared her.

Never had the human body seemed more like a biological machine than it did now, now that it didn't work right anymore.

The *real* David…

"No," Charis protested to herself, shaking her head. "Don't be stupid. That was just a dream."

But she didn't *want* it to have been just a dream. Given the choice between a random sleep-induced fantasy, and having actually found her husband's soul across the boundaries of reality, of course she would prefer the latter. Who wouldn't?

She pressed a hand to her mouth, fighting back the surge of insane hope.

Yes, it was ridiculous.

Yes, she felt embarrassed to even entertain the teeny, tiny possibility of it. And yet…

Oh, God. Wasn't that madness still better than this?

If someone else had approached her with the idea, Charis would have immediately condemned that person as a con artist. But nobody had brought this to her. Nobody stood to profit by this delusion. She'd brought it to herself.

She'd already taken personal time off work, refusing to even consider going back until David was safely settled in the long-term care wing. She'd already spent more time than was probably healthy reading everything she could about comas and head injuries. She recognized that, even if David lived, he could suffer from seizures, memory loss, impaired judgment, more. Worse.

But what she couldn't find anywhere, not in any book or pamphlet, was how to handle this. How to handle any of this.

What did she have to lose in hoping…beyond her self-respect?

Judging by the growing ache in her chest, the growing tightness in her throat, she was heartbroken already.

Decision made, Charis picked up the overly large receiver for the ICU room's telephone off David's bed table and dialed nine to get an outside line.

CHAPTER EIGHT

*D*AVID AND *C*HARIS *have been dating for over a year—a wonderful, fascinating year—when he finally gets just how difficult a time she has letting go.*

Letting go of what's familiar to her. Letting go of the past. And most significantly, letting go of her illusion of self-control.

"I've been offered a promotion," he tells her, leaning against the kitchen island in her town house while she cooks dinner for them. "It's a good one."

She frowns at her cookbook a moment longer and then, as if only then hearing him, she looks up with a growing smile. "You have? Congratulations!"

God, she's beautiful. Not fashion-model beautiful, but real beautiful, deep beautiful. Especially when she smiles, her hair curling around the edges of her glowing face from the heat of the stove. He loves that she's got that special smile, just for him, and he can't help himself, doesn't want to help himself. He kisses her.

After a surprised start—which he finds kind of endearing, considering that it's not like they haven't kissed, and more, plenty of times—Charis relaxes into the kiss, into his embrace.

Then the timer goes off, and she starts away from him. "Sorry," she whispers, turning to move a pot off a burner.

Because heaven forbid the potatoes cook even half a minute longer than they should. She's so funny.

"It's in Paris," Dave announces. When his boss told him that, he'd been thrilled. Paris! The romance capital of the world. What an adventure that will be! Him and Charis…

Watching her opposite reaction—the widening of her eyes, the fading of her smile—Dave realizes just how significant a role Charis plays in his excitement about the idea. Just how important she's become to him.

"Paris…?" she repeats, looking lost. "That's…so far."

"I'm not going without you," he assures her.

She looks confused. "But…you said it's a good offer."

"It's an incredible offer."

"Then are you sure you want to give it up for me?" *Her eyes are so big, and she's holding a ladle without doing anything with it. She doesn't want him to leave her, and that makes him feel immortal.*

"I don't want to give it up for you," he admits.

She presses her lips together, turns toward the oven so that he can't see her expression, but he ducks between her and her roast to capture her gaze. "I want you to come with me."

She blinks, bewildered.

"Marry me," he whispers, *drowning in those eyes, wondering if he will ever, ever be able to swim deep enough to know all her secrets.* "Marry me, and come to Paris with me."

She blinks again, still pole-axed.

He puts his hands on her shoulders. "I'm sorry—I'd meant to do this more romantically. Maybe slip a ring into your dessert, or hire a billboard…."

Her own voice isn't so much a whisper as a strangle. "Oh, please don't."

"Now, with this great opportunity—I don't want to go without you. I want you with me. Married. In Paris."

"But…" She lets the word linger, then ducks around him to check the damned roast.

Dave reminds himself that it's kind of a comfort thing for her, being in control of the meal. He figured that out about her a while ago. Usually, he finds it endearing, but just now…

He asked her to marry him!

"But what?" he insists, brushing her jaw with his fingers in a plea for her to turn her beautiful eyes back to him. *Even when she's schooled her face to show nothing, her eyes give her away. She's frightened. "Tell me why you're scared. Is it me?"*

"I've got a job, too," she reminds him.

"I'll be earning plenty."

"But it's my job. It's what I do. And my friends are all here. And…and I don't speak French. Even if I knew the language, there would be all these cultural differences. I don't want to go to France, David. Please…" Her voice falters before she whispers, *"Please don't make me go to France."*

"Make you?" he repeats, his pulse loud in his ears. *"How could I make you?"*

"By leaving me. It's not you, David. I'm not scared of you." And her face brightens with her own slow certainty of it. *"I'm not scared of marrying you!"*

Hallelujah. *He kisses her again, and she kisses him back, long and grateful and right. And then the uncertainty seems to creep into even that, and she ducks her head into his sternum. "I love you, but I don't want to move away. If you ask me to choose, I don't know what I'd—"*

"You don't have to choose." He rests his chin on her hair, his eyes closed in gratitude. Paris, schmaris. She

wants to marry him, and that's a far bigger thing. "I'll stay here. I'll stay with you."

She sighs, deeply, relaxing more into his embrace than ever. She whispers again, more firmly this time, "I love you, David Fields."

And the world is perfect.

Then the timer on the oven goes of, and she kisses his chin before turning out of his embrace to make sure the meat doesn't dry out....

MAYBE DAVE was a spirit. Maybe he was even a ghost of some sort. But he was still feeling downright skeptical.

He knew Charis, and Charis was too practical to take her friend Diana's advice. He *knew* that. But since it was his only hope of seeing her again, his only hope of speaking with her, he eavesdropped anyway.

Pacing.

He gave his body, in the bed near the window, a wide berth. It still hurt too much—head-crushing, arm-snapping pain—to get close. The two women, friends since before he'd met them, sat in chairs at the foot of the bed…also not that close to his body.

"You've got a couple of options," their friend Diana admitted. Dave had to concentrate to hear her faint, underwater-like voice. "Really."

But she seemed to be pushing the optimism. She'd only marginally recovered from her shock at seeing David for the first time since his accident. He'd recently been moved to the long-term care ward. On the plus side, he finally got to have visitors.

In the minus column, Charis now had to go home at 8:00 p.m. every night.

"Curfew," muttered Dave sourly to himself, "and this ward's one step closer to the nursing home."

He sensed a chill, smelled an acrid dankness and spun to look for the Thing. He didn't see it as often in this wing as he had in ICU, but it still lurked, waiting for him to screw up or—if his understanding was correct—to bleed dark enough emotions to make him worth approaching.

Today, it skulked at a safe distance. It seemed to be watching him, though he wouldn't have thought it smart enough to blame him for its recent low-soul diet. But it wasn't getting anywhere near the golden glow that Diana Trillo cast off.

Interesting.

"Option one," stated Charis, her own voice frustratingly distant now that she was back among the living. "Get my head examined."

Dave glared. Now *that* was the Charis he knew and…and wished would change, for once.

"Enough with the negativity," chided Diana for him. "Belief counts for more than you think."

"Exactly," said Dave.

Charis looked so crestfallen, he would have laughed, except for how serious this was. If their chance of meeting again rested on Char's ability to believe in the supernatural, they were in serious trouble.

But they *had* to meet again. And not just to be together, though that was reason enough.

Dave also had more, well, *pragmatic* reasons than he wanted to admit.

"Option one," continued Diana, "is to have a séance. I don't advise that one."

"Because David isn't dead." Charis didn't make it a question. Clearly, as far as she was concerned, while the body lying there kept breathing he couldn't be a ghost. No matter how ghostly. Charis was a stickler for technicalities.

"Yes...there's that." Diana liked to dress the part of someone who believed in the supernatural. She wore long, gauzy skirts and multiple strands of crystals, and her eyeliner was unusually dark for a blond woman... but it worked for her. Especially when she made a face. "But I was thinking of the fact that we're in a hospital."

"Oh. Stupid horror-movie plot?"

"Exactly. Doing a séance in a hospital is almost as bad as holding one in a cemetery. It's right up there with 'Don't explore a dark basement when a serial killer's on the loose' and 'Never read a book of demon summoning aloud, even as a joke.'"

"Agreed. So what's option two?"

"Well...I'm going on the assumption that since David *isn't* dead, maybe he's having some kind of extended, out-of-body experience," explained Diana. "You said his heart stopped in the emergency room?"

"Yes."

"So chances are he had an NDE."

Charis—and Dave—stared at her.

"Near Death Experience," Diana clarified. "It usually starts with an out-of-body experience, where the subject floats outside his corporeal form."

Both women looked toward the body in the hospital bed.

Dave preferred not to. He didn't like what he saw.

"In fact, many people report that it feels as if they've shed their corporeal form completely. They often describe what they've become, there in the astral plane, as their *true* form."

"Damn," muttered Dave, and sank down onto the room's second bed, currently empty. "Damn, Di, you're good. That's *exactly* how it feels."

Yet another reason he had to talk to Charis.

"Thousands of people have experienced this," Diana continued. "Tens of thousands. And that's just the first of the similarities they've described. There's also the appearance of a tunnel, and the person's departed loved ones, and a bright, bright light."

"But…haven't scientists dismissed all that as a trick of brain chemistry?"

"That's my girl," muttered Dave grimly. They couldn't hear him, of course. Not even when he shouted it, annoyed. "That's my girl!"

Diana didn't quite snort, but she made another face. "Some scientists, sure. But a lot of them think the study of NDE's is completely legitimate. Look at it this way. The same scientists who claim that NDE's are the hallucinatory result of brain functions shutting down? What would they say about the dream you had yesterday?"

Charis bowed her head. "That it was just a dream."

"But it wasn't," insisted Dave. "Char, it *wasn't*."

"And which would you rather believe?" asked Diana.

"Does it matter what I believe? What matters is what's *true*."

"Stop it," said Dave, pushing off the bed to pace to Charis's side. "That's not going to help us!"

But Diana said, "What's really bothering you?"

Like this wasn't enough?

Maybe it wasn't. "It's real now," admitted Charis, a catch in her throat. "With you here. It's…it's real."

Immediately, her friend slid from her chair to crouch at her feet, taking one of Charis's hands between hers. Dave backed up, quickly, to avoid standing in her.

"Oh, honey." Diana pressed Char's hand to her cheek. "Is that why you've been so distant this last week?"

"No! David couldn't have visitors in ICU," Charis reminded her, but Diana looked firmly at the tele-

phone on Dave's bed table, amidst the plastic cups and
tubes and tools. Then she quirked a challenging eyebrow at Char.

Dave hadn't noticed that, despite all the time Charis
had put in at his bedside, she'd made very few telephone
calls. The practical ones, sure. She'd informed his job,
her job. She'd contacted their insurance company.
Charis was great at that sort of thing. But as for talking
any of this over with her friends…

"It's because you didn't want to cry on the phone,"
he said to himself, his throat tight.

Charis nodded. "It's stupid, I know."

"No! It's not." Diana rubbed Charis's hands, and it
occurred to David that this might be the only physical,
human contact his wife had had in over a week.

He felt sick. He wasn't the only one lonely, here.

Diana said, "It's normal to make things more real by
sharing them with our friends, our family. That's one
reason why we invite people to weddings and funerals
and graduations. As long as you kept quiet you didn't
have to admit, maybe even accept what's happened.
And now that I'm here, now that I've had a chance to
see how bad this is, you can't pretend it away anymore."

Dave wouldn't have imagined Char pretending anything. She just wasn't that fanciful. But what Diana said
sounded too true to ignore. Charis had isolated herself
with his soulless body rather than unburden herself on
anybody else. She'd temporarily given up her job, her
schedule, her world, as surely as if he'd moved her to a
new country. But without even him there.

And he'd done this to her. She'd said it herself. He
didn't *have* to pull into that intersection. He was still
glad he'd done it. It had been the right thing to do, for

those kids. But for his wife, the one person he should have protected above all others?

Damn.

"You don't have to go through this alone," insisted Diana, since he couldn't. "You're not the first person to have to endure this, and you won't be the last. You're probably thinking 'if only's' too, right? If only he'd driven a different route to work? If only you'd asked him to stay home?"

"If only we hadn't fought," agreed Charis quietly.

Had they fought that morning? He'd already forgotten.

"It's not your fault, Char," he said. He knew she couldn't hear him, but he had to say it anyway and to hope that somehow, some part of her would get that. "You're not the reason I ended up this way."

For the first time, he felt jealous of Diana. Diana was able to give his wife a hug, while all he could do was…was hover. Almost literally.

His "true form" sucked.

It was Charis who ended the hug first, of course. Charis who pulled back, who wiped at eyes that did look suspiciously damp. Charis who got control of herself.

As ever.

But Dave couldn't help noticing that her aura seemed even less muddy than it had right after their…rendezvous. Just what did *that* mean?

"Well, let's say Dave *is* having an OBE," said Diana, as if nothing had happened. The two had been friends for a long time; of course she knew how much more comfortable Char would be discussing solutions than emotions. "'Out-of-body experience.' That would make him a disembodied spirit. Which, despite that his body's alive, is pretty much like being a ghost. Just…a ghost with options."

Dave glanced at the body he couldn't even get near. Options, huh?

"Then how was I able to see him, in the dream? How was I able to touch him, and talk to him?"

"Look at it this way," Diana tried. "We exist on more than one plane, in more than one dimension, all at the same time. While we're alive and awake we're usually just aware of the physical world. But sometimes, when we sleep, our astral bodies—which were there all along—temporarily leave our corporeal bodies behind. So what seems like dreaming could be a spontaneous form of astral projection. And that's what you want to learn."

"Astral projection."

"Yes. Deliberately leaving your body."

When Charis just stared, not even blinking, Diana clarified, "You let your body relax, and you…you separate from it so that you can move around the astral realm."

"But assuming people can really do that, why *would* they?"

"For the experience?" suggested Diana. "For the adventure. To find out about other beings and other realms."

David said, "To meet with their comatose husband so that he can tell them something important before…"

But as long as she couldn't hear him, he didn't see why he should force himself to say it. Not yet.

Diana dragged her chair closer to Charis's so that she could sit beside her but still hold her hand. "That's probably your best option. Visit his world. On purpose."

"Even if I wanted to, I don't know how!" Charis was shaking her head. That wasn't a good sign.

"I'll bring you some books. But mostly it'll just

take practice in relaxation, meditation, in just…just letting go."

Charis looked haunted. Her distant voice said, "I don't think I can."

David, his heart sinking in disappointment, believed her.

The woman didn't even have the guts to leave the familiarity of her own country for more than short vacations.

Where would she ever find enough sense of adventure to leave her *body?*

*"Why, she's a liar to the end. Where is she? Not there—
not in heaven—not perished—where?"*

—Heathcliff
Wuthering Heights

CHAPTER NINE

It was only as she and Diana walked out to the windy
parking lot together, when visiting hours ended, that
Charis dared ask the most disturbing question about her
reunion with David.

"When I was dreaming," she started, halting. "And
suddenly David was there, and it seemed so real—"

"It *was* real," Diana assured her.

"There weren't just other souls there. There was
something else. A…a monster."

Diana stopped, eyed Charis for a silent moment, then
took her elbow and steered her to her battered old pickup
truck. "Climb in and tell me."

So, safe from the wind in Diana's passenger seat,
Charis did. She explained how the Thing seemed to
mutate from moment to moment—sometimes looming,
sometimes low and wide. She explained how its membranous exterior seemed to be stretched across something lumpy and misshapen and…and foul. And, most
disturbing, she told how it seemed to have melted a
dead man named Rick—and how the old man had said
it ate Rick's soul.

"Is that even *possible?*" Charis asked, hoping it wasn't. All she had left of David was an empty, comatose body and his perhaps inaccessible soul. If his soul itself was in danger...

"I've heard legends," murmured Diana, which wasn't what Charis wanted to hear. Her fear must have shown on her face. "Nothing more probable than stories of vampires and werewolves, though. Really, Char. It's a lot more likely that the monster was a creation of your mind. A nightmare."

"But you said the dream was real."

"Some of it was! But you probably were dreaming before you left your body, and maybe the monster was part of that."

"But it—" Charis silenced her own protest. She'd asked a question, Diana had answered it, and that was that. Whether she liked the answer or not.

"I'll do some more research, see what I can find out," Diana promised her. "And I'll bring those books on astral projection tomorrow."

Charis doubted she'd ever be able to leave her body on demand. But if it were her only chance to talk to David, then she had to try. She and Diana exchanged hugs over the stick-shift of Di's truck, and Charis was surprised at how sorely she'd missed being held.

At how surely the knowledge of David's presence and embrace had colored her world, her future.

Now alone, she climbed out to cross to her own sedan. The wind off the lake seemed particularly cutting tonight, but it also smelled fresh and alive with the promise of spring. It blew Charis's hair off her face, off her neck.

Would David ever again feel something as basic as the wind on his face? Not according to Dr. Smit. And as for Dr. Bennett...

Well, Hank Wells had warned her against doctors who promised more than they could deliver.

Charis hated that she had to go home at night. As she'd told Diana, earlier, it became real now. Up to this point, she'd been avoiding the truth of what her life—and, more important, David's—had become. As long as she'd been holed up with his unnaturally still body, sleeping in the hospital recliner, eating hospital food and keeping her trips home as short as humanly possible, she didn't have to truly face it. But now that she was driving home every night, with twelve long hours to fill before visiting hours resumed…

It meant facing their world without him.

Gassing up the cars had always been David's job. Despite that they'd only been married four years, Charis had gotten used to that. Her route home took her by his favorite restaurant, by the park where he liked to jog and, if she didn't go out of her way to avoid it, right through the intersection where a drunken Todd Vernon had run that fateful red light. Was that glitter by the curb the remains of David's windshield? Was that lamppost the last thing he'd seen, or had it been that tree?

And then there was their house….

CHARIS STARES out the car window at the little brick bungalow-style house. "Well…it's a detached home, anyway. How old is it?"

"From 1925. It's one and a half stories, if you count the basement, with three bedrooms and one bath. You'll love it," David assures her, his eyes dancing.

Charis seriously doubts that. As David leads her up the stone steps to the front door, she leans out to examine the narrow space between this house and its next-

door neighbor. David uses the key that he apparently sweet-talked out of the Realtor, unless...

Her stomach sinks. "You haven't made an offer already, have you?"

"Give me a little credit." He takes her hand—her left hand, with the engagement ring—and leads her into the low-ceilinged front room. "Tah-dah!"

Charis blinks at it, stunned. "The carpet is aqua."

"Carpet can be replaced. Come look at this." As David leads her through the house, Charis is increasingly mystified. The kitchen has old Formica cabinets—not just countertops, cabinets! They're yellow, to match the lemons on the stained wallpaper. The walls in one room have been painted fuchsia, and in another, forest-green. There is only one bathroom, and it has its original, powder-blue tiles. Wood paneling frames the den walls.

"So what do you think?" asks David, after giving her the initial tour.

She wishes she did like it. It's in their price range and, more important, David clearly sees something in it. She desperately wants him to be happy. But... "This is the ugliest house I've ever seen."

He grins. "I know!"

Charis shakes her head, increasingly worried. David was orphaned in his teens, so she never met his family. Did they have a history of mental illness? It's not too late to break their engagement....

Except that she doesn't want to. With David, for the first time, she doesn't always want to do the practical thing. "I don't get it."

"With a house this ugly, we'll have to change everything. Well, except the outside—the brickwork's okay. That means you get to choose everything. The wall color. The carpet. The cabinets. You'll be in complete control."

He leans closer to her, as if he can better judge her expression from inches away. "C'mon, Char. That's gotta curl your toes, doesn't it?"

She never would have thought of it that way...but damned if he isn't right. "And...we can take out that wall between the kitchen and the dining room?"

"Anything you want," he promises.

"Then I love it." And she loves him. Engaged to be married, and sometimes that still surprises her.

"I knew you would," he says. Which unsettles her, somehow. Because she never would have guessed that she would like this place, so how did he?

How can he know her better than she knows herself?

CHARIS LET HERSELF in and locked the door behind her, sliding the chain into place for extra safety. Although she'd lived alone for most of her life before she and David married, she felt unusually vulnerable, now. She had to turn on the radio to break the echoing silence.

But not the TV. That would feel too much like going on with her life without him, to kick back and watch TV.

There was a message on her answering machine. "Charis?" It was her boss. "I just wanted to let you know that we're all praying for David, and...I don't want to push you, take all the time you need. But the temp has another job offer. If you have a guess-timate as to when you might be coming back to work, could you give me a call?"

She erased the message and headed for the bedroom. She couldn't think about going back to work, not yet. Leaving David alone all day; only visiting him after work and on weekends. It felt blasphemous...and horribly inevitable. How long would it be before she cut back to four nights a week, then three nights and Sundays, then…?

No.

Everything in the house reminded her of David. They'd painted the walls themselves, taken down the paneling, stripped the wallpaper and torn down several walls to create a more open floor plan. Between his enthusiasm and her attention to details, they hadn't done badly, despite their inevitable arguments. The bungalow had quickly gone from a house to a home.

Now it was just a house, again.

Charis glanced at the bedroom clock, where it hung between two paintings of the wind-swept moors—another *Wuthering Heights* touch of David's. It wasn't even nine o'clock. But she stripped off her clothes and climbed into bed anyway.

After she took the paintings down and turned them against the wall.

The bed felt too big, without her husband beside her. It felt too cold. She wanted his arms around her. She wanted his body over her, in her. She wanted David, David, David….

She'd hoped she would dream of him.

Instead, she just cried.

"IT'S NOT GOOD," admitted Diana, meeting Charis in David's room the next afternoon.

What about this is *good?* thought Charis. Then she realized what Diana had to mean. "You mean…the monster?"

Her friend nodded.

"You said it might be a creation of my mind." Charis hated the shrill edge to her voice. "A nightmare."

"And it still might. Maybe I shouldn't have said anything. Look, here are the books I promised you."

But of course, now that Diana had mentioned it, Charis had to follow up. "So what did you find out?"

Diana sighed but, resigned, she sat. "I sent some e-mails to people I know. A Wiccan high priestess. A shaman. A medium. The kind of people you never believed in."

Charis had never disbelieved the actual existence of such people, certainly not after the proof of her friend's reality. She'd just never believed they were particularly...sane.

And now she was hungry for anything they could tell her.

Welcome to desperation, she thought.

"Mind you, none of this is scientifically proven," Diana cautioned. "But apparently the threshold between life and death is a traditionally dangerous place. What you described sounds like an entity which prowls around that threshold, scavenging for any morsels of energy they can get. As food, I mean. See, our thoughts, our feelings, our actions—we're always projecting energy, no matter what we do. And apparently, there are some...things...out there that feed on the more negative flavors. Grief. Anger. Despair. And fear—fear is a big one."

Well wasn't that convenient? Charis couldn't help but be skeptical. "Why don't they feed on positive energy?"

"The same reason that healthy people are less likely to catch a contagious illness. People who are joyful and confident tend to be stronger, so parasites have to work harder to get through to them. It's the people who are exhausted by negativity who make easy marks. And apparently there's a particularly nasty kind of entity that targets the newly dead—"

"Like that guy Rick," said Charis.

Then Diana warned, "Or the not-quite-dead."

Like David.

Shaken, Charis reached to her husband and took his hand. Of course, he couldn't squeeze back. His hand was limp in hers. "So…so if this is common, they must have some kind of remedy, right? An exorcism of some kind?"

"Except that it's *not* common."

"But you just said—"

"They've heard of this, yes, but on battlefields or in concentration camps. Apparently they were common in asylums, before the mental health profession cleaned up its act. This sort of Creature can't exist unless there's the right mixture of suffering and death to draw it and to maintain it over a long period of time. They never heard of one in a modern hospital. Never."

Charis shook her head. "Then why this hospital?"

"That," said Diana, "is what we have to find out. While David still has the energy to fight this thing off."

CHAPTER TEN

DAVE MANAGED to venture farther and farther from his body, as the days passed, until he could roam much of the hospital.

He wasn't sure if that was a good sign, regarding his body's health. He wasn't sure that his once-turquoise aura fading to a misty, bluish smear, was reason for optimism either. Probably not. But at least this meant he was able to patrol the E.R. and the ICU again. And not just to stand guard against the Creature.

He'd become increasingly fascinated by the death process.

What surprised him most was that, often as not, it seemed to be a *good* thing.

"Wow," he commented, as one woman sat up from a cancer-ridden body and stretched her astral arms up high over her head. She radiated glittering light. "You seem almost…cheerful."

"Why not?" She swung her legs off the gurney and stood, leaving her less-distinct corpse behind her. "I've got energy for the first time in months. My chest doesn't hurt. I don't feel like throwing up. The hard part's definitely over."

Dave glanced over his shoulder, to make sure the Creature kept its distance. He needn't have worried. If Diana were right, and it only scavenged on negative energies, then this woman was clearly immune. She seemed delighted when the tunnel appeared, doubly so when figures emerged from it.

"Joe!" she exclaimed, flying into waiting arms. "Grandma! And look, Rascal! Hello, Rascal. Hello, boy. Oh, I've missed you so much."

"What about your family?" Dave asked, from his position on the edge of this strange reunion. "Won't you miss them?"

"It's not like we won't always be connected." She looked toward the indistinct figures surrounding her bed and pressed her lips together, marginally more solemn. "I do wish I could tell them not to worry, though. I wish I could tell them I'm okay."

"Don't you worry about them," instructed her grandmother, squeezing her shoulders. "They're strong enough. Now this is *your* day."

As if it were her birthday, or something.

"Bye," called the woman, as the whole lot of them— a waggly tailed Rascal included—vanished into the bright tunnel. Then the tunnel vanished, too.

"Damn," marveled Dave.

Now *that* was a death.

And then, in contrast, there were the hard deaths. Like Kathy Wells, from that first day, these ghosts were often elderly and usually confused and exhausted…because, Dave came to realize, they'd been dying long before their spirits finally left their bodies.

And some of them resented the hell out of it.

"Aw, hell," grunted one old man, scowling at the figure still in his bed. "What a lousy way to go."

Or, "It wasn't supposed to be like this," mourned a thin-haired woman, her faded eyes gleaming with unshed tears. "We were supposed to take a cruise this spring."

These spirits, the Creature liked. Dave was so busy guarding their passage from their corpses to the inevitable tunnel, keeping himself between them and the increasingly aggressive scavenger, that he only half listened some of the time.

That is, until he began to notice the same refrain.

"…If I'd have known it would go this way, I wouldn't have had the operation. I'd at least have had an extra year at home."

"…One week, that's what the doctor promised. Just one week and I'd be back in my garden."

"…'In and out' my aunt Fanny's ass."

"Wait a minute," protested Dave, despite the need to hurry, when a tall, white-haired man made that last comment. "You're saying you were promised a quick recovery?"

"That's right."

And he sure wasn't the first one. "Who was your doctor?"

The man frowned over Dave's shoulder. "Look out, sonny."

Dave spun—just in time to dodge the Creature's silent attack. "Go!" he called to the white-haired man, scrambling back. "You'll be safe when you reach the tunnel!"

"What about you?"

"I'll be safe once you move on," Dave insisted.

But that was only half-true.

As the Creature slimed nearer, emanating such a foul scent that Dave felt dizzy from it, he sensed the increasing danger. These older people had lost some of their spiritual armor as they'd lain there, still hoping for the recovery they'd been promised, dying by inches instead. That's what made them vulnerable.

But what the hell did Dave think was happening to *him?*

With a barely discernible popping noise, the tunnel behind him closed. Good. Dave relaxed.

And it struck.

The sensation of sticky pseudo-mouths closing around his legs screamed through him. He felt as if his life force, his being, wasn't just hemorrhaging from him, but was being sucked out against his will. As if someone had punched through his leg muscles, twisted his tendons and veins and arteries around its hand and yanked.

Dave couldn't stop himself. He cried out. But he also flung himself blindly away from the Thing, quickly enough that—as a horrified glance confirmed—his legs and feet came with him. The Creature slimed after him. Dave forced himself onto his frozen, throbbing feet and stumbled to outrun it.

It loomed behind him, not quite catching him, almost as if it were playing with him.

How could something that big, without legs or even discernible feet, move so quickly and so silently? But it did. And Dave, struggling to keep his own feet moving, staggered in the only direction his pain-addled mind would let him.

He ran for Charis.

Over the last week, especially as she'd studied astral projection and out-of-body theory, Charis's aura had begun to change. She was still depressed, Dave was sure of that. It frustrated her that she still hadn't managed to actually leave her body—almost as much as it frustrated Dave. And yet…

The fact that she had a mission, even if it was studying a process she would never achieve, seemed to comfort her.

To strengthen her.

Dave stumbled into the room where she sat beside his body, reading not *Wuthering Heights* but the even less likely *Astral Projection for Beginners,* and he tumbled to the floor by her feet, panting. He rolled, looked toward the doorway…

And the Creature had stopped. Apparently, as Dave had hoped, it wasn't getting any closer to her.

Charis shivered and looked up. She stared at the doorway, exactly where the Thing lurked in all its misshapen, membranous misery. And to judge by her blank expression, she couldn't see any of it.

Which wasn't necessarily a bad thing.

After a long, threatening pause, the Creature slurped off in search of some other weaknesses to exploit, and Dave was able to lean against the wall, beside Char, and to consider the repercussions of this afternoon.

The Thing had almost gotten him. If he went on this way indefinitely, then the odds were in its favor. Sooner or later, that soul-sucker was going to have him for breakfast.

Charis seemed…okay. No, she wasn't happy. With the exception of her dream visit that one time, he hadn't seen her smile since the accident. But as he gazed at her, memorizing the little line between her brows as she squinted at the page and the way she would unconsciously brush back a strand of hair that hadn't even come loose yet, he thought she would survive this. As some of the spirits who'd appeared to guide loved ones across the threshold had noted—the experience was universal, and loved ones were usually stronger than they thought. So was Charis.

It occurred to Dave that, for once, he didn't resent her composure. Maybe he'd been a selfish jerk for wanting to see her advertise her emotions just to prove her love for him.

Or maybe he was simply giving in to fatalism.

As the throbbing in his ravaged legs eased, David stood and forced himself to step closer to his body. His head immediately began to throb, and his arm, and his chest. He found it hard to breathe—or to mimic breath, since he still didn't know if he needed it here on the astral plane. It felt as if rocks were piled on his chest, crushing him. But he forced himself to stand close for a few moments longer.

He forced himself to really look.

"God," he muttered, through the discomfort. "I look terrible."

His hair, which Charis brushed daily for him, didn't look clean. His jaw was bristly, and his tan had faded sallow. His lips were chapped, despite her best efforts. He was losing weight. And all those freaking tubes! Nasogastric tubes. Endotracheal tubes. The location of the IV was changed every few days, to preserve his veins, and his hands and arms boasted bruises from previous sites, running the gamut from purple to yellow.

When Dave backed away, it wasn't just to escape the agony of pain that the body seemed to telegraph to him.

He bumped into a wall and stopped, shaken by the realization that he didn't want that form anymore.

He was ready to let it go.

With one, no, *two* lingering concerns.

One was the Creature scavenging the halls of St. Emily's Hospital. What kind of a jerk would he be, to move on while it was still loose? He'd heard what Diana had said—that this kind of Thing wasn't likely to exist without a regular source of food, of negative energy. If Dave's suspicions proved correct, and the source could

be traced back to a negligent doctor performing unnecessary operations, then stopping the doctor should dry
up the Creature's main food source, right?

Okay, so that was basing a hell of a lot on specula-
tion. But he was already a disembodied spirit fighting
a soul-eating monster. It wasn't like there was a manual for this, either.

And since he *was* a disembodied spirit, then his only
hope for stopping the doctor lay in his second concern
about leaving.

The woman who sat vigil by his body, struggling
to learn an impossibility in the mere hope of seeing
him again.

Charis....

*"I, DAVID MATTHEW FIELDS, take thee, Charis Elise Sin-
clair, to be my lawfully wedded wife..."*

*David has never suffered from stage fright, but as he
speaks his vows, his voice trembles. He has trouble
catching his breath. She's become that beautiful to him.*

"...for better or for worse..."

*Her wedding gown isn't the romantic sweep of ruf-
fles and train he'd always imagined. Then again, Charis
isn't the kind of wife he'd imagined. The ivory gown she
chose, long and sleek and simple, complements her so-
lemnity far better than would flounces. And the way
she's gazing at him....*

*"For as long as we both shall live," he finishes, and
he means it.*

*Then it's Charis's turn to repeat the words of the min-
ister. Unlike David, she speaks clearly and simply. "I,
Charis Elise Sinclair, take thee, David Matthew Fields..."*

*So maybe she isn't particularly romantic. Maybe she
can learn. But he has no doubt that she loves him.*

"...in sickness and in health..."

The service is small, consisting mainly of friends and colleagues. Neither of them have much in the way of family. But they will be each other's family.

He has family, again. And if he's not careful, he's going to completely blow his macho image by tearing up.

"For as long," she says, "as we both shall live."

DAVE HAD FIGURED "as long as we both shall live" would last a lot longer than four years. But so, he guessed, did everyone who took vows. He didn't want to leave her. Of course not! But did he want this to be the rest of her life, babysitting a vegetable? She excelled in responsibility. And she'd rarely even dated before they met. He could easily imagine her giving up on any social life out of some misconceived loyalty.

Maybe the kindest thing *was* to let his body die. Assuming he even knew how.

It's not like he wanted to risk trying, just yet. And he didn't plan on giving into the soul-for-lunch method.

So, first step? Stop the Creature.

How? Find the doctor.

And as for that...

"Charis," he said, loudly. Like raising his voice would help. "I think it's one of the doctors."

Charis, of course, continued to read.

He said, "One of the doctors may be performing unnecessary operations on the elderly. We need to find out who."

Charis turned a page, continuing to frown at her instruction manual for astral projection.

Damn! Dave planted his hands on the back of her reclining chair, one on either side of her head, and leaned over her. Into her, even. But it didn't feel strange, where parts of them overlapped. It felt right. Like they'd done this before.

"A doctor!" he shouted into her ear. "If it's one of the doctors, we have to stop him! Charis, hear me. Please. I think we're dealing with—"

"A doctor," she whispered, then looked up, startled by her own words.

"Yes!" Dave pushed back off the chair and spun in triumph, then leaned close again to kiss her cheek, even if it felt like an air-kiss to him, even if she couldn't feel it at all. "Yes, Char. We've got to find out which doctor it is."

But a different voice, hollow with distance from the doorway, teased, "You called for a doctor?"

And suddenly, Dave wasn't so sure he was ready to cast off this mortal coil after all.

Because the way Dr. Bennett was smiling at his wife—pleasant enough, but obviously interested—really pissed him off.

"You have left me so long to struggle against death, alone, that I feel and see only death! I feel like death!"
—Catherine Linton
Wuthering Heights

CHAPTER ELEVEN

"THAT WAS WEIRD," said Charis, more to herself than to Dr. Bennett.

"What was?" He came in and began to do his regular look-over of David. He wasn't David's primary doctor, anymore; like Smit, Dr. Bennett did surgery and sometimes responded to the ICU. But he still checked in every few days, even since David's move to the new ward. He'd told her he couldn't just file people away like old projects.

She'd appreciated that, appreciated the familiar face. Sort of. But Hank's comments about a surgeon's promise killing Kathy made her wary. And now…

Why had she just said, "a doctor"? Out loud? As if it meant something.

Just as intriguing, why did the knot in her stomach insist that it *did* mean something?

Maybe her imagination was just working overtime since Diana's visit. Maybe she was an idiot to have bought into all that craziness as much as she already had. Maybe her nightmare with David had been just that. A nightmare.

In any case, she was saved answering Dr. Bennett's question when he glanced at the bright yellow book she was reading. "Astral projection?"

Out of the awkward frying pan and into the fire of embarrassment. Two weeks ago, she would either have stuttered or dismissed it as a joke, but… "Do *you* think it's possible?"

To judge by her first awkward attempts, it was not. Not for her, anyway.

"I believe a lot of things are possible." Dr. Bennett patted David's shoulder, then swung a chair closer and straddled it before sitting. "For example, I believe that more people can recover from head injuries than old-school medicine would predict, if we just change the way we treat those injuries. Fluids are the secret of minimizing swelling, and I—we—made sure your husband got plenty of fluids when he came in. After that, it's just a matter of trusting nature to know what she's doing. I understand that you're probably feeling pretty desperate about your husband right now, Mrs. Fields, but it's far too early for hopelessness."

"What makes you think I'm hopeless?"

He nodded toward the book. "Paranormal diversions could be seen as wish fulfillment. An emotional escape for people who don't want to face reality."

Which was easy for him to say, with his thick blond hair and his golf-course tan and his broad shoulders and his…his…

His being conscious.

"Have you looked around?" she asked, and extended an arm. This was an entire ward full of people unlikely to get better. "Sometimes reality sucks."

"Yes, but sometimes it doesn't suck as much as we think it does at the time. You never know what's going on behind the scenes. Your husband's scans are hopeful, or as much so as can be expected. He's not brain-dead. There's cause for optimism. Don't let anyone tell you differently."

A doctor, she thought again. "Anyone like who?"

Bennett grinned toward her book as he stood. "Anyone you might meet on the astral plane, Mrs. Fields."

Well...*that* was confusing. He'd said nothing to indicate that he was the surgeon Hank had meant, back when Hank called one of the doctors a murderer.

Still, almost as if she'd been asked to, Charis belatedly stood and followed Dr. Bennett out of David's room.

She looked both directions and saw nothing but the nurses' desk. There wasn't even a community area, as none of these patients were particularly mobile. Either Dr. Bennett walked very, very fast, or he was visiting with another patient.

Still unsure why she was doing this, Charis turned left and paced past several rooms. One was dark, its occupants either absent or sleeping. Another was crowded with someone's family, children and grandchildren perched on windowsills and countertops amidst bobbing Happy Birthday balloons. In another, an older woman lay staring blankly at the ceiling instead of the blaring TV.

No Dr. Bennett. Charis retraced her steps to David's room—and, glancing in, noticed just how still he seemed. How quiet.

How empty.

"David," she whispered. "Where are you?"

If he were here, she thought, he would step up behind her and put his arms around her, strong and warm and real. *Yes, like that.* And he might rest his chin on her head—*like that,* she thought again, imagining a weight against her hair so real, she stretched up into it. He would stand that way for a few minutes, anyway. But David couldn't stand still very long, and soon he would be ducking his head, his jaw gently scraping her cheekbone, his breath heating down her neck, followed by his familiar, familiar lips....

She closed her eyes, savoring it, relaxing back into the embrace that felt more right, more necessary, than anything else in her life ever had. "David...."

"Darling," he whispered against her neck. "I love you. You know I love you."

Eyes still closed, she smiled. Yes, she did know it. She would always know it. No matter what.

Then he said, "But we've got this monster thing to figure out—"

And her eyes flew open—to nothingness. Rather, to reality. To the same old, unchanging view of him lying there, corpselike.

Now she was *fantasizing* about him?

"This is stupid," she muttered, blinking back a burning disappointment. But she turned from the room and sped her step, all the same. In the choice of whether to spend time learning a technique that might not even exist, or looking for clues that might not even exist, at least this one got her the exercise Dr. Smit kept recommending.

"—cause for optimism," Dr. Bennett's voice said from a room ahead of her, and Charis froze.

Was he telling everyone on this ward the same thing he'd told her?

Was he lying?

Her pragmatic, prudent side balked at listening in on someone else's medical consultation. It wasn't just unethical, it was probably illegal! And yet, good God, if

Bennett was just mouthing what he thought people wanted to hear…!

She guessed her current situation—hers and David's—had shifted her priorities a bit, when it came to prudence, and she blatantly eavesdropped.

"In light of that, you and your husband may want to prioritize," she heard him continue. "The results of the colonoscopy were disturbing. I don't mean to imply that you were misled. But they aren't yet life-threatening, and there's the chance the blockage isn't permanent. You may want to wait until Leonard has better recovered from his stroke before asking his body to undergo more trauma."

"But what if he doesn't recover?" asked a woman's quavering voice. Charis raised a hand to her own throat, feeling a bond with this unknown, unseen wife, suddenly overwhelmed by the responsibility of deciding her husband's care. "What if he's stuck in this bed until… until he…?"

"That's a different issue," Dr. Bennett reassured her. "People do recover from strokes. We have no reason to believe that Leonard won't. I'm merely suggesting you give him that chance before asking him to recover from a surgery as well."

Leonard's wife said, "Dr. Smit told us that if we wait, he may not survive the surgery."

Oh? Charis could hear her own breathing as she strained for Dr. Bennett's response. "Surgery at any point is a risk," he started. Then something in his tone changed, like he'd given up. "And really, either decision has merit. Please don't think there is a right or a wrong decision, here. Just…be as informed as you can. And ask your pharmacist about Leonard's medications first."

"Thank you. I'll—*we'll* take that under advisement." But Leonard's wife sounded no more convinced than Bennett had sounded convincing, there at the end.

Charis was so fascinated, so *horrified,* that she didn't even bother to back away before the younger surgeon left the room.

He stopped abruptly, recognizing her. "Mrs. Fields! I—did you have some concerns about David?"

"I'm concerned about Leonard," she said quietly, and his face set. "I'm concerned that you aren't telling his wife the truth."

"You know that I can't discuss another patient's treatment with you. Just…go back to your husband and hold his hand, read to him, be there for him. Let this family make their own decisions."

"Without them knowing everything?"

He shook his head and turned toward the stairs, but she followed, protesting, "Why not flat out tell them that his medications might interfere with the surgery? The way they did with Kathy Wells?"

Dr. Bennett, of course, said nothing. He took the stairs quickly, his steps echoing off the close walls.

Charis's accusations echoed, too. "You don't think he needs this operation at all, do you?"

"It doesn't matter what I—" But Dr. Bennett bit back his protest. He used both hands to push out the exit from the stairwell, into the hallway on the floor where David had first been brought in, near the emergency room.

Charis followed. "You're a surgeon! How could it not matter?"

He spun on her. "Because he's not my patient!"

She stared.

"He's not my patient," Dr. Bennett repeated, more evenly. "I can only intercede so far. I can offer general opinions. But I cannot give medical advice, not without risking…"

Again, he shook his head.

But this, this was an area Charis knew. Chains-of-command and hierarchies were all about practicality. And efficiency.

And dehumanization.

"Not without risking another surgeon getting angry at you?" she finished for him.

Dr. Bennett said nothing, but she could sense his desperation, as surely as she'd sensed David's arms around her in the hallway, as surely as she'd sensed David's lips on her neck. *Real? Or merely imagined?*

Oh, hell, what did she have to lose? She chose real.

"His surgeon," she insisted, "who is more senior than you are, and who could get you fired. You don't want to piss off Dr. Smit." It made sense, but she had so much more to understand. Why would anyone advise a patient to undergo an operation he was too weak to survive—or worse and more likely, one he *would* survive, only to slowly die in its aftermath? How could nobody else have noticed such a pattern? And…

"How can you be such a coward?" she demanded.

In contrast to her David.

The wailing of an ambulance, pulling into the bay, interrupted them before Dr. Bennett could answer her—or not answer her, which was more likely. He looked relieved to escape her questions in order to meet the gurney being wheeled into the emergency room.

"Senior citizen, male, found by his daughter," reported the paramedic. "Overdosed on his medication. Possible suicide attempt. Apparently his wife died a few weeks ago."

Then Charis recognized the frail, unconscious occupant under the oxygen mask, and she caught back a cry of dismay.

It was Hank!

CHAPTER TWELVE

IF DAVE hadn't been trailing Charis and Dr. Bennett in some dysfunctional mixture of chaperoning and eavesdropping, the Creature would have gotten to Hank first.

Instead, as soon as Charis cried out the old man's name, Dave readied himself.

And sure enough, here it came. The Creature swayed back and forth by the crash cart, as if its appetite refused to let it sit still. Every bulging, membrane-veiled eye, out of dozens, seeming to focus on the blurry old man and the dark, dirty colors he put off.

"No," said Dave. "No, you don't."

But when he looked down at himself, he noticed that his own aura, once blue, had faded to little more than the ripple of heat on a hot day. *While Dave still has the energy to fight this thing off,* Diana had said.

He had the sinking sensation that his aura was kind of like his battery pack…and that it was increasingly low on juice.

And yet when he heard moaning from the gurney— *clear* moaning, now in *his* plane—Dave wouldn't have cared if he was out of juice entirely. He didn't intend to watch this Thing eat anyone else.

Certainly not someone he knew. Sort of knew, anyway.

"This way," he whispered, placing himself firmly between the monster and the gurney.

"Wha-a-a-t…?" A glance over Dave's shoulder, toward Hank, showed the man flickering in and out of existence while hospital staff worked over him. "Wha-a-a-t the…?"

Then he was gone.

Then he was back.

The old man groaned—and the Creature, intrigued, started to circle Dave.

"No!" Dave reached out and deliberately trailed his fingers through the edges of the Creature's slime, despite its sickening reek, its burning cold. *Broken promises. Broken dreams. Abandonment. Shame.*

A bulbous eye, momentarily revealed, blinked at him.

Dave shuddered, gagged. Shaking the goop from his hand, he backed quickly away. "Come on, you stinking sack of slime."

And it ignored him! Instead, it sludged closer to Hank.

For his part, Hank was sitting up on his gurney, more solid now, shaking his head in confusion. "What the blazes *is* that?"

Hurrying to get between him and the Creature— again—Dave asked, "Where's the damned tunnel?"

But a quiet, strangely familiar voice said, "There is no tunnel."

It was just enough to distract Dave, to spin him back toward Hank, so that the Creature got its shot.

"Look out!" called the old man.

Too late.

The Creature swelled over Dave like a wave. One moment he'd been in the strange twilight of the astral realm, the oddly lit walls and apparatus of a hospital around him, and then—

Impact.

Cold.

Blackness. Or rather…an absence of light.

And pain. More pain than the car accident. More pain than losing his parents. More pain, even, than the time he'd feared Charis would leave him….

Broken promises. Broken dreams. Abandonment. Shame.

Dave became nothing more than endless anger, depthless pain, drowning despair….

"—back!"

Dave gasped as feeble old hands, Hank's hands, tugged him free of the retreating Creature. Dave felt raw, frozen, wholly beaten by life. Not by death; by the inability to escape into the peace of death. He could hardly think, hardly move. But he seemed whole. *How…?*

Then he could see how.

The angel glowed with so bright a gold, her light arcing in rays far into the corners of the emergency room, that she hurt Dave's eyes. What effect she must have on the monster…

Well, Dave could see that in its absence.

He tried to open his mouth, tried to sit up, but had little will and no strength. God, this was as bad as being stuck in his body!

The angel bent over him, slid a hand across his cheek.

Dave's suffering eased immediately, and he was able to see her more clearly. He managed to work his lips around the word, "You." Then his struggling brain arrived at a name. *"Kathy?"*

And it *was* the old woman he'd seen his first day here. New and improved. This woman radiated health, peace, beauty.

And strength.

Aged or not, she had to be the most beautiful human being he'd ever, ever seen.

"Thank you," she whispered to him, while her warmth filled and healed him. Then she turned to Hank, who stared at her. Trembling in recognition. Weeping.

"I told you I would always be with you," she chided him with a happy laugh. "You just weren't listening, were you?"

And suddenly, Hank wasn't the only one of them crying.

"I'M THE ONE who always plans our anniversary," Dave complains, stalking to the front hall for his jacket, his briefcase. He hates fighting with Charis. He needs to get out of here before one of them says something they shouldn't. And before he sounds any more like a woman. "Maybe I'd like just a little indication that it's important to you, too."

Too late.

"Of course it's important!" She says that as if she's made it obvious. At all. She hasn't. Oh, she says the words. She buys the cards. But there's no spontaneity to her. He's beginning to fear that even her passion is by rote.

That he failed to awaken her spirit, after all.

He has an idea. "Then you plan it for once." It'll be great. He'll finally get a glimpse at what she finds romantic. Maybe he'll get a better glimpse of her. "Surprise me."

"I wouldn't know where to start," she says coolly.

"Figure something out." Then another thought occurs to him, one so ugly that he has to turn in the doorway and search her for some hint as to whether it's true. They've been married almost four years. He knows he's been happy. But there are moments when they're talking, when they're planning, even when they're mak-

ing love, that he has the occasional doubt about Charis. Usually he dismisses it. But this is a bad day, so he has to wonder. What if…? "Unless you don't want to."

And she says, "*I* don't want to."

God. "Nice job softening that one, Char." When she plays dumb, he reminds her that, "It takes two to make a relationship work."

"We *are* two people." *Does she have to look at everything like some kind of computer?*

"Sorry, Princess. I meant two people who care."

"I do care!" *At least she makes that much effort.*

"Then show it. Show me something." *He tries to soften his request with a laugh, but it's an awful laugh.* "Show me anything."

She sets her jaw. "Maybe you aren't looking close enough."

Because God forbid she ever be the one in the wrong. It's as if she keeps points. Dave says, "Maybe I shouldn't have to."

That's her chance to agree. For once. But she says, "Screw you."

"Nice spontaneity," says Dave, swallowing back his hurt, "but I'm late for work."

Even then, even as he stalks out to his Firebird— which she also hates—he can't leave it at that. She's his wife. She's everything. He has to keep trying. "I'll call you later," he calls.

But Charis says nothing.

So he drives away. And he's still unsure about her feelings for him even as he's stopped at a green light, waiting for a crosswalk to clear so that he can make a right turn. Surely Charis wouldn't have married him if she didn't love him. It's not like she hasn't said she loves him. But if only she could show it in more than a joint checking account and a shared bed. If only she would make some kind of grand gesture, put herself out there for once, so that he could be sure. Because if their marriage is in trouble...

It's during that moment of despair that he sees the Corvette racing toward the red light—and the kids in the crosswalk.

Dave doesn't think. He just yanks his steering wheel left and hits the gas.

HE *HAD* DONE IT on purpose.

Dave replayed the morning again, even while he watched a still-flickering Hank almost vanish in Kathy's brighter, loving embrace. No, the accident hadn't been some kind of suicide attempt. He wasn't *that* lame. And he was glad to help save the children in the crosswalk; that part really had been instinct.

But all the same, Charis had been right, too.

Even if it had been the absolute right choice, in the broad scheme of things, it had been a bad choice for their marriage. He'd chosen a handful of schoolchildren over his future with his wife. She had every right to be angry about that particular moment of nobility. *She* was the one suffering from it. Especially after he'd said all those things.

He'd been an ass that morning. He'd wanted a grand gesture?

What did he call the constant, daily vigil she'd kept over his body, when even *he* hadn't wanted to get near it? If Charis were as indifferent as he'd sometimes feared, surely she would have gone back to work by now. Marrying him? That had been big. Sharing his bed? That was great.

But giving up every other element in her life to sit,

day after day, by the bedside of a man who was little better than a vegetable? Being there? *Always?*

That was love.

He saw it now, in part because he was seeing it in someone else. Maybe he'd been confused because his own parents had died before he'd learned it from them. But he was seeing it now.

"It's not your time," Kathy insisted, leaning her forehead against Hank's, holding him in her warmth. "You have more to do."

"And you'll be here?" he asked, his voice trembling. "With me?"

"Always, my love. Always."

So he nodded, then grimaced at the body on the gurney. "Whooey," he muttered. "That's not going to feel good."

"You can do it," she laughed. "You always were stronger than me."

"And here I thought angels couldn't lie."

They kissed again, long and romantic and true. Then Hank hitched himself back up onto the gurney.

"Wait!" called Dave, then felt guilty. The man was already flickering between life and death, leaving the love of his life behind. But Dave's love was powerful enough to be selfish. "Tell Charis something? Please?"

Hank nodded.

"Tell her that I know it's Smit," Dave said quickly. "Tell her I have a plan. And—and tell her I love her?"

"I'll do that," Hank assured him. Then, with a grimace of distaste, he leaned back into his body—

And the body seemed to lurch back to consciousness.

Kathy smiled, pleased. When she turned back to Dave he felt awed, as if he were in the presence of a saint or…well, an angel. "You've been kind to us more than once, Mr. Fields."

"Then…" David felt like a jerk for asking anything more, after she and Hank had saved him from the Creature, but this might be his only chance. "Then I have a favor to ask you, too. If you really are able to come back."

"Oh, we're able to come back," she assured him, with a beatific smile.

Dave wanted to get back to Charis, even if it was merely to hold her in her imagination, like he'd held her in the doorway to his hospital room. He sensed, from his pale aura as much as his inability to fight off the monster, that his time was short.

But duty called.

"Then how would you like to help me stop this from happening to anybody else at this hospital?"

"We've braved its ghosts often together, and dared each other to stand among the graves and ask them to come… but Heathcliff, if I dare you now, will you venture? If you do, I'll keep you. I'll not lie there by myself: they may bury me twelve feet deep, and throw the church down over me, but I won't rest till you are with me. I never will!"

—Cathy
Wuthering Heights

CHAPTER THIRTEEN

"ARE YOU CHARIS FIELDS?"

Charis stopped pacing the overcrowded emergency room waiting area, startled in her worry by a middle-aged woman. The resemblance was obvious. "You…are you Hank's daughter?"

"Yes, I'm Jean."

"How is he?" Charis hardly knew Hank Wells, but between the immediate intensity of their brief relationship and her previous experience in this damned emergency room, she felt close to panicked.

"He's fine," Jean assured her, relief palpable. "It was close—his blood pressure dropped so low that his heart stopped for a moment—but he's fine now. They pumped his stomach and gave him charcoal, and he's going to be just fine. He's asking to talk to you. I wasn't sure…?"

"We became friends in the ICU."

Even as Jean led Charis to the curtained area where

Hank was being treated, Charis could hear the old man arguing. "I'll talk to your shrink all you like, but I'm telling you, I did not try to kill myself. It's just…Kathy's the one who kept track of my medications. My Kathy always looked out for me that way. I guess I just got confused."

Passing through the curtain revealed that he was talking to a black lady doctor, who was nodding.

"Daaad." Jean extended the word, her tone a harmony of love, and fear, and frustration. She had to be in her mid-forties, but Charis could suddenly see the teenager she must have once been. "That's why we've been after you to move in with one of us. Or if your independence is so important to you, at least consider an assisted living community."

"I might just do that, Jeannie-mine. But first, I'd like to speak to this lovely lady here. Hello, Mrs. Fields."

"Hank. I'm—" But what could she say? *Sorry you OD'd?* "I'm glad you're feeling better."

"That I am. Better than I've felt since I lost Kathy, truth be told."

The doctor took that opportunity to draw Jean aside for private consultation. Now Charis could finally find out why in the world a man she barely knew would ask to talk to her.

Then he said, low, *"He's just fine."*

For a moment, Charis didn't understand. *He?* Who…?

Then she remembered that Hank's heart had stopped.

David! She clapped a hand to her mouth, catching back a cry that sounded pained to her own ears. But she was glad, so glad to have any word from David, even that pain was a good one.

Hank studied her, curious. How a man with smears of charcoal down his face and shirt could look so wise, she didn't know. "So you believe me? Just like that?"

But it wasn't "just like that." She believed him after having imagined David holding her in the hallway—or not. After having dreamed about him—or not. After any number of moments when she thought she saw something, noticed something, at the edge of her hearing or vision. This faith had taken weeks to build.

So Charis nodded. If believing that David was here, just beyond her ability to see or touch him, was crazy, then she no longer wanted to be sane. But it wasn't crazy.

Either Hank proved that—or they were part of each other's insanity.

"Did he talk to you?" she asked. "Did he help? Did… did you see the Thing?"

Hank shuddered. Apparently he had. "My Kathy sent it packing, I'll tell you what," he said proudly. "But your husband, he bought her the time to do it. He asked for me to give you a message."

Charis nodded, held her breath.

"He said he knows it's Smit. I don't know what that villain's been up to now, but it sounds like Mr. Fields is onto him for something."

Charis wrapped her arms around herself at the idea that David had been there when she talked to Dr. Bennett and learned the key to the hospital's curse. "Then Smit is the one who recommended Kathy's operation?"

Hank nodded, his thin-lipped, black-smeared mouth tight. "I know it's a sin to hate a fellow. And now that I've seen how happy Kathy is, how healthy she is, I suppose I shouldn't hold it against him like I do. But I still resent the time he stole from us, even if we *do* get it back in the next world. He should've known Kathy wasn't well enough to recover, should've known her medication would work against her. I guess I'm just selfish."

"Or in love," said Charis. *Like Heathcliff.*

A love so powerful that a person wouldn't care whether or not they're selfish, so necessary that a person would sell his soul to keep from losing it.

Two different questions—*why would Smit do such a thing?* and *what else did David say?*—warred for priority. Charis went with, "What else did David say?"

"He said he has a plan," reported Hank. "And he said he loves you. 'Tell her I love her.' Those were his words."

When Charis closed her eyes, she could picture it. *Hear* it. In her mind, anyway. It still counted.

She smiled and opened her eyes. "Thank you."

He nodded.

She'd almost turned away before her less selfish side reasserted itself. "Hank—do you have any idea why Dr. Smit would recommend operations on people who aren't as likely to recover from them?"

"Because he's a son of a bitch."

"But it doesn't make sense. It's not like he looks any better if he leaves a trail of corpses behind him."

Hank held her gaze for a long, tired moment, thinking. "Well, it's not like they die on the table," he noted finally. "The operations are almost always a success, on paper. Kathy's death certificate reads, 'pneumonia,' not 'surgery.' As for what caused that pneumonia, it seems the hospital's just as glad to keep that part quiet."

Or they just didn't know about it.

Charis thought of David—not her ghostly companion, but the physical David, comatose upstairs—and her stomach cramped in recognition. The most common cause of death for someone in a coma was infection, especially pneumonia.

Long, lingering deaths had to be one of the crueler

kinds of murder. And while Hank might be old, and tired, and sick from his close brush with overmedication and death, she was not.

"Being a son of a bitch isn't good enough," she decided. "I need to know more."

"You do that." Hank caught her hand with his, old and veined and age-spotted. "And you take care of that husband of yours, you hear?"

"Any way I can," promised Charis, and kissed his cheek.

Since she couldn't do anything about the health of David's body, one way or the other, the least she could do was work toward the safety of his soul.

She had a plan, too.

DR. SMIT wasn't easy to track down. Finally, Charis learned he was scheduled for surgery in half an hour. She made a quick trip by the gift shop, then found the operating rooms and waited as close as she was allowed.

If she had to, she would wait even closer.

As in the emergency room, she felt haunted by bad memories. David, too, had needed surgery—to reinflate his lung and to relieve the pressure in his skull. She'd spent two ugly hours on that leather sofa in the waiting area, where two separate families were clumped together even now, one group holding hands in prayer. God. Was there any wing of the hospital she could enter again, without feeling this weight of dread?

As if on cue, a lullaby tinkled out of the intercom system, signifying that a baby had been born in the maternity wing.

"DON'T YOU WANT CHILDREN?" he asks, deliberately turning their shopping cart down the baby aisle of the su-

*permarket. "You said when we were dating that you
wanted children."*

*She's overwhelmed by all the cuteness around her.
The cute baby faces on jars of food. The teddy bears on
bags of diapers. The bottles, and the bibs, and the teeny,
tiny booties. She imagines holding a baby with David's
bright smile, with his flashing eyes, and it's tempting,
so tempting.*

*But babies, like puppies, are about more than being
cute. They're a big responsibility. As enthusiastic as
David is, is he responsible enough?*

*"You'd have to get rid of your Firebird," she hedges.
"It only seats two."*

He laughs. "You just hate my Firebird."

"They're dangerous. I've read the statistics."

*"They're only dangerous because young, stupid guys
like to drive them."*

*Charis arches a telling eyebrow at him, but he just
grins. "You're changing the subject."*

*"No, I'm not. I just… I don't think it's practical to
have a baby yet. I think we need to be better prepared…."*

Now, with David out of the picture, even the idea of
babies hurt. And not just because, if she'd gotten pregnant when he wanted, he might have been driving a
nice, solid minivan. If she'd gotten pregnant when he
wanted, she might have a baby to live for.

Still, bad memories or not, she waited there. And she
intercepted the older surgeon on his way down the hall.

"Excuse me, Dr. Smit?" She winced at her own po-
liteness, but still removed her hand from her pocket to
shake his when he offered.

"Mrs…Fields? Your husband's that fellow in a persistent vegetative state, right?"

Not his spirit.

"I'm afraid I haven't had a chance to look in on him, lately," Smit admitted. "And I'm on my way to remove a gallbladder—"

"I don't suppose you do much surgery on comatose patients," interrupted Charis deliberately. "Do you?"

Smit checked his watch. "That depends. Sometimes a patient like your husband might need a colostomy, to ease his upkeep, or a tracheotomy, to preserve the moisture in his throat. If you're having a problem, we could certainly set up an appointment."

"But—aren't comatose patients particularly susceptible to anesthesia?" persisted Charis, biting back what she *really* wanted to ask. Somehow she suspected that "Why are you killing off sick people?" would be too direct.

Dr. Smit glanced at his watch again before patting her shoulder. "If your husband is strong enough to survive," he assured her, "he will survive. Now, I really must be going."

And if he isn't strong enough? That's when Charis remembered Dr. Smit's words to her, back in the cafeteria. *You won't be of any use to him if you fall ill yourself.*

At the time his words had seemed innocent, even encouraging. But now that she knew what he'd been doing, the comment took on far uglier implications.

There was a time when she would not have challenged a man like him. He was older. He was a surgeon. She had no proof on which to base her anger.

But over the last few weeks, she'd learned a lot about following instinct—and being a little selfish.

Not to mention, the brand-new miniature tape recorder in her pocket, which she'd gotten at the gift shop, hadn't caught anything incriminating enough. "So if he isn't strong enough to survive the surgery, he might as well die?"

Dr. Smit widened his eyes at her. "Excuse me?"

"Is *that* what you're doing?" But she knew it was, even without him confirming it. So she went with direct after all. "You're getting a reputation, Dr. Smit. You like to do surgery on patients who are elderly or weak. And I've been trying to figure out why."

"I don't know with whom you've been speaking, Mrs. Fields, but I'd very much like to find out!" Warning darkened his tone.

"So that you can have them fired? No."

"I'm going to be late for my gallbladder, Mrs. Fields."

"I don't care, Dr. Smit!" She stepped between him and the double doors into surgery. "Do you understand what you've done? These people think they're going to get better. You *tell* them they're going to get better!"

"People with sense know that any surgery is a risk."

"And you tell them it's a risk worth taking. They want to believe you, to believe there's a chance. And then when they can't recover they just get sicker, and sicker, and more depressed. And what that's created, Dr. Smit…!" She shuddered from the memory. "You have no idea of what you've done."

"What *I've* done? Anybody who can't recover from a simple surgery is someone who would have been a drain on their family, on the system, on society for years, not just months. How do we know how strong we are until we test ourselves?"

And that, thought Charis with a mix of horror and relief, *is the part that's going to lead the malpractice suit against you.* "That's easy for you to say. You're healthy."

"Because I'm smart enough to keep myself healthy. I eat right. I exercise."

He wasn't as old as some of his patients, either! And he hadn't worked with asbestos or dangerous machinery, or in cruel weather, like some of them had. He hadn't been in an accident, like David. Maybe he was smart. But he was also lucky.

"That," said Charis, "is called 'blaming the victim.'"

"No, that," he countered, "is called pragmatism."

It had never sounded like such an ugly word. Charis could think of a few particularly ugly words that might go well with it. But before she could offer them, the strangest thing happened.

Dr. Smit's gaze focused over her shoulder—and his face went white.

White as a ghost.

*"Nelly, there is a strange change approaching; I'm in
its shadow at present. I take so little interest in my daily
life that I hardly remember to eat and drink."*

—Heathcliff
Wuthering Heights

CHAPTER FOURTEEN

"WHAT'S WRONG?" Charis asked, wary—and turned.

All she saw was the floor-to-ceiling window over-
looking a peaceful little courtyard, complete with a tree
and a fountain.

She turned back to Dr. Smit, who blinked, then
backed away a step. "Me? No. Nothing."

"What?"

"I have a surgery to perform!" He broke into a run.

Charis let him go. She had enough information on the
tape recorder to take to a lawyer. It was a start, although
one she feared would take far too long for David's
safety.

David.... Damn. In the excitement of the day, she'd
forgotten for whole minutes at a time that David was
still...was still...

That he still wasn't David anymore.

She felt guilty for that, and looked back at the window. All she could see were the tree, and the windows
across the courtyard...and, of course, her own reflection, superimposed over them. *Something felt wrong.*

Of course, something had felt wrong for weeks now. Something *was* wrong; her husband was in a persistent vegetative state! But she still felt so unsettled, Charis had to go check on David. Now.

Just in case.

"GOOD START," said Dave, to Kathy. "I'm sure he saw you."

The elderly angel kissed his cheek. He felt stronger for it, bathed in her brilliance. "You make sure that wife of yours checks in on my Hank, now and then," she insisted.

"Won't you be there?"

"He could use people in his world as well."

Dave nodded agreement. Kathy turned, walked away—and faded completely, in the space of three serene steps, leaving only the empty, otherworldly corridor.

Dave glanced at Charis and wished he could talk to her about this, but the distance between them was too real. Instead, he followed Dr. Smit to where the surgeon prepared to operate, washing his hands to the elbow, shaking his head as if to clear it of what he'd seen reflected in the window. The slimeball was actually going to do surgery after that? Smit really *did* subscribe to the school of suck it up, didn't he?

But not on Dave Fields's watch.

"So who's next?" Dave called, before an innocent patient could be wheeled in. "Kathy said that there were other people this man helped kill, other people who want to stop—"

Poof! Even as Dave blinked, at least five people stood there with him, all of them strong and bright with the peace of the afterlife. Three elderly types appeared, and a painfully skinny girl, and a young man whose round face and slanted eyes indicated Down Syndrome. They all exchanged solemn looks while, unaware of their presence, Smit extended his hands for a nurse to dry.

"It's a shame," said the young angel, his voice not at all slurred despite his appearance. "But I suppose he does have to be stopped."

One of the older men nodded, and the five of them crowded around Smit.

"Doctor," called the young man. "You have to stop this."

"Doctor," repeated the skinny young woman. "It's enough."

"Doctor Smit," added the older man. Over and over again, they called his name, walking with him into the operating room. *Doctor, doctor, doctor....*

Even Dave found it eerie, and he was one of the ghosts.

At first, he didn't think Smit even heard them. Then he noticed the tightness in the surgeon's jaw, noticed the shallow edge to his breathing.

Oh, Smit heard all right.

The nurse asked something that Dave couldn't hear over the ghostly chorus. Smit responded sharply and glanced upward toward the round, reflective disk of the surgical light.

He cried out, looked away—then winced back.

Dave had to know. He came close enough to see how the concave reflector twisted and flattened the surreal faces of Dr. Smit's victims as they called to him. "Doctor?" "Doctor." "Doctor!" Their eyes seemed lengthened, their mouths wide.

Shaking his head, Smit backed out of the operating room before the patient even arrived. Hopefully someone else could do the gallbladder operation if, in fact, it was needed.

Dave followed Smit into the corridor—and stilled, awash in brilliance.

"My God," he muttered.

The hallway thronged with angels, souls whose time had been cut short by Dr. Smit's conceit, by his misdirection, by his bias. Dave couldn't have hoped to count them, even if his vision weren't obscured by their radiance. There had to be dozens. Scores. Maybe even a hundred.

No wonder there'd been enough misery around here to feed a monster!

The calls of "Doctor?" "Doctor!" reverberated around and through Dave. But now, not just Dave felt it.

Smit was staggering now, turning, occasionally trying to flail one of the ghosts away from him. Dave wasn't sure how much he saw around him and how much he only saw in reflections and at the edge of his vision. But he clearly knew *something* was happening.

"No!" shouted the surgeon, and sped his step, his head down, his jaw set. He was going to ignore them even now?

Dave shook his head. *Reckless.*

Then he realized what direction the surgeon was headed, and he broke into a run.

Charis!

DAVID WAS—well, of course he wasn't all right. Charis feared he would never be all right again.

But nothing seemed to have changed, at the moment.

Confused, exhausted, she sank into the chair near his bed. Only once she realized that she'd been staring at the numbers of his monitor, as if she could change them by will alone, did she shake off that useless funk.

She opened the drawer of his bedside table. It was

time she forgave him for being a hero. It was time she gave him what little she could.

She opened the new copy of *Wuthering Heights* and began to read where the pages had opened. "'He shall never know how I love him: and that, not because he's handsome, Nelly, but because he's more myself than I am. Whatever our souls are made of, his and mine are the same....'"

Her voice broke. She swallowed and tried again, several lines down. "'If all else perished and he remained, I should still continue to be; and if all else remained, and he were annihilated, the universe would...would turn to a mighty stranger...I should not seem part of it....'"

Come on, Charis. It's his favorite damned book.

She cleared her throat. "'Nelly, I am Heathcliff! He's always, always in my mind: not as a pleasure, any more than I am always a pleasure to myself, but as my own being.'"

But it was no use. Tears were running down her face. Charis let the book fall to her lap. She tipped her head to stare up at the ceiling, teardrops sliding into her ears. David wasn't here anymore. No matter what the monitor said about his heart rate and his breathing and his blood pressure, this wasn't David. David was somewhere else, and he'd left her alone.

But he hadn't wanted to. He'd sent word to her.

Tell her I love her.

With a snuffled start, Charis sat up. She understood her feelings of unease, now. What if David hadn't just sent her the message as a loving communication?

What if it had been a goodbye?

"David?" she whispered, reaching across the space to his bed, shaking his arm. Of course it was futile. She knew exactly how desperate she looked, and she didn't care. Even if this shell was all she had left…. "David. You aren't really going anywhere, are you? You can't—"

"What the hell have you done?"

Dr. Smit filled the doorway to David's room.

Charis stood, immediately wary of his hunched posture, his wild expression. "What have *I* done?"

"You're the one making those crazy accusations," insisted Smit. "You're the one who thinks I've done something wrong. It has to be you. Did you drug me?"

She backed toward the head of David's bed, as if she'd be safer there. "Of course I didn't drug you. Why would you think that?"

"I—" He began to laugh, an unsettled, unbalanced sound. "I'm seeing dead people!"

"Oh, God," whispered Charis. David hadn't just sent the message that he loved her. He'd said he had a plan.

When Smit took another wild step toward her, she pressed the panic button beside David's bed. An alarm began to beep.

"And just what dead people are you seeing, Doctor?" she demanded.

Tara, one of the long-term care nurses, skidded into the room. Even as she rushed to David's side, she glanced nervously toward Smit.

"No!" said the surgeon, to nothing at all. Then, "Be quiet. *Stop it!*"

"Whoa," murmured Tara, checking David's pulse—and switching off the alarm. "What's up with His Highness, there?"

Smit backed away from them, out of the room. "I said be quiet! I did it for your own good, damn it. I did it for your families!"

"I'd better go get some help with this," said Tara.

When she followed Smit out of the room, Charis followed, too, both horrified and fascinated.

Smit was talking to himself now, flailing at invisible attackers. "Not my fault!" he snarled. "If you were strong enough to survive…better it take a few months than a few years, right?"

With a ding, the elevator doors opened and Dr. Bennett hurried out. "What the hell's going on?"

With one last, wild look, Smit broke into a run for the emergency exit. He pushed through the double-doors to the stairs, vanished…

And screamed.

When Charis heard his scream abruptly stop, her chest clenched. Tara, Bennett and another nurse ran for the silent stairway. Charis followed more slowly to keep out of their way, almost in a trance.

"He's still alive!" she heard someone call. "We need a neck collar and a backboard!"

She thought of Kathy…and as she backed away from the crisis, Charis didn't feel the least bit sorry for the man. At least he was still alive.

That was better than many of his patients, the ones he'd proven "too weak" to survive, had gotten. Just because people were weak didn't mean they shouldn't get every chance to live. The children David had saved, back in that crosswalk, had been especially in danger because they were smaller, weaker than adults. And David himself, he was weaker now….

Charis didn't want him to suffer indefinitely. And no, of course she didn't want him to die! This wasn't something for her to control, any more than Smit should have manipulated his patients' ability to control their destiny.

What she wanted, now, was whatever David wanted. But…but how could David even tell her what that was?

Tell her I love her.

Charis's throat felt tight with the need to act. She had to find him, had to meet with him at least once more, had to tell him she loved him, too. She had to let him know that whatever he decided...

She looked over her shoulder at David's room—and she knew that as low as her chances at astral projection were, they'd never happen inside the hospital. Not with nurses checking in regularly, not with nearby TVs blaring, not with all the conversations and equipment.

No matter how much she'd read, she didn't want to leave her body. She couldn't help imagining it like a roller-coaster drop without the safety harness.

But she had to see David, the real David, at least once more. She had to try!

Decided, Charis headed for the elevators—and the privacy of her car.

"But the country folks, if you asked them, would swear on their Bible that he walks. There are those who speak to having met him near the church, and on the moor, and even within this house...."

—Nelly
Wuthering Heights

CHAPTER FIFTEEN

"Now that," said Dave, "is what I call vengeance."

Dr. Smit lay in ICU, paralyzed from his fall. He radiated enough muddy gray fear and sulfuric despair to keep the Creature that loomed over him lapping up his pain with its tendril-like tongues for a long, long time. The only thing that would have made it complete would be if Smit could actually *see* the Thing he'd created.

And maybe if he were eaten by it. Slowly.

So why didn't Dave feel better about this?

"It's not about vengeance."

He didn't have to turn to know that Kathy Wells stood at his shoulder. Her voice and her illumination gave her away. That, and the fact that she'd seemed to read his mind.

When the Creature shuddered back from her light, she drew it in slightly, as if she had a dimmer switch.

The monster began to drink Smit's despair again, but its wary, half-hidden eyes didn't leave the angel.

Noting her tolerance, Dave said, "It *looks* like vengeance."

"It's about understanding." She rubbed his back, like his mother used to do when he was little. "Sadly, some people can't understand the consequences of their actions until they experience them."

"But this isn't what he did to his victims."

"Yes, it is. He took away their ability to make an informed choice. He took away their control over their own lives. Now he has lost his own."

"Kind of like when I was hit…" But Dave stopped himself. Charis had been right, after all. That stupid drunk driver had been at fault, but Dave had been given a choice as well.

Kathy looked at him expectantly.

"Okay, so I chose to risk myself," he defended. "It was the right choice."

"Of course it was. Every one of those children, every one of their parents and schoolmates, would agree. Those children have the chance to grow up, to fall in love, to have their own children because you made a selfless, heroic choice."

He liked hearing that. "So why do I feel guilty?"

"Because the one person who *didn't* have a choice is the one person you would not have hurt for the world."

Charis.

Dave thought of her sitting by his body, day after day, a prisoner to his decision, and he cringed inwardly. He couldn't ask her to do that indefinitely.

But as long as he lingered…wouldn't she?

First things first. He gestured toward the Creature, still feasting on Smit's misery. "What about that Thing?"

Kathy laughed. "Isn't this what you so often accuse

her of doing?" she asked, when he frowned at her. "Focusing on practical matters instead of affairs of the heart?"

Her wise-woman routine was starting to bug him. "So I shouldn't do anything about a soul-eating monster?"

"No." As Kathy's smile widened, so did her brilliant golden aura. "But perhaps you could understand her better."

As her light expanded and intensified, the Creature shrank back from her and, by default, from Smit. Dave braced himself. But before it could slither past the edge of her radiance, another angel appeared. Then another.

"Well howdy," said one wise-old-man angel, as if he knew Dave. When Dave squinted, trying to place him through the glare, the angel added, "I see it ain't et you yet."

Only the accent gave him away as Rick-the-businessman's grandfather.

"Y-you…" stuttered Dave. "I mean, how…?"

He probably would have continued to embarrass himself if he hadn't been distracted by a clear, familiar voice.

"David!"

Charis! Dave spun, desperately searched. But he didn't see her. All he saw were several more angels emerging from the bright, spiraling tunnel with which he'd become so familiar.

So why did the tunnel scare him, this time?

The Creature, cornered, writhed in discomfort as a length of light from the tunnel solidified, separated, and became yet another angel. The sweep of light off her seemed majestic.

"Pat Trammell!" this one called, and the shuddering Creature let out a horrible, wrenching screech.

A bright light tore out of it, arched to the angel's side,

and resolved into a hunched, shivering person. One who increasingly straightened, healed, reformed into what he'd been.

"Pat," greeted the majestic angel, looping an arm around the recovered soul's wide shoulders. "Welcome home."

She drew Pat into the tunnel even as another angel called, "Becky Russell!"

The Creature's shrieks almost covered the sucking, slapping sound of its writhing, bucking distress. The membranous, raw wound where Pat had escaped flapped with its shudders. Its screeching pierced the air.

But another soul shot from it, morphing into an old, confused, slime-covered woman.

Dave gulped back his unease at the increasingly shredded look of the monster. It bled rolling eyes and ichor in black splatters. Was it *shrinking?*

Backing away from it brought Dave nearer to the tunnel.

And he felt it!

A sensation he hadn't felt since the day of the accident. Comfort. Beckoning. Drawing….

The tunnel was open to him.

"Mac Harper!" called yet another angel. But Dave was looking past that angel, farther up a line of glowing silhouettes. One leaned out, waved at him, and he recognized her even through her dazzle.

"Mom?" he breathed, suddenly tired, suddenly so ready. And the taller angel behind her…? "Dad!"

Behind him, someone called "Joshua Smith!" That was followed by more air-rending squeals of a dark, dank Creature being burned on the outside and torn apart from the inside.

The Creature was the unnatural part. It was the horror. But nothing could be more right than reuniting with his parents....

Then he heard his wife's clear, desperate voice again—*David, where* are *you?*"

And he definitely felt afraid. And now he knew why.

Dave was scared to face what he had to do next.

But he wasn't scared to face the cause of his uncertainty. Not even close. He turned toward her call like a plant turning toward necessary sunlight.

Just in time to catch Charis as she flung herself into his waiting arms, solid and real. "I did it," she gasped. "I made it. Oh, David...."

Dave buried his face into her hair, held her so tight, so very tight, breathed the smell of her....

And he felt her tremble against him as, for the first time, his usually calm, cool wife wept in his embrace.

Here in a dimension she normally would not have believed even existed.

CHARIS HADN'T THOUGHT she could do it, even in the marginal privacy of her car with the seat laid back. She'd tried again and again, concentrating on the instructions she'd memorized, trying step-by-step to achieve the seeming impossible.

"Relax, focus, envision it. Relax, focus, envision it...."

But willpower hadn't worked. Concentrating hadn't worked.

What had worked was when she gave up, let go...and simply wanted to see David again, one last time, more than life itself.

The first time it happened the sense of otherness, the view of the parking lot rushing past as she was drawn toward the emergency room, had startled her. "David!" she'd cried.

Just before opening her eyes, back in the car. Nothing.

She'd almost given in to despair, then. But despair wasn't, well, practical. She'd done it once, damn it. Twice if you counted the not-a-dream. She would do it again.

And now, here they stood together, bathed in the light of countless... angels?

She didn't care, didn't want to let go.

"I did it. I made it. Oh, David...."

He kissed her head, kissed her cheek, kissed her closed eyes as if he couldn't get enough of her. "Are you *crying?*"

"No," she lied, and laughed because lying didn't seem possible here. When she opened her sticky wet eyes, he was laughing, too. And his dark, intense gaze looked bright.

"Char," he whispered, and again he kissed her.

Body. Soul. *Everything.*

Everything.

The sensation of being alone with him, creating their own world amidst the chaos around them, was rent by more ungodly keening. Charis tried to ignore it, honestly she did. The world could end, for all she cared, as long as she and David were together.

She whispered, "'If all else perished and he remained, I should still continue to be....'" But she said it quietly, in case he thought she was whining about losing him.

David broke first. "What's it going to take to shut that thing up?" he called over his shoulder, past spirits helping other spirits into...

Into a bright tunnel.

She almost *hadn't* made it, had she?

In part to deny the presence of the swirling, inevitable threshold, Charis followed David's line of sight to the most miserable, disgusting puddle of Creature she could ever have imagined.

"Let me…" for some reason, David laughed at himself before he continued. "Let me deal with one more practical detail."

He strode toward the Thing. That's when Charis saw just how tired he looked, how…dull. She didn't see auras the way he apparently did. But she could tell that being trapped betwixt and between had weakened him, somehow. It had diminished him. And small and helpless though that Creature might look…

"No!" she called, and ducked between him and it.

"Wait!" David protested.

"Stay back. You're not strong enough anymore."

"Like hell I'm not!" He sounded like the businessman that had been eaten in front of them, the one Charis now saw being led, shivering, into the tunnel.

She didn't want to think about the tunnel. And since she doubted she could convince him, she did the only thing she could think of. Something rash.

Something David-like.

She turned, crouched—and picked up the cool, rubbery remains of what had been a monster before Dave could get to it. "So this is all you were before that slimeball of a surgeon overfed you, huh?" she asked it.

"Charis!" bellowed David, reaching for the Thing. She twisted it away from him. "What do you think you're doing?"

"I'm letting it go." She slid the sorry, shivering Thing under Smit's bed, where it immediately cowered into protective shadow. Then she stood. "Unless someone like him shows up and starts creating too much misery and death, it shouldn't get big enough to harm anybody else."

David didn't look convinced. "What if it had hurt you?"

Hurt her? *Her?*

"You have *got* to be kidding!" Damn. It really was too easy to speak one's mind on this realm, wasn't it? "What if *I* got hurt?"

To her surprise, David looked chastened. "You're right. Char...I'm sorry. I'm so sorry I created this excuse of a life for you. You're the only innocent victim in this whole thing."

What? "I'm not the one in a hospital bed! I'm not—"

Dying. But she couldn't speak the word. She would never, never speak that word.

"I made my choice. And God forgive me, Charis, I didn't choose you."

That should have hurt a lot more than it did. "No! David—no! You made the right choice. I don't blame you, not as much as I admire you anyway." She framed his jaw with her hands, held his gaze. "You're the bravest man I ever met."

He tried to shake his head no.

"*Yes,* so I'm selfish enough to resent what we lost. Who wouldn't? What we lost was, it was magic. It was *love.* But regret what you did? David, you're my hero. I—" She could barely force the words. She wanted to do anything, anything but to say them. Still, this was why she'd fought so hard to get here, wasn't it? "I love you. I will always love you, no matter what happens. I had to make sure you knew that."

"I know it," he murmured.

"I've always been so horrible at showing it. I'm sorry."

"I shouldn't have doubted you. I was a jerk. I was such—"

She covered his mouth with her own, and not just to silence him. If this was all they had left, the moment shouldn't be spent in regrets. It should be spent memorizing every bit of his soul. Her soul's mate.

"David," called a gentle voice behind him, at the tunnel.

The angel had eyes just like his. This resemblance, too, was obvious. All the other spirits had gone except for her.

And him.

"I can't leave you," said David. "I can't do that to you."

"You can't just wither away to nothing! People work through grief, so I will, too. I'm sure I will." Probably she'd be more convincing if she weren't starting to cry.

David's skeptical gaze said the same thing.

"I'll find that idiot boy and tell him we forgive him," she hurried on, trying to outtalk her closing throat, her burning eyes. "Because it's what you want me to do."

"You're being practical again," he warned.

"Because—" Too late. Her last words came out in an unbecoming wail. *"Because it's the only way to let you go!"*

With a groan, David pulled her back into his chest, back into the only embrace she ever wanted to know. "I'm sorry," he whispered into her hair while she sobbed, noisy and wet and shameless into him. "I'm so sorry."

"If I follow my heart," she slurred, between desperate gasps, "I'll just turn selfish again. I can't do that to you. I can't. I love you so much…."

"Shhh. I love you, too, Char. I don't know how I ever deserved someone like you."

"David," called his mother, again.

AND, AT THE WAIL of a car horn, Charis started awake— or at least aware—in her car's reclined seat.

Alone.

"No," she muttered, shaking off the momentary dizziness of being back in her body. And that's exactly where she was. In her body, in her car, in the rapidly darkening parking lot. "No!"

She had to do it again. She had to go back. She couldn't leave it at that! "Relax, focus, envision."

But a buzzing in her pocket wouldn't let her concentrate.

With a lurch of dread, she recognized the vibration of her silenced cell phone. *No....*

Part of her knew, even as she fished it from her pocket. Part of her understood, even before she saw the number for St. Emily's long-term recovery ward on the phone's display. But she didn't answer it. She couldn't face it. Not yet.

For a few more moments, even as she scrambled out of the car, she made herself focus on the sensation of David's soul in her arms. He loved her. He knew she loved him. That mattered.

She ran across the parking lot in a daze, barely dodging a car that braked and honked. The evening receptionist, who knew her well now, called a hello, but Charis didn't answer. She felt as if it would be blasphemous to speak.

She had to get to David, first.

As she stepped off the elevator and navigated the maze of corridors to long-term recovery, Charis saw several hospital personnel rushing in. A blue light flashed over the door to David's room, signifying an emergency.

Charis sped her step. At least his suffering would be over, she thought doggedly against her growing, selfish fear. At least...at least...

But no. Nothing would make this more bearable.

She broke into a run. Braced, she swung into David's room.

And was confused by the smiles on the doctors' faces. What was there to smile about? Why had they raised the head of David's bed for the first time since his accident.

Then she met his gaze.

Her hands pressed to her mouth at the kick of recognition. Yes, his face was gaunt and pale. Yes, his eyelashes looked spiked and oily from the drops they'd been giving him. But those bright, intense eyes?

It was David. Awake. Alive. *It was David's soul.*

"Ch—" he tried, his words slurred and hoarse. "Char-is."

She began to tremble, staring.

"It's a good sign," encouraged Nurse Tara. "He'll need physical therapy, but Mrs. Fields—this is a really good sign. Your husband's obviously a fighter."

"Fight." David swallowed, obviously in pain, clearly uncomfortable with his recovered language skills. "With me?"

His eyes pleaded far more eloquently. When he said fight, he meant it. There would be physical therapy. Rehabilitation. Frustration. It wouldn't be easy.

"Char?" he added.

With an almost inhuman cry, full of more emotion than she'd believed herself capable of, Charis fell on him. She kissed him, held him, smeared him with her tears and who-knew-what. "Stupid!" she scolded him. "You stupid, wonderful risk taker."

"For. You."

She kissed him.

Then she held him.

"Not in…" He took a deep, deep breath of her, and seemed to relax. "Not in the abyss alone."

"No," she agreed, kissing him again. She loved how his stubble scratched her cheek. She loved his sour breath. She loved the feel of his thick, thick hair as she wove her fingers into it to hold his head under her onslaught of kisses. "Never alone."

And together, they could conquer anything.

Dear Reader,

Some stories seem to fly from my heart to the keyboard. This is one of those stories.

Police officer Amanda Riley thinks she's seen it all—until her boyfriend Jason turns into a wolf right in front of her. A month later, Jason is dead, an apparent victim of the same serial killer Amanda's team has been investigating. Amanda begins to suspect this killer is targeting shape-shifters.

FBI agent and shifter Nick Templeton travels to Fort Worth to investigate his cousin Jason's murder. But will fighting his attraction to his prime suspect Amanda endanger them both, or will each realize they've found the one person with whom love will bring true happiness?

I'd love to hear what you think. You can reach me via my Web site at KarenWhiddon.com.

Best wishes,

Karen Whiddon

SOUL OF THE WOLF
Karen Whiddon

To my brothers Scott and Shawn, and their significant others, Sharon and Mia. And to Alex, because the last one was supposed to be for you.

CHAPTER ONE

"ONCE WE HAVE proof you did it, you'll pay." The voice snarled in her ear. "With your life. Got that?"

"Proof I did what?" Amanda Riley leaned back in her chair, keeping her voice calm, pleasant even. She didn't want the caller, whoever he was, to realize he'd rattled her.

"You know." Heavy breaths. "And you'd better start planning for your funeral." *Click.* Then silence.

Replacing the receiver, Amanda doodled on the notepad in front of her. Another prank call. Third one this month, too. And for the life of her she couldn't figure out which bust had pissed the guy off.

"Hey, Riley, got a minute?"

Amanda sighed. The question was rhetorical. The man asking, Lieutenant Gordon, or Gordy, was her boss. And, since they were both members of the brand-new task force investigating their very own Fort Worth serial killer, of course she had a minute. She had all day, if he wanted it.

"Sure." She blinked, tearing her gaze away from the incredibly detailed coroner's report on the victims. It took two seconds before she noticed Gordy had someone with him. A tall man, not in uniform.

Hastily, she pushed her chair back, scraping the floor with a loud, nails-on-chalkboard sound, making her wince. "Here or in the conference room?"

Gordy flashed a smile, which scared her. It was his shark smile. He never used that smile on her, only on the rookies or the perps. A shiver ran up her back. Who the hell was the guy with him? She stood on the tips of her toes and tried to see around Gordy's bulk.

"Nah, here will be fine." He pushed his way into her tiny cubicle. Since making detective, she'd been granted this one small slice of privacy. It might not seem like much, but compared to the crowded squad room it was nirvana.

The other man followed him. Amanda stared. Normally, she wasn't much for being overwhelmed by a guy's looks, but this guy was something else. Tall, dark and handsome didn't begin to describe him. Though he looked positively dangerous in his black leather jacket and faded jeans, everything else about him screamed "law enforcement."

"Detective Amanda Riley, this is Agent Nick Templeton. FBI Agent Nick Templeton."

The name struck her like a ball-peen hammer between the eyes. "Templeton," she breathed. Templeton had been her former boyfriend Jason's last name. His obituary had just run in the paper yesterday. FBI?

Not caring that staring might be rude, Amanda stuck her hand out. She braced herself when his larger one gripped hers. But he played nice, unlike most other large men she'd met, his handshake firm but not painful. As he slid his hand free, she noticed he had long, elegant fingers. Her mouth went dry. She'd always been a sucker for a man with sensual hands. Like Jason.

They'd tried to kick her off the task force when her former boyfriend had become one of the serial killer victims.

"Jason's last name was Templeton." Amanda heard her voice, noted the harsh tone, all without being conscious of even speaking. "You must be related. I'm very sorry."

His cool gaze gave nothing away. "We were cousins."

Gordy touched her shoulder. "You okay?"

From habit she nodded. All Gordy needed was one tiny excuse and she would be put on R&R. Though Jason and she had broken up a month earlier, his murder had hit Amanda hard. She'd even had to wonder if it had been directed at her for some reason, like the serial killer was now taunting the task force.

Amanda straightened her back. This was her job. Her grief was private. Even if this guy was Jason's cousin. And a federal agent.

"Agent Templeton is here about the murders." Gordy spoke without inflection. His best political, talking-to-the-chief voice. "I've assigned him to you. Fill him in, show him around. He's here for the duration."

Amanda couldn't help it; she let her mouth fall open. "Say that again?"

The look Gordy shot her told her he didn't like it any better than she did. No one liked the feds messing with their investigations. "He's now part of the task force."

"One agent? That's all they sent?"

Gordy shook his head in warning. "Yeah."

Closing her mouth, Amanda forced a smile. She knew that tone. It would be pointless to argue, so she didn't. "Great," she said, not bothering with false enthusiasm. The guy would have to be stupid not to figure out he wasn't wanted. Wait till the other guys on the task force got wind of this. This Nick Templeton was dead meat.

The fed looked at her and Amanda saw two things. One, he realized this and two, he didn't care.

"I'd like to talk to you about Jason." Though the accent was similar, his voice was deeper than Jason's, more raspy. "And I wasn't sent by anyone. We're working too hard on terrorism to spare anyone for a couple of murders in cowtown. I asked to come."

Amanda sat back down and steepled her hands in front of her. From deep inside she pulled out a composure she didn't yet feel. The wound still cut too deep.

"Jason wasn't the first victim." Again, she swallowed. "But I expect you know that."

He indicated the manila file, still open in front of her. "Case file?"

"One of them."

"Mind if I see it?"

One glance at Gordy told her what she needed to know. Share the file. In case she didn't understand, Gordy put it in words. "He's to have full access to all resources."

Fine. Without another word, Amanda slid the file across the desk. He stopped it with one finger, his intent gaze never wavering from her face.

Gordy cleared his throat. "I'll leave you two to it then." Lifting his hand in a wave, he took off. Coward. Not that Amanda blamed him. Most everyone on the task force would avoid Agent Nick Templeton like the plague. And now her, too. Since he was her new partner, she'd be tainted by association.

"So you and my cousin were engaged?"

For the second time in ten minutes, her mouth fell open. "That's news to me," she managed. "Jason and I never talked about marriage." Her heart thudded in her chest, like every beat was a major effort. Suddenly, inexplicably, she wanted to lay her head down on the desk and cry.

Instead, she set her jaw and told herself she would not. She'd fought hard to stay on the task force. She wanted to bring Jason's killer to justice.

His hard expression softened. "You cared about him." He made his question a statement.

She nodded. "Yes."

"Yet you personally covered his crime scene."

"I'm still on the task force." She couldn't keep the bitterness from her voice. "They didn't know who he was. I cover all these particular crime scenes." By particular, she meant victims, potential or otherwise, of this serial killer. Jason had been number four. And they still had no idea who was responsible, or why.

Without another word, he opened the folder and began to read.

Ten minutes later, after Nick confirmed what he already knew—they had a potential serial killer on the loose—Amanda shook her head. "My turn. Why are you here? I mean, I know the feds want a piece of the pie, but Jason was your cousin. Why you?"

He leaned back in his chair, crossing his arms. "It's personal. Jason was family."

He said *family* like he meant *mob*. Nah. It just sounded that way because of his accent.

Looking at him across the scarred surface of her desk, she tried not to notice how muscular his arms were. "We all care, Agent. We all care."

Unsmiling, he dipped his chin. "Call me Nick."

Now was the part where she was supposed to tell him to call her Amanda. But she didn't. Something about this guy set her teeth on edge. Maybe it was the dark sexuality that oozed from every pore. A guy who looked this good shouldn't be a cop. She narrowed her eyes. Or maybe it was just the resemblance to Jason. Damn. The air went out of her in a rush.

"I understand your grief." The moment she spoke, Amanda knew she'd made a mistake.

Nick's expression hardened. "Do you, Detective Riley?" He rose to his feet, the movement oddly graceful for such a large man. "I plan to look around town tonight, on my own time. You never know where a clue might turn up. Since I'm not familiar with the area, maybe you'd like to be my guide."

As invitations went, this one stopped just short of surly. But then he *was* horning in on an investigation already in progress.

"Sure." Amanda leaned back in her chair. She was amazed she'd just agreed to be his guide. "I've been working this case after hours for weeks."

Since he was staying at the Marriott hotel, she agreed to pick him up at nine o'clock. Time enough for both of them to change clothes and grab a bite to eat. Some guys, especially cops, had a problem with a woman driving them around, but he didn't seem to mind. Which was good, since Amanda wouldn't let anyone else drive her new car and she didn't feel like worrying about some damn rental.

Amanda wrote down his room number and pocketed the slip of paper. "Try not to look so much like a cop."

His mouth—well shaped, she thought—tightened. But to his credit, he didn't pretend not to know what she meant. No one who might have information about

Jason's death would talk to them if they even caught a whiff of law enforcement.

The clock showed a quarter till six. Detectives didn't get paid overtime.

Amanda followed Nick from the police station, watching as he got into his rental car. Even that looked like a cop car. Nondescript, blue Ford Taurus. She couldn't wait to see how he adapted to her new silver Volvo SUV. Men tended to feel uncomfortable in such a family-type vehicle. Except for Jason. He'd called it the thrill-mobile. Well, maybe for other reasons beside speed.

Once home, she fed Clause, her inside cat, then fed the outside strays that gathered on her back patio. For some reason her apartment's parking lot was a dumping ground for unwanted cats.

A microwaved T.V. dinner, with salad from a bag as her nod to healthy eating, served as her dinner. She read as she ate and checked her watch three times. They'd agreed she'd pick Nick up at nine, though from experience she knew the Fort Worth night scene didn't get started until after ten o'clock.

Outside, the darkness gathered quickly. Something— a set of glowing eyes—made her spin, heart pounding. It was just one of the outside cats, she realized. With a curse, she yanked the curtains closed.

Sighing, she began rummaging through her closet. Years of undercover work had given her what she called a diverse wardrobe. She could wear anything from early matronly to frankly slutty, depending on the need.

Tonight she wanted to look good. In a knock-his-socks off way. She made a rude sound low in her throat, angry at the truth. Being escorted around by someone as handsome as Nick Templeton demanded she try to look as good as possible, nothing more.

It took her nearly an hour to settle on an outfit. The denim miniskirt was flattering, showing off her long legs. She chose her sexiest heels and a black silk halter top. Yanking her hair from her work ponytail, she combed her fingers through and let it fall where it may. She grabbed a silver choker and dangling earrings and spritzed herself lightly with perfume.

She was dying to see what Agent Templeton would do to make himself look less like a cop. Assuming he could. As she passed the hall closet, she remembered Jason had kept some things in there, something that had happened gradually over the nine months they'd been together. Just in case he'd had to go from her place to work in the morning without a change of clothing.

For a moment her chest felt tight and she couldn't breathe. Sometimes she thought she could still pick up the phone and call him, tell him she was sorry for freaking out and give him a chance to explain. Hell, what had he expected when he'd changed into a wolf in front of her? She still wasn't sure she believed it, but one thing about Jason's death—and all the others—fit right in.

Amanda was the only one on the task force who'd made the connection. Hell, she was the only one who would even consider a paranormal possibility. All of the victims had been killed with a custom-made, silver bullet. According to the Internet, silver bullets were one of the only ways to kill a werewolf. The other way was by fire.

Though she didn't know for certain about any of the

victims, she was working on finding out if they could have been like Jason. If someone was killing these people with unique abilities, she had to stop it. After all, they were people first, people who didn't deserve to die in such a horrible manner.

Jason had been a werewolf. She'd bet her last dime the other victims had been werewolves, too.

CHAPTER TWO

NICK FULLY expected Amanda Riley to be late. In his experience, women who looked like her spent hours planted in front of a mirror. She'd surprised the hell out of him. He'd known Jason liked his girlfriends tall, blond and sexy, so he'd been prepared to find a hooker. But when he'd learned she was a police officer, the news had given him pause. Attractive women had things even tougher in law enforcement. They had to work twice as hard to get men to take them seriously.

Though she tried to downscale her stunning looks, Amanda exuded sex appeal. Nick didn't understand how her colleagues kept from swarming all over her. For all he knew, maybe they did. But she'd made detective, so she had more going on than attractiveness. She was smart and ballsy, too. He liked that in a woman. While he hadn't expected his instant rush of physical attraction, after the few hours he'd spent working with her, he actually *liked* Amanda Riley.

Now he had to find out what she knew about Jason's death.

For the fifth time in an hour he checked his watch. She'd said she'd pick him up at nine o'clock. He thought about waiting in his room and making her come to him. But Nick wasn't a patient man, so he paced the hotel lobby instead. Idly, he wondered what kind of car she drove. He'd learned a lot about people by their choice of vehicle. He was betting Amanda owned something sleek, fast and expensive.

She pulled up in a Volvo SUV instead. Safe and practical? Pushing through the lobby doors, Nick shook his head. That's what he got for thinking with his hormones instead of using his brain.

Reaching for the handle, he heard a click as she disengaged the locks. He climbed inside, trying like hell not to stare at her legs. Lightly tanned and smooth, they seemed to go on forever. The kind of legs that wrapped around a man's waist when he—whoa. Nick took a deep breath and immediately wished he hadn't. Even her scent was pleasing—lightly musky and ultrafeminine.

Damn. "Nice car."

She raised a brow. "Thanks. I bought it as a present to myself when I made detective."

He felt her gaze like heat as she inspected him. Once or twice, early in his career he'd done some undercover work for the Bureau. He could pull off the look if he had to. Still, he relished her surprise.

"I like the jeans. They're torn in all the right places." A trace of humor colored her voice. He decided to ignore it.

"Yeah." He plucked at the denim. "I don't like them, but they'll work. Good thing I'm not from around here, so I don't have to worry about running into someone I know."

Her laugh took him by surprise. A husky contralto, the sound of it rolled over him, raising the hair on his arms. His wolf-self, never far away, became alert.

It took a moment to realize she'd asked him a question. "What?"

"Are you like Jason?"

He froze. Raising his gaze to hers, he saw all traces of humor had vanished from her face. Deliberately he made his voice neutral. "Like him how?"

"With what he could do. Jason told me. Hell, Jason *showed* me."

Careful. "Could do? What do you mean?"

She looked away.

He said nothing, continuing simply watching her. Twin spots of color bloomed high upon her cheekbones. Her pulse beat an agitated rhythm at the hollow of her neck.

At his lack of response, her stern face came back. Cop face. But the cascading waves of golden hair ruined the effect. He felt the urge to change—his wolf-self knew what she was asking and stirred restlessly inside him.

Finally, she waved her hand. "Come on, Nick. I really need to know. It's important."

Important. She had that one right. He made his own features hard. He was a cop, too. He could play the same game. "Like Jason. Hmmm. Well, I'm older than Jason is—was." Deliberately misunderstanding, he also wanted to remind her of their loss. "We weren't close, though we got together at the usual family gatherings. While I've heard we look similar, I don't know about personality-wise."

"That's not what I'm asking." Her voice sounded flat.

He cocked his head. *Spell it out.* "I'm not sure what you mean."

"I'll let it go for now," she snapped. "Only because I've just met you and you're FBI."

Good. Great. Though he'd been granted a reprieve of sorts, he had a feeling next time the subject came up, she wouldn't let him go so easily. She was too good of a cop for that.

"Have you eaten?"

Because the curve of her sensual mouth distracted him, he cleared his throat. "I grabbed a sandwich at the hotel bar." And a couple of beers, too, hoping to dull the edge. But judging from his body's reaction to Amanda, that had been a mistake. He'd need all his mental sharpness to make sure he didn't let down his guard with her.

Though she was a cop—detective—and on the newly assembled team investigating the recently named Fort Worth serial killer, Nick had a hunch Amanda might knew more about what had happened to Jason than she let on.

They pulled into a well-lit, crowded parking lot. Small groups of eclectically dressed people milled around.

"Sundance Square," she said, then laughed at his un-comprehending look. "One of Jason's favorite hang-outs. We'll start here."

He made sure to get out of the car at the same time she did. Manners be damned, no way in hell could he keep from checking out those endless legs of hers if he were to open her door.

Her heels clicked on the pavement as she moved to stand next to him. In her shoes she was as tall as Nick, which made her nearly six feet tall, flat-footed. He noticed a suspicious lump in the side of her short black jacket.

"You carrying?"

Her eyes went cool. "Of course. This is still police work, after all."

"It shows. If I noticed, someone else might. Maybe you should put the gun in your purse."

Cursing, she glared at him. "I knew I should have worn a longer jacket."

He shrugged. He had his own gun in a shoulder holster, but his leather coat hid it.

He waited while she transferred her weapon to her purse. They didn't speak again as they crossed the parking lot. He'd never known he could find the tap-tap of heels so sexy.

Though it was early, the sidewalks were crowded. Amanda took his arm. He felt a jolt, all the way through his leather jacket.

"We're together," she told him. "For cover. Keep that in mind."

He set his jaw against the images that danced through his mind at her words. "Right."

The first place they entered had a cover of ten bucks a person. Amanda stood back and let him pay it.

Once inside, the pulsing music drowned any attempts at conversation. Not a good place to question suspects. Yet Amanda didn't seem to notice—or mind. This was her territory, her jurisdiction. For now, he'd let her take the lead.

He ordered them both a beer, making his way through the crowd to the table she'd chosen. He barely had set the glasses down when she grabbed his hand, pulling him on to the dance floor. Once there, she began to move to the pulse of the music. Despite the fast tempo, her movements were exotic and sensual.

Her mouth moved and he realized she was speaking to him. "What?"

She leaned closer, talking directly into his ear. "Dance. You're drawing attention to us."

He cursed and began to move. Entranced by her, he

hadn't even realized he'd been standing stock-still on the dance floor.

The sea of gyrating bodies threatened to swallow them up. If Amanda's actions had purpose other than tempting the hell out of him, he couldn't tell.

The song ended and Nick breathed a sigh of relief. The jeans clung to him like a second skin and he'd noticed several other women checking him out. He didn't like the new and unfamiliar feeling of being on display.

"Nick!" Amanda laughed up at him. She leaned forward, her breasts pressing against his chest. Of their own accord, his hands came up to circle her small waist.

"Play along." Speaking into his ear as though whispering suggestively, her breath tickled him, causing his body to tighten in reaction to her closeness. Instantly he was hard. Knowing the jeans would hide nothing, he tightened his hold on her.

Her eyes widened as she felt his arousal.

"Sorry. I am playing along," he growled back. "Though later I expect you to tell me what the hell you're doing."

Another song started, a slow ballad this time. Narrowing her eyes, Amanda began to sway against him. Each movement of her slender hips seemed to stroke his erection.

"Damn it." He gritted his teeth. He hadn't reacted like this to a woman since he'd been younger. "Outside." Without waiting to hear her response, he began to move through the crowd, one arm clamped tight around her and keeping her in front of him, her pert little rear nestled against his now raging arousal.

The combination of lust and woman scent roused the beast in him; that part of him that remained wolf even when he was human, even when he led what appeared to be an utterly normal life. Sometimes he counted himself lucky shifters were in complete control of when and where to change.

Once outside, the night air felt blessedly cool. He pulled her around a corner, into a semidark doorway.

"Nick—"

"Shhh." He spun her around, fighting the urge to change, fighting his arousal, conscious only of the need to kiss her, touch her, explore his exploding attraction to her.

She opened her mouth to protest and he dipped his head and claimed her lips with his.

Mine. The word echoed in his mind as he kissed her. Never mind that she wasn't a shifter, Nick wanted her more than he'd ever wanted a female—human or shifter.

The roar of urgent desire had him deepening the kiss, tasting her. Hell hounds, she gave back as good as she got. Her arms wound up around his neck. Her tongue danced with his, teasing, retreating, maddening him.

He heard himself growl. Wolf-growl.

She made an answering sound low in her throat. It took him a moment to realize it was a protest.

He let her go.

She reared back, pushing him away. Glaring at him, chest heaving, she looked like an avenging angel.

"What the hell are you doing?" she snarled, still panting. Part of him liked that she was so rattled.

Though he didn't have his composure back either, he was a better actor. He managed a bland look. "Kissing you."

She took a step back. "Tomorrow I'll talk to Gordy, er, Lieutenant Gordon about reassigning you. I don't want you to touch me ever again."

Nick could scent her emotions better than he saw them. She was lying, for her level of arousal was equal to his.

But she was right. This was the last thing he needed, to lose his head in the middle of a major investigation that also happened to be personal. Not just to him, but to the entire Pack. More than one shifter had been killed—all of the victims had been members of various Packs across the country. Because he was FBI, Nick had been chosen to investigate on behalf of them all.

"I apologize." He meant it. "I don't know what came over me."

"Yeah, right. I'm barely hanging on here by the skin of my teeth." She crossed her arms. "When the task force found out victim four was Jason, they said it was too personal and tried to boot me off. Now I have to constantly prove to them it's not."

"Detective Riley—"

"I'm not finished." Taking a deep breath appeared to give her a shot of strength. "What about you, Federal Agent Templeton? It seems to me investigating your own cousin's death is mighty personal as well. I'm thinking maybe you had to work as hard as I to get the powers that be to allow you this assignment."

Her words hit uncomfortably close to home. "Yeah. So?"

"Could it be that someone, somewhere, might need an excuse to yank you off the case? Any reason, especially a mistake as monumental as pawing a female coworker against her will, would do, wouldn't it?"

"Against her will? You kissed me back."

He was right and she knew it. Nick saw the realization settle in her furious eyes.

"Maybe I did, but what you did was still uncalled for."

"I lost control." Truth, he'd stick to the truth. He admired her honesty. The least he could do was give her the same. "Again, I apologize. Please let me make it up to you, Detective Riley."

Though she stared hard at him, she didn't run. He supposed he should feel lucky for that.

If he'd made her afraid of him, he knew damn well it would be because she sensed the beast in him, the wild animal pacing, brought to life by the force of his desire for her.

CHAPTER THREE

ABOUT TO LEAVE Nick to find his own way back to the hotel, Amanda spotted a familiar face heading her way and froze. Damn. Just her luck to run into Jason's best friend Chris while pretending to be out on a date with Jason's cousin. Chris, short for Christine, would think Amanda hadn't spent any time grieving for Jason. She sure as hell couldn't tell Chris that Nick was FBI and they were working the case.

Resigned, Amanda heaved a sigh. The job came first. Always had. "Chris." She plastered a welcoming smile on her face, hoping she didn't look as ruffled as she felt.

"Hey, Amanda." Wide smile faltering, Chris's gaze slid past her to Nick, no doubt wondering why they were standing so close together, disheveled, in a darkened alley. "What's up?"

Cut right to the chase, that was Chris. Amanda suppressed the urge to sigh again. "Chris, I'd like you to meet Jason's cousin, Nick Templeton. Nick, this is Christine Chartwell, Jason's best friend. And mine, too," she added, tacking the last on as an afterthought.

Expression watchful, Nick shook the other woman's hand. "Jason's best friend was a—?"

"A woman?" Christine smiled pleasantly. "Yes. We went to college together. And you're Jason's cousin?"

She looked Nick up and down. "You're the FBI guy Jason talked about. He looked up to you. Jason liked you. A lot."

Nick glanced at his watch, then at Amanda before looking back to Chris. "Do you have a few minutes to answer a couple of questions?"

"Nick, what're you doing?" Amanda glared. Damned if she was going to let him grill Jason's best friend like she was still a suspect. "We've already questioned Chris."

"Closure." Nick seemed to trip over the word, as if it was unfamiliar. "Maybe talking to Jason's best friend will give me closure."

"Closure, my ass."

Chris touched her arm. "Amanda, that's all right." She gave Nick a serious look. "I totally understand. Anything I can tell you about Jason will help, right?"

"Yeah." Nick nodded. Damn his hide. Still, Amanda stood and played nice while Nick asked his questions. Did the man think her unit's investigation had been so shoddy that they hadn't pulled in every single person even remotely related to the victims and questioned them?

Finally Nick wound down. They were still standing in the alleyway.

"I'm finished." Nick smiled at Amanda, causing her insides to somersault. "Are you ready to move on?"

"Yes. Chris, can I catch you later?"

Chris didn't bother to hide her relief. "Sure. I'll give you a call. I'm meeting someone here anyway." She turned and went into the bar they'd just exited, leaving Amanda alone with Nick.

Amanda waited until she was certain Chris wouldn't be back before rounding on Nick. "What the hell was that all about?"

"Questioning a suspect." He shrugged. "I know you've probably already been all over her, but humor me. I might find something you missed."

"It's possible." But her tone let him know she didn't think it was, not really. "She's not a suspect anymore."

Nick's eyes narrowed. "Until this case is solved, Detective, everyone is a suspect. I would think you of all people could understand that."

The air went out of her in a rush. He was right. As a cop, she couldn't afford to think of Chris as her friend.

"Believe it or not, I think I can help you," he said.

"Me?" She kept her voice as bland as his.

"Not you personally, but the task force. I'm talking about finding the serial killer. That's what's important here, isn't it?"

Grudgingly she had to admit he was right. Again. But still… "Yeah, but we need to settle things between us."

"This is your jurisdiction. I'm a guest, here on your sufferance. The locals always hate the feds horning in. But we have no choice. Like you, we just want to catch the bad guys. Give me a break."

Bam, bam, bam. He'd hit every point square on the head. Every point but one.

"There are personal matters we need to settle."

His brown eyes turned hard. Unfriendly. "I already said I was sorry for kissing you. It won't happen again. Believe me."

The vehemence of his last two words offended her. She pushed that thought away. He still hadn't addressed the werewolf issue, but she wasn't entirely sure there *was* a werewolf issue. For all she knew, Jason could have been an anomaly.

And pigs could fly. Right.

Still, if he wasn't and she came out and accused Nick…the man would think she was nuts. Certifiable. Hell, she'd think she was crazy, too, if she hadn't seen Jason turn into a wolf with her own two eyes. She'd thought she'd seen it all, the worst that humanity could become—until she'd stared down a huge muzzle with razor-sharp teeth and saw Jason in that ferocious, lupine face.

Nick led the way to the next club. Without asking. And, without arguing, she followed him.

The noise level in this one wasn't nearly as loud as the last. Thank God.

They took a small table near the bar. He ordered drinks while Amanda scanned the crowd, looking for someone, anyone, who might look the least bit familiar.

No such luck.

Nick looked totally relaxed, sipping his beer, just a guy out on the town with his date. She hated that he might be better at undercover work than she. Taking a deep breath, Amanda struggled to match his nonchalance. "It's been too long since I did this."

"What do you mean?" His expression reflected polite curiosity, nothing more.

She took a big gulp of her own beer, reminding herself why she never drank draft. Headache city. "Surely you know Jason and I broke up about a month before he was killed."

He didn't bother to lie. "Yes. Mind telling me why?"

Though he'd asked like he might consider even her a suspect, Amanda ignored her resentment. She hadn't spoken to anyone about her reasons for dumping Jason, and the guilt was eating her alive. If they'd still been together, would Jason still be alive? They'd spent their nights together at her apartment, on the couch in front of the television. Not cruising singles bars or roaming the Dallas-Fort Worth streets. But she'd heard after they'd broken up, Jason had tackled that life with a vengeance.

With difficulty, she forced herself back to the question at hand. How to answer depended on how much of the truth she wanted Nick to know. She refused to lie.

"He changed." She watched him closely for a reaction to the stock phrase. "I couldn't handle it, so I asked for time apart. Jason didn't take it well."

If she thought Nick would ask for specifics as to *how* Jason had changed, she was wrong. What worried her was her fear he'd know exactly what she meant without her saying *your cousin turned into a werewolf.* Or, she chided herself, was she letting her overactive imagination run away with her again. Maybe he'd simply taken her words at face value.

"I understand," he said.

They finished their drinks without any more talk. Amanda didn't mind. That made it easier to search the growing crowd without distraction.

In the third club they hit pay dirt. Amanda recognized three of Jason's buddies playing pool. With Nick looming behind her like a broad-shouldered shadow, she said hello. They looked from her to Nick and back again. None of them seemed overjoyed.

"We've already been over everything with the cops," said a stocky blonde with six earrings in his left ear.

"Yeah," another one chimed in. "What'sa matter, can't you read the report?"

Amanda kept her smile pleasant. "This is kinda off the record. Jason was my boyfriend. I want to catch his killer."

Again, one by one their glances slid over her to Nick.
"Jason said you broke up with him."

The third man, who'd appeared to be lining up his
next shot, lifted his pool cue. "We don't know anything.
Leave us alone."

Nick touched her arm. "Come on. Let's go."

Though her jaw ached with the effort to keep her
mouth shut, Amanda spun on her heel and followed him.

Once they were outside, she shook her head. "I don't
know what that was all about."

"They're hiding something."

"Oh yeah?" She lifted a brow, her voice dripping
with sarcasm. "How could you tell?"

He ignored her. "The one in the back especially. I
need to talk to him. Alone."

"Templeton, if he won't talk to me, what makes you
think he'll open up for you?"

"Because," he looked calmly past her at the exit to
the bar, "he's signaling me right now. Wait here."

Without another word Nick pushed past her, disap-
pearing inside with the other man.

Alone on the sidewalk, Amanda felt like cursing
but contented herself with kicking the toe of her shoe
at the ground. While she felt a bit better, all she succeeded in gaining was a scuff mark on her best pair of
black heels.

Someone elbowed her—she was blocking the sidewalk. With a sigh, she moved over to wait next to the
wall, careful to avoid making eye contact with anyone.

After a few minutes that seemed an eternity, Nick returned. Looking, if possible, even more grim.

"Well," she demanded. "What did he want?"

"Not here." Taking her arm, he steered her down the

street, weaving through the crowded sidewalk with the ease of long practice.

Before she realized where they were heading, they'd reached the parking lot.

"What—?"

He shot her a warning look. "In the car."

More and more curious, Amanda located her car keys and pushed the unlock button. She got in and Nick climbed in beside her.

"Where to?"

Not looking at her, he drummed his fingers on the dash. "Anywhere but here."

Starting the engine, Amanda put the gearshift in Reverse. "Nick, what did the guy say?"

"His name is Chet. He told me Jason had joined some secret club."

"Club? That's the first I've heard of anything like this. What kind of club?"

"I don't know. Either Chet didn't know or he wouldn't say. But apparently Jason had been trying to take him to a meeting for months."

"Months?" While she hated that she seemed only capable of repeating Nick's last word, she needed to wrap her mind around what she was hearing. She'd been with Jason until a month ago, and he'd never said one word about any secret club.

Unless… "Was this a guy club? Did they play poker together or something?" God, she hoped it was something like that. Something minor, not serious. Not dangerous.

"No."

Her stomach sank. She put the car in Drive and pulled slowly forward. "None of the other victims belonged to any kind of clubs."

"That you know of. And you're assuming Jason's murder is related. Maybe it's not."

"Of course it's related. You saw the file. The M.O.'s the same." This time she couldn't hide her exasperation. "You know the drill—they're shot with a damn silver bullet, dismembered and then they're decapitated."

"Yeah." Nick went utterly still. "Did you find out where the shooter got the silver bullets?"

Signaling a right turn, she pulled onto the service road. "Not yet, but we're working on it. None of the local gun shops sell that kind of ammo. We've even checked the Internet. No silver bullets, though I have found several Web sites that sell bullets with silver tips. These were entirely hollowed out silver, expensive as hell. Custom jobs, handmade."

She hadn't told him anything he didn't know. Yet Nick appeared lost in thought. Finally, he gave her a sideways glance. "What did your people discover when they talked to Jason's friends?"

"You read the report. You saw. We learned nothing. Jason was an ordinary guy. He worked hard and played hard. He was intense." In every aspect of his life.

Nick went silent again. He fiddled with the radio, finding a classical station that played soothing music. Allowing this, though she hated anyone to touch her radio, Amanda waited for him to say more. He didn't. Finally, she couldn't stand it any longer. "Did you learn anything else?"

He blinked. "No. Chet told me everything he knew."

"Not enough."

"No." He flashed her a grim smile. "But this was only one night. I'll learn more."

She couldn't help but notice he said "I," not "we."

"Where to?"

He glanced out the window, noting the signs directing them to I-30. "You're the driver, you tell me. Let's go someplace where Jason might have hung out."

"This is it for Fort Worth."

"Seriously?"

She shrugged. "It's a small city. Mostly we hung out around Sundance Square, near downtown Fort Worth. But we drove over to Dallas a lot, too. Deep Ellum and Lower Greenville are happening places. And Jason really liked a couple of bars in Addison, which is sort of Far North Dallas."

"Let's go."

"That's an hour from here, or more."

"So." He pointed at the luminous clock on her dash. "It's early yet."

She had to be at a task force meeting at eight in the morning. And, if Nick planned to take part in this investigation, so did he.

"I—" Her cell phone rang, loud in the quiet car, even though it was tucked into her tiny purse on the floor in front of him. It was nearly midnight. This call couldn't be anything good. "Could you hand me that?"

He did and she answered, flipping open the phone. It was Gordy, sounding both furious and exhausted. "Another murder. Eighth Street, over by the hospital. How long will it take you to get here?"

"We're on our way." She closed the phone and reached in back for the bubble light. "Hang on," she told Nick. "There's been another killing. This time you can see the killer's handiwork, up close and personal."

CHAPTER FOUR

"W HO QUESTIONED Jason's friends?"

Amanda barely moved her attention from the road. She'd slapped her bubble light on her roof and gripped the steering wheel hard. At sixty plus miles per hour, she needed all of her concentration for driving.

"I'm not sure. We all work each suspect. Some of us talk to family members, others to friends. Everything should be in the report. We can check at the station in the morning." She spared him a quick glance. "Why? I get the feeling you haven't told me everything. What else did you find out?"

"This club Jason joined. That bothers me."

"You think it's like a cult?"

He shrugged. "Could be. Either way, I have a feeling it was involved with the murder someway, somehow. What also bothers me is that no one mentioned this before."

"If Chet told some other officer, he didn't report it." Now that Nick mentioned it, Amanda did think the omission was odd. Worse, if any of the other victims had belonged to this same group…

Nick shifted. "We'll check the file. I want to talk to this uniform, whoever he is."

"I agree. If someone was stupid enough to let a lead like this go, Gordy needs to know."

Ahead, they saw what looked like a dozen flashing lights.

"Here we are." They pulled up behind an extraordinarily long line of police cars.

"Must be a slow night," Amanda commented as she pushed open her door. "Lots of uniformed looky-lous."

Lifting the yellow crime scene tape, Amanda located Gordy across the sea of uniforms. In the bushes, one cop was upchucking his dinner. She winced. More than once, when viewing the carnage that the killer made of his poor victims, she'd nearly lost it herself.

Gordy saw them coming and met them halfway. "The M.E.'s here. He's done his bit and wants to head to the morgue. I don't think I could get him to hold off much longer."

Amanda lifted a brow at that. "Don't tell me the CSI guys are done already?"

He shrugged. "Just about. They're still taking pictures."

Nick spoke up. "Enlighten me."

Gordy gave him a long look. "You've seen the file."

"Yes, but humor me, please."

When Gordy glanced at Amanda, she kept her own expression bland.

"Each victim is killed by a single gunshot wound. One silver bullet, lodged in the heart. But this guy likes blood. He cuts them up first, then kills them."

"Torture."

"Right."

"Because the blood won't flow once the heart stops pumping."

"Right. The killer savages the body while the victim's still alive."

"Savages?"

Gordy gave a helpless shrug. "That's the best way I can think of to describe it. He rips them apart, limb from limb. Hell, you know all this."

"Yeah, I do. He leaves the body in one place, except for the head."

"The heads are all missing." Gordy's expression was grim. "Every single one of them."

"Trophies."

"That's what we think." Making a dismissive sound, Gordy turned away. "We don't know what he does with them." He walked away before Amanda or Nick could comment.

"Ready?" Amanda touched Nick's arm, drawing his gaze.

"You want to take a look at the body, right?"

He nodded, following as she led the way. Several of the other cops greeted her with a wave or a nod, then looked at Nick, and their expressions shut down.

"You ready?" She touched Nick's arm, trying to prepare him—and herself, if she was honest—for the sight ahead.

Like all the others, the victim had been dismembered. The sight wasn't pretty. Nick found himself watching Amanda for a typical woman's reaction, then remembered she was a cop. Blood and horror were part of her daily routine.

Amanda gave the victim a cursory glance before facing the CSI guy.

"Name?"

"No ID was found."

This was not unusual, though sometimes the killer left the victim's wallet intact. "Personal effects?"

"None whatsoever. No coins, no bills, nothing."

Nick spoke up, his voice intense. "You got a decent set of prints, right?"

Charlie Tate, head crime scene analyst, frowned. "Who the hell are you?"

"He's FBI." Amanda looked for Gordy, spotting him talking to two suits on the fringes of the scene. "Part of our team now."

From the tightening of his jaw, she could tell Charlie didn't like it. "Feds."

"Prints?" Nick prodded, ignoring the way Tate said feds as if it was a curse word.

"We've taken them, like we always do." Charlie lifted his head, his gaze defiant. "I'm sure they're running them now. We should get a match soon." He looked at Amanda and grimaced. "No one's called in a missing person yet. I'm hoping this guy lived alone."

Amanda cursed, kicking her toe at the ground. "He was someone's kid, Charlie. I'm sure he'll have a parent grieving over him. Anything unusual?"

"No. Nothing. Same as all the others."

"Damn." Amanda looked at Nick.

"Let's go." Nick touched her shoulder. "I need to check something out."

Suddenly weary, Amanda let him lead the way to her vehicle.

Back in the SUV, Nick waited until she'd buckled herself in. "We need to go by the station."

Amanda blinked. "Okay. Mind telling me why?"

"To review the file. I want to see why Chet's lead was never mentioned. And, once I find out who interviewed him, I want to talk to that person."

That made sense. She did, too. If someone on the team had missed a clue as important as the one Nick had gotten his first time out, then the person deserved to be kicked off the task force.

Once back at the squad room, she made her way through the area, waving at Officer Hernandez, who was taking a report from a young Hispanic boy. Crossing the normally bustling room, she remembered how much she'd hated working nights.

A lot of the rookies were out on patrol, paired with one or two seasoned cops who claimed to like working graveyard. She pushed in chairs, clearing a path to her cubicle, and located the file exactly where she'd left it, on top of the stack of paper in her in-basket. Handing Nick the binder, she ran a hand through her hair and grimaced. "Knock yourself out. I'm gonna see if the night crew made coffee. You want some?"

He glanced at his watch. "It's nearly eleven."

"So? Are you planning on sleeping any time soon?"

"You have a point." He sighed. "Sure, I'll take a cup. Black."

Black. Of course. Personally, Amanda had to use two packets of sugar and enough nondairy creamer to turn the coffee a vanilla color before she could stomach the stuff. Hot tea was much more to her liking, but making it took too much time at work, so she only drank it at home.

When she brought Nick his mug, he looked up and frowned, waved her closer. "Come look at this."

She set his cup down on the desk next to him. Sipping from hers, she moved behind him to peer over his shoulder. "What?"

"Chet's here." He tapped the paper. "I've made my own list of people who are listed as Jason's buddies, but there's nothing about this club. Nothing at all."

"That's strange." She placed her mug on her book-case. "But then maybe not. I talked to several of Jason's friends myself. Not a single one mentioned Jason join-ing a club. I wonder why."

"Ominous omission."

"Yes. Let me see that."

He slid the binder to his right. Taking it, she went to the guest chair next to her desk and sat. Nick leaned back and watched her.

A quick riffling through the pages showed her what her gut already knew. "Nothing. You're right, damn it."

Regarding her, his gaze was direct and steady. "We need to find out more about this club. This might be the first big link to the killer."

"We've got to notify the team." She reached for her phone. "And Gordy. I should call him first."

"No." He placed his hand on top of hers, hard. "Not yet. Let's pursue this lead and see what we find out. If this club does turn out to be important to the case, then we'll tell everyone else."

"Why wait? I don't like hiding things."

"I think there'll be more people who will talk to me. If Gordy sends someone else in…"

Damn. She blew out her breath in frustration. "Ear-lier I might not have believed you. After tonight…I don't know."

As though he finally remembered he had it, he reached for his coffee and drank deeply, taking several quick gulps of the still-steaming liquid.

Blindly, she mimicked him, both hands around her own cup as she sipped. "You're asking a lot."

"I know. Give me two days."

"Two days? Feeling pretty confident?"

"Just let me have a shot. I want to catch this guy even worse than you do."

"I don't know about that. I cared about Jason, too."

Nick didn't comment.

Amanda looked at the file. Flipping through the paperwork, she finally reached the section marked Jason Templeton. "Let's make a copy of this." She stabbed the list with her index finger. "All Jason's friends. We can start with them."

Nick glanced at her. "I'm doing the questioning."

That rankled. But he was right about one thing. She wanted this killer bad. "Fine." She kept her tone dry, matching his. "No problem. As long as you don't start keeping secrets from me."

His expression gave nothing away. "Two days, Amanda."

"Two days." She laughed self-consciously. "If you think you can perform miracles, I'm all for it. But no extensions. If we haven't found the killer in two days, I'm telling Gordy what we've learned about the club."

Nick held out his hand. "Deal."

She slid her fingers in his, liking the comfortable firmness of his handshake. "Deal."

"Where's your copier? We need to make a copy of this."

She led the way to the copy room, leaning against the door frame watching while he made the necessary copies. Her cell phone rang. Out of habit she checked the caller ID, her heart skipping when she recognized Gordy's number.

"Please don't let him be calling to tell me there's been another murder." After uttering the fervent prayer, she answered.

"We've ID'd the body." Gordy's voice triumphant. "And you're not gonna believe who it is—was. Ryan Humbert. We interviewed the guy several times, most recently after Jason Templeton was found."

"Ryan Humbert." She repeated the name. It sounded vaguely familiar. She searched her memory of Jason's friends, trying to place him or see his face. Finally, she gave up and grabbed the sheet of paper from Nick and searched until she located the name. "You're right. Ryan Humbert was one of Jason's friends."

"Yeah." Gordy's bark of laughter was utterly without humor. "Was being the operative word. Now he's dead. There's a connection here somewhere, and we need to find it."

A connection was the understatement of the year. Amanda kept her face neutral, while she desperately tried to find the correlation.

Looking up, she met Nick's gaze. In his dark eyes, she saw a mirror of her own resolve. They were missing something, something big. How quickly they figured it out might be the factor that saved—or cost—another innocent life.

CHAPTER FIVE

WHEN AMANDA relayed her conversation with Gordy to Nick, he swore and left the copy room. She kept pace with him as he headed for the door.

"The connection has to be that damn organization Jason joined." Frustrated, Nick heard the growl in his voice and winced. Even though his self-control was excellent, moments of stress always brought the need to change close to the surface.

Amanda looked at him sideways. "Are you all right?"

"Yeah. But if this is what I think it is, every second counts."

"What do you think this is?" Her voice, the detached, rational sort of cajoling used by cops everywhere, made him wonder if she *knew* what Jason had been, what Nick himself was. Time to share, he thought savagely. They were partners. If she knew and was thinking along the same lines as he, that was good. If she didn't, then now was a good time for her to learn. He felt a flash of fury, then deadly calm. They needed to settle this once and for all.

"Get in the car."

"Do what?"

"The car. Now. I'll drive. We need to talk. This is important."

She swore, but handed him the keys and headed for her SUV. "It better be."

Unlocking the doors, they both got in. He waited until she'd buckled in before he started the engine. If he remembered right, down the street he'd noticed a city park. Nice, neutral ground for them to share information.

As he shifted into Drive, she turned in her seat to face him. "What's up, Templeton?"

"Nick."

With an exaggerated sigh, she conceded. "Fine. What's going on, Nick?"

He pulled into the park and drove into a slot by a picnic table under some spindly trees. Sensing her frustration, he kept his movements deliberate as he killed the engine and pocketed the keys.

"Nick…" Her voice contained a warning.

He would have given her a fierce smile, but until he knew, he had to keep this serious. "Amanda, earlier you said Jason had *changed*. Please tell me exactly what you meant."

Though she looked outwardly calm, he saw a touch of belligerence in the lift of her chin as she searched his face. "What the hell's up with you? You're freaking me out."

"No, I'm not. Cut the crap. You're a cop. You've made detective and you're not even thirty yet, are you?" At her nod he managed a smile. "I know better, Amanda. You don't scare so easily."

At his words she glanced away. She rubbed her arms up and down, as though she were cold. Then she looked him full in the face, her forehead creasing in a frown. "Okay, Nick Templeton, FBI agent. You asked for it." She took a deep breath.

He waited, pretty sure he knew what was coming.

"Jason was a werewolf. And since I've shared with you, now it's your turn. Are you a werewolf, too?"

The term made him wince. "I hate that word. So I was right. Jason shifted in front of you."

She crossed her arms. "You didn't answer the question. Are. You. A. Werewolf?"

"Shifter."

"Just answer me, damn it. You are, aren't you?"

"Yes."

Now she flinched. "Damn."

At her disgusted look, he rushed on. "How you feel about that doesn't matter, not now. That's personal. We can deal with it later."

"Personal?"

"Yeah. I wanted to get that out of the way, so we could discuss this case like two investigators. We've got to focus on the job."

"I agree, though I don't see what you—or Jason's— abilities have to do with it."

She was still thinking too close to home. Personal. But the case wasn't. "Amanda, I think all the serial killer's victims were shifters. I think someone out there is hunting down and killing my kind."

He watched her expression harden. She went from dazed and uncomfortable to focused detective.

"I had my suspicions about exactly that. The silver bullet angle, you know. But I couldn't find any other connection, until now with the possible club thing. You werewo—er, shifters, are a pretty closemouthed bunch."

"Unless need or circumstances demand otherwise."

He saw her think, start to ask something. Then, evidently remembering what he'd said about separating the personal from the professional, she closed her mouth.

"Hunting shifters. Any idea why?" she drawled.

"That's what we need to find out. And I think it would be best if we started with trying to locate this secret society that Jason joined."

Amanda nodded, glancing at her watch. "It's after twelve. We've got a big meeting in the morning at eight."

He kept his expression neutral. "Up to you."

"We can't skip the meeting. It's required. All the team has to be there."

He didn't comment. Just waited.

She sighed. "Let's go to Dallas," she said. "If we finish up by the time the bars close at two and head back, we'll still have time to grab a few hours' sleep. If we're too tired, we can always take a nap after work before we head back out for the night."

Surprisingly, he sort of liked the way she said *we*. Like they were partners. Which, in a way they were.

Deep Ellum reminded him of the Village in NYC. Funky and eclectic, the place pulsed with late-night vibrancy. Yet, though they wandered from bar to bar, Amanda saw no one familiar. Nick, on the other hand, recognized many of his kind mingling among the crowded bars. Their scent, even over the myriad aromas that filled the air, announced them as Pack. But whether or not they knew Jason, he had no way of knowing. He'd have to pull them aside and question them, one by one.

Once more he scanned the packed bar. "No one here looks familiar to you?"

"No. Maybe I'm just tired." Frustration echoed in her voice.

"Let's go back and get some rest. We can come back tomorrow night."

"Works for me." As one, they turned and headed for the parking lot.

"I want to do some more checking with Jason's buddies after the meeting. Make phone calls, set up some face-to-face meetings."

Amanda shot him a look. "Maybe our original plan needs rethinking. Maybe I should make the calls. Jason's friends are more likely to talk to me."

"Not if they're shifters." Though he hated to bring up the subject again, it had to be dealt with.

"So? I was Jason's girlfriend."

"Was." He put it as gently as he could. "I think most of Jason's friends know you'd broken up. Chet knew."

As they climbed back in the SUV, her shoulders sagged with exhaustion. He felt an impulse to massage her, to see if he could rub out the strained tiredness.

Of course he shook that impulse off. He must be more exhausted than he'd realized.

On the drive back to Fort Worth, neither spoke. Amanda changed the channel and turned up the radio. She'd chosen a classic rock station, playing Lynyrd Skynard. Evidently she didn't like classical music.

They stopped at the hotel to drop him off and he watched from the lobby as she drove off. After riding the elevator to his floor, Nick carefully removed a slip of paper from his pocket. While he'd been talking to Chet, the other shifter who'd been playing pool earlier had handed it to him. There was a phone number, nothing more.

Nick hadn't wanted to call the guy until he gauged Amanda's reaction to shifters—after all, she'd broken up with his cousin after learning the truth. He still couldn't fathom her casual discussion. It had to have been an act.

As soon as he turned the light on in his room, he dialed the number.

Voice mail picked up. No name, nothing but a simple message asking the caller to leave name and number. Without hesitation, Nick gave his cell phone number.

The clock on the nightstand blinked luminous green—3:33 a.m. If he was lucky he could get almost four hours of sleep.

Undressing, he thought of Amanda, wondering if she were doing the same. He wondered what she slept in, grinning as he allowed himself to picture a skimpy teddy of black lace and little else. Then, as his body stirred at the thought, he shook his head. No doubt practical Amanda slept in an oversized T-shirt and panties.

But even that seemed sexy, on her. He groaned out loud, before making quick work of brushing his teeth and yanking back the covers. Praying the hotel clock radio's alarm worked, he set it to wake him at seven-thirty and crawled beneath the sheets.

Thoughts of Amanda, her nipples showing through a thin, white T-shirt, refused to go away. He went from semiaroused to hard instantly. Damn. He glanced at the clock again. A cold shower was not an option.

Tossing and turning, unable to get comfortable, he forced himself to relax, practicing some of the relaxation techniques he'd learned over the years.

Eventually, he must have drifted off.

Only to be woken what seemed like seconds later by the shrill tone of his cell phone ringing.

Disoriented, he reached blindly for the blasted thing. "Hello," he growled, his tone a clear warning that whoever had called him at 5:00 a.m. had better have a damn good reason.

"I was returning your call." Unapologetic, the young male voice was unfamiliar. "Mike Andrews."

"You were a friend of Jason's?"

"Yeah. Jason and I hung out. You're his cousin, right?"

To cut through more preliminary small talk, Nick identified himself by Pack. "Leaning Tree, New York Pack. You?" Packs were as sharp an identifier to a shifter as countries were to humans.

Silence. Nick could have sworn he felt nervousness radiating through the phone lines. What the hell? All he'd asked was Mike's Pack. This was a common form of greeting among their kind.

Finally, the younger man spoke. "That's what I need to talk to you about. Jason and I, we joined the same Pack. A new one. Secret, at least for now."

The secret organization was a *Pack?* Not possible. Setting up a Pack in a new town was simple. One merely contacted the state council of shifters and registered. There was no reason to keep it secret.

Plus, Jason had also been a member of the Leaning Tree Pack. He could understand if his cousin had joined the Fort Worth Pack as a matter of courtesy, though his birth Pack would always hold precedence. But some secret Pack? Why would Jason do such a thing?

Still, Nick held his tongue, waiting to hear what his caller said next.

"We're worried, all of us. Whoever is killing shifters is targeting our new Pack."

"Explain 'new Pack.' You're not talking about the Fort Worth Pack or the Dallas-Forth Worth Council?"

"No. Kenyon—that's our leader—believes we shouldn't have to hide anymore. We're working on a plan to make humans aware of our existence and learn to accept us so we can coexist."

With his free hand, Nick rubbed his eyes. This was the oldest debate in the history of the Pack. It had been tried once several centuries ago, with disastrous results.

He'd bet Kenyon was targeting young kids, like Jason and Mike. Kids who apparently hadn't studied their Pack history. What Kenyon wanted to do would never work.

Humans would always fear their kind. Sure, there were exceptions, like Carson, the human husband of Brenna, Leaning Tree's librarian. Or the wife of Nick's friend Alex, Lyssa. But humans who could accept shifters were few and far between. Not even Amanda, whose job required her to see things that would repulse most humans, had been able to handle it when Jason had shifted.

Mike had fallen silent.

"Are you telling me all the victims of this serial killer were members of your new Pack?"

"Yes. And there are rumors that they all wanted out."

Motive. Despite his racing pulse, Nick kept his tone light. "Where can I find Kenyon?"

Mike gave a nervous laugh. "I'll need to talk to him first, to see if he's okay with meeting you."

The words "obstructing justice" hovered on the tip of his tongue, but Nick bit them back. He'd learned long ago that he'd get more if he had cooperating witnesses, rather than hostile ones. "Do that and get back to me."

"I will. Oh, and a word of caution…"

"Go on."

"The pretty lady you were with tonight? Tell her to back off. There are some who blame her for Jason's death."

The only killing sanctioned among their kind was blood vengeance. If someone truly believed Amanda responsible, her life could be in serious peril. Dangerous territory.

"They'd have to prove it first."

"I've heard there's a few claiming to have proof. If that's true, she's as good as dead."

CHAPTER SIX

THE NEXT MORNING Amanda watched with bleary eyes as Nick strolled into the conference room five minutes before eight. He looked none the worse for their late night, his crisp, professional appearance in direct contrast to how she felt, and probably looked.

He snagged the empty chair next to her. The other cops seated around the long table stopped talking to watch.

"Morning." She inclined her head in a cool nod.

"Yeah. Look, I need to talk to you—"

"Good morning, team." Gordy's hearty voice made Amanda wince.

"Later," she whispered, turning her attention to her boss.

The guys who'd been standing around the room drinking coffee and talking took their seats.

Gordy strode to the front of the room. "As many of you know, there's been another victim. Late last night—or early this morning, I guess—we found another one."

"Same M.O.?" someone asked.

"Yes. Dismembered and headless."

"DNA?" Another cop drummed his fingers on the table.

"Again, none. The spot was remarkably clean of human DNA."

"Gordy?" Amanda watched every head swivel to look

at her. Sometimes being the only female on the task force sucked. "You said *human* DNA. What did you mean?"

A couple of the guys at the other end of the table snickered. A hard look from both Gordy and Nick silenced them.

Still, one wise guy had to make a crack. "You know, human. People. Like you and me."

Amanda ignored him, watching Gordy. "Did you find animal DNA at the site?"

"Yes." Gordy's short answer silenced the room. "Canine. Normally, that in itself wouldn't really be unusual. But the dog didn't disturb the body that we can tell. No teeth marks, nothing besides the head missing. I'll know more after I get the M.E.'s report."

Canine. Amanda stared down at her hands, avoiding looking at Nick. More likely lupine would be a better description, and she was betting once the lab finished their analysis, they'd say so, too.

Why now and not before? Had the others been taken by surprise? This time, had the victim changed in the moments before his attack, the better to defend himself? Did werewolves or, she raised her head to glance at Nick, shifters change back to human form after they lost their lives?

Frowning, Nick looked back at her. "Later," he mouthed.

"That said," Gordy continued, "we are no closer to determining a motive or a suspect than we were when these killings began. We've established the pattern. The killer strikes only on Wednesday nights. And, like always, he's losing control."

"Since the time between kills has decreased," one man muttered.

"Right." Gordy speared him with a look. "The mayor's involved now, the commissioner and the chief are all breathing down my back. We need answers, we need a suspect, *something*."

Gordy swept the room. "Does anyone have anything to report? Breaking news, a new lead? Anything?"

Most of them avoided the lieutenant's stare. Amanda clasped her hands in her lap and stared right back.

Under the table, Nick touched her arm in warning. Apparently he didn't want her to reveal what little they'd learned.

As if she would. If she started spouting off about werewolves, they'd cart her off in a straitjacket.

When Jason had decided she, as his girlfriend, needed to know the truth and had changed in front of her, Amanda had freaked. All her years as a police officer, working in the trenches, had hardened her to a degree, forced her to face a certain, unpleasant reality.

But this—this was the stuff of nightmares. Seeing Jason become a wolf had been the beginning of the end of the relationship between them.

Now, after his death, Amanda had developed an uneasy acceptance. No more, no less.

She resisted the urge to bat Nick's hand away.

One officer cleared his throat. Another coughed. Several chose that moment to take long drinks of their coffee. No one volunteered any information.

"That's what I was afraid of." Gordy heaved a sigh. "They're on my back to wrap this thing up. Before anyone else gets killed."

Still no one spoke. They didn't have to. They were all in agreement.

"All right then. Meeting dismissed."

As they all filed out of the room, Amanda started to head toward her cubicle, but Nick grabbed her arm. She allowed him to lead her outside, toward the parking lot and his rental car. Frankly, she was too damn tired to argue about anything.

Once inside his car, Nick locked the doors but made no move to put the key in the ignition. Obviously he'd wanted to talk someplace where there was zero chance they'd be overheard.

"What's up?"

He dragged his hands through his short hair. "I got a call last night."

Perking up at this, she leaned forward. "Go on."

In a few words he outlined what Mike had told him about the new Pack.

Packs. "You organize yourselves into…Packs?"

"Yes. Each state has their own council. There are county councils and we even have town councils in some towns with high concentrations of shifters."

"I see." She rubbed the back of her neck. "So you think this Kenyon is killing the ones who want out of his Pack."

"It's a possibility worth investigating."

"Is that usual? Killing anyone who wants out?"

His brown eyes looked almost black in the bright sunlight. "No. Despite what we might seem like to you, we're actually quite civilized. Humans kill other humans. Wolves don't kill other wolves."

She supposed she deserved that. "How long are you going to wait for this Mike to arrange a meeting?"

"If I haven't heard from him by noon, I'll call him back. But I think he'll come through. If Kenyon's ever been higher up in a regular Pack, he'll recognize my name."

Narrow-eyed, she studied him. "You're so powerful then, are you?"

He didn't even crack a hint of a smile. "In some circles. But there's more, Amanda."

She sighed. "All right. Let's hear it."

"Mike said there were some who thought *you* might have killed Jason."

Her mouth fell open. "You're kidding, right?"

"No."

"Why would they think that? How could they think that, when his murder fit a pattern like all the others?"

But she knew. Copycat. They believed she'd deliberately made Jason's death look like it'd been the serial killer's handiwork. He must have told his friends how she'd reacted when he showed her the truth about himself.

Great. Just great.

Nick said nothing else, just watched her intently.

"That hurts." Amanda meant it. "I cared for Jason."

"But you broke up with him."

"He changed into a wolf right in front of me. He's lucky I didn't shoot him."

"You didn't handle that well."

"No," she mimicked his bland tone. "I didn't handle that well at all." Her chest felt tight. She resisted the urge to cross her arms. Too defensive. She didn't want Nick to think she had reason to be defensive about anything.

They stared at each other in the front seat of the car, the tension between them palpable. Finally, Nick shook his head. "I've got to know, Amanda. Did you kill Jason?"

She was a cop, through and through. To her very bones she understood why he had to ask the question, but that didn't keep the pain from knifing through her heart.

"I did not." Straightening her shoulders, she looked him full in the face. "I couldn't. First off, I'm a law enforcement officer. I don't go around murdering people. Second—"

He kissed her despite his promise, his mouth slanting over hers, hard and possessive. Just that one kiss, and she was breathless.

"I believe you," he growled, staring at her lips. "Hounds help me, I believe you."

She pressed her back into the door. "I think we'd better go inside." She cleared her throat. "Because if someone saw that…"

"Wait."

Hand on the door handle, she froze.

"Mike said something else. He said you were in danger. The ones who believe you responsible mean to take action."

"Oh, really." She turned her head and smiled brightly. "Then that would explain the sudden rash of phone threats I've gotten since Jason died."

"Phone threats." Glaring at her, he shook his head. "You didn't see fit to mention these earlier?"

"No. Not to you, not to Gordy, or anyone else. Not until I know it means something. I'm a cop, damn it. Things might be different for you almighty FBI guys, but in my job threats come with the territory."

"Amanda." Something in his voice knocked the wind from her sails. "You've never been hunted by a shifter. When a wolf moves in for the kill, he rarely misses."

A warning? Maybe, but Nick spoke only truth.

"I don't have to defend myself." She narrowed her eyes. "Not to you or to anyone else."

"Tell me about the calls."

"There've been three. Same guy, using something simple—hand over his mouth, or a cloth—to distort his voice. He always says the same thing. Once we get proof that you did it, you'll pay."

"Damn."

She shrugged. "Templeton, I've worked a bunch of cases since the calls started coming in. They could be related to half a dozen different people. All cops get calls like this. Seriously."

"There's no way to know if the caller is human or shifter." He caught himself again wanting to kiss her, hold her close, keep her safe. He had a feeling she'd hate that if she knew, so he kept his hands to himself.

"Right. And I can't do anything about the calls, so what's the point in worrying?"

Typical cop attitude. While he could identify, that didn't mean he approved. "Did you try running a trace?"

"No. The caller won't stay on the line long enough."

"Don't you think you should let Gordy know?"

"Hell, no." Expression horrified, she shook her head. "Ever since Jason died, Gordy has been looking for an excuse to take me off the team. No way am I going to give him one."

"I didn't think of that. I had to fight the Bureau to be assigned to this case."

She lifted a brow. "How'd you manage that anyway? A cousin is a much closer relation than a former girlfriend."

"I called in some favors."

She smiled. He found himself smiling back, then remembered the topic at hand. "Amanda, you could be in real danger."

"I know." Her smile faded. He hated to see it go.

"And there's more. A couple of times, I think I've been followed."

"More reason to mention this to Gordy. The team needs to know. This could be the killer."

"Maybe. Maybe not. But whoever was behind me was quick. I never caught even a glimpse of him."

A horrible thought occurred to him. "You're not letting yourself be a target or something foolish like that, are you?"

"Of course not."

Though her denial came quickly, Nick wasn't fooled. He'd seen the truth in the expression that flashed across her face. "Stay armed at all times, you hear me?"

"I always am." The grim set of her mouth had him again inexplicably wanting to kiss her.

He cursed instead. "I just wish we knew if the threat is from a human or a shifter."

"Me, too. But if he's not human, my gun is worthless. I don't have any silver bullets."

Without silver bullets, they might as well be unarmed.

CHAPTER SEVEN

SHE HAD A POINT. Silver bullets were one of only two ways to kill a shifter. Only that or fire could do the job.

If some rogue shifter was hunting Amanda, what would Nick do? Eliminate his own kind to save a human? Hell yes, if she were innocent of Jason's murder. He felt pretty confident she had not killed his cousin.

If she had…that would be a different story.

"Don't we have a lead to follow?" Looking away from him, she glanced out the window toward the station house. "As a matter of fact, we should move. If anyone sees me sitting in a parked car with you, I'll get a ration of crap."

He started the engine. "Where to?"

"Somewhere with food. I need breakfast. Have you eaten?"

"No." He hadn't had time. "Now that you mention it, I could use something."

They ended up at a pancake house. While he ate, he watched Amanda make quick work of her cheese blintzes, scooping up the last of her strawberry topping with obvious relish.

"I think I need to stay with you." He hadn't meant to blurt out the words like that, but once said, there they were. He braced himself for her argument.

Blotting the corners of her mouth with her napkin, she stared at him as if she hadn't heard correctly. "Stay with me? Why? Is your hotel kicking you out?"

Nick grinned. "Right. Soon as they learned I was a federal agent, they booted me. Come on, I'm serious. If a shifter is actively stalking you, I need to stick to you like glue."

"Why?" The cop expression was back. Her eyes had gone hard and cold. She didn't return his smile.

"Protection."

"I can protect myself."

"I knew you'd say that. Of course you can protect yourself, *Detective*. Against a human enemy. Not against a shifter."

She had no ready reply for that. How could she? She didn't have the slightest idea what she was up against.

"Also, if I'm around we might stand a better chance of catching the guy and finding out what he knows." That would appeal to Amanda, he knew.

A second later, he saw he was right.

"Okay." She nodded. "You want to stay in my apartment? With me, correct?"

"Exactly."

He expected an explosion. Instead, she reached for the coffee carafe and poured herself another cup. When she'd finished doctoring it up with creamer and sweetener, she raised her gaze. "Do you know what kind of crap they'd shovel on me at work if I let you stay with me?"

"Don't tell them."

"You're serious about this."

"I am."

"Nick, don't get me wrong, but I don't know you that well. You're a great guy, for a fed that is, but…"

"I'm not suggesting we sleep together," he said, and watched the color rise in her face.

Elbows on the table, she leaned forward. "You kissed me."

"It was only a kiss."

She swore. "There was no 'only' about that. You haven't lied to me so far. Don't start now."

Nick tugged at his collar, forcing his hand back to the table when he caught himself. Damn it, she was right. Still… "We're both adults. Nothing has to happen if we don't want it to."

"Yeah, I know." She gave him a rueful smile. "The problem is, deep down inside I think we both want it."

At her words his body stirred, the wolf part of him restless, the human part aroused. If just hearing her admit she wanted him could do this to him, how could he resist her if they were together night and day?

She frowned. "Look Nick, I appreciate your wanting to protect me and all, but I can take care of myself."

He sighed. "Somehow I knew you would say that."

His cell phone chirped. He answered it, unsurprised to hear Mike's hesitant voice.

"Kenyon's agreed to a meeting."

"When?"

"How quickly can you be at the Broken Shackle?"

"The Broken Shackle?" He repeated the name for Amanda's benefit. She nodded, letting him know she was familiar with the place. "Hold on." He covered the phone with his finger. "How far is it?"

"Twenty minutes. Downtown Fort Worth."

He gave her the okay sign and then made arrangements to meet Kenyon. Luckily, the waitress had already brought their check so he tossed a couple of ones on the table. "Let's go."

With Amanda providing directions, they made it to the Broken Shackle with a few minutes to spare.

The place lived up to its name. Tucked between a Vietnamese market and a bail bondsman, the Broken Shackle bar looked exactly that—broken. A cracked cement exterior that had once been painted red matched the dirty glass window and flickering neon beer sign. Burglar bars covered the window and the door.

Nick looked at Amanda. She shrugged. "Bad part of town."

Pushing on the front door, Nick found it was unlocked. It swung open with a loud creak and jangle of dirty metal blinds. The only light came from a small, dingy lamp on the bar.

A man stepped from the back room. He pointed a gun at them. Beside Nick, Amanda stiffened. He knew without looking that she was about to draw her own weapon.

He touched her arm. "Don't."

With a curt nod, she gave him her agreement. The set of her jaw told him how little she liked it.

The other man watched silently. Finally, he gestured with his free hand. "Follow me."

In the back room the light was even dimmer. Nick's shifter eyes adjusted automatically, though he could tell by Amanda's squint she wasn't so lucky.

In the corner, another man sat in a large chair on a raised platform. Three more bodyguards flanked him. Kenyon. The setup looked so much like a throne Nick was startled, but years of training kept his face expressionless. No point in antagonizing the man before Nick even questioned him.

Kenyon spoke first. "You're here about my people?"

"About their deaths, yes."

"If killing them was your retaliation or a warning of some kind, you are a dead man." Kenyon took in Amanda, standing silently at Nick's side. "As is your human mate."

Nick's every sense tingled a warning. "Retaliation?"

"Which Pack council sent you?"

Ah, now Nick understood. Kenyon was under the impression that Nick had been sent as an enforcer, someone who hunted down lawless renegades and exterminated them. This had been the practice for centuries, though of late the United States Pack Council had practiced more human methods, much like the current human court system. The New York State Pack had sent Nick as investigator, rather than enforcer.

"I work for the FBI. I'm here in conjunction with the Fort Worth Police Department. We're investigating the killings."

Kenyon's broad face creased into a frown. "You haven't answered my question."

Nick kept his eyes locked on the other man. "The New York State Pack asked me to investigate my cousin Jason's death. The FBI was sending someone, so I volunteered."

"Just one person?"

"Every resource in the Bureau is dedicated to terrorism, these days."

At that, Kenyon growled. The menacing sound raised the hackles on Nick's neck. He stifled his own growl, fighting the urge to change, forcing himself to appear unmoved. Human.

The goon who'd led them in the room continued to

keep his gun pointed at them. The three who flanked Kenyon were also armed, though they kept their weapons holstered. For now.

Despite the implicit threat the armed guard offered, Nick didn't think Kenyon would be so stupid. Killing a federal agent—and a cop—would bring down wrath from every law enforcement agency in the state, not to mention the U.S. Pack Council's wrath.

"What do you want, Investigator?" A wealth of sarcasm resonated in Kenyon's baritone voice.

"Answers. I need to know if your…" he hesitated. "If your *Pack* has any enemies."

"You. Your kind. The council."

Nick took a deep breath. Every nerve tingled a warning.

Kenyon leaned forward. "Let me ask *you* a question. Did you kill my people?"

"No. Did you?"

The other man reared back, revealing shock for the first time. "You dare…" he roared.

Nick stood his ground. "Did you have them killed because they wanted out of your Pack?"

Kenyon snarled. Nick snarled back, unable to help himself. The three men surrounding the throne drew their weapons, their lips pulled back in identical, animalistic grimaces.

"Enough." Amanda stepped forward, her own gun drawn and pointed at Kenyon.

"Amanda." Nick kept his own hands in plain sight. "What are you doing?"

"Someone has to put a stop to this." She didn't even glance at him, keeping her gaze—and aim—on Kenyon. "Put your weapons down or I'll shoot him."

"You're outnumbered." The man who'd led them in spoke from near the doorway, off to their right. "You'll die."

"Yeah, but I'll take him down with me. Then the rest of you can try explaining why you killed a federal agent and a Fort Worth detective."

Kenyon snarled. Then he signaled his bodyguards with a wave of his hand. "Lower your guns."

Instantly, they all complied. All except the one by the doorway.

"Antoine." Kenyon's low-pitched voice contained a warning. Reluctantly, Antoine holstered his pistol.

"Good. Thank you." Keeping her own weapon still trained on Kenyon, Amanda stepped forward. "Are your guns loaded with silver bullets?"

"Silver bullets?" Kenyon recoiled. "Why would we do such a thing?" Then, as the implications of her words dawned on him, he grimaced. "We do not kill other shifters. Only those humans who foolishly threaten us."

"So you couldn't have killed Nick then."

"No, but we could make him hurt. Badly. And," he leered at her, "we could have killed you."

Amanda stared back. Slowly, she lowered her gun.

"We've heard a rumor that the victims were all members of your club."

"Pack. Yes, this was no rumor. These were all my people."

"Did they want out?"

Kenyon cocked his head, appearing to take her seriously. Still, Nick kept ready for attack from any direction.

"Not all of them." Leaning forward again, Kenyon rested his elbows on his knees. "What about you, pretty cop? I've heard you killed Jason when he changed in front of you."

"Not true."

"That would be a good thing for you if it's true." Kenyon's smile looked pleasant, though his eyes remained cold. "But there are some who don't believe you. You are being hunted, even now."

Hunted. That explained the tingling at the back of her neck, the shadowy shapes she'd imagined she'd seen from the corner of her eye.

"Hunted I can deal with," she said, trying for nonchalance, and very nearly making it.

"Can you?" His smile told her he wasn't buying it. "Just don't let yourself be caught."

CHAPTER EIGHT

Hunted by a werewolf. In her years on the force, Amanda thought she'd dealt with every kind of threat. But if she remembered how Jason had shimmered, how his image wavered in front of her shocked eyes, how when she'd blinked he'd become a huge, predatory, animal—the idea of something like that stalking her made even her toughened heart quail.

Still, she managed to meet Kenyon's unwavering gaze with a smile. "Since I didn't kill Jason, I have nothing to worry about."

He studied her for a moment, the color of his eyes an odd, yellowish-brown. His bodyguards stared straight ahead, as still as muscular statues.

"Kenyon." Nick's voice drew the big man's attention. "We have a few questions we'd like to ask you."

Kenyon frowned. "No. If the council wants to bring me up on charges, let them try. I've done nothing wrong."

Amanda took a step closer and lifted her chin. "May I ask one question?"

Kenyon narrowed his eyes. His full lips curved in a sneering smile. "Even if you don't like the answer?"

"You don't know the question yet."

He laughed, a short bark of sound. "Go ahead. Ask."

She took a deep breath, straightening her shoulders for courage. "Did you kill your own people because they wanted out of your club?"

Kenyon growled. The bodyguards reacted. Even without them taking a step toward her, Amanda knew they'd gone on full alert.

"You've already asked that."

She hadn't; Nick had. She saw no reason to point that out.

"Not an answer. Did you kill those five victims?"

"I did not," Kenyon snarled. Though in human form, his teeth looked sharper than normal. Amanda watched while he visibly calmed himself. "Interesting that you suspect me while I," he looked from Amanda to Nick and back again, "suspect you."

"But—"

"Enough." His roar seemed to echo in the unkempt room. He made a hand gesture, dismissing them. "Donte will show you to the door."

The look Nick gave her told Amanda he thought they should count themselves lucky.

As they were escorted out, Kenyon called out after them. "I will learn the truth." Neither responded out loud. When Nick looked over at Amanda, frowning, she grinned.

Once inside the car, he let go. "What the hell were you thinking, asking him that? Did you really think he was going to look you in the eye, admit to the murders, and then let you walk out of there alive?"

Amanda shook her head. "I wanted to see his reaction."

"He's a shifter. He's had years to practice hiding things."

"Besides," Amanda continued, as though Nick hadn't

spoken, "if Kenyon is behind the killings, he didn't do them with his own hands. More likely one of those goons he had with him performed the deed. I watched them, too."

"So did I." Nick's admission sounded grudging. "But they're shifters as well. Not one of them so much as blinked."

"I noticed." She glanced at him sideways. "But they reacted. Very subtle, but they were ready for action."

He shook his head. "We were outnumbered. I can't protect you against so many."

"This is getting old, Nick." She swallowed back her anger. "I didn't ask you to protect me."

He sighed. "I know you didn't. Let's go back to the station. I need my computer to see what I can dig up on this Kenyon."

They turned right. So did the Mustang behind them.

"Someone's following us."

"I noticed." Nick grimaced. "Either he's an amateur or he wants us to see him."

"This makes no sense. Kenyon already gave us a clear warning."

As Nick opened his mouth to speak, she heard the sharp pop of gunfire. The back window shattered in a spray of glass.

Nick swerved. "Get down." He floored the accelerator. The Taurus shot forward. "There's another car."

"What?" She popped her head up. "Where?"

"Get down." He cursed again. "There's no way we can outrun them in this rental."

Using the seat as a shield, Amanda hunched over. "Two of them? This doesn't make sense."

"I agree." He jerked the steering wheel to the right,

sending them careening into an alley. "It's too damn obvious. Maybe it's not Kenyon."

"Someone else. Great."

The rental car creaked and rattled as they tore over potholes.

"If not Kenyon, then who?"

Nick flashed her a grim smile. "That's what we're about to find out."

Amanda inched herself up far enough to look over the back of the seat. "They're gaining on us."

Another window exploded.

"And still shooting. Though their aim's not getting any better." Nick's dry tone made her glance up at him. His mouth curved in a ferocious smile. With his taut expression, focused on driving, he looked in his element.

"Which one?"

He barely glanced at her. "What?"

"Which one is shooting at us?"

"Don't know. Maybe both." He jerked the wheel. "They're shooting at the other car, too. Unbuckle."

Without question, she did.

"When I grab you, keep your head down. Don't get out from behind the car."

"Don't get out—are you crazy? No way am I leaving you without backup. I'm a cop, damn it. Get that through your thick head."

He glanced at her. His eyes glowed amber. "If these are shifters, your backup isn't worth crap. Stay behind the car."

That stopped her cold. For half a second. But she had no time to argue. At the end of the alley, he flipped the car around to the right. Hard. The tires screeched as the Taurus fishtailed. Nick kicked open his door and dived out, pulling her after. They hit the pavement rolling.

Brakes squealed as the other car tried to stop. "They're going to hit us. Move. Now!"

Together, Nick and Amanda leaped out of the way. An instant later, there was a sickening crunch of metal slamming into metal as the Mustang hit. A second later the other car slammed into the Mustang's back end, pushing both into Nick's car. The rented Taurus shuddered and caved in.

Taking shelter behind the corner of a building, both Nick and Amanda drew their guns. No one emerged from either the Mustang or the other car, a brown Chevy. She looked at him. He cocked a brow. "Ready?"

She nodded. Crouched. Peered around the building at the wreckage. "Police. Come out with your hands up."

No one moved. The Mustang sat silent, engine dead. Steam rose from the Chevy—steam or smoke—telling them they had to act fast.

Together they crept closer. "We've got to get them out. Looks like the driver might be unconscious."

"It might be a trick. Don't relax your guard."

The Mustang's driver appeared to be alone. The passenger seat looked empty.

Nick moved closer, his weapon still on the suspect. Amanda covered him, alternating between watching him and the Chevy.

Yanking open the door, Nick felt for a pulse. "Nothing."

"He's dead?"

"He took a clean shot in the head. Right between the eyes."

Dead. Beyond help or questioning. Carefully closing the door, Nick left the body in the seat. Weapons ready, they moved to the second car.

The brown Chevy also contained a single person. Female, if the long blond hair was any indication.

"Alive." Unfastening the seat belt, Nick lifted the woman from the car.

Amanda stared. "That can't be…"

But it was. The Chevy's driver was Chris Chartwell, Jason's former best friend.

TWO HOURS LATER, hand cramping from the ream of paperwork required, Amanda stretched and looked at Nick. "Any word from the hospital?"

He checked his watch. "Not as of twenty minutes ago. She's barely awake, groggy. They say she's up for questioning. We should get over there now."

"So we can personally take her statement?" Amanda was definitely ready to get out of the station. "Let's do it."

Though they'd found a gun on the seat beside the dead guy in the Mustang, there were still a lot of unanswered questions. Amanda hoped Chris would have some answers.

When they got to the hospital, they found Chris alert and talking.

"Hey, girl." Chris held out her arms to Amanda for a hug.

With a shake of her head, Amanda hung back. "We have a few questions for you."

Nick stepped forward. "Why were you following us?"

The way Chris looked him up and down put Amanda on edge. Her appreciative smile and feminine sigh had Amanda gritting her teeth.

"Well hello to you, too." Chris smiled. "I recognize you from the other night, when I ran into you and Amanda in the alley. Jason's cousin, Nick."

"Special Agent Nick Templeton." He pulled his badge from his pocket and handed it to her. "Now please answer Detective Riley's question."

"Fine." Pouting as she handed the ID back to him, Chris turned her attention to Amanda.

"I saw you two leaving the Broken Shackle bar. Some guys were following you."

"How many of them?"

Chris blinked. "I don't know. Two or three? Tough-looking guys. They followed you out of that bar. One of them was tailing you in that Mustang. I was only trying to warn you." Her lower lip trembled. "I didn't know he was going to start shooting. I could have been killed. I just learned how to use a gun."

"Ever think of using your cell phone and calling me?"

Chris looked down. "I would if I'd had it. I lost my cell phone last night. I was going to go over to the Sprint store to get a new one today."

A nurse came in, her soft-soled shoes making her approach soundless. "I'm sorry, but you'll have to leave. We've got some more tests to run."

Letting her head flop back on the pillow, Chris groaned. "I hate tests."

Amanda and Nick turned to go. "We'll be in touch," Nick said, glancing once more at Chris.

"Yeah." Chris looked at Amanda. "Call me later."

Amanda managed a pleasant smile. "Will do."

They walked to the elevator in silence. Nick punched the button. Amanda brooded. "Something's not quite—"

Holding up one hand, Nick gave a slight shake of his head.

The elevator doors opened. They stepped inside. Nick touched her arm as the doors slid closed. "Something about Chris's story doesn't ring true." He punched the stop button. The elevator shuddered, halting between floors.

"So you think she's lying, too. But why?"

"Did she lie? Did she know the dead guy? That was one hell of a lucky shot."

"Seems unlikely."

"So was she trying to warn us? Is she merely a dumb blonde or is she a damn good actress?" He shook his head. "Damned if I could tell. You know her."

Amanda felt hot. The elevator seemed too small, too confining. Standing next to Nick, she had the strongest urge to touch him. Hell, she wanted to rub her entire body against him. *Pay attention to the subject at hand.* "She was more Jason's friend than mine." To her chagrin she sounded breathless, as though she'd been running full out. "Are you going to keep us in this elevator forever?" Amanda gave him her best glare, but found herself focusing on his mouth.

"Maybe." He took a step closer, but made no move to touch her. Which, she thought faintly, was a damn shame. She positively *ached* for his touch.

"Chris," she said faintly. "We're talking about Chris."

"Right. Chris. There's something else I've been meaning to ask you about. Was Jason sleeping with her?"

"Chris?" Amanda found it difficult to think. "I don't think so, though I confess I'd wondered the same thing myself." She shrugged, working hard at keeping her rising agitation from showing. "I asked Jason once if he'd ever slept with her. He said no. He said he thought of her as one of the guys."

Which was *not* how she thought of Nick. She clenched her hands to keep from touching him. "Damn."

Nick seemed to be having similar difficulty. His eyes had dilated so the pupils seemed huge and black. "One of the guys? She's a tall, leggy blonde. Curvy in all the right places."

Ignoring the twinge she felt at his words—it couldn't be jealousy, after all—Amanda forced a smile. "True. But Jason claimed I was all he needed."

"All he needed." Nick echoed her words. "He believed you were his mate. Our kind mate only once, for life."

An undercurrent in his voice made her shiver. She had to say something, anything to break Nick's intent stare and her traitorous body's heated reaction.

Nick took the last step. Reaching out, he pulled her against him, letting her feel the force of his own arousal. "Jason was wrong." He breathed the words in her ear.

Her knees went weak. "Ex-excuse me?"

"You were not meant to be his mate."

Holding herself absolutely still, Amanda let her breath out in a slow whoosh. Her breasts tingled where they pressed against his chest. But if she moved, it wouldn't be to pull away. She wanted to wrap herself around him like a starving cat. "Why do…" She licked her lips, hardly recognizing her own voice. "Why do you say that?"

"Why?" He lowered his mouth to hers. "Because you were meant to be mine."

CHAPTER NINE

WHILE HIS MOUTH moved over hers and her soft, pliant body molded to his, Nick knew he was in trouble. Big trouble. But for the first time in his life, his body controlled his mind. He couldn't help himself.

And, judging from her heated response to him, neither could Amanda.

Her small hands tore at his shirt. Calling on every ounce of will he owned, he forced himself to stop touching her and captured her hands with his. Lifting his mouth from hers, the savage part of him felt gratified when she whimpered.

"If we keep this up, we'll be going at it in the elevator."

He watched as sanity returned to Amanda's eyes.

She pushed herself away. "Why is it every time we touch, I feel like we're an uncontrollable freight train headed for a wreck?"

"From the way you're glaring at me, I can't help but wonder if you think I've somehow put a spell on you. Or if you're still repulsed by the idea of shifters."

"Don't be ridiculous," she snapped.

Still, he had only truth to offer her. That didn't mean she'd like it. "I'm beginning to believe there's a reason for our attraction."

Still staring, she lifted a finger to her swollen lips. "Let's hear it."

"I've already told you. You're my mate."

She took a step back. He felt it like a silver shard straight through his heart. "We are so not mates."

Nick had to force himself to be rational when he wanted to yank her back and prove how wrong she was. "Oh yeah? Are you sure?"

"I don't even know you."

"We think the same. I know what you're going to say before you speak. You feel it, too, don't tell me you don't."

"We have similar backgrounds. Law enforcement training."

"True. Yet I've had partners I couldn't stand. Don't tell me you haven't."

He was right and she knew it, so she breezed past his comment. "Work. That's different."

"True. But I'm not talking about work. Even though," he flashed her a smile. "We spend sixty percent of our waking moments working."

She swallowed. "You're FBI. From New York."

"So? The Bureau has an office both in Dallas and Fort Worth." He heard his own words with a faint sense of shock. Then a feeling of rightness clicked into place.

"Don't transfer on my account," she snapped. "You don't even realize what you're saying." Her face had gone very, very pale. With a choppy movement, she leaned over and punched the elevator button again. An instant later, the doors opened on the lobby floor.

"Come on." Amanda strode from the elevator without looking at him. "We've got work to do."

IF AMANDA had been stunned by her body's reaction to him, she was even more stunned by the way she felt about his words.

Mates. Gave her a warm, fuzzy glow in the heart.

Stupid. But true. Oh, God. She wanted to cover her face with her hands. She had it bad for Nick Templeton. Her former boyfriend's cousin and another…shifter.

Odd how the idea no longer seemed so out of the ordinary to her.

"Amanda." Nick's voice, deep and sexy and full of masculine authority, made her stop. She turned, watching as he crossed the sidewalk to her.

"We'll table this for now."

She nodded, punching her remote to unlock her SUV. "I agree."

"But later, when all this is over, we have to settle it."

"I can't tell if that's a promise or a threat." She climbed up into the driver's seat, pulling the door closed behind her. Going around the back, he did the same. "I don't like to be threatened," she said.

Nick didn't rise to her bait. Instead, he fiddled with the radio station, finding a classical station and humming along to the music.

"Muzak." She punched button three, for alternative rock. An old Toadies song blasted through the speakers.

"Much better."

He only shrugged.

Amanda glanced at her watch and groaned. "Do you know what tonight is?" Without waiting for him to answer, she rushed on. "Halloween. One of our busiest nights. All the crazies come out and run wild. Wanna bet this killer decides to take another victim?"

"If he does, he'll be stepping up his schedule dramatically." They both knew the killer had already done that. The last victim had been killed less than a week after Jason.

"Even if he doesn't, plan for a long night. Most of us pull at least a twelve-hour shift."

"Not detectives. Surely they don't make you guys work the street."

"There's a serial killer on the loose." She gave him a serious look.

"Are you going to start the car?"

"I will in a minute." His voice had been low, almost a growl. Something in his face… Amanda froze, concerned. "Are you all right?"

"Fine." He started to nod, then winced. "Tonight I would have preferred to be somewhere else."

"Somewhere else? Why? What do you mean?"

"The country. The woods, preferably, though an isolated field would do. Just because tonight is different. The earth pulses with power, the moon's pull is strong…." He swallowed, his dark eyes intense. "On All-Hallows' Eve, most of us change into our wolf-selves."

To her surprise she felt sympathy. Not horror, or revulsion, or even shock. "Are you going to be all right?"

"Yes. I will. I have to be."

Halloween. She'd never really thought about the possibility of the supernatural being well, *real*. Until Jason had showed her the truth. What had once scared the hell out of her, now seemed…acceptable. Normal even.

Damn, she'd lost her mind. Maybe if she took some time alone, away from the force of her attraction to Nick. "You don't need to go to the station. If Halloween's bad for you, take off. Do what you have to do.

We need to check out the clubs near Sundance again, especially Broken Shackle Bar. I can head out to Fort Worth alone."

"Hell no. I have to go." Though less of a growl, he still sounded husky. "If the killer's looking for another shifter, I want him to choose me. I'm bait."

She locked gazes with him. "Or maybe I am. Some of your kind still believe I'm the killer."

"Another reason for me to go with you. I'm not leaving you unprotected."

Because she'd told him before and her words had made no difference to him, she didn't bother to point out she was a trained law enforcement officer. An armed policewoman, with backup a radio call away.

She checked her watch. "It's nearly dark. Let's roll. If the killer's going to strike again, he'll do it before midnight."

"Wait." Something in his voice stopped her as effectively as a gunshot. "If it turns out to be Kenyon, you may have to take cover. Or leave."

"Leave?"

Nick came closer, a muscle working in his cheek. "If Kenyon has killed other shifters, he'll have to answer to Pack justice, not the laws of mankind. I won't be bringing him in."

A cold, hard weight settled in her chest. "Explain Pack justice."

"I'll kill him."

"Nick, you can't—"

"I can. I will." He looked at her and she saw in his gaze how serious he was.

"Nick—"

"If Kenyon is not the one, if the killer is a human, then the laws you uphold will apply."

She lifted her chin. "You're sworn to uphold them, too. Or doesn't the FBI go for that anymore?"

"Pack law takes precedence." Nick looked at her, reached for her keys, thought better of it, and dropped his hand to his lap. "Believe me, I'll only do what I have to. You don't have to be there. You don't have to be a part of this."

"You're asking me to turn my back on all I believe in. I can't do that."

"No, I'm not. This won't be like a normal arrest. If Kenyon is discovered, he'll change. He will fight me as a wolf. He will know death awaits, whether by fire or silver bullet. He knows the laws of our kind."

As a wolf. Everything within her froze. "You'll have to change, too, won't you?" Despite her best efforts, the words came out in a whisper. She'd thought she'd accepted this, believed she could handle seeing Nick morph into an animal. Now…she wasn't too sure.

"Yes."

"You know, Halloween might be a night for strange happenings, but how can you expect me to deal with this now? In the middle of an intense investigation, to be partnered with an actual *werewolf?*"

"Shifter," he said. "I thought you'd learned to deal with this."

She sighed. "I care about you. I don't know why, or how it happened in so short a time, but I do. What about me, Nick? What am I supposed to do while you fight him? I can't shoot him, hell, I don't have a silver bullet."

He touched her, and she felt his hand on her arm like a brand. "That is not our law. I must handle Kenyon."

"You honestly expect me to stand around and watch you two fight to the death?"

"Assuming Kenyon is our perp, yes."

"I can't promise anything." She moved closer, willing him to understand. "I'm an officer of the law. That's what I'm about, more than anything else."

"I won't break any laws. And with you, he will still be innocent until proven guilty."

"You plan to be his judge and jury."

"If he was the one who killed my people, yes."

She shook her head. "Despite all this craziness, all I can think about right this instant is how badly I want to hold you, to keep you out of this. Safe. Must be the cop in me."

The tight line of his mouth blossomed into a smile. "Not cop. Mate."

She shook her head, not quite ready to admit that much. "Stay safe, okay?"

"Amanda, I—"

"Later." Lifting his hand from hers, she brushed a kiss against his palm. "We've got a killer to catch."

CHAPTER TEN

ALL THE PARKING LOTS around Sundance Square were full. It looked like everyone under the age of forty in the city had come out to party on Halloween. Amanda ended up parking her Volvo in the bank garage. "It's a bit of a walk, but we should be safe."

"All kinds of beings stroll among mankind this night." Hunched into his jean jacket, expression bleak, Nick looked dangerous. Not law enforcement dangerous, but bad guy dangerous.

Despite herself, Amanda shivered. "I don't want to know."

They reached the crowded square without incident, merging into the costumed throng of people. When Nick took her hand, Amanda didn't resist. For the first time in her life, she felt comfortable having someone else at her side.

The night pulsed with life. Witches in stilettos and pointy hats strolled alongside astronauts and gangsters. Amanda counted three wizards, a ghost, some sort of bondage costume, seven vampires of both sexes and a couple of authentic-looking werewolf costumes. If only they knew.

Smiling, she caught herself glancing at Nick. He dipped his chin to their left.

There. The Broken Shackle bar. One of Jason's favorite hangouts.

Kenyon had cleaned the place up since Amanda had seen it. Around the corner from the popular Sundance Square, the place was enough off the beaten path to be ignored by the tourists. Maybe the bar was more than an unprofitable front for his Pack business. Muted yellow light glowed from behind the sparkling glass storefront. The place looked packed. Amanda squeezed Nick's hand. A muscular bouncer dressed like an extra from an X-rated movie guarded the door.

"Kenyon's goon."

"I recognize him from earlier. I wonder if he knows the Mustang guy who shot at us."

A small line had formed at the entrance. They waited patiently, both of them continually scanning their surroundings. Nothing appeared out of the ordinary—other than the costumes. People laughed and talked and strolled. A bunch of partiers, out to enjoy the darkest night of the year.

But something was different. Wrong. Amanda sensed it. She could tell Nick felt uneasy, too, though he might be dealing with feelings peculiar to shifters.

At last they reached the front of the line. If Kenyon's bodyguard recognized them, he didn't show it. Face impassive, he took their ten dollar cover fee, stamped their hands and waved them through, behind a woman in a gauzy harem costume who had to be freezing.

Barely squeezing inside, her hand firmly in Nick's, Amanda searched the room. The noise level, while loud, still seemed subdued compared to a club with a live band. At least she could hear herself think. "I don't see him."

"Kenyon? If he's out prowling for a victim, he won't be here."

"Or if he adheres to your traditions," she felt obliged to point out, "he might have gone to find himself a nice, isolated pasture. Let's ask for him."

"Are you out of your mind?"

She yanked her hand free. "You know, you ask me that a lot. I'm getting tired of it. I'm here on official police business. If I want to see a suspect in a crime, I have a right to ask to see him."

"Tonight's crime hasn't even been committed yet."

Opening her mouth to ask him how he knew this, Amanda swallowed back the words. Hell, even *she* sensed whatever was to come had yet to happen. And she didn't have Nick's extra senses.

"Kenyon will be here shortly." The man's voice, flat and without inflection, came from behind her.

Amanda spun. "Who—?"

A tall, gaunt man stared back at her with eyes so black they seemed bottomless. He wore the costume of an old world gypsy, the clothing so worn that it looked authentic.

Yanking Amanda away, Nick growled. "Get away from us."

The man held up his hands in the classic gesture of appeasement. "I meant no offense."

"None taken." But Nick's thunderous expression didn't match his words. He stared after the other man until he'd disappeared in the crowd.

"What was that all about?"

"You don't want to know."

"Yes, I do. Who was that guy?"

"A very ancient vampire," he said, unsmiling. "I'm

not sure why he's working with Kenyon, but this can't be good."

"A vampire. As in, costume?" Even to her own ears, Amanda knew her question sounded weak. As Nick started to respond, she shook her head. "Never mind. You're right…I don't want to know."

Nick stiffened, frowning. "We need to go outside."

"Why?"

"I don't know. Maybe I'm just suffocating. Or maybe it's gut instinct." Turning, he pushed his way back to the door. Amanda followed.

Once outside, he turned in a slow circle, breathing in the cool night air. Around them the crowd flowed and surged, laughter and the murmur of small talk filling their ears.

Amanda glanced around, too. "Do you sense something?"

"That's just it." Frustration colored his tone. "I don't know. All I know is if the killer is a shifter, he will feel compelled to kill tonight."

About to comment, Amanda spotted a familiar face entering the Broken Shackle bar. "There's Chris Chartwell."

"Out of the hospital already?"

"She should have been under guard." Amanda punched automatic dial on her cell phone. A few words with the team member on station duty, and her stomach clenched. She clicked the phone shut. "She discharged herself. They couldn't charge her with a crime, so they had to let her go."

"That's odd. Wouldn't you think she'd have gone home instead of bar-hopping?"

"Yeah. And this particular bar…too many coincidences. Let's go talk to her."

He touched her arm. "No, wait. If she's meeting Kenyon, his guards will have told him we're here. I don't want to alarm her into running."

"Meeting Kenyon? Why would—?"

Someone screamed.

Amanda started forward.

The scream became a laugh. Someone else growled. Another person made a ghost sound. Playing.

"Halloween."

Shaking her head, Amanda managed a shaky laugh. "I'm a bit tense. That's not good."

"Look." Nick ducked behind a large metal suit of armor used as a statue. "Over there, by the door to the back. Chris. She's with one of Kenyon's bodyguards."

Tall and slender, Chris's blond hair shone in its single braid. She wore some sort of warrior princess costume, like Zena or Wonder Woman. As they watched, she slipped her arm around her date's waist. Drink in hand, he leaned down and spoke into her ear, sending her into a fit of giggles.

"What the—" Swearing, Amanda started forward. "She said some men were following us when she chased us in her car. Now she's dating one of these guys? We need to find out what Chris is up to."

Chris and the bodyguard disappeared around the corner. Still, Nick hesitated. "They're heading toward the movie theater."

"Let's follow," Amanda said.

"Keep a few people between us. You don't want her to see you."

Amanda nodded. Counting to ten, she took Nick's arm. Together, they strolled around the corner.

There was no sign of Chris or Kenyon's goon.

The wind gusted from the north. The solitary street-light had burned out, leaving this stretch of pavement dark and cold.

"Where the hell did they go?"

"I'm worried." Amanda tightened her grip on Nick's arm. "What if she's not dating that guy? What if he's forcing her somewhere?"

Nick covered her hand with his. "Did she look like she was being forced?"

"No, but—" Nick was right. She swallowed. "One step at a time. Come on." She tugged him down the sidewalk. "We've got to find them first."

"How far is the theater? Maybe they've already reached it."

"This quickly? It's two blocks up, so unless they ran, they wouldn't be there yet. They must have turned up one of these side streets. Come on."

Still he didn't budge. "Could they have taken a shortcut?"

"Nick, either you come with me, or I'm going without you." She started forward. He grabbed her arm, spinning her to face him.

"Amanda…" Face intent, he cautioned her. "You're a cop. Think. We've got to be extremely careful. There are a lot of innocent civilians around, especially in a movie theater. If a gun battle breaks out—"

She pulled free. "Gun battle? Do you really think Kenyon's bodyguard would do something that crazy? Here? Now?"

"If he plans to hurt Chris, he might."

She stared. "Hurt Chris? You just said she looked like she was there of her own free will. On a date. Why would you think he'd hurt her?"

He looked down. "Remember when I told you some shifters think you're responsible for Jason's death?"

"Yes."

"A few more of them are watching Chris. She was his best friend. If she did anything to hurt him, they'll be on her like fleas on a dog."

"Watching Chris. Don't you think you should have shared this before?"

"I just found out."

"When?"

"While you filled out paperwork at the station earlier. I heard from Mike Andrews again. He seems to consider himself my informant. And then, I thought it was nonsense."

Only slightly mollified, she shook her head. "I thought we were partners. Partners don't withhold information from each other."

"Amanda." He grabbed her chin. "I'm sorry. I made a mistake."

Taking a deep breath, she pushed away her fury. Out of place, overmagnified. But still… "We need to go. Get Chris out."

He grabbed her arm. "Wait. We need to hold off until the movie starts. Nothing will happen there—they'll have to leave. We'll have to watch the theater."

He had a point. "So we wait." She couldn't keep the grudging tone from her voice. She crossed her arms. "You know, there are severe holes in your logic. If Chris killed Jason, then she would've also killed the others. All the M.O.'s were the same. While I agree that we could consider Chris, I think Kenyon's a much more likely suspect. One of his bodyguards is with Chris. She could be in danger, especially if Kenyon thinks she's the murderer."

"If she didn't kill Jason, then she's not in danger. Kenyon wouldn't act without proof."

A sound from their right, close, around the back of an old warehouse, made them turn. Amanda looked at Nick. He stared back. Both of them recognized that sound. The muted pop of a gun fitted with a silencer. Then a crash and the awful thud a body made hitting the ground.

"Chris," Amanda whispered.

They ran.

CHAPTER ELEVEN

ONCE AROUND the corner, Amanda skidded to a halt. The bodyguard was on the ground and Chris stood over him with a gun aimed at the man's chest.

"You!" Amanda struggled to hide her surprise. She didn't shock easily, but the scene in front of her was unreal. Tall, slender Chris had bested the burly bodybuilder. How—especially if he was a shifter? And why?

Tossing her hair as she lifted her head to glare at them, Chris snarled. "Yes, me." She saw Amanda look at the bodyguard and laughed. The sound sent chills down Amanda's spine.

So did the sight of the pistol Chris clutched in her left hand and pointed at Nick.

"You're the killer?" Amanda still didn't believe it.

Chris smirked. "Yes. I slipped something in his drink. Takes a while to work. Nothing to it, just like all the others." She glanced at Nick. "You shifters are not the brightest."

"Why?" Nick asked, his voice unemotional and calm. "Why'd you kill them?"

"Because I can. And now that you know, I'll have to kill you, too." That was no answer, and they all knew it. But criminals, especially killers, liked to boast. If Amanda could get Chris talking…distracted, then

Amanda might have a chance to go for her own weapon. She flexed her fingers. Dare she?

Chris kept her gun pointed at Nick, though her gaze flicked to Amanda. "Try it and he dies. I have silver bullets."

Damn. Amanda gave a slow nod to show she understood, then she glanced at the body, pretending fascination. "You're damn good, Chris. One shot, straight through the heart. Amazing. You obviously know what your victims are."

"So do you." Chris pursed her lips. "Jason told me. He showed you. And you didn't want him."

Nick had gone silent. With a major effort of will, Amanda kept herself from looking at him.

Jason. She focused on Chris's words. "You killed Jason?"

With a frown, Chris jerked her head once. Yes.

"You were Jason's best friend. Ever since college. You two were inseparable. Why kill him?"

"Because of you." The other woman spat the words. "I loved him, more than you ever could. He belonged to me. In more ways than one."

Now Nick spoke. "You were lovers?"

"Lovers? You could call it that. Jason did what I told him to do. He was my slave."

Nick spoke. "You were his mistress?"

Chris's smile was cold. "In every sense of the word. But I didn't realize he had the upper hand until too late. He used me. For sex. Not lovemaking." She mocked the word. "He liked it rough. Lots of his kind do." Her furious eyes burned Amanda. "Bet you didn't even know that, did you?"

"No." Amanda managed to push the word out past her suddenly dry throat.

"Not all shifters like it rough." Nick answered Amanda's unasked question, though he spoke to Chris.

"Jason did. He liked to play wild and loose. Two women, or men, the more the merrier. He helped me kill the first victim."

"Jason?" Amanda couldn't contain her shock.

"Yes." Chris grimaced. "The first time was an accident. It happened in the heat of the moment."

Nick took a step forward. "An accident? You ripped his limbs off."

Amanda quietly did the same.

"Don't come any closer." Chris's voice went shrill. "Or you'll be my next kill."

"You're not one of us." Nick never took his gaze off the gun. "You're human."

"Human," Chris snarled. "Not good enough. I wanted to be like you. But Jason refused to obey and make me a shifter. Gave me some story about how it was inherited."

Amanda noticed Nick didn't point out that Jason had spoken the truth. She inched a little closer. "If you shoot Nick, I'll take you down."

Chris's gaze darted from one to the other. "He'll still die."

"So will you."

"I hate you, Amanda." Chris spat the words. "Jason thought he loved you, not me. And you didn't even know him. I accepted what he was, but he was going to propose to you. I tried to stop him, told him how I felt, and he rejected me." Venom and rage rang in her tone. "I wasn't good enough for him."

"So you killed him?" Amanda kept her expression

neutral. Dangerously unbalanced, Chris still had her gun aimed at Nick's chest.

"I've never been good enough." Chris's face started to crumple. For half a second, then the icy mask came back. "Jason helped me, at first. The kinkiness got out of hand. When it did, other things got out of hand. In the midst of all this, Jason changed into a wolf. That's when I knew what I wanted to become—a werewolf. Jason lost control—you should have seen what he did to that guy's body. I thought if he bit me, if he drew blood, then I'd be able to become a wolf, too."

"Have you?" Nick asked, as though it were even a possibility. According to what he'd told Amanda about shifters, it wasn't.

Chris stared at him. Amanda took that opportunity to move a few feet closer, unnoticed.

"Not yet." Chris kicked at the dead bodyguard under her feet. "I've tried and tried and tried, but I haven't become a wolf."

"Why'd you kill the others?"

Lifting her head, Chris's nostrils flared. "I want their power. When I become a wolf, I'm going to be a strong one. Jason told me how, in the Pack, the power of the dead can transfer to the living."

"That's why you dismember them?" Nick sounded fascinated rather than repulsed. Amanda hoped that was only a ruse. If it wasn't, she didn't want to know. But if Nick could keep Chris's attention and keep her talking, maybe Amanda could get close enough to take her down.

It was worth a try. She scooted a bit forward.

Chris glanced at her and Amanda froze. "Yes," she said hurriedly. "Why cut off their arms and legs? And what do you do with their heads?"

"I do what Jason did as a wolf. I feed on their power. I eat their flesh, drink their blood. It fills me with power."

Amanda didn't dare look at Nick. But the idea that Chris had Jason's head and the heads of all the others, and kept them as trophies, infuriated her. "You're insane."

Chris bared her teeth. "I'm a wolf," she snarled. She swung her gun around to Amanda.

"Now!" Nick shouted, moving forward.

Amanda kicked up, glad for all those Tae Bo classes she'd taken. Her shoe connected with Chris's arm an instant before Chris squeezed the trigger.

The gun went off. The bullet went into the air.

Amanda's momentum carried her forward. Chris went down with an oomph. Her head made a sickening sound when she hit the pavement. Amanda slapped cuffs on her and then felt for a pulse. When she finally found one, it was unsteady and weak.

"Is she dead?"

"No." With Chris safely captured, Amanda opened her cell phone and dialed 911. Nick snatched the phone out of her hand. He looked positively savage.

"Pack law takes precedence."

Though her heart skipped, she kept her expression calm, her voice steady. "Let me call an ambulance. She's barely alive. I can't let you take her. She's not a shifter. She'll die."

His eyes were dark, his expression unreadable. He closed his hand over her phone. "She's a killer."

Amanda cursed. "Yes. But she's human. Not Pack. Human justice is what she gets. She'll die without medical attention. Even she doesn't deserve death without a trial."

Nick didn't appear convinced. Was he considering

taking Chris anyway? Amanda couldn't tell by looking at him. Though he stood quietly, he looked dark and dangerous, his expression remote. Tension radiated from the set of his shoulders.

Amanda had the strongest urge to wrap her arms around him and draw some of that tension away. She shook her head to clear it and held out her hand. "I've got to call 911, then call in the arrest. Give me back my phone."

"The victims deserve justice."

"*Human* justice. She'll get it." Amanda held out her hand.

On the ground, Christine lay unmoving. Amanda couldn't tell if she was still breathing.

"My phone, Templeton. Please."

"She knows about the Pack."

"She's insane. They'll never believe her." Speaking with conviction, Amanda held out her hand again, fighting to keep her arm steady. "They'll know she's crazy. You heard her. She *ate* the victims."

Nick stared, then looked back at Amanda, down at her hand.

Amanda held her breath.

Finally, he tossed her the phone. "Call 911. Then notify your team. I need to call in myself." And he turned his back to her.

In a few minutes, they were surrounded by police. An ambulance, lights flashing, arrived too late to save the bodyguard. Chris's shot had been clean through the heart, killing him instantly. They loaded Chris up in the ambulance and sped off.

Gordy was pleased—shocked to learn the perp was a woman—but glad to be able to disband the task force and notify the police chief and the media that the killer had been captured.

After he'd congratulated Amanda and shaken hands with Nick, Gordy ordered Amanda to take the rest of the week off. For once, she'd agreed. Once she filled out the necessary paperwork, she promised to go straight home.

When the last police officer had left and the bodyguard's body had been transported to the morgue, only Amanda and Nick remained, surrounded by yellow crime scene tape, watching the flashing lights fade into the night.

Nick didn't speak. No doubt he was still furious she'd interfered with Pack justice.

Shoulders aching with tension, Amanda swallowed against the tightness in her throat and turned to go.

She half hoped Nick would stop her.

He didn't.

Nearly to the car, she realized she'd never been a coward before. She didn't want to become one now. She needed to turn around and talk to him. If the short and wild heat that had blazed between them was over, she owed them both a better goodbye than that.

Confused, she stopped. She wanted to look back to see if Nick was watching her, waiting for her, but her courage again deserted her. She didn't know what to do. Keep going? Get in the car and drive away, back to the safety of her sterile existence? Or turn around and confront him? Fight for what she wanted more than she'd ever wanted anything else in her life.

She'd always been a fighter.

Amanda turned, ready to run to Nick if he'd open his arms.

But she was too late. Moving so silently she hadn't heard him, Nick had gone.

CHAPTER TWELVE

HE'D THOUGHT his heart would shatter as he watched Amanda walk off. Away from him, rejecting all that he was, all that they could be together, rejecting *them* without a word.

He'd never known a woman's silence could be so cruel. Watching the tense, military straightness of her shoulders, the choppy confidence of her walk, the breezy way her long hair swung around her shoulders, made him want to growl and go after her. Make her talk, make her look him in the face and explain.

Instead, he ran. He'd noticed a park past one of these darkened streets. He'd find it, slip into the comforting shadows of the trees, and change. Only as an animal could he give in to such awful feelings of loss. Only as a wolf could he howl his agony to the moon.

He ran as a man, faster than human men. Always conscious of his surroundings, he reached the edge of the park and slowed his pace.

Another stepped out from under the trees. Kenyon.

"We've caught the killer," Nick said by way of greeting. Kenyon growled low in his throat when Nick finished relaying the rest of the tale.

Finally, Nick ran out of words. Feeling awkward, he bounced on the balls of his feet, aching to change. He glanced toward the trees. Not many, but enough. Kenyon would understand.

"I've got to go." He started for the woods.

"What of your mate, Amanda?" Kenyon called after him.

Nick froze. Even hearing her name made his chest hurt. He cleared his throat, turning slowly. "She doesn't want to be my mate."

"Unbelievable." The other man sounded truly regretful. "She rejected you, just like Jason?"

That stung, too. But maybe Kenyon was right. He tried for a shrug. "She couldn't handle Jason being a shifter. I don't know why I thought she'd feel differently about me."

"Maybe she does." Kenyon pointed. A few blocks away a lone spotlight illuminated a woman, walking toward them fast. "It's your Amanda. Lift your head, use your nose. I can taste her scent on the breeze."

Heart thumping in his chest, Nick could only stare. Helpless to move, to run, he barely noticed as Kenyon faded back into the shelter of the trees. He watched Amanda come closer and did the only thing he could think of.

He changed.

AMANDA WATCHED Nick change. As before, when Jason had shifted and totally altered her perception of reality, Nick's form wavered and shimmered. Sparkles of light, reflecting off each other and the moonlight, surrounded him, became him, and then faded. When the mist cleared, a huge black wolf stood where a moment ago Nick had been. Eyes gleaming in the moonlight, the wolf watched her approach. She could have sworn she saw a flash of teeth.

Wolf. A natural predator. Dangerous, her mind screamed. No. This was Nick. It wasn't easy, but she kept moving. Unfaltering, each step carrying her closer to the man/beast—shifter, she told herself fiercely—closer to the shifter she loved. For she knew that now, knew it with a certainty from the core of her being. She loved him. Nick.

He lifted his muzzle and scented the air. It might have been the angle of his head, or the way the moonlight bathed him, all shadows and angles and black, black fur, but she again saw a flash of his teeth. This time, she could have sworn he grinned.

Finally, a foot away, she stopped. She held out her hand, as she would when approaching a strange dog, then shook her head and dropped down to her knees in front of him. Her heart pounded and sweat dampened her palms. He had to smell her fear. All she could hope was that enough of Nick remained inside the wolf to keep him from hurting her.

Unmoving, he continued to watch her. Not warily, no, but not welcoming either. Aloof, perhaps, as though he didn't really care what she did.

Amanda knew better than that. *Mates,* he'd called them. They were mates. That was what she wanted, more than she wanted to breathe.

Still the wolf—Nick—watched her. Unmoving. She realized then he wouldn't come to her. She'd have to go to him.

On her knees, she crawled the last few inches that separated them, wrapped her arms around his neck and buried her face in his fur. Nick's scent was here still, and she hugged him close and prayed she could communicate her love.

"You are my mate, Nick Templeton. I love you." Her voice was fierce but certain. He cocked his head, as if he hadn't heard her, so she raised her voice and told him again.

"I love you. All of you, what you are now and the man you are before you shift. You were right, we're mates, and I'd like nothing better than to stay at your side for the rest of my life."

Absolutely still, he listened. Then, with a fluid twist of his lean body, he slipped from her grasp, and walked to the edge of the trees. There, he looked at her over his shoulder, his lupine form sinuous and powerful.

Rejecting her?

Aching, she held out her arms, conscious of the hot tears running down her face, of the need that showed in her eyes, and not caring. "Nick…"

If he slipped into the shadows of the trees now, she'd know she'd waited too long to show him her acceptance, too long to take what he'd offered, too long for them to have a chance at happiness. She could only pray that wasn't the case.

He didn't walk away. Instead, he changed. This time, when the twinkling lights and shimmers faded, the human Nick stood staring at her.

Beloved. Licking her lips, she spoke the word out loud. "Beloved."

Though he didn't respond in kind, she waited, admiring his lithe, athletic, naked body and hungering.

Without self-consciousness, he walked to where he'd left his clothing on the grass. Still looking at her, he stepped into his pants, pulling them over his lean hips and fastening them at the waist. Bare-chested, he rolled his shoulders, flexing his muscular arms while his unwavering gaze locked on hers.

"Say it again," he demanded, hoarse-voiced. With each word he came closer, until he towered over her.

"Beloved," she said.

He held out his hand.

Gazing up at his face, she repeated her earlier words. "I love you." Slipping her hand into his, she let him help her to her feet. She opened her mouth to tell him all she felt, all the emotion and longing and love inside her, but the instant she was standing, he pulled her into his arms and captured her mouth with his.

Neither of them spoke for a long while.

Finally, Nick lifted his head. "Mine," he growled, his eyes glowing. "Mine."

Her eyes filled with tears. "Yes, yours. And you're mine." Then again, "Mine." Her throat closed, full with emotion. Standing on her toes, she placed a fierce kiss on his mouth. "I love you, Nick Templeton. All of you."

Later, after he'd kissed her so thoroughly her head spun, they ran for her car. Laughing and eager, they couldn't keep themselves from touching even as they ran. Once inside with both doors closed, Amanda heard only the sound of their breathing and the rapid pit-pat of her heart.

"I want to make love to you." Nick leaned across the seat, capturing her lips again and stealing what little breath she had left.

"Not here," she finally managed, fumbling to place her key in the ignition and start the engine.

"Where?"

"My place."

"The hotel's closer." He pointed.

Agreeing, she turned left.

Heart in hands, eyes, voice full of love, they barely made it to his room.

Everything you love about romance...
and more!

Please turn the page for Signature Select™
Bonus Features.

Bonus Features:

Author Interview 4

A Conversation with Linda
Winstead Jones

A Conversation with Evelyn
Vaughn

A Conversation with Karen
Whiddon

Author's Journal 18

Astral Projector for the
Meditatively Challenged
by Evelyn Vaughn

Author's Journal 25

A letter from John Stark (The hero
of "Forever Mine") by Linda
Winstead Jones

Alternate Ending 29

FOREVER MINE
by Linda Winstead Jones

Top 10 Movies about the
Supernatural 35

Signature Select™

BONUS FEATURES

BEYOND THE DARK

Author Interview:
A conversation with
LINDA WINSTEAD JONES

Linda Winstead Jones is an award-winning author who's been writing romantic suspense, fantasy and historical romance novels since 1994. Recently we

4 *spoke to her as she took a break from writing her latest book.*

Tell us a bit about how you began your writing career.

Like so many other writers, I was a reader first. I have always loved books, and stories. I was a young mother when I began to think that maybe I could write some of my own stories. I had a rough start. First I tried to write at the kitchen table, but my manuscripts usually ended up being decorated with oatmeal or SpaghettiOs. I finally moved my "office" to the bedroom, where I used an ironing board lowered to the proper level as a desk. It was a very unstable, shaky desk, but it worked for a good long while. The book I wrote on that ironing board won't ever see the light of day (be very, very grateful <g>) but it was a valuable learning experience.

What's your writing routine?

The routine varies from book to book. Some stories come quickly, and I can't type fast enough. Others come more slowly, and I have to take my time. The one constant is that I most enjoy writing in the morning. That's when the creative side of my brain seems to work best.

How you do develop your characters?

Sometimes I feel like the characters are developing me! Seriously, when things are going well, they can take over. I remember more than one instance where I wanted to change a character's name or hair color or perhaps an annoying trait—and they wouldn't let me.

If you don't mind, how did you meet your husband?

We were both trombone players in our high school band. I met him the summer before my first year of high school, and we dated all through those years. We got married a month after I graduated. We've been married thirty-three years now.

What are your favorite kinds of vacations?
Where do you like to travel?
I love the water. The beach or a lake, a little sun and a book. That's my idea of a relaxing vacation.

Do you have a favorite book or film?
Moonstruck and *Shakespeare in Love* come to mind first as favorite movies. Favorite books are more difficult for me because there are so many.

Any last words to your readers?
Thanks for taking the time to join me in this (hopefully-not-too) scary ride!

Author Interview:
A conversation with
EVELYN VAUGHN

*Evelyn Vaughn believes in many magics,
particularly the magic of storytelling. She began
writing stories as soon as she was able to hold a
crayon. She's been at it ever since. Recently, she
chatted with us about her writing career, how she
comes up with ideas and some of her favorite
things.*

**Tell us a bit about how you began your writing
career.**
I began my writing career with crayons. Really!
My mother informs me that I did not leave
spaces between any of the words at first, though
I don't remember that part. I do remember that
the idea of writing stories seemed natural to me
from the very start, whether because of past-life
influence or because my parents were both avid
readers (my dad was a great storyteller, too).

At the age of twelve, I published my first short story, which won a local newspaper contest, called "Gohst [sic] in the Graveyard." I won an AM radio for that, but my attempts at publication afterward floundered; even with the help of *Writer's Digest*, a teenager can only do so much unless she's a prodigy, and I was no prodigy. Luckily, by the time I was in college, a friend put me in touch with the North Texas Romance Writers of America, and doors to the publishing world opened for me. I didn't walk through those doors until nine years later when I sold my first novel. *Waiting for the Wolf Moon* was the first of four books that I wrote for Silhouette Shadows and, again, it was a paranormal. Hmm... I'm beginning to see a pattern here!

Was there a particular person, place or thing that inspired this story?
"Haunt Me," the story of Charis and David, was inspired by several things. Part of it was my continued interest in things paranormal— magic, time travel, alternate worlds and, yes, astral projection. Part of it was my continued love for the novel *Wuthering Heights*, despite what a jerk Heathcliff is. But part of the inspiration was much sadder, so feel free to skip to the next question if you don't want to be

saddened! Last year, my dad's surgeon convinced him to have an operation, the recovery from which should only have taken four days. But things went horribly wrong, not the least being that medications my dad needed in order to breathe properly inhibited the healing process! A projected four days turned into two months of hospitalization, a second operation to correct mistakes from the first, two grueling weeks in ICU and my father's eventual death.

Everyone who has done the hospital deathwatch knows how surreal the whole experience can be, and of course the grief of losing one's parent (or for my mother, one's spouse of fifty years) is catastrophic for anyone. While I was still reeling from it all, my friend Maggie Shayne wisely urged me to work my way through my grief and anger by writing. So I did, mixing these diverse inspirations to come up with the basic idea for "Haunt Me."

What's your writing routine?
Life would probably be easier if I had a routine, but I don't. I often joke with friends that I "don't live in real time," but it's only half a joke—I actually mean that more often than not. When I'm excited about a story, I can write for hours a day, although my job as a full-time English instructor at Tarrant County College takes

precedence Monday through Thursday. When I'm not excited about my work, I'm far worse about spending too much time in front of the TV (a fictional world is a fictional world, and I do love alternate universes). And when I start to push a deadline, it's almost like living somewhere else completely.

How do you research your stories?
Research is one of my favorite forms of procrastination. Mostly I use books and the Internet, but some TV channels—like The History and Discovery channels or PBS—are also very useful.

How do you develop your characters?
I think of writing as opening a portal to someplace else. So I learn about my characters by starting to write about them and seeing what they do while I'm there. When I'm lucky, they emerge fully formed by chapter three, and it's easy to rewrite their earlier, less distinct presentation. When I'm not so lucky, I have to nudge them some. It helps to figure out what a character wants most, and what is most likely to keep her or him from getting it.

If you don't mind, could you tell us a bit about your family?

I come from a large, wonderful clan that moved a lot. We lived in Virginia, Illinois, Arizona and Louisiana. Once we got to Texas, though, we stopped and stayed. My mother lives about an hour from me, and my younger sister and her husband live barely two miles away. I have a brother and sister-in-law with four children in Louisiana, another brother and sister-in-law in South Dakota, three half siblings in Oregon and some wonderful cousins in New England. And let's not forget the friends who are just like family! My own household, however, consists of just me, my elderly cat, Simone, my silly cocker spaniel, Kermit...and of course, all my imaginary friends. They live here, too.

If you don't mind, how did you meet your husband or partner?

I'm a never-been-married, barely-been-looking. For whatever reason, it works well for me... maybe because it gives me even more time to spend with my fictional friends. The closest thing I have to a man in my life would either be the aforementioned Kermit, or my handsome, sexy and beloved Phineas. But Phineas is, ahem, make-believe.

When you're not writing, what are your favorite activities?

Two things. One is teaching—I teach college-level English, mostly literature and creative writing, and I adore it. The other is television. Wow, am I addicted to television. The invention of cable and VCRs and whole seasons on DVD... did I dream this up, too? Because it's what I would dream of, if it didn't already exist.

What are your favorite kinds of vacations? Where do you like to travel?

I used to adore travel. As a teenager, I longed to see Europe and have adventures. Then, in my twenties, I did just that! It was everything I'd hoped (although I did learn that adventure becomes increasingly uncomfortable the older you get). But my beloved cat got older, and I began traveling less and less so that I could keep an eye on her. I'm hoping to get my second wind in a few years and set out again, but even then, my idea of a vacation will be nowhere near as fast paced. Time on a beach...that's a vacation. Or staying for a week in a London or Parisian apartment, instead of using that week to see Edinburgh, London, Paris, Brussels, Amsterdam, Munich and more. I'm going for depth over breadth, this time.

Do you have a favorite book or film?
I have several, and they tend to fluctuate depending on what month it is or what mood I'm in. One of my very favorites is the musical play *Man of La Mancha*. Another is the movie *Labyrinth,* and a third is the book *A Little Princess* by Frances Hodgson Burnett. I particularly enjoy series: everything from the Amelia Peabody Mysteries by Elizabeth Peters to the Little House books by Laura Ingalls Wilder. That may be because I like going back to visit old imaginary friends so much.

Any last words to your readers?
Don't discount the importance of something just because other people don't see it or understand it. Believing is half the battle. And training yourself to have a positive state of mind can be more important than we often think it will. Really.

Author Interview:
A conversation with
KAREN WHIDDON

Karen Whiddon started weaving fanciful tales for her younger brothers at the age of eleven. Growing up in the Catskill Mountains of New York, then the Rocky Mountains of Colorado, she found enough magic in the rugged peaks to keep her imagination fueled for years. Recently, she took time out from her schedule to talk to us.

Tell us a bit about how you began your writing career.

I've always been a voracious reader. When I found out I had to have surgery and would be off work for six weeks, it was a natural thing for me to attempt to write a book. I had an old electric typewriter (this was before computers), and I'd never heard of RWA or submission guidelines. I typed 140 single-spaced pages over those six weeks—my first book! I promptly mailed it in to Harlequin. I still have that dusty old manuscript—and my first rejection letter.

Was there a particular person, place or thing that inspired this story?
Nick Templeton, the hero in "Soul of the Wolf," came to me in a dream after I watched Thomas Jane in *The Punisher*. Nick's sort of the reverse—a bad boy gone good, but he still wanted to find out the truth about his cousin Jason's murder. He also has his own, dark secrets.

What's your writing routine?
I write Monday through Friday, 7:00 a.m. until 10:00 a.m. I work at a day job also, so at ten I have to go in to the other office. I take weekends off mostly, except when under deadlines (which is all the time here recently).

How do you research your stories?
For the police/DEA/FBI research, I have various sources. I have research books and I use the Internet. I also attended a course offered by our local police department, Citizen's Police Academy. One of the officers I met there had worked undercover for the DEA. He has been helpful in the past in answering questions. The FBI has a great Web site, as do most police departments.

How you do develop your characters?
Sometimes I dream them, sometimes they whisper in my ear. Most times I fill in a character chart for reference, listing physical characteristics, background information (where they grew up, family, etc.) and any other pertinent information I need for the story.

If you don't mind, could you tell us a bit about your family?
Sure. I've been married to the same man for ages—we've been together for twenty-two years. I have a grown daughter who teaches fourth grade in a nearby public school district. I have two fur-faced children, Daisy and Mitchell, both miniature schnauzers. I live in north Texas and love to travel.

If you don't mind, how did you meet your husband or partner?
I met my husband at work—a long time ago. We were friends before we got serious and we're still best friends to this day.

When you're not writing, what are your favorite activities?
I love to camp—my husband and I have a travel trailer and we love to spend weekends near lakes where we can fish. I also like to read and

listen to music. Oh—and my husband says I have a degree in shopping !

What are your favorite kinds of vacations? Where do you like to travel?
One of the best vacations I've had in a long time was this past summer when my husband and I went to Vancouver Island, BC, Canada, and stayed at a salmon fishing lodge. It was beautiful and rustic and I caught an eighteen-pound king salmon. We had a wonderful time and plan to go back next summer. I also enjoy (for a different type of fun) Las Vegas.

Do you have a favorite book or film?
Gosh—there are so many... I have several books I read again and again. Most are romance, as are my favorite movies.

Any last words to your readers?
I hope you enjoy Nick and Amanda's story. Two strong people who find everlasting love while thwarting the bad guys—one of my favorite kind of stories.

Astral Projection for the Meditatively Challenged
by Evelyn Vaughn

Yep. Astral projection is a real technique. Think of it as a deliberate out-of-body experience (OBE), in which a person allows their body to rest and then move around in their spirit for a change. Floating up and out of the body, a person can then explore a version of reality that's remarkably similar to our dreams. In fact, most experts believe that we astrally project in our sleep all the time, so this version of existence may *really* be our dreams!

You can find many excellent books and Web sites on this psychic ability, so I'll keep my redundancy short. Most of these experts will suggest some basic steps to be practiced over a period of time....

1. *Safety first.* Protecting yourself is key. Not only should you say a prayer, cast a circle or envision yourself surrounded by

protective light, you should also
remember to lock your door.

2. *Relax!* For one thing, if you're scared,
then you're probably not ready. For
another, you have to relax your body to
the point of forgetting about it, in order
to leave it behind. The projection is
natural (dreams, remember?). It's only
the *awareness* of it that we're controlling.
Some people relax themselves one body
part at a time. Others count backward, or
imagine themselves in an elevator going
lower and lower into their subconscious.
Whatever works for you.

3. *Moving out.* Once you're relaxed, imagine
your spirit floating upward or, in some
instructions, rolling out of your body.
Most practitioners describe an
indestructible, slim silver cord connect-
ing their spirit to their body. Take a look
at your body as proof that you're outside
it.

4. *Explore!* Try to have a destination in mind,
or else your journey may be as random
as your dreams. Some people use astral
projection to meet with spirit guides.
Others use them for "remote viewing,"

glimpsing activities hidden from our physical selves. Don't worry; experts consistently report that there are few dangers in the astral world, just as there are few dangers when you're dreaming. If you even imagine you've run into a problem, just think about your body, wiggle your fingers...and you're home.

Pretty cool, huh? I really hope to manage it someday.

Yep. I confess. Part of the problem is that, frankly, I don't have the time or dedication to prac-tice, practice, practice. Part of the problem is that I'm an Aries and don't have a lot of patience for meditation—if it weren't for moving meditations like Tai Chi and yoga, I'd be in trouble! Part of my problem may even be that I'm fairly suggestible, and so the daily conditioning which insists that we live only on *this* plane, in *this* world, works pretty well on me. I haven't managed a solid astral projection, yet....

Or have I?

Here's the nonredundant part, and why I've called this piece "Astral Projection for the Meditatively Challenged." The more I've studied this topic, the more convinced I am that we all astrally project—and not just in our dreams.

Experts may laugh at me (go ahead; laughter's good for you!). But I firmly believe that getting lost in a good book or an excellent film is a form of astral projection. I think playing computer games, or even spending a lot of time in a chat room are forms of astral projection as well.

Follow me...

1. *Losing Oneself in a Story*
Have you ever been so involved in a book, or a movie or a TV show that you lost track of your physical being? Perhaps the dog barked, or the phone rang and suddenly you were back in your body—and you felt momentarily disoriented? Why do you think that was? *Where were you* just before the dog barked or the phone rang? The more I write, the more convinced I am that the zillions of alternate dimensions where stories "live" are part of the astral plane.

Yes, a skeptic would argue that "that's just fiction." But some fictions, from *Star Trek* to Santa Claus, do have their own reality and one which many of us share. Audiences discuss these worlds and characters as we would our own friends and our own memories. We sometimes find ourselves spending as much thought on them as we might on our vacation plans.

The world of stories is not our physical reality, true. Few people believe it is. But neither are fictions completely false. They just have a different *kind* of reality. Perhaps it's an astral reality.

2. *Techno-Projection*

One of my favorite definitions of *cyberspace* is that it's where we go when we're on the telephone. Think about it. When you're having a long, involved phone conversation, your body may be where you left it, but your spirit? Your spirit is somewhere else. That somewhere else is hard to define, but then, so is the astral plane. Being in the astral isn't quite like turning invisible and wandering around. If we think in that mode, we're still anchoring ourselves to *bodily* reality. Being in the astral, by all accounts, involves senses that can't be described by earthly means. Some psychics that use terms like "I see" or "I hear," mean it—but sometimes, as in when we "hear" a familiar author's voice in a book we read, they're using those terms metaphorically.

Imagining ourselves as a spiritual *body* is a construct to give us something to visualize, and for many, it works. But remember that astral projection is an *out-of-body* experience.

So when you're having a deep phone conversation, or are heavily involved in a chat room, do you lose track of the time? Do you forget about your headache or toothache for minutes at a time? Do you not notice what's playing on the radio? Forget to eat? If so, why aren't your senses keeping track? It might just be because your bodily senses are temporarily off-line.

This is all the more real with some computer games. Again, people rarely believe that they are physically in the game. We achieve what Coleridge called the "willing suspension of disbelief." But in doing that, part of us—a part real enough to be emotionally invested, a part that is honestly cheered or depressed by the game's outcome...part of us is there.

So who knows? Maybe I'm just rationalizing things. Certainly plenty of respectable people have reported out-of-body experiences far more similar to those in "Haunt Me" than they are to reading a good book. I don't mean to imply that OBEs are a distinct phenomenon, and very much worth the practice, practice, practice. I've yet to give my own studies. But maybe, just maybe, I'm also correct.

We astrally project when we dream, sometimes experiencing things so powerful that we hate to wake up in the morning or muse about them all day. That part's already accepted by those who believe in astral projection. So why is the mildly dissociative experience of getting lost in a book or a video, or in an online chat, all that different? Is it because we aren't doing it all by ourselves?

If so, I've got news for you. Although we like to believe otherwise, there's very little in our lives that we do all by ourselves. Even when our bodies are alone...those are just our bodies.

I'd love to hear what you think. Feel free to write me at *Yvaughn@aol.com.*

And safe journeys!

Author's Journal

A Letter from John Stark
(The hero of "Forever Mine"
by Linda Winstead Jones)

Dear Reader,

Do you believe in ghosts? I do.

If you think about it, believing makes perfect sense. Every culture, in every time, has involved some sort of belief in the afterlife and in the apparitions that sometimes seem to haunt us. British folklore gives us the bogey, our mischievous bogeyman sent to scare little children into being good, and the barghest, a spectral hound who appears as a death omen, among many others. The Japanese tell of the seventeenth-century ghost of Sakura, and of *buruburu,* the ghost of fear. They even have *tsukumogami*—ghosts who inhabit tools. (No wonder I never much liked chain saws.) Many Native American cultures revere the dead, and the spirits who, on occasion, make themselves known to the living. The Eqyptians, the Greeks, the Romans, the

Celts—they all knew that the living did not, and do not, walk this earth alone.

In the nineteenth century there was a revival of spiritualism. Mediums contacted deceased loved ones, talking boards were all the rage and associations for the express purpose of studying psychic phenomenon were formed, either in the manner of secret societies or as academics. Some of those associations continue to exist even today. Many of our ghost sightings have been dismissed as illusions, and others have been proved to be out-and-out hoaxes. And yet there remain those sightings that cannot be explained away.

Children see many things that we do not because they have not yet learned that they shouldn't. They talk to invisible friends, they laugh at jokes we do not hear, they blame a spilled drink or a lost toy on someone who isn't there. We write these interactions off to imagination, or a child's boredom or simple mischief, and we ignore what these kids see every day. We ignore what our minds cannot accept as real.

I believe in ghosts. I've seen them, talked to them, even sent them on their way, with a little help. (Ghosts are not my specialty, but when one presents itself there's not much I can do but go along for the ride.) I realize that many of you who are reading this won't take my word about something so important—or about anything else, for that matter. If you don't believe in ghosts, you might have a hard time with buying psychics, too. I don't mind, really. If I wasn't one I probably wouldn't believe, either. We live in a society where we're taught from birth not to believe in anything we can't touch, or see or smell. If it's not tangible, it can't exist. Right? Besides, it's often easier to live in a world where everything can be explained away. It's neat and tidy.

We do explain things away when they threaten our neat and tidy world, don't we? A cold spot in a room is certainly just a draft; what sounds like laughter or crying or the softly spoken sound of your name must be the settling boards of a creaking old house; the shifting of light out of the corner of your eye is explained away as a trick of tired eyes or an oddly positioned shaft of light coming through a window. When those keys you were so sure you placed on the end table turn up in the kitchen, it's easier to believe that you placed them there yourself and forgot rather than to even consider that a poltergeist might be playing tricks on you. Yes, very often we'd prefer insanity over accepting the presence of visitors from beyond.

Insanity might often be preferable, but take my word for it—we are not alone. The spirits of our deceased loved ones visit us often, to check on our progress and to shower us with love. The trapped ghosts of sad, lost creatures walk the same earth we do, searching for happiness or justice. There are mischief makers, most of them simple and lively, while still others possess a darkness most of us (fortunately) never see. And while these spirits cavort among us, we go blindly about our business, giving all our attention to those things that we can see.

Open the door to your world a little bit wider, if you dare. The next time a small child starts to talk about friends you cannot see, or you misplace your keys or you feel a chill in an otherwise warm room, stop what you're doing. Let yourself believe in the impossible, for a moment. And if you smell a hint of Grandma's perfume or Gramps's cigar while you're standing there contemplating what cannot possibly be, well, all the better.

I believe. Do you?

John Stark

ALTERNATE ENDING

Forever Mine
by
Linda Winstead Jones

After reading "Forever Mine" by Linda Winstead
Jones, did you wonder how the story would have
ended if there was a sign that the ghost was still
around? If so, read on and find out what could
have been....

"So, Mr. Stark, what are your intentions? How are you going to take care of my friend? If you're a gigolo planning to live off of her money, I swear…"

"I have a job," John said. "I don't want Miranda's money."

"A job," Elyse snorted. "What kind of a job?"

John didn't answer, but instead looked at her and waited. Miranda smiled. "John is a psychic," she said. "An extraordinarily talented psychic who makes a very good living helping people. I feel quite confident that he cares nothing about the Garner family money."

Elyse was silent for a moment. "A psychic," she repeated softly.

"Yes," Miranda answered. "A psychic." She would never deny him again. Not in this life, not in any life to come. They were past that challenge, at last.

"And what are *you* going to do in Atlanta while he's…psychicing?" Elyse asked.

"I'll help out around John's office and travel with him on occasion." She'd never thought it would be possible to walk away from the home she had loved for so long, but she wanted to be with John, wherever that might be.

"But…" Elyse began.

"I love John," Miranda said before her friend could come up with another argument. "I love him, and I'm going to marry him, and eventually the two of you will be the best of friends."

Elyse was not so sure about that, and neither was John.

But Miranda knew that one day her husband and Elyse would be friends. She wasn't sure how she knew with such certainty that this would come to pass…but she did. She was beginning to sense things in a way that was entirely new to her, as if she'd taken a small parcel of John's talents deep into herself and they had taken root in her soul. He was truly a part of her, in a way she had never imagined.

When they were alone once again, Miranda gratefully pulled John to her and melted against him. She was in love with a good man who loved her back, and she saw a bright future waiting for her—something which had seemed impossible

32

just a couple of weeks ago. "You really are forever mine, aren't you?" she whispered.

"Yeah." John pressed his hand against her back and kissed her throat, and she closed her eyes to drink in the sensations.

While she was in that relaxed state, her mind uncluttered and unfettered, she had her first true vision; a vision of what was to come. An image formed in her mind, clear and precise, as if she were watching a movie. It should be frightening, but thanks to John, who held her so tenderly, it was not.

Miranda found herself standing in a cozy nursery, with pink stuffed animals lined up on a slightly crooked shelf she knew John had hung himself. She heard a *coo* and smelled baby, clean and sweet and innocent, and she even felt the swelling of maternal love in her own heart. She walked to the white crib with the pink bedding and butterfly mobile, and reached inside to touch the baby, her daughter, John's daughter. Everything she wanted, everything she needed, was here in this home she and her husband had made together.

And then she heard a crack of thunder outside the nursery window, and her eyes were drawn there just in time to see a white face illuminated beyond the glass.

Tony.

She jerked and gasped, and if John had not been holding on to her she would have fallen to the floor.

"He's coming back," she said breathlessly. "Tony. He's gone for now, but he's going to find his way back, one day."

"I know," John said softy. "I saw, too. Don't worry. We'll fight him together, when the time comes. He won't win this time, Miranda. We won't let him."

"But…"

"If I have to fight for you every day for the rest of our lives, I will."

A sense of true comfort and safety washed over her, and she was able to smile. She didn't know everything of what the future would bring, but she knew all that mattered. She had love, and the rest would come one day at a time.

On the horizon, the rumble of an unexpected thunderstorm reminded her that every day would be a new adventure.

TOP TEN

Movies about the Supernatural

by Katherine Gortnar

Who isn't fascinated by the unknown? Here are 10 great movies about the supernatural that are sure to entertain.

1. Truly, Madly, Deeply (1991)

Starring Juliet Stevenson, Alan Rickman

Set in London, this is the story of Nina, a young woman completely overwhelmed by grief when her partner suddenly dies. Her anguish is so fierce that he feels compelled to return to her as a ghost, albeit a very real one. Their relationship will have you alternately laughing and crying in this charming film that benefits not only from a superb cast, but also an excellent script and wonderful direction by Anthony Minghella. A superb movie that reveals the universal truths of love, loss and letting go.

2. Wuthering Heights (1939)

Starring Merle Oberon, Laurence Olivier
One of Hollywood's all-time classics, this is the first film adaptation of Emily Brontë's literary masterpiece. During a raging storm, a solitary traveler takes refuge at Wuthering Heights, a desolate house on the English moors, but finds little comfort there when he hears a ghostly female voice outside his window and feels the icy grasp of her hand. He is then told the tale of Cathy and Heathcliff, two star-crossed lovers separated in life by societal position and jealous obsession, and again by her premature death. Filmed with haunting beauty, this is one of the best romantic dramas depicting eternal love, pride and passion between two tragic soul mates.

3. Ghost (1990)

Starring Demi Moore, Patrick Swayze, Whoopi Goldberg
Probably best known for its unforgettable sexy scene between the lovers at a pottery wheel, this thrilling romance is the story of a man who dies of what seems to be a random act of violence. Now a ghost, he learns that his girlfriend is also in grave danger and must

communicate through a psychic to warn her. Supernatural chills, spiced with great comic moments combine perfectly in this memorable love story.

4. The Ghost and Mrs. Muir (1947)
Starring Gene Tierney, Rex Harrison
Determined to live her life the way she wants, newly widowed Lucy Muir declines her in-laws' demand that she live with them and moves with her daughter (a young Natalie Wood) to a seaside cottage going cheap due to its haunting by the gruff yet handsome sea captain, Daniel Gregg. When Lucy's independence is threatened, a deal is struck between the two one night allowing her to stay in the house and the ghost to materialize only in her bedroom. As the captain spends more time with the determined and beautiful Lucy, a bittersweet romance evolves between them in this magical tale of immortal love.

5. Sleepy Hollow (1999)
Starring Johnny Depp, Christina Ricci, Miranda Richardson, Michael Gambon
Inspired by Washington Irving's classic tale, this delightfully creepy film combines horror, fantasy and romance that brilliantly come

together under the dreamy vision of director Tim Burton. Set in 1799, Ichabod Crane, an eccentric and earnest constable from New York, is sent to the village of Sleepy Hollow to probe a series of murders, allegedly committed by a terrifying headless horseman. There he encounters a string of extraordinary characters, but is most affected by the young Katrina Van Tassel who appears to dabble in mysterious spells.

6. What Lies Beneath (2000)

Starring Michelle Pfeiffer, Harrison Ford
A suspenseful, supernatural thriller reminiscent of Hitchcock's filming style, it is the story of a happily married couple whose life takes a dramatic turn when their daughter moves away to college. The wife, Claire, begins to hear mysterious voices, is haunted by the wraithlike image of a young woman and becomes suspicious of the couple next door. As she gets closer to the truth behind the ghostly presence, it seems the apparition is determined to come back for Claire and wreak havoc in her marriage. This movie will keep you on your toes throughout its multiple plot twists and "jump out of your seat" scenes.

7. Ladyhawke (1985)
Starring Michelle Pfeiffer, Rutger Hauer, Matthew Broderick

Set in medieval France, a spell of vengeance has been cast upon Etienne Navarre, captain of the guard, and the beautiful Lady Isabeau D'Anjou. She is transformed into a hawk by day, he a wolf by night, so the two lovers are damned to wander the wilderness, always together, eternally apart. When Etienne enlists the unexpected help of a young pickpocket so that he may confront the evil source of the curse, there seems to be hope on the horizon. This film features some beautiful photography and has become a classic historical romance.

8. The Seventh Sign (1988)
Starring Demi Moore, Michael Biehn, Jurgen Prochnow

When Abby and Russell Quinn rent the apartment over their garage to the mysterious David, bizarre events begin to occur, and Abby becomes suspicious that their strange tenant is trying to endanger the life of her unborn child. She seeks help from the only person that believes her, a young rabbinical student, and becomes reluctantly involved in an epic battle between good and evil. This supernatural thriller crafts an intriguing story based on the prophecies found in the final chapter of the Bible.

9. The Lost Boys (1987)
Starring Jason Patric, Kiefer Sutherland, Dianne Wiest, Corey Haim, Jami Gertz

An eighties brat-pack classic, this film stylishly combines horror, comedy and romance. Recently divorced Lucy packs up her two teenaged sons, Michael and Sam, and moves in with her eccentric father who lives in the picturesque coastal town of Santa Cruz. Michael becomes infatuated with a beautiful girl who brings the two brothers in to the world of her biker gang, and they soon realize that the gang's members are more dead than alive. A hip vampire movie filmed with an MTV-like sensibility that explores the impassioned teenage desire to be cool.

10. Brigadoon (1954)
Starring Gene Kelly, Cyd Charisse, Van Johnson

This lush adaptation of the Broadway musical depicts the story of two American tourists, Tommy Albright and Jeff Douglas, who stumble upon an enchanted Scottish village. Every 100 years, the people of Brigadoon awaken for a single day, then go back to sleep for another century, while the village itself vanishes in the mists. When Tommy falls in love with one of the village girls, he must decide before night falls whether to stay or return to his fiancée and jet-setting lifestyle back in New York. This lighthearted film features lavish sets and costumes, with exuberant dancing choreographed by Kelly, himself.

Note: Originally published on
www.eharlequin.com

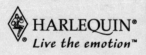

SHOWCASE

Two classic stories in one volume
from favorite author

FAYRENE PRESTON

In one house, secrets of past and
present converge...

SWANSEA LEGACY

Caitlin Deverell's great-grandfather had built
SwanSea as a mansion that would signal the
birth of a dynasty. Decades later, this ancestral
home is being launched into a new era as a
luxury resort—an event that arouses passion,
romance and a century-old mystery.

PLUS, exclusive bonus features inside!

Available in November 2005.

COMING NEXT MONTH

Signature Select Spotlight
IN THE COLD by Jeanie London
Years after a covert mission gone bad, ex-U.S. intelligence agent
Claire de Beaupre is discovered alive, with no memory of the brutal
torture she endured. Simon Brandauer, head of the agency, must
risk Claire's fragile memory to unravel the truth of what happened.
But a deadly assassin needs her to *forget*....

Signature Select Saga
BETTING ON GRACE by Debra Salonen
Grace Radonovic is more than a little surprised by her late father's
friend's proposal of marriage. But the shady casino owner is more
attracted to her dowry than the curvy brunette herself. So when
long-lost cousin Nikolai Sarna visits, Grace wonders if *he* is her
destiny. But sexy Nick has a secret...one that could land Grace in
unexpected danger.

Signature Select Miniseries
BRAVO BRIDES by Christine Rimmer
Two full-length novels starring the beloved Bravo family.... Sisters Jenna
and Lacey Bravo have a few snags to unravel...before they tie the knot!

Signature Select Collection
EXCLUSIVE! by Fiona Hood-Stewart, Sharon Kendrick, Jackie Braun
It's a world of Gucci and gossip. Caviar and cattiness. And
suddenly everyone is talking about the steamy antics behind the
scenes of the Cannes Film Festival. Celebrities are behaving badly...
and tabloid reporters are dishing the dirt.

Signature Select Showcase
SWANSEA LEGACY by Fayrene Preston
Caitlin Deverell's great-grandfather had built SwanSea as a mansion
that would signal the birth of a dynasty. Decades later, this ancestral
home is being launched into a new era as a luxury resort—an event
that arouses passion, romance and a century-old mystery.

The Fortunes of Texas: Reunion
THE DEBUTANTE by Elizabeth Bevarly
When Miles Fortune and Lanie Meyers are caught in a compromising
position, it's headline news. There's only one way for the playboy
rancher and the governor's daughter to save face—pretend to be
engaged until after her father's election. But what happens when
the charade becomes more fun than intended?

SIGCNM1105

Signature Select™

LINDA WINSTEAD JONES

would rather write than do anything else. Since she cannot cook, gave up ironing many years ago and finds cleaning the house a complete waste of time, she has plenty of time to devote to her obsession for writing. Occasionally, she's tried to expand her horizons by taking classes. In the past she's taken instruction on yoga, French (a dismal failure), Chinese cooking, cake decorating (food-related classes are always a good choice, even for someone who can't cook), belly dancing (trust me, this was a long time ago) and, of course, creative writing.

She lives in Huntsville, Alabama, with her husband of more years than she's willing to admit and the youngest of their three sons.

She can be reached via www.eHarlequin.com or her own Web site www.lindawinsteadjones.com.

EVELYN VAUGHN

believes in many magics, particularly the magic of storytelling. She has written fiction since she could print words, first publishing a ghost story in a newspaper contest at the age of twelve. Since then, along with four Silhouette Shadows (republished as DREAMSCAPES miniseries), she has written four historical romances and a handful of fantasy short stories, some under the name Yvonne Jocks. She loves movies and videos, and is an unapologetic TV addict still trying to figure out both how to time travel and how to meet up with some of her favorite characters. Even as an English teacher at Tarrant County College in Fort Worth, TX, Evelyn believes in the magic of stories, movies, books and dreams. Luckily, her imaginary friends and her cats seem to get along.

Evelyn loves to talk about stories and characters, especially her own. Please write her at Yvaughn@aol.com, or at P.O. Box 6, Euless, TX, 76039. Check out her Web site at www.evelynvaughn.homestead.com.

KAREN WHIDDON

started weaving fanciful tales for her younger brothers at the age of eleven. Amidst the Catskill Mountains of New York, then the Rocky Mountains of Colorado, she fueled her imagination with the natural beauty of the rugged peaks and spun stories of love that captivated her family's attention.

Karen now lives in north Texas, where she shares her life with her very own hero of a husband and three doting dogs. Also an entrepreneur, she divides her time between her business and writing contemporary romantic suspense and paranormal romances that readers enjoy for the Silhouette Intimate Moments line. You can e-mail Karen at KWhiddon1@aol.com or write to her at P.O. Box 820807, Fort Worth, TX 76182. Fans of her writing can also check out her Web site at www.KarenWhiddon.com.